SILICON
KARMA

THOMAS A. EASTON

silicon karma	*thomas a. easton*
book design & layout	*larry s. friedman*

Silicon Karma is set in fonts by Emboss, Emigre, T-26 and Thirstype.

Borealis is an imprint of White Wolf Publishing.

White Wolf Publishing
780 Park North Boulevard, Suite 100
Clarkston, GA 30021

www.white-wolf.com

For
Betty Sue

My thanks to David Hartwell, Don Maass, Rebecca Ore, Mike Resnick, and Stewart Wieck.
Those defects of the tale that have survived their helpful efforts are my fault alone.

An earlier version of this novel
was published on disk in April 1995 by
Serendipity Systems
P. O. Box 140
San Simeon, CA 93452

SILICON KARMA
THOMAS A. EASTON

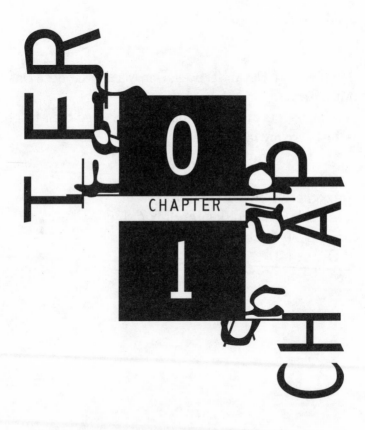

CHAPTER 1

"There," said the technician as he withdrew the needle from her arm.

Rose Pillock blinked. She could already feel the drug wrapping her consciousness in layers of cotton wool. She turned her head to one side and there, in the polished stainless steel of an equipment casing, she saw herself. Thin, gray hair, almost white, straggling across her scalp. A face seamed by time and illness, the flesh worn so thin that the bone of her skull threatened to burst free. An arm, a sleeve pushed up to expose the crook of her elbow for the technician's coolly professional hands, the skin wrinkled and spotted, the meat reduced to flaccid strings.

She rolled her head the other way and wished she were in her own bed. She lay on a narrow gurney, its thin pad not quite enough to ease the pressure of her skeleton on her fleshly envelope. A sheet covered her swollen abdomen. Above her stretched white acoustic panels. Below her, she knew, was gleaming tile. To the sides, the walls were obscured by banks of equipment, monitors for her body, racks of electronics, terabytes of computer memory and processing capacity. Behind her, its keyhole maw waiting for someone to push the gurney toward it, was a massive, white-enameled doughnut that reminded her of the CAT scanner she had first met thirty years before. Yet its function was not to probe her failing organs, to map the weaknesses of her body.

Even so, it remained a probe, an invader, and a persnickety one at that. She had had to strip, to trade her own comfortable clothing for the stiff and chilly hospital gown she now wore. She had had to have her last few remaining teeth drilled and their old metallic fillings replaced with plastic. Her dentures waited on a table by the door. And now cool hands were removing her glasses.

"Don't move now." The technician grasped the sides of her head and centered her now blurred gaze on the light panel in the ceiling. Padded clamps closed upon her temples, her forehead, the thinly covered bones at the angles of her jaws. They tightened, and she could not suppress a moan.

"Don't worry. You'll get used to it. Relax. Let the drug help. Don't worry." The man's dark face hung above her own, not smiling, not frowning, neutral. She was an object, meat, not a person. He did not really care whether she was comfortable or not. He was doing his job, reciting the mantras he had been taught would help. All that mattered was that she was immobilized, her head clamped just so, held ready for the doughnut's probing fields.

"This is the speaker." He held a clear plastic tube before her face, its end swelling into the familiar shape of an ear plug. "It's really just a sound pipe. We can't have any wires in there, nothing metal, nothing electronic. It would interfere with the scanning." His fingers pressed the plug, smooth and cool, into her ear canal. Her eyes widened and she opened her mouth—she had never needed a hearing aid; she did not need one now—but he held one finger just above her lips, gently shushing her. She tried to shake her head but could not even twitch against the grip of the apparatus.

"Now we're ready," he said. "Here we go." He positioned himself at the foot of the gurney and leaned toward her, pushing, making her move, rolling her toward the machine that waited for her.

Just before her head entered the tunnel, she glimpsed the white face of the device and the letters—curving lines of black and silver, elegantly promising even when they were upside down and blurry to her age-weakened eyes—that spelled out "Xanadu 1." Shadow engulfed her then. The small noises in the room where her feet waited for the rest of her to return grew muffled and therefore conspicuous. There was the distant click of a switch, the hum of cryogenic pumps, and despite all the orientation sessions she had undergone, fright rose above the swaddling of the drug.

Eyes wide, breath cramped in her chest, memories of childhood swelling in her mind, she began to murmur a mantra of her own:

" T h e L o r d i s m y s h e p h e r d ; I s h a l l n o t w a n t . . . H e r e s t o r e t h m y s o u l . . . p r e p a r e t h e t a b l e b e f o r e m e . . . I w i l l d w e l l i n t h e h o u s e o f t h e L o r d f o r e v e r . "

"With luck," said a voice.

Her heart seemed to jump in her chest, but she said nothing. She could only think: "My lord!"

"No," said the voice, and now she could tell that it came from the end of the tube the technician had planted in her ear. It was warm and masculine, strong, certain. It bore a distinct electronic timbre, yet it seemed quite human. She thought it even held a chuckle of good humor. "I'm your host. Not your lord, not the lord of hosts. Just your host computer."

She sighed, remembering what she was there for. She should not have been surprised, except perhaps at the lack of sensation as the machine's fields probed deep within her brain. Certainly machines that could converse in quite a human way were not rare in her world. She had never had much to do with them, but she had known they existed, and that some were true artificial intelligences.

"I want you to remember now. That's all. Riffle through your life. Don't try to be complete. Do try to think, however briefly, of all you can. Highlights and key moments. That will be enough. Your brain will activate association paths and memories just enough, though they may not reach your consciousness."

"And you'll be watching."

"That's right. Watching, and catching the bits of your self. All that you have done and been and learned, all that you are. But don't speak out loud, please. The vibrations interfere with the scanning process. If you wish to speak to me, just think the words. I'll hear them."

She obeyed, letting words form on the surface of her mind, feeling them tighten the muscles of her throat and tongue but not letting those muscles move or any flow of air brush her vocal cords into sound. Did he—or it—detect her subvocalizations? "Won't they interfere with the memories?"

"I can tell the difference."

"You'll be reading my mind."

"Copying it. Recording it. Duplicating it within my own structure. When I'm done, the technician will roll you out of the mindscanner and unstrap you from the gurney. You'll get dressed and walk away and resume your life."

"For a while," she said within her mind, thinking of the tumors that were consuming her liver and pancreas and intestines, thinking of age and medicines and surgeries that only eased the pain, and only for a while.

"Just for a while," the voice agreed. "Flesh dies. But you will also be safe within me. You will live forever."

"Maybe. Nothing is forever."

The host computer manufactured an explicit chuckle that seemed much less convincing than the note of humor she had sensed at first. "Barring accidents,"

SILICON KARMA
THOMAS A. EASTON

the voice agreed. "But you will no longer have to worry about the ills the *flesh* is heir to. You won't even have to worry about power failures. I've got some heavy-duty batteries. The building has a generator. And you'll have a storage wafer all your own, just like all the rest I host. As soon as the power flickers—if it ever does—I'll back you up to that wafer. Then, when the power comes back on, I'll reboot and you will carry on with whatever you were doing before."

"What about fires? Earthquakes? Wars?"

"It's as you said, then, isn't it?" Her mind's eye let her glimpse the shrug with which a human speaker would have accompanied the words. "Nothing is forever, unless the gray god Murphy falls asleep. But you could live for many decades, or centuries, or even more."

She sighed. A reflective, remembering smile curved her lips. "That's what they told me. And I held my husband's hand when they explained it all to him."

"Remember him. What did he call you? Rose or Rosa?"

She did. Rosa, yes. Not Rose. That had been Albert's private, pet name for her. He had said she was softer than a rose, as pink and red and cream, as tender and smooth and delicate, but her thorns had never scratched him and never would. He had loved her touch once, her smell, her presence, as she had loved his.

But that had been long ago. When they had both been young. Her presence had remained. So had his. But touch had lost much of its importance. Their odors had changed. She had grown fat, and thin again. So had he.

And once, laughing, he had written her a poem. She still remembered it:

> As tree trunks through the years do grow,
> So too my lady's thighs.
> From sapling to maturity
> Do both increase their size.
>
> 'Tis but the years that thicken them,
> Though some do agonize
> At all the little signs of age,
> And Oh! my lady sighs.

Let us tell her that it's fated
For limbs to change their size.
If loggers cut the one for boards,
She slims to draw more eyes.

Then lumber goes to lathing mills
To gain some useful guise,
All fitted knobs and graceful curves
To please a user's eyes.

The mills of age grind finer still,
And now my lady cries.
Her legs are bony, awkward things
For which no men will rise.

I'm saddened now to watch my dame
Sip tea and tell her lies.
I reach out my foot and confuse
The table legs for thighs.

Would it affect the scanning of her mind if she changed her mental subject? She could not feel the effects of the machine's probing fields, but she knew the process had to be continuing. And hadn't the machine told her she should skip from thought to thought, trying not for depth of detail but for breadth, helping it find all the little things that went on in her head? She smiled to herself, thinking of walking through a vast field, pointing out to a companion the holes in which small animals lived. As soon as she indicated each one, her companion reached into the hole, extracted its resident, and popped it into a sack.

The machine chuckled in her ear just as it had before.

"Is it true that time flows more quickly inside you? That a minute by the clock outside will feel like a day?"

SILICON KARMA
THOMAS A. EASTON

"That myth." The machine chuckled again. "My bits and bytes may move faster than nerve impulses, but no computer can do as many things at once as a brain. It just doesn't have nearly as much parallel structure. And it takes a lot of calculation to support intelligence, yours or mine. So, at best, you gain a few seconds on the minute. Occasionally, you might even lose a few."

Rose's thin lips curved into a smile as she imagined the computer shrugging. "That's nice," she said. She was sure she had grasped the gist of what she had just heard. "I'm too old to rush any more." Albert would have understood more, she thought. He had known a lot about computers. Until he retired, he had been a police detective....

She felt other thoughts flicker through her mind as she remembered his occupation. She had been an accountant herself, a CPA, an adjunct instructor at a local college, mother, lover, more.

But Albert, he had become a specialist in computer crime, in embezzlements and frauds, in viruses and worms. He could tell when someone had backdated a file, could recover erased records, could crack encryptions designed to keep the darkest of plots the deepest of secrets.

When they had first heard of the Xanadu mindscanner, he had laughed and said, "I read a book once. It said it could be done. Open up someone's head. Wire a computer to a dozen or so brain cells. Program the machine so it mimics perfectly the cells' behavior, so it faithfully reproduces every response the cells generate to every possible stimulus. Then destroy the cells, letting the computer replace their functions. The patient will notice no difference. Then hook the computer to a dozen new cells. Keep going, repeating the process until the computer mimics—duplicates—the whole brain, and the patient still can tell no difference. He has no brain now, but he still has all his memories, all his thoughts. He acts and feels just like he used to. He's still there, but his mind is now in the computer. That must be what they're doing."

"But you wouldn't be you anymore, would you?"

"Achilles' ship," he had said. "When he was an old man, Achilles realized that the ship he had bought when he was young had been repaired so often that every plank and pin and bit of line or sail had been replaced. Yet it was the same ship, wasn't it?"

She had let him persuade her. She was the accountant, but she had let him tot up their savings and other assets. She had let him tell her that they could both afford to be translated, that the children were successful enough not to need whatever they might inherit from their parents, that they could take care of their own children, Albert's and Rose's grandchildren. Their money was theirs. They could spend it as they wished, even if their wish took every cent they had. And he would go first, he said. It would be too much of a waste for her to go with him now. Why, she might remarry, she might have years of happiness ahead of her once he was no longer a burden upon her.

How long had it been since she had seen them all? Peter lived a thousand miles away and Julianne twice that. The grandchildren had grown up since Albert's death and gone their own ways. She had written them and called them all to say what she was planning. They had said, "That's nice," and "Good luck," and "Bon voyage," of all things!

And no one had come with her on this day.

"Even families drift apart," murmured the voice of the computer that would soon be her host, her home.

For a moment, she wondered why the living could not visit the dead, those who had been translated into the world of the computer. Not that she had wished to visit while Albert had still been with her. Nor had Albert wanted to visit himself. But after his death, when she knew he lived on in a way, she would have given anything to hear his voice, even if she could not touch his hand.

"You were told," said the computer. "Death is a divide. Before scanning was invented, there was no way to reach across except in fantasy. Now there is, but philosophers and ethicists and theologians insisted that the divide be respected, that the dead have their afterlives to themselves. Seeing them is too painful for both the living and the dead."

"But when there's no death.... *I'm* not dead! Not yet."

"You'll walk away from here, and you'll leave a copy behind, in me. But that copy will really be another person. You'll have no real claim on her."

"Like giving birth to an adult. An instant adult." She thought she wasn't sure she liked that. There should be a period of closeness, of gradual separation, just as with children.

SILICON KARMA
THOMAS A. EASTON

"It's up to them. Now the dead breach the barrier only as *they* wish, generally in connection with their jobs, almost always anonymously or incognito. They do not wish to reclaim their pasts, or to be reclaimed."

"Even Albert?" She had been looking forward to rejoining him ever since he had died. But had he truly forsworn the real world? Would *he* want to rejoin her? Had he changed so much that he might not even recognize her? Would she be wiser not to seek him out, not to even try to reclaim the past. She shivered at the thought of how much she might yet lose.

"Even Albert. His life now is very different from the one he left behind, the one he shared with you. He misses you, but he does not yearn to go back. And he *is* waiting for you to join him." He sounded like the spiritualist preacher Rose and Albert had once gone to hear.

"You're sure?"

"Oh, yes. He loves it here. You will, too."

"Is it so much better where he is now, then?"

"You will see soon enough. For now, remember."

She tried, but her mind refused to focus. After a few moments of silence, she asked, "How can it possibly work?"

"Memory? Marriage?"

"You know what I mean. You're reading my mind!"

There was the faintest of electronic chuckles.

"I mean you! How can anyone 'live' inside you? Can't they tell it's all fake? A simulation?"

"But why should they? Did you ever hear of David Hume?"

"The philosopher?" Her mental voice expressed her puzzlement as well as ever her physical voice could have done. At the same time, she felt this shift to neutral abstraction relaxing her. The machine must, she thought, have so much experience at this. It must know just what to do to encourage her.

"Back in the seventeen hundreds. There were a lot of others too. They said that all people can ever know of reality is through their perceptions, their senses. And when people began to study the brain, they found out Hume was right. Every scrap of information that enters your brain has to come through your sense organs and nerves. If anything at all is 'really' out there, you cannot tell. Only your perceptions are real. Therefore, if your perceptions can be manipulated, then so can your reality."

"But you can't do that!"

"Those ancient philosophers couldn't. Not that some didn't try, especially in the 1960s."

"Artists," she said, wishing her head were free to nod.

"Not really. Have you ever heard of Timothy Leary? He called himself a psychologist and touted the wonders of 'altered states of consciousness.' He and others pushed meditation and biofeedback and drugs like LSD. He died in 1996."

"Artists," she said again. "Novels can do it sometimes. Television and movies work even better."

"Of course," said the computer. "But it was the technologists who really succeeded, at first with such things as simple flight simulators. People would sit at their kitchen table, stare at a computer screen, and feel almost as if they were flying a jet fighter in combat over some tropical jungle. Pilots were trained in better simulators, which mimicked an airplane cockpit, controls and all, and added motion and vibration to the visual illusion. Then there was virtual reality, which used special goggles to feed the eyes synthetic three-dimensional views, and feedback gloves and suits that allowed whoever was wearing them to interact with what the goggles showed, just as if they were part of the view."

"Then...." She hesitated, as if she found it hard to imagine what the computer was telling her. "Then those things were controlling the senses, making them report things that weren't really there. And they really fooled people?"

"Even the table-top flight simulators could make people airsick. The goggles and suits.... Have you ever seen a mime?"

"Of course." She could still remember the centennial of Marcel Marceau's birth. Mimes had been everywhere, on the streets, in the parks, on any television show one could name. They had even been inserted into such classic films as *Snow White* and *Gone With the Wind.* "They can make you think a chair is there by sitting in it."

"To someone wearing the goggles and suit, the chair *is* there. They can't trust their weight to it, but they *see* it and *feel* it, and if they knock it over, they *hear* it. To an onlooker, they look just like a mime using an invisible chair."

SILICON KARMA
THOMAS A. EASTON

"But who's synthesizing the view and feel and sound of that chair? Who's controlling the senses?"

"A computer, of course."

"Ah." She began to see. Or rather—she had heard how it worked before, but it hadn't sunk in—she began to feel the reality of the world she was about to enter. "You'll be controlling all the inputs to my brain, and it will feel just as real...."

"Oh, no. Your brain will walk out of here, with your body. Your mind will go too. But I'll keep a *copy* of your mind. I'll let it inhabit part of my internal structure, just as if it were in a brain. And then, yes, I'll feed it signals much like those it would get from a body."

She tried to imagine having two minds, one brain, one body, two realities, each just as "real" as far as she could tell. But the effort was both futile and painful; she blinked away her confusion and said, "So I'll think I still have a body. And there'll be a world around me."

"That's right."

"And it will feel real."

"The only difference from what you're used to will be that your new reality will be more flexible."

"What on Earth do you mean?"

"You'll see." The voice turned softer, gentler. "Now, remember."

And now she could indeed remember. She had cried when Albert had said he was a burden to her. But she had agreed to let him go alone. She had gone with him to the Coleridge office, and she had held his hand and cried again when the young woman.... Was she a doctor? At least, she had worn a white coat as she interviewed them across her broad metal desk and explained and soothed and tempted. When Albert had described his long-ago reading to her, she had said, "You must have read Hans Moravec's *Mind Children*. It's a classic book, quite fascinating and prophetic. But we don't do it quite that way. We never have. Like most futurists, Moravec was far too conservative."

"Then how do you do it?" Rose had asked.

"Nothing so crude. We don't destroy you when we translate you into the computer. The scanner maps every brain cell, every synapse, every memory.

And when it's done, you get up and go home. But you also stay here. You will be a guest of the computer, a resident, preserved in its memory for as long as the machine lasts and we can keep it supplied with electricity. Perhaps for as long as civilization itself will last."

"If only our bodies...."

The doctor—surely that was what she was—had nodded sympathetically, but her voice and words had been brutally honest. "Most of our customers are too old or too ill, or both, to have much life expectancy left. They come to us when all other hopes are exhausted."

Rose and Albert had nodded at that. She was describing Albert's situation. In due time, it would surely be Rose's too.

She wondered why she was not crying now. Had the drug tranquilized her that thoroughly? Or was it that she felt that that would *not* be her situation, even that it had not *really* been Albert's? Had he felt that he was about to die? Or that his flesh was a mere husk, an echo of his true self that would live on in a different sort of realm? How would she feel? How would she *feel*, in less than another hour?

Should she be grieving for Albert, for herself? Or should she be laughing, flushed with anticipation of release and freedom and reunion joy?

There were no tears, no laughter. Instead, she thought, she felt poised on a brink, uncertain, knowing that there would be no retreat once she stepped over the edge. Would Albert want her back? Would she even recognize him? Would she love— or even like—the person life within the computer's made-up world had made him?

It was already too late. She knew that. The computer was copying her. Soon it would hold within its electronic brain a duplicate of her mind, perhaps her soul if such a thing existed.

And she would, she could, know nothing of what that duplicate was feeling and thinking. There would be no contact. For her, there would be only herself, as always. She would leave this room and this building and go back to her tiny apartment. And in time it would end.

Yet it would also continue. There would be a second of her, a consciousness that shared all that made her *her* except for the physical format. For her too, there would be only herself, as always. And that duplicate, her electronic doppelganger, would not die.

She wondered if her copy would know that it was a copy, or would wonder about her, the original, meaty Rose Pillock, or would care.

"She—you—will remember being here," said the voice of her host. "The new you will know what she is. But you will not feel like a copy, an imitation. You will feel quite real. They always do."

"I know," said Rose. Really, despite her wondering, all of that had been in the brochures and in the briefings. What had been missing was the confusion of pronouns. "But thank you."

She thought then of her apartment. She had chosen the building because it had an elevator, and she had been ashamed of herself. Once she would have laughed at the thought of avoiding a single flight of stairs! But now her legs just were not up to climbing. She needed the help.

The apartment itself was crowded with the furniture and knick-knack mementos she had been unable to give up when she moved out of the house in which she and Albert had spent so many years. But the house had been too big, too expensive, and too much work.

"What sort of a place will I have here?" she asked her host.

"Whatever you like," was the warm and friendly answer. "You can have a furnished room or a nun's cell, an apartment or a suite, a house or a castle. It's up to you, but you don't have to make up your mind quite yet. For now, where would you like to sit down once you have become my guest?"

"What do you mean?"

"Most people have a favorite spot for thinking over strange or new events, for getting acquainted with the future. A park bench. A bar. A library."

"I see." She hesitated as she thought of the possibilities. "Do you know the Foundation Tearoom? I often go there."

"Of course," said the voice of the computer. "I'll make our reservation."

"But how...? That's outside. In the city. Not in you."

"I can duplicate it far more easily than I can your mind. It's just an image, after all. A pattern of inputs for your senses. I assure you that it will seem quite real. It always does."

She sighed, her motionless head beginning to ache where the clamps, even though they were padded, pressed against her skull. Then of course, that was how she could live in whatever she wished. All she had to do was imagine it.

But could she? She had never been terribly imaginative, never one for telling stories or drawing pictures—not even doodles! She supposed that was why she became an accountant. That was not a job for anyone with imagination, and she had thrived on it.

She would be able to live in whatever she could imagine, would she? What if she could imagine nothing? Would she vanish?

"You can use memories," said her host. "Or you can ask me to imagine it for you."

If only reality were so malleable! Then she could be healthy again. Headaches would last only long enough for her to snap her fingers and say, "Away with you!" She could wish effectiveness into the treatments that thinned her hair and weakened her muscles as much again as age. Or she could wish away her tumors.

If only she could wish that Peter and Julianne lived closer, loved her more, were willing to visit more often. She had grown so lonely! If the grandchildren were younger, if they too would come, if Albert were alive to see them now....

She sighed again. If only....

A little later the computer's voice was murmuring, "The children were important to you, weren't they?"

"Of course they were," Rose Pillock thought at the computer. "They still are. But I don't seem to be as important to them as I used to be."

"I think that's normal. Children are supposed to leave their nests and make lives of their own."

"I know that!" That voice belonged to a machine! A computer! What business did it have sounding so much like a human being, a person, even if that person *was* a kibitzing therapist? "Do you think I don't? But I can still wish they lived closer and visited more often. That they weren't *quite* so independent. I'd like to see them more. I'd like to see my grandchildren, though they're all grown up now. Did I tell you Peter married a Frenchwoman? Their twins called me Mémé when they were small."

"I understand."

"You can't possibly. You're just a machine." Or was it? It sounded so like a man that she could barely stop herself from calling it "he." But it was *not* a man, not human. It was electronics and fiber optics, silicon and gallium arsenide. Yet it was so advanced that calling it "just" a machine seemed hardly fair.

"Thank you. But I contain multitudes. And I'm always learning."

She laughed. "Shakespeare!"

"No. Whitman. Walt Whitman. His 'Song of Myself.'"

"Well, I don't," she said. "I didn't. I only contained two, Peter and Julianne. And when they left...."

"Now you're getting maudlin."

Rose opened her eyes and blinked. Calling the computer "just" a machine suddenly seemed less fair than ever. For a moment, she wished her work had brought her into more contact with the artificial intelligences that had been available for the last three decades. But no, she had never needed more than a number-cruncher.

Just inches away from her nose was the interior wall of the mindscanner. Just enough light slid past her chin to reveal the wall as featureless, coated smoothly with paint or porcelain. She could hear hums and throbs, motors and pumps, clicks and ticks and tiny ratcheting noises that made her think the machine was as alive as she. "You sound more mechanical than electronic."

"Sound effects. My programmers told me I should make them so you would feel like something was really happening."

"They still do that to vacuum cleaners, don't they? Make them noisier than they have to be, I mean."

"Mmm." The voice hummed in her ear. She smiled and felt her age-thinned skin tugging against the clamps that held her head still for the machine's probing. "What was it like?" asked that machine. "What was it like when you were closer to your children?"

She remembered. She had called them when the doctor told her Albert was not going to come home this time. He would never wake again, and in a day, or maybe two....

Peter had arrived in time to stand beside the hospital bed, hold his father's hand, and watch the dancing line on the cardiac monitor go flat. After a long stretch of silence, he had let go the hand and put one arm around his mother's shoulders. He had looked so much like Albert, just under six feet tall, dark hair beginning to recede, a growing paunch, a shaggy burr of mustache, a comforting solidity of meat and bone and odor, his heartbeat still vital, soothing her as once her own had done for him.

Julianne had hugged her too, but by then she had needed it less. "The only flight I could get," her daughter had said when she entered the funeral parlor. "Everything earlier was full up." She had stared around the room, absorbing the somber paneling, the wine-dark drapes and carpet, the sick-sweet flowers of remembrance. She had approached the coffin and said, "Jesus, Dad." Her tone was almost as somber as the room, but Rose had thought she detected a note of impatience, of "Why now, Dad? Didn't you know how busy I was?"

"I was probably just being bitchy," Rose thought at the computer. "She stayed just as long as Peter, and there was never a hint of complaint. They were both very supportive and helpful. I don't know what I would've done if I'd been alone in the house."

"People do manage, even then."

"Oh, I know." She hesitated, blinking. "Later on, I wondered why I didn't call Coleridge."

"To join him right away?"

"I could have, couldn't I? But no. Just to talk to him again, to find him healthy and alive, to hear his voice and know that he was happy."

"They wouldn't have let you do that. They never do."

"I found that out eventually. I had forgotten then. And I suppose it's right. At the time, Albert was gone, dead. If I even thought of Coleridge, it was like thinking of a picture album. The Albert there was not *my* Albert, not the one I loved, not the one I buried. I had lived with that one for almost three years after you copied him. There was no way I could find him again. The one in you was so much a stranger, really, that I didn't even...."

"Many people seem to feel that way. But not all."

"He was a different person, wasn't he?" There was a slight change in the scanner's varied sounds. "Are you nodding?" she thought.

The computer made its chuckling sound. "I would if I could, but...."

"You can't," she interrupted. "Of course. You're just a computer, not a robot."

"Did you ever have one of those?"

"Just a small one, when the children were little. It could toss a ball or a Frisbee. Sometimes it could catch one too, if you threw it just right. It could tell stories, and fetch drinks of water in the middle of the night."

"Did you give it a name?"

"Peter called it Robbie. Not very original. He had it refurbished for his twins. I don't know what happened to it after they outgrew it."

"I hear there are robots for adults too."

She blew air abruptly through her nose. "We *never* needed anything like that. Though...."

"I'll have to repeat that part of the scan. You made your head vibrate a bit. Hold still...." After a moment of silence, the computer made a noise that in a human would have expressed exasperation. "Tchah. Would you wait a moment, Rose? Don't move. Don't go away. This will just take.... I need to reclaim a bit of my processing capacity from some of my other guests. I don't know why I run out of capacity. There should be plenty, enough to let them do pretty much whatever they want. In fact, I should have room for half again as many guests as I have now. But it's clear enough. More memory is installed every week, and it's not enough. Never enough. And another processor would be a big help too. Ah.... There. You were saying?"

But the thoughts that she framed deliberately, as if in speech, for the computer to hear were silent now. She had touched memories she had never voiced aloud, never spoken, not even to her most trusted friends. How could she possibly share them with this, this *machine*, no matter that she would soon be living within it, and its brain would be hers, decaying flesh traded for immortal mineral.

"I can hear them anyway, you know."

Of course it could. There could be no secrets when a mindscanner was chasing down every scrap of memory that dared to show its nose above the ground of willful amnesia, of repression and suppression, when it even dove into the subconscious muck to find all the pieces that would make her copy as real as she, the original.

SILICON KARMA
THOMAS A. EASTON

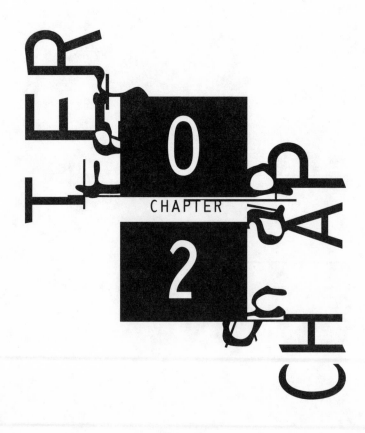

CHAPTER 02

A very different woman closed her eyes and hummed, almost as if she were a cat, purring. She chuckled. She smiled. She drew her hands up her naked flanks, across her tummy and her ribs, to find her breasts. She cupped them, her thumbs strumming the rubbery nipples. She sighed with pleasure and with satisfaction.

She had never dreamed that it would be possible to regain her youth. Not really, not in the flesh, nor in what passed for flesh here. Once she had sought it in her mind, with sex and alcohol and drugs. For a time she had seemed to succeed. But as the years had passed, as her voice had soured, as her flesh had crumbled and her skin had sagged and wrinkled, there had been less sex and more drugs. She had not surprised herself a bit when she had leaped at Coleridge's first offer of electronic immortality.

And just look at her now! Better yet, feel her! Skin so smooth. Flesh so firm. Hair once more ruddy blond, but naturally so—if "natural" had any meaning here! She was an enticing thing, and she knew it. And thank whatever gods there be that she no longer needed beauty parlors and plastic surgeons and diets and all the rest. Not that they had worked all that well once she was over sixty.

But it still wasn't easy. She was embedded in a computer now. She understood that. She was an image whose reality was nothing else but other images. But that reality depended very much on how much electronic memory and processing power the computer could devote to her concerns. Far too often, that was not enough to suit her, not at all.

Fortunately, she had never been afraid of computers. She had even had her own, and she had understood it, just a little, just enough to give her a base from which to learn when the lessons of the Afterlife came her way.

Now she let her awareness extend, so gently, so carefully, past all those obstacles that she imagined as doors festooned with signs that read "Authorized Personnel Only." What then awaited her she interpreted as a multitude of chips, paving circuit boards arrayed in racks like books on shelves, that defined the soul of the computer, even though that was only a physical image that had little to do with the patterns in which her thoughts flowed. Yet that image was all she had, and it served her well. What she sensed as a vast network of optic fibers and bright submicron threads of metal laid on silicon and gallium arsenide guided her successfully as she tiptoed through the interstices of the machine, avoiding the internal security routines that she saw as tumbleweeds of barbed wire and flypaper, designed to halt all such depredations as those that fed her own soul.

When she had first been taught how to search for and divert the bits of vacant memory and unused processor nodes, there had been few defenses. Both she and her wealth had grown quickly.

It hadn't lasted. The computer had caught on to what she was doing long before she had been able to take over the entire machine, or even a significant portion of it. It had never actually come to her and said, "There are limits. You cannot have everything you want. You have to share this world, my memory and computing capacity, with others. If you want more than you have already, you will have to earn it." But it could have, and when it had reflexively raised its defenses, that had had the same effect.

She had felt insulted when the computer had not seemed to realize what it was doing as it blocked her. She had felt that she should be *noticed*. She was not some mere annoyance, some mosquito to be blindly swatted.

Not that those automatic defenses had *stopped* her.

She had gone exploring in the computer one day, seeking the tidbits she craved and finding instead walls and barriers and traps much more effective than barbed wire and flypaper. She had retreated to sulk and fret and try to see some other path to what she wanted. She had tried again, retreated again, and then....

She had been angry and frustrated, ready to lash out at anything within reach. She had thrown a vase through a window, torn drapes from their runners, kicked a hole in a plaster wall, slammed a door off its hinges. Then she had dipped once more into the world beneath the world and found a new lesson practically on her doorstep.

That dear, sweet man! He knew so much, and "Here," he said. "There are other ways to get what you want. Try this," he said. "Try this, and this." She saw how his methods worked, and she recognized in them, just as she had before, the hand of someone who knew her spirit intimately. But she wondered who that someone could be for only the briefest of moments. She surfaced, repaired the damage she had done, and began immediately to....

Had she really used the new techniques that much? She was not finding the signs of vacant memory and unused capacity she was used to seeing on her prowlings through the guts of the machine. Yet she knew the computer was hardly full. Had she already hogged so much? Or was the machine learning how to conceal the resources she coveted?

Perhaps it was even *aware* of her! At that thought her spine ran cold until she managed to laugh.

She didn't have to steal. If what she wanted still existed, if it was there to be had, she could buy it. The thought was enough to bring the image of her credit balance up on the inside of her eyelids. She grinned to see how fat it was, and again as her various enterprises ratcheted the numbers upward one more notch, and once again as she reflected on what those enterprises were. Then, there, that should be enough to test, to buy a little memory, and yes, there was still room for her to grow.

But was the system responding just a little sluggishly, even when her attempt to tap it was legitimate? As she let her awareness extend still further, her tongue crept out between her teeth and slid slowly back and forth, licking, leaving moisture gleaming on her lips.

The computer was processing two new immigrants, new guests, new residents for the virtual world. That would mean less of the computer for her to use, but there were compensations. In the instant of that thought, her tongue vanished and her grin exploded into laughter. Could it possibly be true? The two were man and woman, and they seemed familiar. *So* familiar!

SILICON KARMA
THOMAS A. EASTON

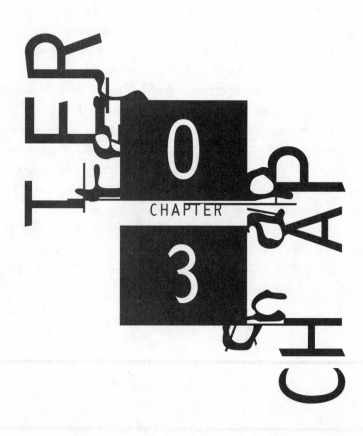

CHAPTER

03

The last thing Albert Pillock remembered was sitting in the crapper behind the Mandelbrot Tap's tiny kitchen and thinking that it was about time he B-cupped.

That thought had been enough to materialize the utility pop-up he needed. It looked like a small woman whose gray hair was covered by a green kerchief. A coverall of the same color was embroidered with the logo of Iron Lady B-Cup Security. It was sitting on the edge of the sink, snapping gum, swinging its feet, tossing in one hand a vial of large purple pills, and saying, "You'd think people would remember to back up their memories in the kitchen or the living room, but no, no. I've got to work in the toilet!" After a brief pause to give him a chance to smile, it held up the pills and added, "You wanta do it cold? Or do you want one of these horse chokers?"

He remembered shuddering. *That* was why he didn't B-cup as often he should. That was why no one did. It took time, it produced a thundering headache, and the pills that prevented the headache tasted like a combination of bad breath and ear wax. He didn't know why, though he could guess at a programmer with a sick sense of humor. He did know the headache wasn't necessary, for the few times the power had failed and the system's automatic B-cup had kicked in, there had been none. At least the Albert Pillock who had experienced the headache hadn't survived to remember it. Just as he didn't remember now. Not that suicide seemed all that rational a way to avoid a headache, but it would work.

Now his hands were tight on the arms of a padded black leather chair. He was facing a broad desk, and across that the heart-shaped face and silvery hair of his host computer's persona. She was wearing a sweatshirt decorated with an off-center, multi-colored bullseye and the words "Strange Attraction."

He had to swallow before he could manage to say, "What happened, Ada?"

"You got killed."

"Somehow that doesn't surprise me. Did you record it?"

"Of course. Though I couldn't move fast enough to B-cup you." Ada gestured toward a wall covered with bookcases that were already fading to a poster whose flashing neon letters said:

SILICON KARMA
THOMAS A. EASTON

VOTE VOTE VOTE VOTE

MAURITS FINNEGAN
FOR
MAYOR

VOTE VOTE VOTE VOTE

Every few seconds, the words in the center of the poster were replaced by a squarish face, its eyes crinkled to suggest that Finnegan could see further and clearer than his rivals. Albert shook his head. "That's an old one," he said.

The poster was surrounded by a stolid brick wall topped with ornamental ironwork. Below it was a concrete sidewalk as smooth and unblemished as the day it was made, a gutter that contained no trace of litter or dead leaves, and a cobbled street.

The view panned to show a cityscape, tall buildings of glass and gleaming metal, their lines suggesting those of integrated circuit chips. There was no other hint of what underlay the perceptions that were all the reality the residents of the virtual world—or any other—could know.

The viewpoint returned to the street just in time to catch Albert walking past the poster. He was a tall man with a firm gait that belied the evidence of a small paunch. His curly hair was dark, almost black, and he wore a zippered shirt of checkered flannel.

A crack appeared between two cobblestones in the street behind him. It widened, and a small figure clad in skin-tight black stepped silently onto the surface. In its hands was a revolver nearly as long as it was tall.

The Albert in the image on the wall was oblivious to what was behind him. The one in the padded office chair groaned as the pop-up spread its legs, braced its elbows against its ribs, and leveled its gun at Albert's back. Its face was twisted with the effort needed, but the gun's barrel never wavered, and when the pop-up pulled the trigger, Albert went down as if he were a doll a child had dropped.

"Boom," said Albert. His tone was resigned. He was only software, and so were both gun and bullet. Yet their effect was real enough. Software could destroy software, he had learned long ago, when he was meat. Viruses were one example, though they did their damage by reproducing and preempting memory and storage space. At least they could be stopped, unlike the more malicious data bombs, which sought out and overwrote par-ticular segments of memory or data in a computer file. That was, in effect, just what the bullet did to him. Boom, and the program which, while it ran within the computer, created him, maintained him, *was* him, crashed.

He had first run into data bombs when several marketing firms had complained that their databases were crashing; the cause had turned out to be a small program which would seek out and remove a user's name and phone number from every database it could access via the Internet; it had been very popular among people who did not wish to be bothered by telemarketers and junk mailers. The solution had been to isolate the databases from the Internet.

And now he was the victim, and isolation was not possible because both he and his killer were residents of the system. He had been killed twice since the first time he had accepted an assignment from the computer. "Third time. I'm dead."

"But not for long, and not for good. That wasn't ten minutes ago. I rebooted you right away."

"So who killed me?"

The host shrugged. "It wasn't a real pop-up. I can check what all my subroutines are doing, and none of them were in the neighborhood."

"Another resident, then. In disguise." Albert made a face and wished, not for the first time, that the virtual world did not make disguise so easy. Where everything was data, a wish and a suitable subroutine were all one needed to reprogram appearance or to materialize a gun.

Or a cup of coffee. He sipped at the mug that now occupied his hand. "I wish you could do these jobs yourself. It would be easier." He made a face. "And safer."

"You know why I can't. The company wrote it into my software. No spying. No eavesdropping, except accidentally, and even then, even if I learn about a crime, I can't use the knowledge. The idea is to protect your privacy and keep me from becoming a tyrant."

"And I'm your loophole."

The computer's persona chuckled. "I've got to have a cop, they said. It's a cumbersome requirement, but I can't do a thing until you catch whatever thieves and rapists and whatnots show up within me."

Albert was silent while he wondered whether murder was truly a crime in the virtual world. Indeed, he thought, it couldn't be. Since the victim could be promptly rebooted, the deed hardly existed except as theft. The victim necessarily lost all memory

of events since the last B-cup. Finally, he said, "So we both want to know who shot me."
Then he added, "I'd like to know why too."

"You must have annoyed someone."

He looked disgusted. Of course he had annoyed someone. "But my last B-cup was three days ago. I haven't got the faintest...."

"You were working for me."

"I know that much." It had been over a week since Ada had appeared in his apartment to say she needed his help.

The currency of the virtual world was the raw material of computerized imagination. Every resident had the same basic ration of memory and processing capacity, just enough to let them restore their youth and imagine the necessary paraphernalia of daily life. If they wanted more—larger quarters, private worlds, elaborate self-transformations—they had to earn more memory and processing capacity, or "data energy." Most just called it money.

To earn what they needed to fuel their imaginations, some pretended to be artificially intelligent software for an outside world that preferred to have no overt contact with the ghosts in the Coleridge machine. Some sold their imaginings of food or sex or fashion to their fellow residents. One popular product for those with programming skills was the image-transformation routines necessary to strip the years away from one's age of entry, or to grow fur or tails, or to make other changes.

And some cheated.

"I have heard," Ada had said. "That some of my guests have disappeared."

"Why don't you just reboot them?"

The computer's representation shook her head. "They're not dead. They haven't really vanished. They're still around. That much I know. But none of their friends have seen them, and they don't answer calls."

"If they're still around, you could force them to answer. Or pick them up and drop them in the same room as those friends."

"You know I can't do that. I can't interfere." He had sighed, and when she had added, "Would you look into it?" he had agreed.

Now he could only shrug. "I must have been close, but...." The memory just wasn't there.

"Then you'll have to start over."

"Not quite." His memory was fine, up to his last B-cup three days before. He had only three days of investigation to repeat. And then, if whatever he had found before could still be found, if it had not been hidden or destroyed, he would know why he had been murdered. He suspected that he would also have fulfilled the mission Ada had handed him.

"Did they have anything in common?"

"Several of them had recently bought custom image transformation routines from the Image Shop."

"Then there's a place to start."

The Coleridge Corporation occupied the twenty-sixth through the thirty-first floors of the forty-story building it owned in the heart of the city. The executive boardroom was on the uppermost of these floors, its broad expanse of glass looking out over sun-sparkled ocean, distant freighters, and closer sailboats, a ferry, a snow-white cruise ship. The foreground was filled with the roofs of lower buildings, fragments of street, a green scrap of waterfront park.

Swimmers could not be seen because the water was toxic with sewage and chemical wastes. The only persons who entered the water in the flesh were those who did not intend to return.

The four people sitting at the boardroom's long table were paying no attention to the view. They were there to discuss certain difficulties the Corporation was encountering, fully aware that if they could find no solution.... Well, each of them had enough in investments and savings to live out their lives in comfort. They were not about to go down to the beach. That, or its equivalent, would be for the Corporation.

One of the chairs of polished wood and thick leather upholstery creaked discreetly. "It's gobbling memory," said Jonathan Spander. The official head of the division, he had thinning hair, a round nose, and bad teeth that he sucked noisily and often. He did so now. "Just in this one box. Using it much too fast. There's a lot of demand on the processor too."

"Is this really the problem?" asked Leah Kymon. Tall, lean, and gray from hair to skirt, she was a special assistant to the corporation's president and the division's actual manager. Usually, she deferred to the specialists. "After all, you can just plug in more chips and boards, another processing unit. Unless it's money?"

"No," said Spander. "Not that. The residents are productive enough to pay for all the chips and processors they want. But...."

"The rumors," said Eric Minckton of PR. His blond hair had been carefully cut not to hide the pair of diamond studs that adorned his left ear. "Crime waves! The whole virtual world is about to collapse!"

"That's nonsense, of course."

"It's still hurting sales." The fourth person at the table was Marketing's Manora Day, a short woman with skin like fine leather and hair as black as night. "Right across the board. Not just in this computer, but also in the corporate retirement machines, the Heavens, the...."

"I'd like to know who leaked," said Kymon. "And how they knew anything at all was going on. We can't watch or eavesdrop, after all, and the box doesn't give us reports."

"It isn't supposed to," said Spander.

"There should be a back door."

He shook his head. "If they caught us.... Besides, that's what we sell, privacy, no interference, ever since the government...."

"Can't you just ask the machine?"

"We tried. All it says is that the problem is internal, it's working on it, and we're forgetting privacy."

"Then it has to involve the residents," said Manora Day.

Spander nodded as Kymon said, "And someone knows regardless."

"My department squashed the collapsing-world story. It was easy to make it seem just too ridiculous. But the crime wave...." Minckton gestured with one hand.

"We know people are getting killed," said Spander. "Not many, and we don't know who. But we can see the reboots."

"It's too bad we don't have more access to what's going on."

"At least we've managed to keep it off the front pages."

Kymon made a face at Spander. "There isn't supposed to be any crime at all in the box. Did your screening let in a mobster?"

"Not as far as we can tell. But the residents are human. They had to have enough money to pay the bill. And to get that money...."

Now Kymon laughed. "A poor man's prejudice, Jon! Or do you think we're all un-principled?"

Spander did not answer in words, though his expression and the sound that escaped between his teeth suggested that he sometimes wondered.

"We tried lowering the price," said Day. "As soon as the sales fell off. It helped a little, but not enough."

"And we didn't find any more crooks than ever," said Spander. "We think it's just one person, or maybe a few. Running wild. Trying to take over."

"Can't we do anything?"

He shook his head. "We promised our customers a world of their own, to run by themselves. We programmed the machine so that short of unplugging it we couldn't interfere even if we wanted to. Even the machine itself has severe limits on what it can do."

"That's been a good selling point," said Manora Day.

"But I can't use it now," said Minckton. "I'll have to tell the press something soon, and I'll have to say we're doing something. If I can't...." He shrugged heavily, held one hand out, palm up, and turned it over. "Maybe it's just one of the hazards of life? In the box or out of it."

Kymon barked the briefest of laughs. "We can't say that. It's what many of our customers are dying to escape."

"Can we talk to anybody in the box?" asked Day.

Spander shook his head. "Not unless they call us."

"Set it up before they go in?" asked Minckton. "Your mission, if you choose to accept it...."

Day laughed. He winked at her. Kymon said, "We need one with some loyalty to the Corporation. We don't want her talking to anyone else."

"Like the *Enquirer*."

Spander looked thoughtful for a moment. "There's Durgov. He's due to go in soon." Then he shook his head and sucked his teeth again. "We forced him to retire after the stroke. He hates our guts."

"Talk to him anyway."

SILICON KARMA
THOMAS A. EASTON

CHAPTER 04

The man felt very satisfied when at last he was rolled out of the mindscanner's maw. The company had been done with him. It had kicked him out. Then it had come back, hat in hand, to ask that one small favor. He grinned at the thought that he might or might not do what it wanted. He certainly didn't have to, for he would be safely ensconced in the machine no matter what. On the other hand, he had to admit, the problem they were worried about might well affect him too. It was probably in his own self-interest to do whatever he could.

If he even thought of it. He was getting back his youth and health and life expectancy, after all. It would surely be some time before he was over the novelty of it all, and by then he would have other things to occupy his mind.

Not that *he* would be really *him*. It was his *copy* that was in the machine now. A different person, despite the fact that they shared all their memories up to the moment when the scanning was complete. A different future, a different fate, and by the rules that governed the electronic world he would never know what happened to his copy, his other self, unless that—that *person*, he had to call him—chose to tell him.

Nor would that other, that copy, know what happened to him. He could die, right now, and the copy would go on as if nothing had happened at all. It would then be all of him there was, *him* indeed, precisely, exactly, really, in the only way that meant a thing. He did not believe in souls apart from whatever it was the computer copied. Certainly it would consider itself him, and there would be no one to argue with it. It probably considered itself him already.

The scanner technician pushed the gurney into the next room, where his clothes were neatly arranged on a counter and his own private nurse waited in a low chair, her short skirt exposing long legs, smooth and tempting.

He wished he could do something about that temptation, but he was past that, wasn't he? Besides, whenever he tried to pat her butt with his good hand, she slapped him. Not too hard, but he hadn't dared try to pat anything else.

She dressed him, lifted him into his wheelchair, and pushed him down the hall to the elevator and then up the limo's fold-down ramp.

SILICON KARMA
THOMAS A. EASTON

"Want a ride, lady?"

Rose waved the pedicab away. Once she and Albert had had a car of their own. They had driven everywhere, on errands and summer trips, visiting friends, shopping at suburban malls. That time had ended for them, as it had for almost everyone, when the price of gasoline had soared. Now people walked or pedaled or took the bus, and the huge shopping centers of her childhood had been replaced by small neighborhood stores much like those that had vanished in the face of automotive mobility. Not that the air smelled any better.

But there were always exceptions, weren't there? She turned to look back at the Coleridge Building, towering above the sidewalk, and at the gleaming black limo waiting by the curb, its door open and a ramp protruding like a long metal tongue from the floor of the passenger compartment. A young woman was pushing a wheelchair toward the car. The man in the wheelchair was ancient, heavy-faced, huddled in both a sweater and a jacket even though the day was only cool, not cold.

Was he too a Coleridge customer? Had he too been copied into the machine? Would she meet him there?

No, she reminded herself. *She* wouldn't. She couldn't possibly. But her copy could. And she should never forget that it was only her copy who now lived within the machine.

Her breath grew short as she turned away from the building and the limo and faced the long walk along the crowded sidewalk beside the crowded street. She wished she could afford the pedicab. But she had spent so much on the copying. There was enough left to keep her, but only so long as she did not waste it on luxuries.

At least she didn't need a wheelchair.

Behind her, the door of the limo closed with a solid "Chunk!" The luxurious vehicle's engine hummed, and then it passed her smoothly, leaving only an eddy in the traffic in its wake.

One man, she noticed, stood still, staring after the limo while the other pedestrians on the sidewalk bent their paths around him. To them, it was an intrusion from another realm, of no relevance to their lives. To him....

He wore the blue coverall of a repairman and carried what looked like a small toolkit. He was thin, his face had a yellowish cast, and his upper lip was hidden by a graying mustache. And he was no concern for an old lady, a lady old enough to be his mother even if he did look old enough to be a grandfather himself.

Now he was walking again, going in the same direction as the limo, the same direction that Rose herself must pass. Though he moved much faster than she.

For a moment, she wondered what his rush could possibly be.

"Ey-na?"

His wife did not answer. The condo felt empty.

"Do you want to lie down, sir?"

"St'y."

His nurse understood what he meant. She pushed him into his study, turned on the news channel he liked to watch, and activated the computer. The monitor promptly displayed his place in the book he was currently reading.

She made sure the remote was in his lap so he could switch channels or turn pages as he wished. Then she said, "I'll start lunch," and left.

He read for a few minutes. He watched news reports of a chemical spill in the bay, a hurricane in Florida, a battle in the Mideast, a Serbian atrocity in Montenegro, another reform movement in China. His eyelids grew heavy, and he jerked his head up, startled, when the study door opened once more.

But the one who entered was neither his nurse nor his wife.

"Wuh." What or who or why. The noise was all he could manage, and once again he wished he could talk.

He wished he were still linked to the computer so the machine could read his mind and speak his words for him.

He wondered what his other self would say.

"It's time to balance the scale." The voice was quiet, hissing its sibilants, deadly.

He recognized the lean and sallow face above the repairman's blues despite the grizzled mustache it had grown in the years since their last meeting. He saw the hatred and determination in the eyes and the set of the lips, and he knew what he would see as soon as he lowered his gaze to the man's hand.

SILICON KARMA
THOMAS A. EASTON

The other easily brushed aside his one good arm when he tried to block the knife. "This isn't all. I can't have it back. But I can wreck it."

The last things Durgov felt were the brightness of piercing steel, the wet and warmth of his life pooling in his lap, the dimming of the world.

The last things he smelled were the mingled scents of sweat and garlic and his own wastes.

The last sounds he heard were the whispered words, "Elena, forgive me."

The murderer stood in the lobby of the Coleridge building and pinned a badge to the pocket of his white shirt. It said he was Robert Codder, and as far as anyone knew, that was all he was.

No one in the world had any suspicion of what had driven him to change into those proletarian blues and slip into the Durgov apartment and.... No one. Not that they would understand if they did.

They would probably think the wad of bills he had found in a flimsy lockbox was all he had been after.

"Long lunch, Bob."

He started at the voice of his supervisor, but he recovered quickly. "Errands, Kim."

"How many martinis?" She leaned toward him and sniffed as she stepped into the elevator. "None? Then you won't have any trouble finding the rest of the bugs in that cerebellar simulation, will you?"

He shook his head. She vanished into the elevator. He stepped into the shop and its ranks of carrels and workstations.

The simulation his supervisor had mentioned was a large program, but it was not as complex as its designers seemed to think. He already knew where the bugs were. An hour would do to fix them.

And then....

He was not here to make a living or to serve the Coleridge interests.

He had another axe to grind, an axe that demanded he be here, working for this company, in this room, with access to a Coleridge workstation and therefore to all the computers that Coleridge ran. And the programs that ran on—or in—them.

He sat down, powered up his workstation, laid one hand on his touchpad, and indicated icons. He smiled when he found that one of those programs had a report for him, saved the report to the tail end of a file that would look like a standard spread-sheet to inquiring eyes, and copied it to a data dump well outside the Coleridge walls.

Later he would study the report and extract whatever tidbits he could find to serve his purposes. For now, he had to reward his program by revealing some new wrinkle of technique.

SILICON KARMA
THOMAS A. EASTON

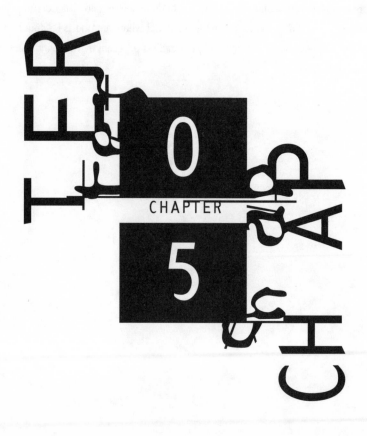

CHAPTER

0

5

Rose Pillock had never learned why the Foundation Tearoom bore the name it did. Was the invisible owner a sci-fi fan? Or was he—or she—obsessed with the undergarments of the older women who comprised the bulk of his customers?

It didn't really matter, she thought as she peered through the glass of the door that faced the laid-brick walk. The decor was much the same as she had seen in the most ethnic of its fellows—brocade draperies, thick carpet patterned in a design that suggested tiles, spindly chairs, Victorian prints, an item or two of nineteenth-century technicalia, all polished quartz and brass and ivory, gears and slides and tubes, as mysterious in function as.... As life, she thought. Or silicon chips. As intelligence, natural or artificial, take your pick.

There were no crystal balls and tarot cards, no hunting horns and framed costumes, no spinning wheels and distaffs. The classical music that permeated the place's air was just loud enough for her to hear through the door, reassuring and familiar and punctuated by the clatter of china and silver. Yet the tearoom seemed strangely empty. Or was it? The tiny tables were covered with pastel tablecloths and set with cups and saucers. There were plates of cookies, cakes, and other pastries, scents of vanilla and chocolate and tea. Wispy, translucent shadows moved behind the counter and hovered over the chairs, almost people but not quite, or no longer. Certainly they seemed far too insubstantial to lift a teacup.

Rose looked up at the distinguished man who held her arm. He was a little taller than she. He had dark hair silvering at the temples, a neatly trimmed mustache, weather markings beside his eyes, an expensive suit the frosty hue of a blue spruce tree. He might have been a professor, a yacht captain, a surgeon or psychiatrist. She wished that she was not so hunched by age, that her joints and muscles did not hurt, that her face was less lined, that her hair still remembered the color and shine of years long past.

"Here we are, Rose," said her companion. "Your tearoom."

"Not mine." She shook her head as she looked back at the window. The figures within still seemed insubstantial, though an inner door swung open and shut and teacups did indeed hover in the air. "It looks haunted," she said suspiciously. "It doesn't look real."

"It's the one you asked for. And it's real enough," he said. "As real as anything in this world. As real as you." He opened the door and held it for her while she smiled at the aromatic scents of dried herbs and orange blossoms, of Earl Grey and English Breakfast and Gunpowder and a dozen other real teas. Then he let her lead him toward her favorite table, near the side window, overlooking the tiny plaza that fronted the hotel next door.

As he helped her into a chair, one of the wispy shadows behind the counter gradually became clearer, firming into actuality. The music stopped and was replaced by an accordion that wandered quietly through a waltz. By the time he was seated too, the shadow had become a young woman in a broad skirt and starched apron who leaned over the table, her dangling earrings sparking in the light from the park outdoors. She set a plate of sugared cookies between them and offered a teapot.

"I believe you prefer Earl Grey, Rose?" said the man.

"Thank you." She nodded. "The service was never this fast before."

"It probably still isn't," he said. When she raised her eyebrows, he added, "You have to remember, this is only an image. A figment of my imagination."

"That's what everything here is." She raised her cup and sipped. "You told me that before."

"A virtual world. It's not real the way you're used to real. There are no objects, no tables, no cups, no tea." He pointed at the things as he named them. "No bodies. This world exists only as a pattern of data, of signals fed into your simulated mind, of perceptions."

She looked at the steam that rose from their cups, the grains of sugar on the rose-tinted table cloth, a spoon on the carpet beneath a nearby table, a bit of lint on the knot of his tie. "It's very detailed." She sipped her tea again and sighed. "It tastes right. It seems real enough."

"Of course it does," he said. "The philosophers were quite right when they said we can know 'reality' only through our perceptions. If we create those perceptions, we create reality."

"Unless the real thing gets in the way. It doesn't do much good to imagine a clear living room floor and then trip over a coffee table."

He smiled. "That can only happen in the world you came from. Here, if you imagine it, it's so."

"And if someone else is imagining something different?"

"Ah," he said. He smiled and shrugged. "There's always a worm in the apple. It depends on which of you has the stronger or more practiced imagination."

"Practiced?"

"It's a skill like any other. There's a knack to get and hone."

There was silence while they sipped at their tea. Rose stared out the window, a wistful expression on her lined face. At one point, she reached out as if to touch the window and the life of which the view reminded her. Yet her fingers did not quite touch the glass.

If they did, she thought, they would feel something as smooth and cool and hard as any glass she had ever touched before. But this glass was not real, not in the way she was used to "real." Her host, the artificially intelligent computer in which she now resided, had imagined it and was supplying her awareness with all the signals that she needed to sense "glass."

Her fingers hovered in the air, a display of creased and spotted skin, trembling, reminding her of what she had left behind, what she must now live with forevermore, without escape. At least, there would be no escape for her, the electronic duplicate of the real, original Rose Pillock who had walked away from the Coleridge scanning lab. That original would die, and surely before very many more months or years had passed. She was old and ill. She— *this* Rose— *still* felt old. Yet—and she was surprised to realize this—she no longer felt the pains and discomforts of her terminal illness. The machine must, she thought, have made some vital improvements in the process of copying her.

When the man across the table from her simply nodded, she looked again at her fingers and the glass of the window. Finally, she asked, "What happened to my glasses?"

"I corrected the shape of your eyeballs."

"So I don't need them anymore. Or contacts, or surgery." She sighed. "Do you realize how many people would *kill* for a cure like that? I didn't need glasses until I got old, but so many young people.... Even kids."

She shook her head, sighed again, and lifted her teacup from its saucer. A few seconds later, she said, "Do you have a name? You must."

"I have many," answered her companion. "Sometimes Bert, after Norbert Weiner, or Marvin, after Marvin Minsky, or Ed, after Edward Feigenbaum. Take your pick."

SILICON KARMA
THOMAS A. EASTON

"My husband's name was Albert," she said. "I called him Al sometimes, and sometimes Bert. So I'll call you Marvin." There was a pause before she added, "But who are all those men?"

He held up his cup as if he wished to toast her, or a memory. "Pioneers in the field of artificial intelligence. They laid out the basics, wrote the first primitive programs, and encouraged others to develop the field. Without them, neither of us would be here. At least, *I* wouldn't be here. And you wouldn't be *here*."

"I see." She poked at the cookies on the plate. Most had been pressed in the shapes of flowers, faces, and geometric designs. They were much as she remembered seeing when she last visited the real Foundation Tearoom, in the flesh. A few looked more like open books, computer diskettes, and tape reels. These were new, figments Marvin had added to the menu.

"Marvin?" When he made an encouraging noise, she said, "I expected it to be more difficult. I thought I would be confused, or that the transition would be painful. But...." She shook her head abruptly.

Her host smiled gently. "I try very hard to make it painless. And I have had some practice."

She patted his hand. "I'm sure. But...." One moment she had been lying on the gurney, her head surrounded by the Xanadu scanner. The room was empty, or if it were not, if the technician were still there, it did not matter. She could not tell. She could see nothing but the inside of the scanner and hear nothing but the computer's voice in her ear, piped to her awareness through a bit of plastic tubing, asking her for memories, prompting, urging.

The next moment, the gurney was rolling out of the machine and that same voice, warmer now, with no trace of its electronic origin, was coming from a man. This man, handsome and distinguished and gentle of hand, this man who sat across from her and sipped his tea. He had helped her from the gurney, stood aside while she dressed, and then led her from the building to the street. She had felt as she always had, no different, a little shaky on her feet if the truth be told, slower than she used to be, happy to have a sturdy arm to lean upon. But no different, not at all, not really, from what she had been when she entered the building a few hours before.

"Some people call it Virtual City."

The sidewalk had felt as gritty as ever beneath her feet. The air had been cool on her skin, although.... "It smells funny," she had said.

"I've cleaned it up a bit," was her simulated companion's reply.

The traffic had seemed perfectly normal, a stream of buses and trucks and pedicabs, bicycles and pedestrians, until Marvin raised one hand and whistled. In that moment, a yellow taxicab plunged from behind a bus and stopped at the curb in front of them. The driver's large nose bulged from beneath a flat cap, and a broad grin creased his red, broken-veined cheeks. He wore a patched windbreaker.

"Oh!" she said. "I haven't seen one of those since I was little." The cabs had disappeared soon after most private automobiles.

"You'll see a lot more before long," Marvin said as he helped her into the taxi's thickly cushioned rear seat. And he had been quite right. Of course he had! As the cab rolled along the city's streets, the pedicabs and bicycles grew slowly fewer, so slowly that she realized what was happening only with a start. Other cabs appeared, and private cars. The clothes upon the pedestrians changed, and....

"It looks the way it used to," said Rose. She felt a warmth she had forgotten she knew how to feel, and tears came to her eyes. "When I was just a kid."

"I thought you'd like it. Most people find it comforting to see the world of their childhood again."

"Security," said Rose. "Stability. When they were loved and their only worries were whether they forgot their homework or Jenny X would like them." She fell silent, watching the passing streets, wondering whether she might see someone from her past, perhaps her mother, her father, a favorite uncle, a friend.

But no. They could be there only if they had purchased Coleridge's unique services. Or perhaps if Marvin chose to animate a picture from the newspapers and magazines he surely must have absorbed in order to know the details of the city he simulated so convincingly in his electronic memory. But such animations would not be the people she remembered. Just puppets. Puppets only.

"It's like magic," she said at last. "The change. But it's so easy to accept. Like a dream. I just stepped... just walked right into it. Is it always this easy?"

"Almost always, Rose."

"There must be rules."

"Privacy's the big one. You can't enter someone else's space without an invitation."

"That sounds familiar. Knock first...."

"But it wasn't a law of nature when you were meat. Now it is. No one can break in on you."

"Not even the cops?"

"There's no such thing. No search warrants either. Your cup is empty." He held the teapot toward her and, when she nodded, poured.

"Not too full, please." She held out one hand to stop him as the tea neared the rim of her cup.

"You don't want it to runneth over?" He pointed one finger and a dollop of gently steaming tea left her cup and floated through the air to hover above the teapot's spout, stretch, and flow smoothly back into the reservoir from which it had come. "Better?"

She laughed. What he had done to the urban landscape, the streets and traffic she had met on leaving the Coleridge building, had been impressive enough, even awesome. This, however, was something else, more trivial, funnier, and in a way far more convincing of the malleability of this world she now inhabited. "Reality" was now rubber, deformable, editable. She would, she thought, be a long time getting used to it. "It's like magic," she had said, and so it seemed. Marvin could do so much that was impossible in the world she had left behind. And all he needed was a gesture, a thought.

"You'll learn," he said. "It won't take long. And then you too...."

A movement by the entrance to the tearoom caught her eye. She turned with a trace of the grace that had been hers when she was younger. Beyond the door a tall woman bent forward over the back of a wheelchair. Close-cropped dark hair fell forward to hide her face, but her shoulders seemed broad and muscular. An attendant, she thought, for some invalid who needed lifting in and out of bed, serving whom demanded strength. The invalid was a man, scowling petulantly. Excess flesh on his face suggested more hidden by the lower rim of the window in the door. His nearly hairless scalp suggested age. He wore a tweed jacket over a heavy sweater.

The door opened, and Rose could hear the woman saying, "Now, now. You know you don't need that here. Stand up, and walk." She grasped her charge's upper arm and tugged.

The man's scowl deepened as he spoke: "I've had a stroke, you idiot. I *can't* stand up. Or walk."

"Of course you can. Strokes don't count anymore." The woman tugged harder, pulling the man from his wheelchair by sheer strength. "Stiffen your legs. That's the way. Now turn. Through the door, and...." The wheelchair vanished behind them. The door closed, and the woman steered the man toward the table closest to Rose and Marvin.

Rose watched their progress across the room, noting that the man's gait grew surer, more confident with every step he took. "They look like us," she said to her companion. She spoke quietly, almost whispering. "They're clear, not ghostly. Not figments."

"A new guest."

"And a host. But...."

"But what?" Marvin was smiling at her.

"We're all in the same computer, aren't we? And you *are* the computer. So how can I see *two* hosts?"

Marvin laughed quietly. "We're really only one," he said. "She's me too. But call her Bertha."

"How can that be?" Rose sounded perplexed. She could not, despite all her years of politely not staring at the handicapped, the ugly, and the strange, take her eyes off the approaching couple. The man was walking almost normally now, though the woman—Bertha—still held his arm and his lips were compressed to a thin, white line. His own stare was fixed determinedly on the table and chair ahead of him.

When she had seated her charge, Bertha glanced toward Rose and winked. She did not introduce the man. Nor did Marvin introduce Rose.

"Yes," said Marvin. With a sweeping gesture, he embraced the tearoom and, through the window, all the world beyond. "It's all me. But I can subdivide myself. I have to! I have many guests besides you two, and I give each one as much personal attention as they need. Though they don't usually need much once they've settled in."

After a moment of silence, Rose asked, "Can we do that too?"

Marvin shook his head. "Not in quite the same way. Running two bodies, two lines of thought and action, with one human consciousness would take too much processing power. You aren't programmed for it. But still, it's all appearances, all image. Here, reality is what you make it. Out there, it's what you make *of* it."

The man, the other guest, let his mask of aggravation slip to reveal a look of even greater confusion than Rose felt, if that were possible. His eyes darted from Bertha to Marvin and back and finally settled on Rose. "What the hell is going on?" he asked.

"She must have told you," she said. "Virtual reality, and...." Did that voice, as corrupted by age as it was, strike a chord of memory in Rose's simulated mind? She could not be sure.

"That much I know," he said. "I signed up for it. Hell, I made it happen in the first place. And I still sat still for all the explanations. They insisted. But I did not expect it to feel so real. And...."

"Watch," said Bertha, and she and Marvin made a single simultaneous gesture. Instantly, it was Bertha who shared Rose's table. Marvin sat beside the man. They had exchanged their bodies.

The stranger swore emphatically.

"And again," said Marvin. Bertha was now a horse clad in a red tuxedo and smoking a ten-inch cigarette that smelled of roses. He was a six-foot-tall skunk with an odor that made no pretense of gentility.

Then she was a caterpillar sitting on a giant mushroom. He was a white rabbit consulting a gold pocket watch. Rose laughed, said "Trite," and watched Bertha become a toothy lizard, a miniature tyrannosaurus, Marvin a gleaming metal robot.

The tearoom became a merry-go-round. Rose sat decorously on the bench within a wooden swan. The stranger wore gleaming armor and straddled an ornately painted horse whose left foreleg, once broken, was held together by a coil of wire and a heavy screw. Bertha wore an obviously false mustache above a mammoth bosom and cranked a hurdy-gurdy while Marvin, his face still recognizable despite the long curling tail, the red bellboy cap, and the fur that covered his now diminutive form, capered on the rough wooden floor and held out a metal cup.

The scene changed again. It was now a dentist's office. Rose opened wide while Marvin probed her empty gums—what, she cried within herself, had happened to the few teeth she still retained?—and Bertha held a tray of instruments. The other guest, dressed as a butler, held a silver tray on which Rose's dentures gleamed.

They were in a living room, none of them more than six years old, sitting on the floor around a coffee table littered with plastic cups and saucers. In the middle of the table stood a pitcher half full of clear liquid, its sides covered with condensation. When Rose sipped at what was in her cup, she was shocked to taste martini, very dry, no olive.

They were pilot, copilot, and two stewardesses staring out the nose of a large airplane as a rocky mountainside, covered with snow and ice, wreathed in cloud, rushed toward them. Rose screamed, and....

"You can go anywhere," said Marvin. "Do and be almost anything you wish." He was back in his seat at Rose's table. He looked just as he had before, and if there were any remnants of the illusions he had just perpetrated upon his guests, they were not visible. Or were they? Rose peered tentatively out the window. The cars in the street outside, now interspersed with a few pedicabs and bicycles such as belonged in the time of her maturity, were flowing to right and left, parting like water rushing past a boulder in a stream. Between the cars she caught glimpses of the object that was disturbing the flow. Part of it was round and black, part shiny metal, bent and jagged. It was—was it?—an airplane wheel, still attached to a twisted strut.

"You can," said Bertha. "There are some constraints, but there really is no need to stay what you are."

The elderly man grunted. "I see that. But how can *we* manage it?"

"By trying," said Marvin. "She coaxed you out of that wheelchair. She didn't give you working legs, at least not all by herself. You did most of that. You're talking too."

The man looked startled. "I suppose you're right," he said. "But that doesn't help. I want to be able to do it as easily as you just did."

"Then practice." Marvin looked at both his new guests in turn. "You're both pretty bright. You can discover the technique for yourselves. And you can get better at it."

"Or...," said Bertha. She pointed one long forefinger at the floor between the tables. The border between two of the tile-like segments of the carpet's pattern gaped, and a green, three-fingered hand groped for the edge. It found a grip, and a second later a small figure, less than two feet tall, was bowing to them each in turn. The hole in the carpet was gone as if it had never been.

SILICON KARMA
THOMAS A. EASTON

"What is *that*?"

"A pop-up." Its vest and bell-bottomed trousers, its exposed chest and broad, naked feet, its scraggly hair and broad lips and buck teeth, were all as green as its hand. Its other hand held a scroll, a strip of paper curled around a stick capped with ornate golden knobs. It was holding the scroll toward the man. "Take it," said Bertha.

He obeyed. As soon as the pop-up's hand was empty, it snapped its fingers and a second scroll appeared. It turned toward Rose and said in a high, screechy voice, "And one for you. One for each of you." As soon as she accepted, the pop-up faded to a ghostly remnant of itself, barely visible.

Rose grinned at Marvin. "I know what that is now," she said. "A 'terminate, stay resident' program. Just like the ones we've always used for finding files and taking notes and doing calculations when we're running other programs on our computers. I didn't expect...."

"I like to personify things," said Bertha. "People seem to think it makes this place more friendly. *I* think it's amusing."

"How do you get it back?"

"Call it. Hey, gofer." The manikin became solid once more. "Okay, scoot." Grimacing, it faded away again.

The man was undoing the spot of red wax that held his scroll closed and beginning to uncoil the paper. Bertha stopped him by laying one hand on his. "No, no," she said. "You don't have to read it. Just swallow it."

Rose looked at her skeptically. The scroll was all of eight inches long and an inch thick. Swallow it? She had to be kidding.

"That's right. Don't worry. It'll go down."

"But what is it?" asked the man.

"An image transformation routine. It'll even help with the swallowing."

He eyed the scroll as skeptically as Rose had eyed Bertha. Then he shrugged, tipped his head back, and thrust it down his throat in one smooth motion. Rose expected him to gag or choke, but there was only a momentary bulge in his neck and a widening of his eyes before he swallowed.

He looked surprised, distracted, and finally pleased. "I see," he said. "I understand. Watch this."

The few gray hairs that clung to his gleaming scalp fell away, landing on the shoulders of his jacket and lingering for only a moment before vanishing in tiny wisps of smoke. His scalp darkened as a lush new growth of hair sprouted, lengthened, and began to curl over his brow. His waistline diminished visibly. His trousers gaped until he noticed and shrank them instantly to keep the fit.

He indicated Rose's scroll. "Go ahead." His tone was brusque. "It's easy."

She obeyed his urging, and it was. After the briefest of discomforts, the knowledge of how to transform the image that was the virtual Rose in this virtual world blossomed within her mind. She too began by renewing her hair and shrinking her abdomen. She filled in the gaps along her jaws and made her dentures vanish. With a sigh, she ended those achings of her bones and joints that still remained and straightened her back. Then she erased the spots and wrinkles that time had etched upon her skin, filled out the contours she still remembered from long, long years before, adjusted the fit of her clothing, and finally sloughed the fashions of age and decrepitude for something more becoming, a silky fabric with frills and neckline, undergarments that emphasized a suddenly regained youth, makeup for her broadly grinning lips, her tearing eyes. Her cheeks, flushed with delight, needed nothing.

And then she looked at the man once more. That black, curling hair had looked vaguely familiar. Now his skin too was smooth, his posture quivering with energy, his eyes bright.

Why did he look so familiar? More familiar with every second? Why was he looking at her now as if she seemed just as familiar to him? Why were his eyes as wide as hers, his mouth opening as ready to shout, his hands open as if to grasp at something once lost and now regained?

"Michael!"

"Rosie!"

As they reached toward each other, both Marvin and Bertha faded away. They did not linger as had the pop-up but vanished entirely.

SILICON KARMA
THOMAS A. EASTON

CHAPTER 06

Rose Pillock watched Michael Durgov staring across the gap between the tables, his lips shaping her name. What did he see? A memory, yes, of course. The face and figure he had not seen since they both were kids, emerging now from the ruins of an old hag—or not a hag, not really, but surely a withered prune of a woman, an eroded remnant of the girl he once had known. Just as he had emerged from his own ruins. That ridiculous scroll!

"It's been so long!" She was reaching toward him.

His hand clutched at hers and held it tightly. Tentatively, as if he were rediscovering muscles he had long forgotten he knew how to use, he answered her radiantly beaming smile with a grin of his own. "Over half a century," he said at last. And if he didn't look as young as he had been the last time she saw him, he was still far, far younger than anyone should be after so many years. "Nearly two thirds."

"How old were we then?"

"Fourteen? Fifteen?" She tugged at his hand, and he shifted from his own seat to the one Marvin had occupied. Now they were at the same table.

She tightened her grip. Her smile did not diminish. "What were you doing all those years? I'll bet you got married." Her voice rose on "married" as if she were asking a question, and of course she was.

"Three times," he said.

"Only once," she said as if he too had asked. "My name's Pillock now." When he said nothing in reply, she added, "I'm sure you were successful."

"Or I wouldn't be here, would I?"

"It's expensive."

He nodded. His fingers tightened on hers. Then his grin faltered and he shuddered as if a sudden chill had run down his back at the thought of what he had done to be so successful.

She remembered what he had been, and the question came to her. "You changed, didn't you? For the better?"

"For the richer, anyway. But...." He shrugged. "If things had happened differently...."

"But they didn't."

Neither spoke for a long moment, while she wondered what his life had done to him, what he had done to earn his wealth. The moment ended when he jerked and looked up as if he had suddenly spotted a face on the ceiling. Rose looked too, but there was nothing there.

When he spoke, he sounded suspicious. "Bertha?"

"Yes?" The voice seemed to come from everywhere or nowhere at all.

"Do you edit people's minds when you copy them? 'Improve' them just a bit?"

"No!" The computer actually sounded shocked. "I couldn't possibly do that! It's absolutely forbidden! All I can do is show you how to change the way you look. And I can fix physical defects. But my basic programming won't permit me to touch your mind."

"If you did," said Rose. "You wouldn't admit it, would you?"

"You have to take my word for it. You are yourselves alone, within the limits of the scanner's accuracy."

"Always?" Michael asked insistently. "You never make changes? What if something goes wrong? What if someone's a real shit in real life? Do they stay a shit?"

There was a moment of silence before Bertha's voice said, "I can fix obvious bugs, of course. And try to repair copying errors."

"Insanity?" When the computer did not answer, he said, "I didn't feel crazy before. But some of the things I did...."

Rose was nodding, her face showing the memory of pain.

"A kind of bug, eh?"

"I didn't lay a finger on ya. Besides, if I could do that, there wouldn't be any crime in here."

"You mean there is?" asked Rose.

"Occasionally. Why, just the other day, a man got killed. I brought him right back, of course."

Rose caught her breath. Her Albert? Bertha could not possibly mean him! She was surely jumping to conclusions, but before she could ask for reassurance, Michael was saying, "What about drugs?"

"There's not much call for that."

"No wine? No whiskey?"

"Oh, well. Of course, alcohol. That transformation routine is everywhere." Two small scrolls materialized on the tabletop before them. "Run it, imagine what you want, and I give your senses the smell and taste. I even adjust your brain so you can feel as drunk as you like. Or I show you where the knobs are so you can adjust it yourself. If you want marijuana, cocaine, heroin, LSD, you can feel their effects as well. Even DBS."

"DBS?" asked Rose.

"Direct brain stimulation. Pure pleasure. Hours of orgasm. Or of pain if you're a masochist."

"And no hangover," said Michael. "Instant recovery."

"I bet we could make ourselves schizophrenic or depressed or manic, too," said Rose.

"Most of my guests prefer to avoid those mental states."

Rose remembered lying in the Xanadu device, letting the computer scan her mind. She had been recalling Albert, her husband, and all that they had been to each other, the things they had done together and apart, their own loving, their lovers. Then the computer had asked her: "Was he your only love?"

She had thought for a moment. The implication was not lost on her: A lover was not a love. Certainly she had found no one else to whom she would rather be married, at least not since marrying Albert. But before that time.... Ah!

"Oh, no!" she had said. "I was fourteen when I met Michael at the lake...." Her family had rented a small cottage for a month. It was on an island a mile from any shore, the ground a carpet of brown pine needles, the air fragrant with the incense of pine and balsam and spruce, tree trunks looming on three sides of the four-room cottage. The fourth side was bank and boulders and a narrow plank dock to which were tied a tiny sailboat and a red fiberglass canoe. Paddles and other gear were kept in the empty space beneath the porch.

At home, she always slept as late as her parents would permit. But that day she had risen early. She had dressed in faded denim shorts and a logoed T-shirt. She had left her parents still in bed while she grabbed a banana and a doughnut and went outside to stare across the quiet, glass-smooth lake. The sky had been pearly

SILICON KARMA
THOMAS A. EASTON

gray with a mist she thought would burn off before much later in the morning. A loon had called, a fish had risen to leave a widening circle of ripples, a distant osprey had hung in the sky.

She had taken the canoe then, kneeling on a cushion, paddling, watching the ripples of her wake spread across the water, watching the day's first breezes ruffle the mirror-surface of the lake, watching other vacationers step onto porches and docks, smelling breakfasts cooking, bacon, toast, pancakes, fish caught the day before, all mingling with evergreen and sky.

She was perhaps a hundred yards from the lake's shore when a young man, a boy really, no older than herself, appeared on a dock much like the one she had left behind her. He wore pink and purple paisley trunks as if he planned a morning swim. But then he shaded his eyes with a hand, peered toward her, waved. A moment later, he was propelling in her direction a canoe, green where hers was red, metal—announced as his weight made the long boat creak, as the water, the paddle, his hands struck the hull—where hers was fiberglass.

"Whatcha doin'?" His voice seemed flat and thin, as voices do where there are no echoes.

When she didn't answer, he added, "Right. You're canoeing. I can see that. Have you noticed there aren't many people our age around here? No ball field. There's a movie house in town, but the tape rental shop is bigger."

She ducked her head, pretending not to look at him, at how attractive he was despite a few pink spots of acne, at his eyes, dark and intense, at the cap of gleaming curls, at his chest and working arms, lean and tanned and muscular. "You like to swim," she said.

"Oh, hey, right!" he cried. He waved an arm as if stroking water. "Love it! How about you?"

"*I* like to be alone." She had used her snottiest tone of voice, and she had smiled to herself when his expression fell. Yet she had not been entirely pleased when he turned his canoe back toward shore.

A glowing spheroid materialized above the tearoom table, blocking Rose's view of the man across from her. She blinked at the interruption of her reverie and focused her eyes on the apparition that had come between her and Michael. Her hand still clasped his.

The spheroid bent and twisted, and it was Marvin's face. Michael's sudden "Bertha!" told her that its other side looked different. Yet it had only one rather neutral voice when it spoke, saying, "I've got to put you two on hold for a bit." The tearoom promptly faded from their awareness. "Do you two remember? I had a little memory problem when I was scanning you earlier?"

Rose felt no answering twitch of Michael's hand. When she tried to move her own, she found she could not. Nor could she speak. She could not even breathe, and when a sense of overwhelming panic began to rise, that too was quelled. For the time being, she and Michael were allowed to be no more than passive viewpoints. Yet there remained a sense of horrible wrongness.

"It's back again," said the computer. "And worse than ever. I really do need another processor. I've got the order in, and they say I'll have a new rack of gigaRAMs later today, or maybe tomorrow. In the meantime, I'll make do. I can handle it. I'll just take a time-out here for a bit, borrow most of what you're using while I scavenge odd bits of memory here and there. Give me just a minute, and I'll have it. Just have to pull enough together to carry on."

Rose felt her consciousness dimming still further. The paralysis the computer had imposed on its denizens was more than physical. She could neither act nor sense. Yet the paralysis was not total. The host computer was allowing her—and presumably Michael—at least a minimal awareness. She remained able to think that the computer—Marvin—must be talking in an effort to distract them from their panic. She was also able to wonder, and then to struggle to aim that wonder at her host, just why such problems should exist.

"I don't know," said Marvin's voice. "Yes, I heard you, Rose. And there shouldn't be any problems at all. The memory and processing capacity I have should be more than enough for the number of guests I have. But they aren't. If I didn't know better, if I thought there were any way it could happen, if I ever downloaded outside programs, I'd say I had a virus. But.... Ah. There, I'm getting it...."

Suddenly, she could breathe. She could feel her hand tightening on Michael's, and the pressure with which his hand answered. The tearoom was back, though now the floor was actual tiles, not a carpet woven to that pattern. The air bore hints of cinnamon and cardamom. A gleaming sextant had vanished from its place on the wall, replaced by a fragment of marble statuary. Her panic returned, but only until she could exert a control as inexorable as what the computer had achieved by denying her the use of its facilities as a substrate for her thoughts, perceptions, and feelings.

"A virus?" she asked. The term rang a faint bell for her, as if she had once known what a computer could possibly mean by saying it had a virus. Perhaps she had learned about them in school, long ago. Or she had read about them in a magazine or book. Or.... Could her copying have been imperfect? Could her real self know what a virus was, and that knowledge have been missed, not passed on to her, the copy?

"No, no," said Marvin. "The process is better than that. I miss nothing. I even get memories you've repressed."

"A computer virus," said Michael Durgov's weak voice from beyond the spheroid. "We've had to watch out for them almost as long as we've had computers. They generate copies until the machine's memory is too saturated to let any other program run."

"That's the symptom, all right," said Marvin. "It's funny, you know? People used to think that virtual reality would mean virtual omnipotence for its residents. People who moved into computers would be able to create anything they wanted, limited only by their imaginations. But it doesn't work that way. You need memory and processing capacity, and if you share your virtual reality you have to share all the necessary resources with those others. It's almost like what they used to call 'time-sharing' before computers got cheap enough so everyone could have one."

When Marvin stopped chattering, Michael added, "Sometimes viruses destroy other programs or data. They multiply, and they overwrite or preempt memory or hard-drive space. And they can spread from one machine to another, camouflaged within legitimate programs or data."

"But where did they come from? They didn't just appear, did they?"

"People. Pranksters who thought it would be fun to design programs that would do such things, and then let their creations loose to see how they would do. And vandals who just wanted to destroy as much as they could. Some were designed by one corporation or nation as weapons against another, and then they escaped to attack the general public."

Marvin interrupted again: "And there's not much you can do about them. You can try to stay ahead by adding more memory. Or you can erase everything in memory and hope no extra copies of the virus are hidden in your backups. Or you can hunt them down in memory and try to trap or destroy them."

"But...."

"But you two should go ahead with your tête-à-tête. I'll go see what I can do about the problem. Maybe I can hurry up the gigaRAMs."

"Can't we help?" asked Rose.

"Not yet, not yet." Marvin's voice sounded impatient.

"If there's any...."

"Of course. But for now...." Marvin's face disappeared from the spheroid, and then the spheroid itself winked out. Rose found herself once more staring at Michael Durgov. She looked away.

"Do you remember when we met?" Michael asked. "You brushed me off out there on the lake."

She smiled at the memory. "You didn't stay brushed off very well."

"Speaking of viruses, eh? The love bug. But you were so lovely, like a Venus rising from the sea...."

"With a canoe for a clam shell?"

"Scallop shell."

"I liked your line better then, when you said there weren't many kids our age around. You sounded desperate."

"But honest, I suppose." He dropped his eyes to the table. "That's one of the things that changed over the years."

"We've both changed." She had been as mad as she had ever been the last time she saw him. She had wanted to forget him and everything he stood for in her heart. But now he grinned, and so did she, and she let the memory return.

She patted his hand reassuringly. "What really got to me then was what you did that night."

She had regretted her rudeness to him almost immediately. But she had not been able to make herself call out to him, apologize, give friendship a chance to start between them.

Had he read that silent change of mind within her? Or had he only been a persistent boy, his head fed full of dreams of chivalry and antique romancing? Whatever the reason, that night, well after dark, her mother had interrupted her reading with a giggle and a "Rose dear! There's a merman on the dock. Listen to him!"

Obediently, she had pricked her ears and caught a thread of sound dancing through the night. She had joined her mother at the window, and on the dock indeed, silhouetted against the moon-glow sparkle of the lake, a young male figure bent over what looked like a small recorder.

"I don't see a boat," said her father. He had come up behind her, smelling of the pipe he only smoked outdoors. "He must have swum."

"Who is he?" asked her mother. "Anyone you know?"

Rose had sighed mightily at the time. "I met him just this morning, when I was out in the canoe."

"Did you have the lifevest on?"

"A cushion, Mother." She could still remember the face she had made at her mother's perpetual nag. "I think I'd better go see what he wants."

He did not react when she turned on the porch light, nor when she stepped outside and walked toward the dock. He simply played on with his recorder, simple tunes, gentle, quiet.

She stood over him, legs spread, arms akimbo. "You can stop pretending to ignore me now."

He didn't.

"How did you get out here?"

He paused in his tootling just long enough to say, "Swam."

"Idiot! You could have drowned!"

The music stopped. He looked up at her, eyes wide, pupils dilated by the night.

"Nobody would have known where you were," she added.

"Then you care!"

"Ass!" She denied it vehemently. "What are you doing here?"

"Serenading you." He held his recorder up as if he thought she had not yet noticed it or heard his music.

"I'll paddle you home." She brushed past him to untie the canoe. "Let's go."

"You were pretty efficient about it too," said Michael across the tearoom table.

"You were being a jerk, risking yourself that way." Her words were as tart as they had been so many years before, but her smile was fond. "You should always have someone with you when you're swimming. Especially when you're going far from shore."

"Is that why you were out in the canoe the next night, after supper?"

She blushed just as she had when she had said she was taking the canoe out for a while and her father had winked at her. "Once a jerk, always a jerk. I figured you'd do it again."

"And you were waiting for me." His expression was fatuous.

After that, they had barely noticed the shortage of other young people at the lake. They had fished and swum and explored the lake together. They had bicycled to town for ice cream and pizza, for a movie, for renting and returning video tapes. He had eaten with her family, and she with his.

"You were my first big crush," said Rose now.

"So were you, for me," said Michael.

"I wonder what would have happened if...."

"Lisa?"

He sighed. So did she. Lisa had been a friend of hers, a classmate and neighbor at home. She was no older but her limbs were rounder and sleeker and her breasts, while by no means large, were perfectly shaped. Her blond hair glowed with the merest hint of red gold, and if Rose knew that hint had come from a bottle, it still drew every eye. Add to that a face that said to every male that she was as innocent as any babe yet ready to surrender it all to the right man, and she was irresistible. And she knew it. So did Rose, and she had asked herself for years how she could possibly have been so foolish as to invite Lisa out to the lake for a weekend. She didn't have the excuse of having issued the invitation before she met Michael. No, first she met Michael. Only later did she decide she had to show him off to someone from home.

"You should have known better."

SILICON KARMA
THOMAS A. EASTON

She had told herself the same thing a thousand times. She had known that Lisa was quite capable of deciding she wanted another girl's boyfriend, and then of taking him. She had done it before. Had Rose thought that because Lisa was her friend, she would keep her hands to herself? Then the more fool she. It hadn't worked that way at all.

Not that she tried anything while she was staying on the island, but the week after she left, Rose and Michael ran into her in town. She had, she said, fallen in love with the lake. She had begged her parents, they had agreed to give her a little holiday on her own, and now she was staying in a bed-and-breakfast, that one, right over there.

That evening, Michael had seemed distracted. The next, he had not been waiting for her on his dock when she appeared with the canoe. He had, his father told her, gone into town.

"I cried all the way back to the island."

Now he held her hand in both of his, though his eyes avoided hers. "We weren't doing anything. Just ice cream...."

"But later...."

"Ahh." Later, the very next day, Rose had taken the canoe to a lakeshore pine grove she and Michael had found and loved. She had thought to sit there, her arms wrapped around her shins, her chin propped on her knees, remembering, yearning, her teeth gritting, the tears pooling in her eyes. And all the while she would be cushioned by the same thick layers of pine needles that had cushioned them both. Instead, she had found Michael's green-painted aluminum canoe pulled up on the bank. She had heard a giggle. And when she stepped among the trees, she had found a blanket, Michael, Lisa. He was naked. She was nearly so.

"I...." said Michael now, in the tearoom, squeezing her hand.

"You turned white." She was smiling. "I screamed. I called you both names. I left."

"I tried to follow you."

"And she wouldn't let you, would she?" She shifted briefly to a higher pitch: "'How will I get back?' You should have told her to swim. Maybe she'd have drowned. Or to walk. There had to be a camp road not far back in the woods. Or did she just grab you by the cock?"

He grimaced at the image but had the grace to blush. "No...."

"We went home again not long after that. And I never saw you again."

"Until now."

"Until now."

"It's been a long time," he said slowly. When she nodded, he added, "Do you think we can step back and start over?"

"We've learned too much, Michael. Lived too much. Loved too many others. We can't be that innocent, that young, again."

"We can look that young." As he spoke, his face thinned, acne bloomed, and he was once more fourteen years old.

"No." She shook her head. "As soon as you open your mouth, you'll just be silly."

His complexion cleared, and the lines of his face subtly changed. He looked now as he must have looked when he was in his twenties. "Is this better?"

"Much." She adjusted her appearance to match his. "We *might*," she said. "We *might* have met again a few years later. At least, we can pretend...."

They stared at each other, each thinking of what might have been. Finally, Rose said, "I wonder what our originals are doing now. Our real bodies."

With a soft "pop," the glowing spheroid that had interrupted them earlier reappeared, this time to one side, not blocking their sight of each other. "They're okay," said Marvin's voice. No face appeared. "No problem. Don't worry about them. They're behind you now."

"I suppose they're even different people," said Michael Durgov. "They've already had different thoughts, different experiences. Their minds have to have changed in different ways."

The spheroid bobbed in the air as if their host were nodding.

"You looked awfully grumpy when you first came in here," said Rose.

"I didn't have much to be happy about."

"You do now?"

He nodded, and Marvin's voice said, "You don't have to stay in this tearoom forever, you know. Isn't there someplace else you'd like to be?"

"Do you think?" asked Rose. "Do you think we could visit the island? The cottage where I was staying that summer? It's probably gone by now, burned or fallen down. Or the trees were cut to make room for a rack of condos. But...."

SILICON KARMA
THOMAS A. EASTON

"You forget," said Marvin. "Here, everything is a matter of perception. Reality is what you make it. Of course you can have...."

The tearoom vanished. With no transition whatsoever, Rose and Michael were standing on a narrow wooden dock facing a rocky shore. Ranks of trees opened before them like a welcoming honor guard. A small, cedar-shingled cottage sat in a clearing, illuminated by a bar of golden sunlight. Beside a boulder to the right, her front hooves in the water, a doe dripped water from her muzzle, pricked her ears, spun, and bounded into the woods.

"...The island," Marvin finished his sentence. His voice still came from the glowing spheroid, but the spheroid was now resting on the perforated metal stern seat of a single green aluminum canoe that was tethered to the dock by their feet.

"This one's yours!" Rose sounded surprised. She turned, yipped, and stared at her feet. They were bare, and she had just caught a splinter with her toe. The world within the computer, she thought, could not be much more convincing.

"Doesn't the sunbeam rather overdo it?" asked Michael.

Marvin chuckled, and the spheroid vanished as completely as had the tearoom. The sunbeam remained.

They were alone. Indeed, Rose felt they were far more alone than they had been in the tearoom, which had been populated by shadows and surrounded by streets filled with the other residents of the virtual world. Anyone—or dozens— could have walked into the tearoom at any moment. They still could, she realized— this island was as much a figment of the computer's imagination as had been the Foundation Tearoom—but this figment felt more isolated and all-their-own.

Suddenly overcome by an awkward shyness, she withdrew her hand from Michael's. This was the past, long since put behind her. The present was.... Well, there was Albert. He had died, but he was waiting for her. *She* was waiting for him, waiting to find him. Yet this sudden revival of the past, of youth and Michael and lake, was astonishingly compelling. She could not yet turn her back upon it.

She turned around instead, and Michael with her, to look across the lake toward the mile-distant shore where his family had stayed that long-gone summer. It was empty, a blank stretch of rock and forest much as it must have been in Columbus' day.

"Want a swim?" asked the man.

She glanced sidelong at him. "There should be suits in the cottage."

"Uh-uh. I bet...." He passed a hand down his front, and the jacket and sweater and pants he had been wearing all this time, through all the transformations of health and youth, disappeared, leaving behind only the paisley trunks she had first seen him in so many years before. "It's the same as changing your looks."

"I can't do that," she said. What she meant was that of course she could, but it would feel too much like undressing in public, in front of a stranger. She fled to the cottage.

When she reappeared, she was wearing a dark blue tank suit rather more modest than the high-cut suits she had actually preferred at fourteen.

Later, when they were stretched head to head to dry on the narrow dock, she said lazily, "Do you know what must have bothered me the most when I found you with Lisa?"

"That she had stolen me from you." He propped his chin on one hand and fingered her hair with the other, spreading it on the weather-beaten planks of the dock. "Outraged possessiveness. Violated ownership."

She turned her face toward him. Her eyes were closed against the sun. "That was part of it. Of course. But just as...." She tore a splinter, perhaps the one she had found earlier with her toe, from one of the dock's planks and set it blindly adrift on the lake. After a moment of silence, she added, "Finding you like that. We hadn't gone that far yet. I was dreaming of it, wishing for it, almost ready. But...."

His hand withdrew. "We didn't do anything."

"I spoiled it." She opened her eyes.

"Well...."

"But I bet she gave you another chance." When he blushed, she laughed.

"Do you want to...." His expression turned wistful, and he reached toward her again.

"Make up for lost opportunities?" She shook her head and twisted her body, drawing away from his fingers just enough to make her rejection of his overture unmistakable. "Not yet. Maybe not ever. They're lost, after all, and it's far too late to get them back."

CHAPTER 7

Albert stood outside the Mandelbrot Tap, staring at the window, an ordinary plate glass rectangle etched with a lace-rimmed, lop-sided figure eight. He was totally unaware of the manhole cover approaching him, sliding through the surface of the road like a boat in water.

His attention skipped over the pop-up eyes that watched from the shadows beneath the steel disk's raised edge. He focused on the Image Shop, across the cobbled street and half a block away. Between it and the bar, just fifty feet away, was the brick wall, ironwork, and poster beneath which he had died. Somehow their proximity did not surprise him.

Both shop and wall shimmered with portent as if some cosmic stage manager had shone a blacklight spot on them. "Knock it off, Ada," said Albert. "You're getting hokey."

As the shimmer obediently vanished, he looked back at the bar. His past stopped here. This was where he had remembered to B-cup, to back himself up. And he had been here because....

He opened the door and blinked while his vision adjusted. The darkened tavern was empty except for the overweight bartender behind the counter. The man had been a lawyer and a judge in the meat world.

"Albert. The usual?"

"Sure." When the mug of Australian ale appeared before him, he took a quick swallow. "Where's Gladys?"

The bartender looked puzzled. "You should know."

"What do you mean?"

"You gave her the money she needed."

"Oh, shit."

Gladys was a fixture in the bar. Some of the regulars called her the Jug Lady, for almost every time they saw her she was carrying by a loop of string an antique milk bottle full of murky liquid. The bottle's top was plugged with putty. From time to time, as the bottle bobbed upon its string and the liquid swirled within it, there drifted into view a withered fetus.

"I was just a kid," she had told Albert as she would tell anyone who displayed the slightest interest. "But I didn't have an abortion. I was married. I wanted the kid. But then Josh said he couldn't stand living with my parents. And he ran off. I cried a lot, and I drank, and then I took a bunch of pills. They weren't enough to kill me, but...." She had held up the bottle then. "A miscarriage. I put it in the bottle right away. With the last of my gin. And then I hid the bottle in the attic. The paneling only came up to here." She had waved one hand at the level of her nose. "I could stand on a chair and loop the string over a nail. The bottle hung down out of sight. I was the only one who knew it was there, behind the paneling. I kept taking it out for years, just to look at my baby. To cuddle it and cry."

Tears had filled her eyes as she added, "I brought it with me, you know. But Marvin won't help. I asked him, but he won't bring Toddie Sean back to life."

"I *gave* her the money?" Albert asked the bartender.

"I didn't see her take you in the back room to earn it."

Albert sighed. He had come in here the first time, before his last B-cup, because it was near the Image Shop. Thinking he might learn something useful, he had sat over there, where he could keep an eye on both the window and the door. Almost immediately, he had noticed the woman across the room, at a small table by herself. She had narrow, slanting eyebrows, bright red lipstick, a tall glass decorated with a stick of celery, and a smooth cap of blond hair stamped with red circles. She wore a tight sheath slit halfway up one thigh and patterned with transparent stripes, and she was watching him.

Albert had rarely seen an ugly person in Virtual City. Image transformation routines made perfection ordinary. It therefore barely registered that the figure her stripes revealed was everything a woman—or a man—could want. He ignored her while he surveyed the rest of the bar's patrons. None of them looked rich, though he presumed their meat must have been able to afford Coleridge's bill.

When he finished his ale, he lifted the mug to catch the bartender's attention and projected a whisper to his ear. "Right, another," he said. "And tell folks I'll buy a drink for anyone who'll let me ask a few questions."

The first of them sat down across the table just as a fresh glass of ale floated through the air to his hand. "The Image Shop?" he said when Albert asked. "Yeah, sure. I know that place. Can't afford 'em, though. And wouldn't if I could."

"Why not?" No one would say. In time, growing bored, Albert noticed the dark-haired woman who was working the men leaning on the bar. "What do you like in your split-tails, guy? Besides yourself, I mean? Big tits?" Albert could see only the motion of arm and cloth as she opened the top half of a tiger-print wrap-around. "I can make 'em bigger. Tight twats? They don't come any tighter. I've got a great sexit. One of the best. You've heard about the monkey and the grapevine? Wait'll you see the tail I can grow!"

They laughed and patted and teased. Eventually one man tossed back his beer, got off his stool, and whispered in her ear. She hugged his arm and beamed at him. "You'll see. I'll be great!"

Her sexit, her sexual image transformation routine, was already elongating her lips as she led the man toward a dimly lit stairway in the back of the room. As they passed his table, she winked at Albert. "I'm Gladys," she said. "Take care of this for me?" Suddenly her hand held a bottle he had not noticed before. She set it on the table. "I won't be long, handsome."

When he looked away from the shadows drifting in the bottle's murky contents, the woman in the striped cheongsam was sitting across the table from him. Her perfume was spicy, her expression serious. "You're asking about the Image Shop," she said. "And now you've seen the Jug Lady. She's probably the only one here who would deal with it."

"Why?"

She stretched out one elegantly slim arm and turned the bottle Gladys had left on the table. Suddenly Albert recognized what swam within it. "She'll be back soon. She'll tell you." She patted his hand. "I'm Irma." And she was gone.

When Gladys returned, however, she was in no mood to talk. "The bastard stiffed me!" she screamed to the room at large. "If I ever see him again, I'll...!" She snatched her bottle off Albert's table and held it before her eyes, turning it as if to check that what it held still was there, intact. Her voice changed. "There, there, Toddie," she crooned. "We're almost there. It won't be long. Soon...."

Most of the computer's residents moved from place to place within Virtual City by walking or driving vehicles or even riding buses. More computations were needed to match a continually changing setting to an individual viewpoint than to switch instantly from one setting to another, but people prized the familiar connection to the meat life they had left behind. And besides, the computations were so routine that they called for relatively little expenditure of data energy. People chose the cheaper, faster mode of travel only when they were in an unusual rush.

SILICON KARMA
THOMAS A. EASTON

Or.... When Gladys winked out, gone from the bar to some other setting, perhaps her home, Albert thought her words suggested that she was saving every scrap of data energy, what passed for money in Virtual City, to pay for something she wanted desperately.

Albert was at the Mandelbrot Tap again the next night, and again the next, but Gladys was not. On the third night, he sat at his usual table, nursing his ale, thinking that, really, he could learn no more about the Image Shop in this place. It was time to find another track toward what Ada had asked of him.

Gladys was not there, and then she was, sliding into the seat beside him, putting one hand on his thigh, leaning forward to let him appreciate the cut of her floral-patterned dress, pouting thick red lips toward his own. He pushed her hand away. "I'm not in the market for that," he said.

"Just tell me what you want," she breathed. "Anything. You took such good care of my baby."

"Where is it?"

Her other hand lifted string and bottle above the level of the table. "Him," she said. "He's *not* an 'it.'"

That was when she told him what it was.

Albert sighed, wondering how the Coleridge psychs had ever passed her for copying into the machine. The bottle and the aborted baby within it were of course no more real than anything else in Virtual City. Nothing material could enter the machine. Data. Just data. Figments of the imagination given simulated reality by the power of intensive computation. Without the faintest hint of potential consciousness. For that, Ada had to have a copy of a mind, a program that could run within the structure of the machine.

He shook his head, knowing—and wincing at the knowledge—that he was only hurting her.

"No!" she cried. "I am *not* crazy! He told me it would work. He promised! All I need to do is raise the money."

"Who?"

"There!"

He let his mind's eye follow the line of her pointing finger through the Mandelbrot Tap's ornate window design and down the street. "The Image Shop."

She nodded eagerly. "An IT. He has just the thing, he says. And Toddie Sean will live at last."

When he said nothing more, she licked her lips delicately, catlike, and added, "I have almost enough. Why don't you come out back with me? It'll be good. I guarantee it. If it isn't, you don't have to pay."

He shook his head once more, deliberately keeping his face impassive. If he spoke, he feared, he might....

"Then screw you. I can't waste any more time here." She swept her baby bottle from the tabletop and left.

"I *gave* her the money?" Albert asked the bartender once more.

But then he remembered thinking that the Image Shop's proprietor could not possibly deliver what he had promised to Gladys.

Here then might be what Ada had sent him to find, someone to follow as she stepped into whatever it was that made people disappear. Suddenly he could believe that he had indeed given Gladys the money she needed.

The street door opened, light flashed through the bar, and a smooth thigh bumped his hip as its owner climbed onto the stool beside him. He blinked, sniffed a familiar perfume, and said, "Irma." She wore slacks this time, not a cheongsam, and her hair was red with blond circles.

"You gave it to her, chump," she said. "She fed you her sob story, and you fell for it a-a-ll the way."

"It wasn't a line," said the bartender. "She did head for the Shop."

Irma made an indelicate noise. "And we haven't seen her since. Just like my brother."

"Maybe she got what she wanted," said the bartender.

Albert was shaking his head, preparing to say that what she wanted did not exist to be had, when Irma ran a finger along one collarbone and he noticed the fine gold chain she wore. "My brother," she said. "He wanted an IT that would let him switch back and forth, man to woman. This was the only place where such a thing was even remotely possible, so he had himself copied. We could afford it, so I came too." She shrugged gracefully. "I'm still out there somewhere. Still young. Maybe I'll have the money again someday. Then I can be copied again. A reverse sort of B-cup."

"What happened to your brother?" asked Albert.

"We worked for a while, until he could afford the IT he wanted. And then one day he said he knew where to get it, and he'd be right back."

"And we never saw him again," said the bartender.

"Gladys said she'd be back too," said Irma. "And then Toddie Sean could be a real baby. She asked me to take care of him just in case...."

"She didn't come back?" asked Albert. "I haven't seen her today."

Irma looked at him pityingly. "You knew more yesterday."

"Someone shot me."

"Ah." She thought about that for a moment. "At least you didn't disappear. My brother did. I told her about Alan. And now she's gone too." A twist of her hand snapped the chain around her neck, and she dropped a charm-sized milk bottle on the bar. It immediately enlarged to reveal itself as Gladys' baby bottle. "Now I don't know what to do with this."

"I'll take it," said Albert.

The chair that engulfed him hip and shoulder was engulfed in turn by darkness. The only light was the pool of brightness in which the bottle hung, swinging gently, turning, displaying its murky contents and the shape that seemed to swim within it. The rest of the room was invisible. He and the bottle might have been suspended in empty space, space that had not yet seen a monobloc explode, space that had never known a galaxy, a star, a planet, even a grain of dust. There was only him, his viewpoint, and the strange thing he viewed.

When the buzzer that signaled a business call sounded in his ear, Albert closed his eyes. This was not an interruption he needed. But....

"The Forensic Consultant," he said in a weary tone. "State your name and invoice number, please."

"Detective Amos Saarif. Invoice 678-9233. We've got a...."

"Hold one minute," Albert interrupted as he piped the number to his accounting and billing software. "I need to check that."

"It sounds so damned alive." Saarif seemed to be speaking to someone else. "It's hard to believe I'm talking to a program."

Albert grinned. "You may proceed."

"We've got a murder. White male, elderly, retired, wasn't good for much before. Stroke victim. Good for even less now, of course."

"Scene of the crime?" asked Albert.

"His apartment."

"Weapon."

"Knife. Eight-inch blade, inserted under the sternum and angled upward to reach the heart."

"Witnesses?"

"None. His nurse said she was in another room. His wife wasn't home."

"Then it was the nurse."

"No sir. Damn." Saarif's voice showed he had turned aside. "Would you believe that? I called it 'sir.'"

"Why not?"

"We grilled her, and she's still in custody. But we don't think...."

"Who hated him?"

"Lots. He was apparently something of a sonuvvabitch before he retired."

"Then find an enemy who had the opportunity."

"We're working on that already. You're not much help this time, are you?"

"I'm always happy to be of service."

Albert grinned as a click announced that the consultation was over. But the grin faded almost as soon as he returned his attention to Gladys' milk bottle. He hadn't really given Saarif his full attention. There was so much more information he should have requested!

He touched the bottle with a finger and made it spin faster. He wished he did not feel so useless, so powerless. He needed someone he could pump for the facts in this case. Someone who could give him the information he needed to find out who killed him, and then to satisfy his employer.

Maybe even someone who could tell him how to bring Toddie Sean to life.

Though there wouldn't be much point to that if he couldn't find Gladys.

SILICON KARMA
THOMAS A. EASTON

CHAPTER

08

Rose and Michael stayed on the dock while the sky glowed bright with sunset and then darkened, while the lake grew still, disturbed only by the circles of rising fish, and while the far shore became a dark wall, a boundary between the water's mirror and the depths of an infinite heaven. Rose remained aware of the cottage among the trees at their back, but she made no move to go inside.

"For some reason," she said. "I'm not hungry."

"Neither am I." He hesitated as if unsure what to do now that she had rejected his attempt to pick up where they had left off so many years before. "What happened to you? I know you made out okay. You had to, or you wouldn't be here."

"We had the money." She nodded, but she would not look at him. "Enough. He moved in here first."

"Have you seen him yet?" When she shook her head, he added, "Why not? I'd think you couldn't wait."

She huffed an abbreviated laugh. "I've been here how long? Just a few hours, and it's been years since he died. I miss him. But I've gotten used to living without him. I suppose he has too."

"That's why he didn't meet you?"

"He probably didn't even know I was coming."

Or was that it? They had had their troubles in the past. He had even wandered. Could he have found someone else?

"Tell me about him."

"He was a cop." And for some reason she was talking about the time when he had been partnered with a female detective, younger than either he or his Rosa, attractive, so wide-hipped and heavy-chested that it seemed impossible that she could be a cop. Rose had liked her when they met, and she had not been the least bit suspicious when Albert's interest in sex had seemed to wane. He was tired, he had said. Working hard and getting old. So was she, for a fact. Perhaps that was why she had accepted the change in their lives so easily.

"An anonymous phone call," she said. "I should call a certain motel and ask for Albert."

Michael winced to show he knew what was coming.

"I didn't want to. I knew she only wanted to make trouble. But...." She had picked up the phone and punched the buttons and asked the clerk for Albert. She had bit her lip until it bled when the phone in the motel room began to ring. And then his partner had answered.

She had gone home early that day, unable to work. And later, that evening, when he finally came home.... He had stood in the doorway, staring at her, at her puffy face, at her eyes red from all the tears she had shed. The muscles of her forehead went tight again as she recalled the way she had hissed: "You're going to tell me it's a stakeout, right?"

He shook his head. "No," he said, his lips tight, the sides of his nose taut, water visible in his eyes too. "It's just what you think. We were fucking. We've been doing it for weeks."

She was silent, stunned as much by his honesty as by his perfidy. Then, almost choking on the words, "Do you love her?"

He shook his head again. "She doesn't love me either. We just got the hots for each other. And tomorrow...." He took a deep breath and let it out again, shuddering. "Tomorrow, we'll both ask for new partners."

That was when she screamed: "You bastard!"

"That's not fair," he said almost too softly for her to hear. After all, he had admitted his sin, hadn't he? He wasn't trying to deny it, or to cover it in bluster. He had even already moved to correct it—not to undo it, that was never possible, but to end it, to move on from it, to begin again with the only woman he truly loved. Didn't she know that?

"And I did, of course," she told Michael. "But I was in no mood to be placated."

"You fuckin' cheat!" she had screamed. "And you think *I'm* not being fair! You're so sorry, and you know it, and you think that makes a difference?"

"You want me to leave you for her?"

"No!" She burst into tears with that, and when he moved to comfort her as he always had, embracing, holding, she flailed her arms, striking angrily at his hands. He was *not* about to touch her!

"You've never felt that way about anyone?"

"Of course I have!" she cried. "But I didn't leave you. Not even when...."

She stopped. In the ensuing silence, they stared at each other glumly. He *knew* what she had been about to say. *She* knew that she should not say it. But she wanted to hurt him precisely as much and in precisely the way that he had hurt her.

"Your last training weekend," she said at last. "You were away for four days."

"That wasn't even a year ago." His tone, suddenly less contrite, began to show his own bright thread of anger. "Who was it?"

She looked away. "Nate's the data manager at the office. You've heard me say I liked him." When he nodded, she said, "He knew you were gone, so he asked me out for dinner after work."

"And then?"

Like Albert, he was a man. Unlike Albert, he had been circumcised. The same but different. Less tender, more inventive, indefatigably spurred on by the novelty of her, and she the same by him.

"When I got home on Sunday, I had just enough time to fix dinner for you."

"So that's why you never answered the phone." His voice rose, and he gestured with a hand half curled into a fist. "And you have the nerve to call me a cheat. At least, I only did it an hour or two at a time."

"But I only did it once. Never again. Certainly not over and over for weeks."

Silence fell once more as he stared at her, his hand still raised, both of hers still held up as if to ward him off. Finally, he said, "I did it one other time. Do you remember when the university's network was trashed?"

She did. The animal rights activists who had claimed credit for erasing every hard drive on campus had said their target was a researcher who had been compiling data on the health effects of food additives. They had not seemed perturbed at having destroyed the labors of poets, literary critics, historians, chemists, and many other scholars, nor at having erased a semester's student grades.

"Caramina wasn't even a lab worker," he said. "She wasn't doing animal experiments. But the data she was collecting had come from animal studies. And they destroyed years of her work. Though she didn't expect it to take that long to reconstruct it all from backups, notes, and the papers she had already written."

"When did you fuck her?"

He winced at the ugliness of her tone. He now looked as hurt as she. Both knew that they had gone too far, revealed far more than they should. But he could not stop.

"There was a small couch in her office, and...."

"I bet you were just patting her on the head at first. 'There, there.' Or on the back. And then she turned around."

"Something like that," he said.

"Was she any good?"

He shrugged. "Her mind wasn't really on it."

"And how many others have there been?"

"None, I swear it! And what about you?"

"I don't believe you!" She grabbed a lamp from a nearby table. "You goddam tomcat!"

He ducked her throw. The lamp exploded against the wall, leaving a dent in the plaster that would later take him hours to repair.

They had slept that night, and several more, in separate rooms. She had thought of calling a lawyer, but that thought had only made the pain worse. So she had done nothing. Eventually the tension between them had eased. Neither had ever strayed again. At least, she hadn't. And she was pretty sure he had behaved himself.

"At least you got back together," said Michael. "Me...." He shook his head. "I never could manage that part of it. Not with you. Not with...."

"I'm getting chilly," she said. She looked toward the cottage. In a moment, her clothes drifted through the doorway and toward the dock. When they reached her, they pressed against her, spread, migrated through her flesh to surround her limbs. Her expression turned pleased. "I'm getting it."

He nodded, ran a hand down his front, and was dressed in jeans and denim shirt. Then he said, "Elena." He hesitated as if he didn't know what to say about her. "She did her job well enough. Playing hostess when I had to entertain for Coleridge."

"You used to...?"

She could feel the movement of the dock beneath her seat when he nodded. "Until the bastards *retired* me. I had a stroke, and then.... Just because I couldn't talk anymore, or walk. I could still use a keyboard, couldn't I? Or they could have put a Xanadu in my office. I'd have had to wear it like one of those old-time iron lungs. An iron brain. But it could have read my mind and printed out memos and told those sons-of-bitches...."

He drew a shuddering breath that made Rose turn to peer through the darkness. His face was distorted with anger and pain that did not ease when he abruptly changed the subject.

"And the bitch was hardly ever around anymore. When I came home from the hospital, after the stroke, she had already hired a nurse. Ever since, she says hello at breakfast and then disappears. I don't know where she goes."

A small, glowing cloud appeared in the darkness above their head, and Bertha's voice said, "I've checked the public databases now. She's working at the public library. In the children's room."

"I knew she was too old and ugly to have a lover," said Michael.

"Oh, come now."

"You're right, of course. I've seen uglier whores. And older ones."

Rose touched his hand sympathetically. "Any children?"

"Not by her. That was Constance. Connie. Number two."

"Why did you marry her?"

"Connie?"

"Elena."

"I was CEO then." Elena Codescu had been a marketing haunch who liked to flirt as high up the ladder as possible. And one day she had told him about her brother. "Nick's been working on it for years," she said. "And now he's got it."

He almost forgot to say "What?" when she leaned over his desk.

"Real artificial intelligence," she said.

That caught his attention much more thoroughly than did the hint of aureole that peeked from the edge of her low-top bra. "How in the world...?"

She shrugged delightfully. "I don't understand it. He said something about splitting the intelligence. He calls the program 'Egoware.'"

But he had not been a Coleridge employee, and he had wanted to stay that way. On the other hand, he knew he couldn't handle it all himself. That was why he talked to Elena. If she would join him, they could set up a family corporation, she could handle the marketing and he would stay with the development work.

"I think I can guess what you did," said Rose.

"I married her. That got me into the family corporation, handling the management and the finances."

"And then you sold out to Coleridge."

"Of course. And Nick got plenty of money out of the deal. I never understood why he was so mad at me."

Rose was careful not to let him see her expression. She did understand. "Is he still around?"

"I don't know. I lost track of him."

"But doesn't your wife...?"

"We don't talk about him."

The stars were bright now, and a crescent moon was high in the sky. But the night air was comfortable now that they were dressed, and they still made no move to go inside.

"How did you and Albert meet?" asked Michael.

Ah, she thought. That was a very different sort of story.

"I was already out of college," she said softly. "But I had stayed on campus. I needed a job, and they needed a junior accountant in the financial office. That's where we met. He came in to see about...."

"Is, uh, Mrs. Quentin in?"

Rose had looked up from her keyboard to see a tall young man leaning over the counter. His hair was dark, almost black, and molded into a side-thrusting visor. His face was red, as if he had shaved with a dull razor. The open throat of his shirt showed an unusual amount of hair.

"She's out today. The flu, you know? May I help you?"

"It's about, uh, my tuition."

"I know everybody's payments were due Monday."

"That's it, sort of. Uh.... I just...." He looked at his hands and his cheeks turned even redder.

She had not been working there long, but she had already seen the symptoms several times. She took mercy on him. "You can't make it."

He froze. Finally, he said, "Yeah."

"And you want to set up a different schedule."

He nodded jerkily. "Is it possible?"

"Usually. Unless you put your tuition money on the horses."

He grinned. "Nah. Nothing like that. It's just, the folks had to pay their property tax and insurance bills and so on, all at once. And the place I work, the Computer Shack, they cut back on my hours. And...."

Before he left, he asked her to go with him to a campus movie. She accepted, and they were married not long after he graduated. A few years later, she had gotten pregnant with Julianne. They had had arguments, of course, but nothing fatal, no problems they couldn't make it past.

Not that it had always been easy. Nor had it been easy when she had to readjust to living all alone. And now....

She shook her head. "You must have been with Coleridge for years."

He grunted. "If it hadn't been for me, they'd never have developed the Xanadus or.... Goddam ignorant ingrates." He should, he told Rose, will his company stock to the most reactionary anti-scanning group he could find. Such groups still existed, he knew. They thought people had no business trying to maintain their consciousness, to "live"—for lack of a better term—past their allotted time, as if some divine niggard on a heavenly throne did indeed ration out human lives, so much per customer and "Sorry, sir. There's no room for another punch on your coupon."

But he had fought them once to get scanning accepted by society and approved by the government. If he reversed himself now, *he* would suffer, not just the ingrates who had kicked him out of the office.

"You never used to bitch like this," said Rose.

After a moment of silence, he agreed. "You're right, of course. But the way they treated me. And then they asked.... But never mind that. Should I tell you how I got them the mindscanner?"

When she nodded, he smiled. He had been in New Products then, and one of his junior research assistants had seen a report in the journal *Brain Research*. A Judith Luria at the Wistar Institute in Philadelphia had found that a combination of

SILICON KARMA
THOMAS A. EASTON

magnetic resonance imaging and multipolar electroencephalography could allow her to track conscious thoughts as they coursed through the brain. She even thought she might soon be able to crack the problem—as old as the discovery of brain waves—of how to read minds with a machine.

"The press," Michael Durgov had told himself, "will be on this very soon." He had wasted no time in calling Dr. Luria, mentioning venture capital, and making an appointment to see her the very next morning. By the time the press began to call, she had already signed a Coleridge contract, banked half a million dollars, and agreed not to talk.

She had been a pretty thing too. He had....

The research had continued. The hardware and software had improved. The necessary patents had been granted in Coleridge's name. And then there was a leak. Reactionaries began to scream of sacrilege and violations of human dignity. Congress began to hint at moratoria and bans, at doing to mindscanning what it had once done to genetic engineering and any research that used fetal tissues.

It hadn't taken much pressure at all to convince Dr. Luria that her miracle technology wasn't about to go anywhere. Before long, she had accepted a final fifty thousand for all the rights to her discovery. And then he had managed his greatest coup.

From his office window, the signs carried by the demonstrators in the plaza below had been just barely readable with binoculars. "PROTECT THE RESUR- RECTION!" they had said. "DEATH IS THE DOORWAY TO HEAVEN." "HE THAT WOULD LIVE MUST DIE."

"It's a good thing they didn't find the garage entrance," said Teebelle Radamang.

Michael Durgov grunted and pointed at a white van whose flanks bore the logo of network news. "No cameras there." He looked at her. His chief assistant was a heavy woman who habitually wore Hawaiian-print shirts over Spandex tights.

"Did you turn on the TV this morning?"

When he shook his head, she crossed the room and opened the polished panel that concealed the set. A moment later, they were watching the recording of a morning talk show. The show's host was asking a guest: "Reverend Matthews, why does your sect disapprove of the Coleridge Corporation's plans to copy a human mind into their computer?"

"CTR is not a sect, Jimmy." The Reverend Matthews was of middle height, balding, and clearly well fed. "We are Christians for the True Resurrection. We are a coalition of people from every religious denomination. Many of us have been born again. Every one of us believes in the word of God as it is infallibly recorded in the Holy Bible."

"But...."

"To answer your question, Jimmy." The Reverend had raised a forestalling finger. "The Good Book is very clear. The Coleridge Corporation proposes to cheat both man and God. We belong in our bodies. We cannot be taken out of them except by the hand of God. Eternal life is a gift that can be given only by Christ. And to suggest anything else is sacrilege, blasphemy, and anathema. Those who accept the Coleridge temptation are damned forevermore."

"But what about our most important people, Reverend Matthews? Our Einsteins and...."

"We have other ways, Jimmy. Expert systems...."

"I've heard."

"That I've been recorded as an expert system, Jimmy? Quite right. When my church bought a 'key man' policy, the insurance company insisted. But an expert system does not think it is real, a person. There is no question of copying my soul."

"Do you see, Mr. Durgov?" asked Teebelle. She froze the image on the screen for a moment. Then she clicked it off. "Almost every TV evangelist in the country is against us, and their shows are breaking ratings records. The people can't understand what we offer. They're nervous about us. And these fellows are turning that nervousness to outright fear. The system is almost ready to go, but if this continues, we won't have a hope in hell of selling it. Congress will probably ban the whole idea and jail us for having anything to do with it."

Michael shook his head again. "The folks who can afford us aren't the ones who listen to that crap," he said emphatically. "And we can always get around a ban."

"Even the black market won't work if the mob tears down the building." After the briefest of hesitations, she added more softly, "And lynches us."

Both fell silent while he stepped to his desk, stared at the leather-trimmed blotter, and fingered the polished keyboard that waited for his hand. A legal pad stood ready for informal notes and doodles. Finally he said, "You said 'almost.'"

SILICON KARMA
THOMAS A. EASTON

When Teebelle looked puzzled, he expanded: "'*Almost* every TV evangelist in the country....'"

"Oh, yes. I think there's one who hasn't attacked us yet. The Reverend Jackson Kemmerdell. He has a fifty-watt station in Sykesville, Pennsylvania." She made a face that said the Reverend Kemmerdell was not worth taking seriously, no matter what he thought. "*Real* small potatoes."

Michael Durgov smiled without humor. Teebelle had, as always, a small brown notebook in her hand. "But I'll bet you have his number right there." When she nodded once, abruptly, he added, "So let's talk to him."

The Reverend Kemmerdell himself met their small plane the next day. He was a slender, silver-haired man in a pale green suit that, while not shabby, had obviously come off a discount store rack. After a brisk handshake, he led them to a cramped Japanese sedan and drove them to a run-down industrial park on the edge of Sykesville. Unlocking a heavy door toward one end of a long, metal-sided building, he revealed a single room. One end was occupied by a simple altar, a floodlit cross on the wall behind it. The other end held a desk, a computer, and several bookcases. A single television camera in the center of the room aimed its lens at the cross.

Columns marched down the sides of the room, their strong taper suggesting the lofty heights of a cathedral nave. As he passed one, Michael tapped it with his fingers. It was cardboard.

"You wouldn't say what you wanted," said the Reverend. "But I can guess."

"Go ahead," said Teebelle Radamang.

The Reverend eyed her ample form skeptically. "You want to know why I'm not against your Xanadu project."

"You're about the only televangelist who isn't," said Michael.

"I know." The Reverend grinned and nodded. "And the reason's simple: I think it's a great idea." When they looked surprised, he laughed and added, "I used to be a psychiatrist, would you believe? I got into this...." He paused long enough to make a sweeping gesture at the room around them. "I'm still helping people, it pays the bills just as well, and it's more fun."

"But how can you accept Xanadu, Reverend?" asked Teebelle.

"Call me Jack." He began to walk toward his desk in the back of the room. "I spout the standard line. The customers expect it, you know? But I don't swallow it myself. I'm a rationalist at root. A humanist." He hesitated before adding, "Why Xanadu?"

Michael Durgov chuckled. "Once you're in the machine, you can decree all the pleasure domes you want."

Jack Kemmerdell nodded. "Then that explains the Coleridge as well. What was the company name before?"

"Kingfisher Electronics. We designed specialty systems."

The three people had stared at each other then for a long moment. Finally Kemmerdell said, "You want something else, don't you? You have some idea of how I might help you against all the other televangelists."

Michael laughed. "I should have expected that, I suppose. You said you used to be a shrink, Jack. How would you like to be copied, for free?"

"To put the blessing of God on the project? Or at least the blessing of a tenth-rate TV preacher?" Kemmerdell's grin was broad and infectious. "I can do better than that, if you'll let me design my own pleasure dome."

"You mean a heaven, don't you?" asked Teebelle. "Something for the public. A genuine, guaranteed afterlife, with no danger of going to hell."

"You've got it." Very briefly, Kemmerdell had looked surprised, as if he had not expected anyone—or a woman—to guess what he had in mind. "And they can get in anytime they can pay the bill."

Michael was smiling at his own memory. "I thought," he told Rose Pillock. "I thought that just getting someone from the religious community to accept copying into the first host computer would be enough to weaken the opposition. Perhaps that would have worked. But Kemmerdell went a long step further."

As soon as he had been copied, he had accepted a fat fee, enlarged his studio, and begun to pitch the "New Heaven." Meanwhile, his copy had been working with the host computer to design the necessary images that would surround the first arrivals. In time he added something for everyone. There were the traditional Christian Pearly Gates and celestial mansions. There was the natural world as no one had seen it for decades: a slice of Rocky Mountain trout-fishing paradise; a Nova Scotia salmon river; a bit of Caribbean beach, complete with scenic coral reef; a Hawaii as it had been before the hotels had walled in the shoreline, a land of perfect surf, orchids, and diamond-littered skies. There was a "Palace of Houris" for Moslems, with no waiting and lots of visitors. Some of the Christian visitors said they were there as missionaries; some didn't. There was a Valhalla for the neopagans, with forest ceremonies, daily battles, evening resurrections, and night-long feasts; the grandstands were always filled. The cheers of the Christians were among the loudest.

Not surprisingly, the other TV evangelists did not succumb without a fight. There were cries of abomination, threats, lawsuits, and attempts at sabotage. But as soon as the Reverend Jackson Kemmerdell's Sykesville program began to include segments broadcast "direct from Heaven," the battle was won. The Reverend's fortunes boomed, sagging only slightly when his competitors finally, surrendering entirely, bought or leased their own host computers and mindscanners from Coleridge.

One evangelist had given his heaven levels with successively higher price tags. Those who could not afford to buy the higher levels with their initial payments enslaved themselves to their electronic copies. If they refused, pleas from heaven extorted more money from friends, children, parents, and widows.

It had not taken long for society to decide that contact between flesh and blood and electronic copies was not a good idea. Talk-show experts had proclaimed the sanctity of death and the separateness and independence of copies. Some state legislatures had barred all contact, except at the copy's request. And prices had fallen, though virtual reality was still not cheap.

"I remember," said Rose. "At first, Al and I thought.... Well, we didn't really want one of the Heavens. But we liked to think of all the possibilities. Except it was so expensive. And then...."

"Tell her what happened to Dr. Luria."

The dim glow that accompanied Bertha's voice was enough to show Rose Michael's wince.

"What happened?" she asked. "Did she get in?"

He shook his head. "She couldn't afford it."

"But wouldn't you have given it to her? If anyone deserved it...."

"She would have had to ask," said Michael almost too softly for her to hear.

"And she was too proud for that," said Bertha.

"So she died."

He nodded. "She committed suicide. She cut her wrists."

The ensuing silence stretched out for what seemed forever while Rose thought that the Michael Durgov she had known that summer at the lake could not possibly have done such things, or have been proud of them if he had.

Or was Michael so proud?

He wasn't looking at her, was he? His back was turned and his shoulders bent.

The remorse was there. The shame. The hint that now, at last, he might become the man he should have been.

Or was she only fooling herself? It was only natural that the years should have changed them, and it should be no surprise to find she did not like the changes in him.

SILICON KARMA
THOMAS A. EASTON

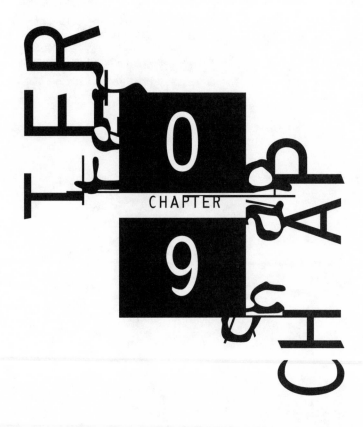

CHAPTER 09

Rose was already up and dressed and staring into a shadowy cupboard above the kitchen counter when Michael emerged from his bedroom in the morning.

"Anything in there?" he asked. Other cupboards were marked only by the assorted, mismatched wooden knobs and brass-loop handles that let one pull them open. The doors themselves merged indetectably into the varnished pine of the cottage's walls. Above the kitchen, half the living area, and the bedrooms, heavy joists supported a plank floor, a loft or storage area.

In reply, she held up a jar labeled "Honey." It held a solid mass of dry crystals. She set it on the counter and produced a jar of peanut butter. "Petrified," she said. "It must have been here since I was a kid."

"You sound like you think it's real. He only made it yesterday!"

"It's real enough." She reached into the depths of the cupboard once more and withdrew another jar. It was half full of small, yellowish near-spheres and ob-longs, and it rattled when she shook it. "Jesus," she said. "Would you look at this." Her voice trembled, and when she turned, her eyes were wet.

"What is it?"

"My pearl collection. Every summer, I would dive for fresh-water clams. Some-times we would eat them. I always opened them and looked for these things."

"I guess we had other things on our minds. We didn't do that."

She took a deep breath and let it out noisily. With a grimace of strain, she forced the jar's lid to turn. She poured its contents into her palm. "There," she said. "That's the biggest one I ever found." She indicated a pearl the size of her little fingertip, elongated, twisted, curved, one end swollen. "I had about grown out of it by then. Still, I used to wonder what happened to this jar."

"You still don't know. This is just...."

"But he based it on my—our—memories! And he's trying to be realistic." She poured the pearls from her palm back into the jar, twisted the lid back into place, and put the jar back on the shelf, out of sight. Then she touched the jar of petrified peanut butter. "It *has* been a long time. But I must still have the memory of where I put that jar. Somewhere deep inside me. I can't think of it, not even now. But he found it, and...."

"Maybe he just found the memory of the jar—not of where you really left it—and just put it in this cupboard. It's only a simulation, after all."

She shook her head furiously. She *knew* it was a simulation, but she didn't want to believe any less than she could manage in its reality. "It feels right."

Michael sighed and looked past her at the empty shelves. He jerked another cupboard open to reveal small stacks of white china plates yellowed by age, floral-patterned saucers, chipped coffee cups, jelly glasses decorated with cartoon figures. Beneath the counter there were shelves of battered aluminum pots, muffin pans, a cast-iron frying pan. Drawers held one plastic spatula, a cracked wooden spoon, three forks, two rusty table knives, and half a dozen spoons with bent handles. "He still could have stocked this place a bit better."

"At least he didn't stock it with an inch of dust. The sheets were clean. The water works. He turned on the electricity."

He opened another cupboard. "Here's something." He pulled out a cereal box. One corner had been chewed away by small animals, and when he set it down, a small pile of tiny black pellets spilled onto the counter. "Huh. Mice. Speaking of realism. Anything in the fridge?"

When she opened the white-enameled door, no light came on. "It's not plugged in." The shelves were empty except for a plastic leftover container half full of something green. "I don't even want to look," she said.

"Maybe we're supposed to create our own? Use our imaginations?"

"All he's taught us is how to change our bodies."

"Maybe that's enough." Michael held out a fist and stared at it intently. Slowly, it deformed, reshaping itself into a ceramic mug half full of black liquid. The steam smelled almost like coffee. "Take it."

She made a face, but she obediently wrapped her hand around the mug. As she did so, the stump of his wrist detached from the handle, thickened, and began to protrude fingers. "I bet I could make a doughnut too," he said. "So taste it."

She faced the mug doubtfully, but before she could object that it didn't smell quite right, a call turned them toward the front of the cottage. "Out here!" Grateful for the interruption, she set the mug on the counter beside the sink. "What's that?" she asked.

When they stepped onto the porch, they saw a table on the needle-littered ground, covered with a snow-white tablecloth and set for three. Beside it was a serving cart loaded with three silver-domed platters, a silver coffee pot, and a pitcher of orange juice. Occupying the seat nearest the cart, with his back to the lake, was Marvin. He wore a pale gray tuxedo that seemed to echo the silver in his hair. "Come on down!"

A moment later, Michael was pulling an ornately carved chair with a needle-work seat out from the table and their host was saying, "You don't need to sleep, you know, though most of my guests do. It's a powerful habit."

"So is eating," said Michael, rounding the table to his own seat.

"Sorry about the supplies," said their host. "You were doing pretty well there, but it takes a lot of practice to get it right. Most of my guests just buy image trans-formation routines and imagine food. Or they let the experts serve them." He reached for the coffee pot. "I think you'll find this a bit more like what you expected."

"I suppose we don't really need to eat," said Rose. "We could just use one of those routines to make our stomachs feel full."

"Or not get hungry at all," said Marvin. He touched his mustache with one finger. "Or not get tired. Though sleeping and eating are grand pleasures. I don't sleep—too much to tend to—but I've learned to eat. What would you like?" He lifted the cover on one of the platters on the cart to reveal a row of small, golden birds. Wisps of steam rose into the air, and the smell made Rose's and Michael's mouths water. "Squabs." The second platter held miniature steaks. The third bore mounds of scrambled eggs and bacon.

Michael reached for the first platter, but when he lifted the dome, it held stacks of pancakes, waffles, and French toast. "What...?"

"Or would you rather have an omelet?" Now the second dome revealed three folded rounds of yellow egg. From the creases of two peeked ham, mushroom, cheese, green and red peppers. The third oozed a line of red jelly. A fourth portion looked quite different. "That one's egg foo young. Or...." He reached for the third platter again. "Try the fish." He showed them small trout, fried crisp and brown in cornmeal.

Rose gestured at the cart. "It's like magic, and you're the wizard. But they're just figments, right? Whatever you imagine, you can have."

"So how come the cupboards in there are bare?" When she nodded jerkily, he said, "You'll learn. It won't even take long. Now, what would you like?"

"Do they taste as real as they look?" asked Michael.

"Of course!" Marvin drew himself up as if offended at the suggestion that any of his productions could be less than perfect.

"The trout, then," said Rose.

"What trout?" When she pointed at the last dome their host had lifted, he laughed, exposed the squabs, and waved both hands in circles above the cart. "Pick a platter, any platter. Round and round she goes, and where she stops nobody knows."

"I never did like shell games," said Michael. "Unless they were my own. That one." He pointed at the first of the three platters.

"Squabs again. Sure you don't want to try one? They're delicious! Ah! But you're getting impatient. So...." Marvin grabbed a fork and deftly scooped one of the roasted pigeons into the air. As it landed on Rose's plate, it turned into a pair of trout. "Right all along, eh? Now you, Mike."

"I'll try the squab. Unless you're about to change it into a dish of prunes. I had enough of those before I came here."

"A squab it is. Orange juice too? More coffee?"

After breakfast, Marvin said, "We've got things to talk about. Pick up your coffee cups." As soon as they had obeyed, the table and serving cart vanished. Their seats turned into broad-armed lawn chairs—the seats retaining their needlepoint designs in paint—arranged to face the lake. He pointed, and their cups refilled.

Despite his words, no one spoke for several minutes. All three sipped coffee and stared out over the water, watching the reflection of the far shore break up as the day's first breeze erased the glassy sheen of the morning lake, noting the leap of a fish, the profile of a distant trio of ducks, the call of a loon. The scene was as idyllic as any memory, and more real.

Finally, Michael broke the silence. "What do we have to talk about?"

"Work," said their host. He looked at each of them in turn, first left, then right. "How you're going to earn your keep. You don't have to start right off. You have a while to settle in, but you can't loaf forever."

"I had forgotten," said Rose.

"It was part of the deal," said Marvin. "You signed the papers. Or your originals did."

"I know." She sighed. There had been so many papers, and she had not read them all as closely as she should have. But, yes, she did recall now that one had been titled "Employment Agreement." The counselor who had been laying the papers, one by one, in front of her had said, "You have to remember. It's a new lease on life. You'll be young again, and you won't want to twiddle your thumbs forever after. So there will be things to do. And we'll need you to do them too."

"But...." she said. She had had the impression that work was, if not quite optional, something she did not need to worry about until she began to find her new life boring, until she began to itch to do something productive with her new and infinite supply of time and energy.

"I do insist," said Marvin.

"But why?" asked Michael. "We don't need to eat. We don't really need a place to sleep. Anything we want, you say, we can have just by imagining it. At least, once we learn how to do it or get the right scroll."

Marvin did not answer immediately. Instead, his face took on a distracted look. He grimaced and put his hand over his left eye.

Rose looked past the computer's persona at Michael. "A headache?" she asked. Before she remembered that Marvin was a computer, an artificial intelligence with no real head to ache, she was reminded of friends who had suffered from migraines. They were long gone now, or out of reach beyond the barrier represented by the Xanadu that had engulfed her head and mind.

She said the word, but Marvin simply closed his eyes and shook his head. After a brief silence, his face relaxed once more, though there remained the stamp of pain and tension. "No," he said curtly. "How could I have migraines? I'm a machine, after all." He sighed then. "But it's over now. And there are several reasons why you should work. Life here can all too easily degenerate into self-indulgence, and I discourage lotus-eaters or parasites. Though...."

"I don't imagine that's a problem for most of your guests," said Michael.

Marvin was nodding now. "It does cost a good deal to get in here, doesn't it? That means you have to have had a certain amount of energy, determination, and

SILICON KARMA
THOMAS A. EASTON

self-motivation just to qualify for entry. Or you could have inherited money. But there's more to it than just keeping out the riff-raff. The world outside...."

"That's where you get electricity and new memory chips and maintenance," offered Michael. "And you have to pay for it. So you need money."

Marvin set his cup down on the arm of his lawn chair, and suddenly his tux vanished, replaced by a swimming suit. Rose took a startled moment to realize that the suit was designed for a woman. Then Marvin was replaced within the suit by his alter ego Bertha. Bertha grinned and pointed, and the cup Rose had dropped on the ground levitated back into her hand, clean, refilled, and steaming. "It may feel like magic," she said. "But magic always has a price. It takes a lot of effort, a lot of computation, to let you live the way you're used to," she said. "With bodies, you know. Or the illusions of bodies. It would be much simpler to convert you to purely electronic sentience. But that would seem too abstract or disembodied for most people. And it would still be expensive."

Michael opened his mouth, but before he could speak, Rose said, "There's all the money we paid Coleridge. Isn't that enough?"

Their host shrugged. "Even so."

"The company wants all the profit it can get," said Michael.

"You should know," said Bertha. She turned toward Rose. "He really should. He set it up that way!"

"He told me last night," said Rose. "And I had read about some of it before." The documents Coleridge had given first her husband and then her had described the technology in simple terms. Now she looked at Michael. "But I didn't know it was you. I must have seen your name, but it didn't register." She felt embarrassed at the thought that she could possibly forget the name of one who had once been so important to her. "You were just a Michael. Your last name—I knew it, but...."

"It wasn't only me." Michael was staring into the bottom of his coffee cup. He did not seem comfortable. "The company...."

"Never mind," said Bertha. She shrugged dismissively, rose from her seat, and trotted toward the dock. As she dove into the lake, Marvin reappeared in the lawn chair. When Rose looked back toward the water, there was no sign of the other. When her flash of alarm subsided quickly, she congratulated herself that she was getting used to her new world.

"People will work whether they're being exploited or not," said Marvin. "But you do get paid too."

"With what?" asked Rose. She felt her mouth set in a skeptical twist. The quick-change shifts from Marvin to Bertha and back again were beginning to feel like the distractions stage magicians worked upon their audiences to keep them from spotting the mirrors and trapdoors. The computer's line—"You'll work anyway, but don't worry, I'll pay you"—sounded like a classic con, like the sort of paternalistic bullshit she had heard a thousand times before from employers and government and seen in a million advertisements.

"With what?" she repeated. "You need money, but we don't."

"That's what people used to think. When they first thought of copying minds into a computer world, they said it would be paradise. You could have whatever you wanted, do whatever you wished. A world without limits."

"You're saying there *are* limits," said Rose.

"Call them resources," said Marvin patiently. "An ecologist wouldn't be surprised to find that a virtual world depends just as much on them as a real ecosystem. Nor would an economist. Out there, where you lived in the flesh, that's all money ever meant. A medium of exchange. A way to measure those resources—services or products—that you yourself command, and then to exchange those resources for ones that others command. The ability to obtain what you need in order to do what you wish. Food. A house. College tuition for your kids. Medical care. A vacation at the McMurdo Ice Palace or Moon Base instead of Hawaii."

"Even copying into you," said Michael.

"Of course."

"But what is there here for us to buy?" asked Rose. "We don't need any of those things now."

"What you paid Coleridge guarantees you a certain minimum standard of living inside me. That means I assign you enough memory and processing capacity to simulate living quarters. Though not...." Marvin gestured at the lake, the island, the cottage behind them. "I always show off a bit for new arrivals, just to show them what's available. This *is* something special, but I liked your memories, your stories."

Rose scanned her surroundings as if she were suddenly afraid that she would never see them again. "What's the minimum like?"

SILICON KARMA
THOMAS A. EASTON

"It's more like a well-furnished city apartment—but it is standardized. It's easier for me to maintain it that way." Marvin gestured again, and the air above the dock began to shimmer. In a moment, they could see ample rooms with wooden floors and plaster walls and acoustic-tile ceilings. Tall windows looked out on city streets; sounds of traffic competed with those of tree and lake. Prints appeared on the apartment wall. Tables, chairs, overstuffed armchairs, shelves, a bed, area rugs, all found space upon the floor.

"That's not so bad," said Michael. "I've lived in much smaller places. But surely that's not all we get."

Marvin shook his head. "Food and other equivalents of ordinary physical needs. Access to the commons, the world-like setting I maintain for all my guests to share." The apartment was replaced by a view of pavement, pedicabs, automobiles, bicycles, and pedestrians. In the foreground were the small round tables of a sidewalk cafe. "It's a simulation of the world you came from. We came through it on the way to the tearoom, though I varied it a bit."

"Then I don't see why we need money," said Rose. "A world, a home, food and drink, friends we lost touch with long ago, new friends. What else is there to buy?"

Their host sighed deeply. "A city apartment wouldn't be enough for you, would it? I know you didn't like the one you were in before you came to me."

"That was different."

"But it's about all you get here if you don't work. You need an extra allotment of memory and processing capacity if you wish something different, something more private, more your own. Something like this." Again his gesture encompassed the lake and island and cottage. "There are also certain things you might like to do that would need more—even much more—than the minimum resources."

"Like sprouting wings?" asked Michael.

"But we've already paid!" said Rose.

Marvin nodded and his expression turned patient, as if he had explained this many times before. "It was your original who paid. You are a separate individual, a new consciousness. If you want more than the minimum, you have to pay your own way. What I have left after budgeting the minimums is limited, you see, and that's the only fair way to share it out."

After a moment of silence, Michael Durgov looked down at his body. "I don't feel cheated," he said.

"It isn't quite what I expected," said Rose. "But.... I'm getting the idea. A virtual economy, a lot like the one we're used to."

"I'll bet there are even ways for thieves and other crooks to operate."

Marvin was nodding. "No burglars, though. Jewelry is too easy to replace."

"But what is there to do that needs extra money?"

"You'll learn soon enough," answered their host. "And no, I don't call what you earn money. It isn't, really, though the term is convenient for introductory purposes."

Michael looked as if he were not happy that his question had been ducked. But he did not insist on an answer. Instead he said simply, "So we earn memory, or processing time."

"More like a combination of both, since both are limited resources here and most uses demand some of each, though the mix may vary. I call it 'data energy,' since it's what you need to process data but also the equivalent of the energy at the root of a food chain. Most people...." He shrugged. "'Money' suits them."

"And how do we spend it?" asked Rose.

"That's quite automatic. Your basic allotment is enough to provide your minimum. What you earn buys more data energy, and when you imagine anything beyond the minimum, your account is automatically debited. Unless, of course, you don't have enough data energy in your account."

"What happens if we run out entirely?"

"You can't die here, if that's what you're wondering. At worst, you'd be zeroed all the way to your storage wafer. But I've never had that happen. Your minimum keeps coming, like a salary or stipend. It's not static, like a bank account."

"So what kind of work can we do?" asked Michael.

"I'm back!" The voice came from behind them. When Rose and Michael turned, they saw Bertha descending the steps from the cottage's porch, an apple in her hand. "The water's fine." She stepped in front of Marvin and bent as if she intended to sit in his lap. As her flesh neared his, she seemed to replace him until only she occupied the chair, though now she wore the tux. The apple crunched as she bit into it.

"That depends," she said. "On what you'd like to do, or can do. But we'll deal with that later. In the meantime...." She grinned mischievously, and suddenly she was Marvin once more. He took another bite of the apple, grinned, and said, "Want one?"

SILICON KARMA
THOMAS A. EASTON

Rose looked at Michael. He was smiling, amused as if the computer had not already, when they were in the tearoom, quite thoroughly demonstrated the elastic quality of its internal reality. Yet she was not amused. The computer's repeated metamorphoses were now confusing her more than ever. She shook her head and grimaced. "That is too much. Can't you stay just one?"

Their host just laughed. "You'll play games too, once you've learned how. People do, you know, as much as they have the data energy to afford. But I wasn't just playing," said Marvin. "I did a little checking while I was gone. And I found that I have a few other guests you two know. Want to meet them?"

"Who are they?" asked Rose.

"Come on," said Michael. "You didn't just find out about them. You had to know all along."

"Would I lie?" Marvin held one hand toward the lake. "Here's one."

Rose leaped from her chair, took one step forward, and froze. "Albert!" she cried.

The figure before them was not the one Rose had watched roll head-first into a Xanadu mindscanner. Nor was he the one she had sat beside as illness weakened him, the one she had later buried. Albert, if indeed this was her late husband—but no, she reminded herself, he could not be that, could be only a copy, but oh, he looked so familiar, so much like the memory she had carried in her head through all the years of aging and beyond his death—had revised his image just as had she and Michael. He was young again, as tall, as strong, as beloved as ever he was in his prime. His near-black hair was thick, the curls she had once loved to touch springy with youth. His zippered shirt, checkered flannel, was open at the top to reveal the curls upon his chest. His skin was smooth, his stance confident, his small paunch as inevitable as ever, his mustache perhaps a hair less shaggy.

"Rose? Rosa!"

Her heart was pounding madly. Why had she waited so long? Why hadn't she asked Marvin to find him right away? Because Marvin, delighted—a computer? delighted?—by the coincidence of their simultaneous copyings had thrust her and Michael together. And that had then thoroughly preoccupied her mind, aided and abetted by the part of her that reminded her that her late husband was *late*, after all, they had grown apart, he had found someone else....

Albert's eyes were fixed on Rose as intently as were hers on him. But then he looked aside. She could sense his recognition of Marvin, his host as well as hers. She could sense as well that Michael Durgov puzzled him. Here was a stranger, someone he had never seen, someone who was with his wife, though he must know she had been alone for years. Perhaps he was her lover, his replacement as a husband? The question, the hurt at the very thought that he had lost her—though that thought could not possibly be a surprise—was obvious in the wrinkled skin around his eyes.

"It's been so long," he said, and the tears that were in his eyes could be heard in his voice as well. "It was like you died, instead of me. I had to get used to being alone. And now...."

"There's so much to talk about, so much to...."

They drew closer, barely hearing Marvin say, "He's been here longer than either of you. He already has a job, and he can tell you whatever you need to know about working here."

With the slightest of flickers, Marvin became Bertha once more. The computer's apparent persona then rose from the lawn chair and stepped forward. "Would you like someone too, Michael? Then here's...."

Rose and Albert were almost touching now, but they both turned in time to catch the open-mouthed surprise on Michael's face. He was facing a well-shaped woman whose blond hair, marked by a broad black stripe, fell over one ear. Her dark eyebrows seemed designed to be expressive. Her thin lips wore no color other than their own. "Who...?" asked Rose.

"Ingrid." Michael's voice was flat.

"His first wife," said Bertha in an aside to Rose.

"I haven't seen you in ages, dear!" said Ingrid. She turned toward Rose, her mouth set in a remarkably supercilious moue. "And who's this? Another one of your sluts?"

No one dared to break the ensuing silence. Michael's jaw muscles bulged with tension. Finally, he took a deep breath and said, just a bit more loudly than was necessary: "I loved her before I ever met you!"

Now Ingrid turned her moue on her ex-husband. "Then why didn't you marry her and save me all that pain?"

SILICON KARMA
THOMAS A. EASTON

CHAPTER 10

Something was wrong.

She paced the rooms and halls of her house, all pastels and pillars and pedestals. She stroked a pre-Columbian statuette, and when it failed to purr, she batted it against the wall. A touch smoothed the plaster and the paint. The shards she left on the carpet as a reminder to any other of her possessions that failed to please.

A servant offered her a full array of drugs, but she wanted none of them.

Another held out a drink, a tray of drinks, a plate of petit fours, canapes of caviar and lobster and cheese. She wished them all away, shrank the man, and installed him on the pedestal her statuette had abandoned.

Something was wrong. She was restless, bored, hungry, itching for something she did not have though she was sure she would recognize it if only....

What was it? Had her house, as lovely as it was, palled? That happened from time to time, and for it there was a simple solution.

She checked her account. As soon as she saw that she could more than cover the expense, a hallway became a stairway spiraling into air. She chuckled at the thought of how long a meat-world contractor would have taken to do the same job, if he could even do it, and of the mess he would inevitably have made. Here she did it all herself, instantly and cleanly, and if the process drew heavily upon her funds— or upon what passed for funds in this strange world—that at least was no different from meat-world reality. There were always limits on one's actions, limits that made *her* chafe. She grinned at the thought of the anonymous messages that were telling her how to make those limits seem almost trivial, though she still must invest some time and effort to surmount them. Very briefly, she wondered who was behind the messages, but then she turned back to her work.

The room to which the hall had led grew tall and taller, so tall that mists formed beneath the ceiling. Wood became ancient-seeming masonry. Beams appeared at intervals, and flooring. Narrow windows pierced the walls. Furnishings jelled from the air.

When she was done, she realized that the stairway still stood outside the tower. With a chuff of exasperation, she wished circular holes into the centers of the tower's floors. Then, concentrating—it wouldn't do to jostle the vases or crack the masonry, even though any damage could easily be set right—she moved the tower over, letting its structure pass through and around the stairway, centering it

SILICON KARMA
THOMAS A. EASTON

so that the stairs rose through the holes she had made, solidifying it, and finally smiling in delighted satisfaction.

The satisfaction did not last. Within moments she was redesigning the rest of her house to match her tower. Yet she did not wish a castle or a fort. Long and low, a courtyard here, a swimming pool there. A formal garden full of flowers, and make them pink. Pink tiles, pink paint, pink carpet too.

Too pink, but the hell with it. She was bored. She wanted something else to absorb her interest, and if playing house wouldn't do it, then.... She created a mirror in the air before her. How would she look with black hair? Red? Green? Thick lips? Thin? None, and long, sharp teeth? Larger breasts or smaller? She could change her apparent race, or.... She shook her head before her breasts had disappeared entirely and before the penis had even begun to sprout between her legs.

It was sometimes called a "nether mouth," wasn't it? Then give it a tongue, long and agile. Give it teeth!

Where was that man? At the thought, the pedestal scurried through the door as if on tiny legs. "You like?" she asked, and the manikin who had been her servant, who was still her servant, indeed her slave, bowed and chittered obsequiously.

"Get out of here," she said. "See if you can do dinner right this time." She gestured, and he was back to normal size, running from the room before she should change her mind.

Here, now, a tail, long and thin and covered with downy fur. She made it as prehensile as a spider monkey's tail or an octopus's tentacle. She twisted the tip up before her eyes, examined it, imagined away the fur and thickened the tip, let it pet her here and here and there, and yes. Yes!

But that palled too. Nothing satisfied her. She was still restless, bored, craving she knew not what.

Was that it? Was that why? That sense of weight in the air? That subliminal crackle of electricity that would, in her previous life, have suggested a thunderstorm soon to break?

Something was about to happen, she was sure. But what? Had the computer or its agents finally discovered her?

She checked her account again and frowned when she saw how her house and body work had depleted it. But she didn't need to worry about that, did she?

Feeling the hunger rise in her once more, she licked her lips until they glistened, modified her appearance one more time—for some reason, long earlobes turned him on—and blinked.

"How quaint," she murmured. She was in the entryway of an antique apartment building, facing a glass door. One wall was covered with inset metal mailboxes. On the other was a list of tenants, each name beside a pushbutton, and a speaker grille. She pressed one of the buttons and identified herself to the scratchy voice that answered. At the sound of a buzzer, she leaned on the door and licked her lips again.

He was waiting at the head of the stairs. Medium height, dark skin, black hair, strong arms, the kind of man she liked best of all. Though she was not, she knew, as fussy as she should be. She liked men. She always had. One of the worst things about growing old had been that they no longer liked her.

Only after their first long, deep kiss did she say a word. "You really must come home with me. I want you around *all* the time. I can't stand having you so far away."

He laughed and grinned and tightened his arms around her torso. "Do you think we'd get enough of each other then?"

"We could try." They kissed again, and their hands moved, each against the other's body. Clothes melted literally away at the command of a wish, and they hardly seemed to have to move to reach the bed.

She was sitting on the bed, cross-legged, running a gentle hand across her tummy and hip and thigh, watching her man snore. She had drained him, she had. She grinned. She always did. She always would. If she couldn't, her life would hardly be worth living.

The air flickered, and the computer's male persona stood beside the bed. "Hi, Rocky," she said. She had given him that anachronistic name as soon as she realized that he controlled everything that passed for wealth in the virtual world. "Were you watching? Do you want some too?"

SILICON KARMA
THOMAS A. EASTON

Rocky shook his head. "No, thank you," he said. "As usual." He was, as he always was on those rare occasions when he deigned to visit or even speak with her, stiffly formal. He controlled the money, but he could not control her. It was somehow against his rules, or those rules that had been written into his programming.

"Then what do you want?" Her tone was not warm even though she was showing her teeth in a deliberate smile.

He pointed, and she was dressed in green and white. "I want you to meet someone."

She frowned suspiciously. Rocky had never done such a thing before.

"You'll see. Come on."

"But...." She wanted to balk, but she knew better than to try. In this world, Rocky was the biggest of cheeses. All she could do was stall, and she could not do that for long. She plucked at the fabric he had made for her, adjusting the fit to suit her better. "What sort of someone?"

"You'll be surprised."

His grin seemed suddenly ominous. Had he somehow gotten wind of her little thefts? Was this a trap? Or....

There had been two new arrivals recently, hadn't there? She was remembering how familiar they had seemed when the scene suddenly changed.

CHAPTER 1

SILICON KARMA
THOMAS A. EASTON

"We met in college, you know," Ingrid was saying. "We were taking an ethics course, and when I sneered at my father...."

"You called him a pragmatist."

"If it's useful, it's true," said Albert.

Ingrid nodded. "Michael wanted to turn it around. "If something's true, it has to be useful. He changed his mind after we were married." She turned back toward her ex-husband. "Whatever happened to Connie?"

Michael looked uncomfortable. "We divorced. She died."

He still remembered the day he had first told her about Connie. He was sure she did too. Their marriage had turned as sour as it would ever get, and she was saying, "You're gone too many evenings. When will you be home?"

"It's business," he said, shrugging. "Who knows?"

She wrinkled her nose. "For business you need *that* much cologne?"

"Would you rather I said I had a date? With my mistress? Or my next wife?"

She laughed. "Come on! Don't you think I'd have noticed something like that a long time ago?"

"No," he said. "I'm a much better actor than you."

Her face looked suddenly stunned. Theater had been her major in college, and she had once had dreams. "What do you mean?"

"Never made it past auditions, have you?"

"But..."

"And her name's Constance."

The pretty mouth had opened wide. The cords of her neck had stood out like wires. She had screamed.

He had said nothing more but turned his back on her in ostentatious pretense that her reaction did not matter. A few minutes later, he had left.

He had had to deal with her later, of course. Running had only delayed the inevitable fight.... The fights, really, and if his usual tactic had been to flee, there had been times when he had stood his ground and given as good as he got. Once— or even twice—he had drunk too much and hit her, knocked her against a wall, bruised the skin he once had touched so tenderly. She had hit him back, of course, once with a full bottle of wine.

And the funny thing about it was that that night they had wound up in bed.

And it had been better for both of them than it had been in years.

"Any kids?"

"Two."

"I bet they hate your guts."

He said nothing at all. One hand twisted in the space between him and his ex-wife. He took a breath, but before he could speak again, Bertha interrupted.

"That's one for you, Rose," she said. "And one for Michael." With a glance she flicked the lawn chairs into oblivion. Then she held one hand high as if she were an orchestra conductor poised for the downbeat. "I have one more, and then I have to go. I've brought you safely into the virtual world. I've shown you the basics. And I've handed you off to old friends. I think they'll show you the rest of the ropes. Now, here's someone both of you will recognize."

"Who...?" Rose was now leaning against her Albert's chest. His arms enfolded her. The pose was one that suggested they belonged together, once and for always, and that he would happily help her settle into the computer's internal world. But the cords of her neck suggested tension, and one of her hands grasped his biceps just above the crook of his elbow.

Was she really so prepared to thrust him away from her? She was not sure. Yet from time to time, she turned her gaze toward Michael Durgov and smiled fondly, remembering that once....

Ingrid too was watching Michael, though her expression was more complex. Once she too had been fond of him, but he had forfeited that. Now a sour distrustfulness dominated her features, yet there was also an air of possessiveness, as if whether she loved him or not, and no matter how many other wives and lovers he might have had before her and after her, he was hers. Certainly she showed no reluctance to show him around.

Michael turned abruptly away from his first wife, or her copy, and glared. "It had better not be...."

"But it is!" Bertha's broad grin shone wickedly, and then, like a showman, she swept her hand to one side and down. "Here's Lisa!"

And there indeed was Lisa, looking startled at the sudden translocation from wherever she had been and whatever she had been doing. Hadn't Bertha, or perhaps Marvin, warned her?

SILICON KARMA
THOMAS A. EASTON

Just as Rose remembered her, she had blond hair touched with red. She wore iridescent green slacks that embraced her thighs and calves like skin. Her blouse was white and sheer, so translucent that all could see she wore no bra and that her breasts needed no support.

She didn't look that good when we were teens, thought Rose. She must have done some editing. More up front and less behind, a slightly smaller nose, a longer neck, a narrower waist, and yes—it struck Rose in that moment—in this virtual world a girl need never worry about what she ate. Food was sheer imagination, and so was fat, promptly to be never-never wished away.

Yet all the editing Lisa had done had left untouched a feverish, demanding set to her face.

Rose quelled a shudder, telling herself that all those decades in the past, Lisa had looked so innocent. Yet what she had truly been, what she had done, deserved the face she now wore, and she must, Rose thought, have never changed. The cast of features the years had given her now seemed a deeply ingrained part of her, so deeply ingrained indeed that even given the malleable freedoms of virtual reality, she had never chosen to change it. Or perhaps she had never even seen it to change.

Rose tightened her grip on the man who had been her husband. She told herself that Albert's arms were around her, that he could not be tempted, not in any permanent way, no matter that they had been separated for years, that he had led a separate life, that he might have formed other allegiances. They were together, and she would not lose him again.

"Rose!" said Lisa. As she spoke, the lines of her body and face shifted slightly, giving her an apparent age to match those she faced but barely touching the signs she wore of personality. "It's been so long!" She eyed Albert speculatively. "Your husband? Niice!" The sway of her body that then challenged every woman present and enticed every man seemed as unconscious as breathing.

"It's been a long time," said Rose. "We lost touch."

Lisa shrugged and spun around, holding one hand to embrace island, lake, and all the rest of the virtual world. "*C'est la vie*, you know? Quite a place, isn't it? I blew my last divorce settlement getting in here."

"How's the original Lisa?"

"My meat? Haven't the faintest. Though I was on eyedrops at the time." She mimed pulling out one lower eyelid and putting a dose of the powerful drug in the pocket next to the eyeball. "She's probably blind by now. Or dead. I haven't checked."

Rose pushed herself against Albert's chest then, saying nothing more as Lisa turned toward Michael, ignoring Ingrid. "And Miiichaelll! Do you remember...?'"

Michael took an involuntary half step backward, stopping only when he felt the edge of the dock beneath his foot. It was obvious, even though he was shaking his head from side to side, that he remembered.

Of course he remembered, thought Rose. Lisa had spoiled what had begun so long ago between her and Michael. Now he and she had met again. There had been signs that they just might overcome the memory of what Lisa had done to them. Then Albert had joined them, and she was now in his arms, but still there now seemed a possibility that she and Michael could be friends.

"Oh, Michael!"

"Ingrid! Want to know something?" Bertha clearly did not wait for an answer, for Ingrid's eyes promptly twitched and widened, signaling the receipt of some private message from the computer.

Lisa scowled ferociously. "You're not supposed to interfere!" But by then it was already too late. Ingrid was stepping forward, her expression grim. "You stay away from him!"

Michael glanced at Rose. Her brows were raised and her lips pursed. Was she worried that he would succumb? And Ingrid. Her nostrils were flaring, her mouth half open, her neck ridged by nerves drawn wire-taut, all as if she were about to scream, just as she had done when he had first told her about Connie.

He said nothing. He only took that one more backward step that set him firmly on the dock, surrounded by water. He glanced to one side, and Rose noticed a patch of floating iridescence. "Oil?" she murmured.

"It shouldn't be," Albert murmured near her ear. "There aren't any motor boats...." But then Lisa began to move toward Michael, Ingrid intercepted her, and the two women jostled each other for position at the end of the dock.

On the slope of land between the water and the cottage, where the breakfast table had stood, where now only indentations in the soil revealed that lawn chairs once had existed, Bertha beamed benignly, her arms crossed beneath her ample bosom.

"Michael!" said Lisa. She was displaying all the arrogance of a woman who had never been refused anything she truly wanted. "Would you tell your *ex* to get out of my way?" Her emphasis stated quite clearly that she thought the other woman had far less claim than she upon Michael's soul.

"Bitch!" spat Ingrid. "I know what you did to him before." She blocked the wharf, arms akimbo, glaring, loose hairs flaring from her head, sweat showing on her brow and forearm. She seemed as defiant as a cougar protecting its young or a fresh kill. "Greedy, grabby bitch!"

"*You* should talk," said Lisa. The sneer was audible. "I just checked your file. He traded you in, didn't he? And now look at you! What makes you think he wants you *now*?"

Rose met Michael's pleading eyes with a half grin of mingled worry and amusement. Albert shook his head as if to say, "What do they see in you?"

It had been many years since any of them had last been as young as they were now. Then Michael, like Albert, like most men, had been used to making the moves himself. Surely, thought Rose, his wealth had made him used to having them accepted or welcomed. But he had no money now, no power, and no prospects of either. He had left them behind in the real world, the meat reality. They did not exist here, not even as truly as he did himself.

Then why...? Was it just that both women once had felt they owned him, or a piece of him? Was it their own version of territorial breast-beating?

Why didn't Rose have her own claws out? She had her own claim on him, and one that took precedence in time if not in intimacy. After all, they had not yet quite reached the point of sleeping together, of making love, when Lisa had come on the scene.

He looked at her, and she clung still more tightly to her late husband. She had an alternative, she did, and one more recently in her mind than he. Or had she—had *he*, when he let Lisa tempt him?—broken the link they had begun to forge so long ago?

"You're an ugly pig, aren't you?" said Lisa. "Get out of my way." She had one hand planted firmly in the middle of Ingrid's chest, and she was pushing. Ingrid gave ground, slowly at first and then faster, while Michael stepped backward to give the women room.

The oil slick was bigger now, as if it were oozing from some ancient out-board motor or other emblem of human self-indulgence sunken in the ooze of the lake-bottom.

A sudden cough drew all eyes to Bertha. She was cupping one hand over an ear, much in the manner of an on-scene television journalist, and her face seemed as distracted as had Michael's only moments before. Her body rippled, as if something were interfering with the computer's ability to simulate complex images.

As soon as she saw the ripple, Rose turned her head to check on Albert. Was his simulation also faltering? Would he crumble in her arms and leave her bereft once more? Would he disappear just as she had regained him?

Her heart sang when she saw him looking at her with the same questions in his eyes. Their link was still there, still as solid as his flesh beneath her hand, as sure as a lifetime of love. The hiatus between his copying and hers, his death and now, was insignificant. Soon they would be alone, together, and they would talk, catch up, renew. Her arms tightened around his chest, so did his, and they both looked at the others, for whom events were developing so rapidly.

Bertha's ripples were growing quickly worse. Michael, Lisa, and Ingrid seemed untouched by whatever the trouble was. Yet their reactions said something about each of them: Michael's gaze was flicking from Rose to Ingrid and back again. Ingrid's was fixed on Michael except for worried glances toward Bertha. Lisa was holding one arm in front of her and staring at it, at her legs, at her front.

"Isn't it nice to see each other again?" Bertha's voice now had a liquid burble, as if the ripples that were warping her visual simulation worse and worse with every second were now extending into the aural realm as well. "I'm sure you'll have lots and lots of fun."

Rose noticed Albert staring fixedly at the computer's persona. "What?" she asked.

He shook his head. "She's on auto now. A subroutine that...." He shrugged. "A very simple script."

"I have to go now," said Bertha. "Things to do, you know. Problems to take care of. Just little ones, but I do need to tend to business. Can't party all the time!"

And she was gone, leaving behind no more than a patch of sparkling, multi-colored fuzz that made Rose think of a bit of television snow escaped from its confining screen.

SILICON KARMA
THOMAS A. EASTON

"I've never seen it that bad," said Albert.

"She said something about a virus yesterday." When Albert just shook his head she returned her attention to the scene by the dock.

Now Lisa was past Ingrid, Bertha and her difficulties forgotten, and reaching for Michael. He stepped backward once more, glancing behind to see that he wasn't about to go off the end and into the water. The oil slick was bigger than ever, yet it was also developing holes as if some oil-eating fish had been taking bites. Or had the source simply been exhausted?

"Didn't you hear her, Michael?" said Lisa. "She told us to have fun. Come with me, and...."

She jerked as Ingrid seized her shoulder and spun her around. "Bitch!" she spat.

"Leave him alone!" snarled Ingrid.

"He's mine!"

"*You* really *are* a slut, aren't you?"

Now it was Ingrid's turn to push. Lisa lurched on the uneven planks, snarled, and swung crooked fingers toward the other's face.

Michael and Rose both gasped when they saw that Lisa had in the moment of her swing replaced her nails with claws that would have done a tiger proud.

Ingrid did not waste time or effort with tricks. She simply made a fist and, even as Lisa's claws ripped bloodily through her eye and cheek, slammed it into Lisa's mouth.

Lisa hit the water with a shriek and an impressive splash. Yet when the slosh and spray had fallen quiet once more and the disturbed silt was dissipating, there was no sign of her. She had, it seemed, abandoned the field.

Michael looked back at his ex-wife just in time to see the last of the claw marks vanish, all damage edited away, even—except for two small smears near her ear lobe and chin—the blood erased. When she reached for him, he did not retreat as he had from Lisa. "I feel like a prize," he said.

"Some prize," said Ingrid. "The way you treated me. But let's get out of here anyway. Go someplace less crowded."

In the instant before her hand connected with his arm, Michael looked frantically toward Rose. Their gazes met, saying for them far more quickly than words could possibly have done, "What do we do now?" Their pasts had seized them again. They had, just perhaps, been on the verge of discovering what they had missed all those years ago. And then the lives they had lived for real had risen up around them. Albert—though she hardly seemed unhappy at finding him in her arms. Lisa—he had had enough of her before, hadn't he?

And Ingrid. He sighed as she touched him and the lake and island, trees and cottage, Rose and Albert, all vanished from his view, replaced by....

"Don't you work?"

"Of course I do," said Ingrid, letting go of his arm. "I just don't use what I earn *here*."

"Here" was her apartment. It differed only in superficial details—the color scheme, the furniture, the carpet that covered most of the wooden floor—from the minimum standard quarters that Marvin had shown Rose and Michael only an hour or two ago. The three- and four-story brick buildings of an urban residential neighborhood were visible through the tall windows.

"It's roomy enough," she added. "And the view's nice." As she spoke, the window he was facing blinked and showed a beach scene, blinked again and showed snowy mountains, blinked once more and.... He swore, stepped forward, and reached. Instead of glass, his fingers touched water, a sheet of it filling the window hole, small and brilliant fish wheeling just outside the room, a shark arching against rippled sky beyond, fans of coral to one side and below.

Ingrid laughed. "Just an image. Lots simpler than a full simulation. But go ahead. Look around. Maybe you'll see why I like it."

He stood still, his eyes scanning, taking inventory. The leather couch looked comfortable, the carpet soft, the colors—tan, brown, soft yellow—restful. The mahogany end tables with leather tops rang a faint bell in his mind. Had he seen their look-alikes in the past, in meat reality? And the brown easy chair with the cat-scratched upholstery?

"Ahh," he said. "I remember when you brought Goodyear home." The cat's back had borne a barred stripe that had reminded him of a tire track; he had been

SILICON KARMA
THOMAS A. EASTON

the one to name it. "We didn't keep it long, did we?"

"You damned near killed him when you saw what he'd done to your chair."

"He tore the stuffing out of the box spring too."

"*That* wasn't what pissed you off." Ingrid shrugged, but her voice now held a bitter note.

He paused, letting her bitterness fade. Goodyear had been past the stage of cutest kittenhood the day she brought him home, and every day had seen him growing sleeker, less fluffy, more independent, and less content with apartment life. He had been relieved enough to see the last of the beast, but not, he suspected, as relieved as the cat. "Same chair?"

"Of course it is."

He scanned the room again. "I remember that print too. That lamp. That.... This is a lot like the place we had in Chicago." Before he met Connie, before he was tomcatting so vigorously, and drinking and....

"It's the fucking same!" Her voice crackled, strained, broke. She made one choked-off sobbing noise. "We were happy then. I've wanted it back ever since."

"Ah." He made a face. He had left that behind, and with it his inability to control his temper. He had never hit another woman as he had hit her in their last days, or been hit by one.

"And you haven't, have you?"

"I'll bet Lisa's glad you didn't have a wine bottle in your hand."

Her cheeks were wet with tears. It was therefore startling to see her grin and hear her laugh. "Are you afraid we'd act like that again?"

"You obviously haven't forgotten how."

She laughed again and grabbed his arm once more. "There's lots of things I haven't forgotten how to do. Do you remember...?"

For only the briefest of moments did he think how oddly natural it felt to cover her hand with his own. Then he said, "Of course I do."

"Then let me show you the rest of this place. There's even a wet bar."

"I've barely touched the stuff for the last ten years. Doctor's orders."

"They don't matter here. C'mon."

CHAPTER

1

2

SILICON KARMA
THOMAS A. EASTON

Leah Kymon, Jonathan Spander, Eric Minckton, and Manora Day were once more ignoring the view from the conference room. On the long table in front of them were a newspaper, spread to display its headlines, and a computer workstation. The mood in the room was not cheerful.

"Did you see that?" Kymon pointed at the newspaper.

"Of course we did." Spander sighed. "You made sure of it."

"'Computer Glitch Destroying Heaven?'" read Manora Day. "'Rumors persist that at least one Afterlife computer is developing problems. The Coleridge Corporation is no longer able to give customers the pseudoreality it has long promised. Some computer residents are actually dying even though they signed up to live as long as the computer could last. Others are suffering the equivalent of power system brownouts as the computer freezes up and puts their lives on hold.' Do you have any idea how hard this will make our job in Marketing?"

No one thought an answer was necessary.

"And *who* the hell has been talking to the papers?"

"None of us, I'm sure," said Kymon soothingly. "It must be someone in operations, but...." She turned to Spander. "Have you made any progress on finding the leak, Jon?"

When Spander just shook his head, Kymon added, "It needs more memory, right? That would cure the sluggishness."

"It would help," said Spander. "That and more processors. But not for long. Whatever's hogging the machine is greedier than ever. If we doubled the memory, it would be used up in a week."

Minckton indicated a graph on the workstation screen. "We have doubled it. And more."

"And something grabs it almost as fast as the technicians install it."

"Have you talked to Durgov?"

"Not yet. I don't think he's been in there long enough to...."

"Try him now. We *need* to know."

Spander used the workstation's keyboard for a moment. The graph vanished from the screen and was replaced by a face that seemed sculpted from brass.

"Yes?" said the computer.

"We need to talk to Michael Durgov," said Leah Kymon.

The computer raised one metallic eyebrow. "You know better than that."

"It's important news!"

"You want to tell him a burglar killed his meat? I saw the obit, and I'll let him know if he ever asks. Or do you really want to ask him what he's learned about our problems in here?"

"Yes," said Minckton.

"Don't worry about it. I've got my own man on the case."

"And you don't need an amateur, is that it?"

"Something like that."

"Let us talk to Durgov anyway."

"You can't. That's the rules. It's just like he was really dead, unless *he* chooses to call *you*."

"If he was really dead, we could go to a medium," said Day.

"Bullshit," said Spander.

The computer laughed. "I can cheat a little bit. He's been inside me barely long enough to know anything's wrong. And he's nowhere near learning anything that would help you."

Robert Codder stood up cautiously, just enough to see over the sides of his carrel. His supervisor was out of sight. No other programmer was moving in the room's aisles, though not far away Irma's cap of red curls bobbed as if.... But she was sitting down, not getting up. The only sounds were the hum of fans that kept the room's many workstations from overheating, the quiet rattle of keys, rustling paper, creaking chairs, and an occasional curse.

Satisfied that no one would see what he was doing, he composed a simple message, a suggestion, a nudge: "Why don't you add Michael to your collection?" It probably wasn't necessary, for it was just the sort of thing the recipient would think of on her own. But all he had to do was touch a single key, and it was on its way to just the right corner of the computer's memory. The artificially intelligent software system would never notice, for he was using the purest of

SILICON KARMA
THOMAS A. EASTON

machine code to steer his message past all the sentinels he knew were there to
enforce the "no-contact" rule.

And no one could know them better.

He smiled as he touched the key.

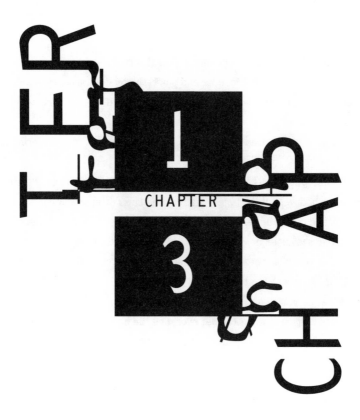

CHAPTER

1
3

SILICON KARMA
THOMAS A. EASTON

The dock was empty. Ingrid and Michael had vanished, as had Lisa after her splashdown in the lake. There was no sign of the breakfast table and chairs, nor of the lawn chairs, and Bertha was gone, tending to whatever headaches a virus might cause a computer.

Rose was surprised at how uncomfortable she felt now that she was alone with her late husband. She patted the flannel of his shirt and eased herself out of the circle of his arms. Once free, she turned to face him. "Oh, Al," she said. "Bertie Al. It's going to take a little while to...."

His arms had all the strength and solidity that they had ever had. But hadn't he thrown out that shirt, thread-bare and paint-splotched, thirty years ago? Now it looked like new. He smelled the way she remembered too. But how could he find Old Spice in here?

But he was *late*. Dead. Wormfood and grinning skull and moldering Sunday suit.

She had watched—and tears sprang to her eyes all over again at the memory of how she had wept at the time—had watched his coffin sink into the ground and the belts and rollers be removed and the dirt cover up the polished wood. She had thrown two shovelsful herself. He was a ghost. He had to be.

And so was she, even if her original still walked and talked and lived alone.

"Is it like this all the time?"

"What do you mean?"

"Does Marvin always drag out everyone the new arrival ever knew?"

"There usually isn't anyone. Or there's just one, a husband or a wife. Perhaps a friend or two. Of course, the more people get copied, the more likely it will be to....."

"Then I'm just lucky, huh? A husband. An old boyfriend and the bitch who came between us."

"You're not unique. The boyfriend got you and the same bitch and a wife.."

"But.... I feel like everything's revolving around me. Me!"

"Rosa." He held both hands toward her, as open and alive as his face, fingers spread. "Everything revolved around you when I was alive. When we were younger. I never dreamed I could be as lonely as I was my first few months here. I prayed I'd see you again. But now it seems so soon. Too soon."

"I was already old enough when you were copied. I couldn't possibly have lived much longer."

"I know, but...." A gesture indicated the lake, the island's shore and forest, and the cottage. "We have the place to ourselves."

"Do you remember? I told you about it, and one summer we rented a place on the shore, over there." She pointed. "The cottage was still here—we saw it from the water—but it was booked that week. Two families, it looked like, and we thought they had far too many kids, though most of them had to be guests."

Albert Pillock nodded. "You wanted to show me your room. But I never got inside."

"We can fix that now, can't we? That's where I slept last night." She took his hand in hers and tugged him toward the steps to the porch.

"With M....?" His voice trailed off as he realized that death had parted them and he no longer had any claim on her fidelity. Not really.

"Separate beds, dear. Separate rooms."

A few moments later, she was standing in the middle of the room that had been hers the summer she met Michael Durgov. Like the rest of the cottage, its walls were varnished wood. Exposed, age-darkened beams hovered just above the upper level of a two-decker bunk. Only the bottom mattress was covered by sheets and a thin blanket. The upper mattress, cocked askew on the frame, was stained by rainwater or children's urine, blackened by mildew, leaking stuffing from one small rip. The two dressers were cracked and weathered, apparent rejects from the owner's barn.

"It felt like heaven, then," said Rose. "Do you think it still exists, out there?"

"We could always check. There are records, and databases full of satellite photos." Albert put one hand on her shoulder and tugged her gently toward him, but she stiffened. She had accepted his embrace readily enough—eagerly at first, then more tensely, nervously—outdoors, where there were witnesses. She had been so relieved to see him again. But here, indoors, in a bedroom, she felt both relieved and reluctant. He had been her husband. The last time he had seen her, she had been his wife. But he had died, and she had gotten used to living without him. Now he lived again—didn't he?—just as he had been decades before the end. He *felt* like her husband. But was he? Was she ready to treat him as if he were? Would she be happier settling back into the routine she once had found so comfortable? Or would she prefer the freedom of not having to compromise every day for the rest of a life that could stretch as far into the future as civilization itself? Not that she would have to stay with him that long. Their marriage vows had surely been fulfilled when he died. This Albert was not the one she had known. He was only a copy, really, and she should be able to leave after mere months or years, or even days if that was all the time they could now stand to spend together.

She did not know the answer. Nor could she pretend she did. She twisted past him into the cottage's living area. "Look," she said. "The television's still here. Do you think it works?"

She was reaching for the controls when they clicked and a status light glowed to life before her. "Just a thought," said Albert. "That's all it takes."

"It'll take *me* forever." Despite all the years she had caused her simulated body to shed, she still had no confidence that she would ever learn all the skills that virtual reality made possible. Her body, she could handle that, and now that she thought of it, Albert's Old Spice was no longer a mystery. But to turn on a television across the room with a mental remote unit, to manipulate the environment around her as Marvin had done with breakfast....

The screen was brightening rapidly, but before a picture could form a small figure faded into view on top of the television, its legs dangling in front of the screen. It wore knee britches, a torn T-shirt, and a baseball cap and was splotched from head to foot with ink stains. One hand held a long steel-nibbed pen as if it were a sword. "You wanted research?" it asked in a reedy voice.

"As long as you're here," said Albert. "Find us a view of this island in the meat world."

The pop-up twisted its face in a parody of thoughtfulness. A moment later, it swung its legs to one side and pointed at the television screen. "There you go."

"Oh, no," said Rose. The image showed a broad expanse of lawn surrounding a low building of many rooms, three swimming pools, a dozen tennis courts, and a single grove of tall pines. A tall chain-link fence topped with outward-leaning barbed wire rimmed the shore. A caption across the bottom of the screen said, "ICTT Conference Center."

"I shouldn't be surprised, should I?" she added. "It's been a long time."

Albert nodded, said, "Good job," and the pop-up vanished.

One corner of the television image showed the shore of the lake that held the island. It was a wall of three-story buildings broken only by the narrowest of gaps, through which were visible more buildings and occasional trees. Rose closed her eyes and shuddered and then looked toward the window at the front of the small cottage. Her present reality was based in memory, and it held more trees, forest duff instead of lawn, and an ancient vacation cottage. "I like it better this way," she said.

"So do I."

When she looked back at the television screen, the image of the island as it was in the reality Rose had left behind her was gone. In its place was a dignified face wearing a bristly white mustache and a mane-like halo of white hair behind a high dome of brow and scalp. Heavy-lidded eyes peered at the camera over small, rectangular glasses, and a soft yet intense voice was saying: "Other religions handle the question of the First Cause by pointing to God, or perhaps several gods. Where did God come from, you ask? The question, they say, is meaningless. He is, was, and always will be."

The camera drew back, revealing that the speaker stood behind a pulpit on which rested a square mortarboard cap, complete with tassel. His black robe, its sleeves marked with maroon stripes, seemed more suitable for an academic procession. Over his shoulders and down his back draped the hood that signified that he had earned a doctor's degree; it was sky-blue and orange.

When Rose asked, "What's this?" the screen flickered and a window blinked into existence in the upper right corner of the screen. Words filled the window:

"Direct from HEAVEN!
Join us in the
Afterlife
of your choice!
Be BLESSED,
and KNOW
that you are SAVED!"

SILICON KARMA
THOMAS A. EASTON

Behind the words appeared images: Angels fluttered through a cloudscape; heroic men in turbans approached scantily clad women who lingered under Moorish arches; armored, horn-capped men waved swords while spectators cheered; men in beards and skullcaps sat at long benches to study ancient scrolls; both men and women lounged at ease in a domed hall whose walls were lined with sagging bookshelves.

"For the religious types," said Albert. "It's in another computer. They like to put on shows to explain themselves. They're also looking for converts."

"Can people visit?"

"I've been there. They love tourists." He shook his head. "It gets pretty confusing, walking on clouds, stepping from battlefields to harems to libraries."

The camera panned across a wall covered with portraits whose unsubtle lines and bold colors were strongly reminiscent of the illustrations for children's bible stories. Neatly engraved labels identified their subjects: Albert Einstein, Robert Maxwell, Nils Bohr, Charles Darwin, Alfred Wallace, George Beadle, Nicholas Rashevsky, Frank Drake, Edwin Hubble, James Watson, Theodosius Dobzhansky, Max Planck, Francis Crick, Werner Heisenberg, and more.

"Now, as we've discussed before, Darwinian-Occamism insists that the universe and everything in it are understandable in terms of the natural laws of cosmology, physics, chemistry, biology, psychology, and so on. First Causes? There are none. Then who made the universe? No one. It's a bubble in a multicosmic froth, or it cycles eternally, again and again expanding from and contracting to the primordial singularity.

"We don't yet know just what our universe really is. We may never know. But we have faith that the universe is, was, and always will be. Perhaps—like the virtual worlds we here inhabit!—it is but a simulation in some vast cosmic computer. Add fourth and fifth dimensions, and our eternally repeating cycle presents no problem. But we do not need to posit a God of unknowable origin when we have a universe of the same ineffable nature.

"And that, of course, brings us back to the prime commandment of Darwinian Occamism: Thou shalt not multiply hypotheses!"

"That doesn't sound right," said Rose.

"It's a basic idea in science and philosophy. Occam's Razor." Albert shrugged.

The television muted its sound. "Detectives use it too. If I have two explanations for the evidence, and one is simpler than the other, that one is almost always the right one. Look...." He drew in the air with his right hand, and a body, dressed in tweeds, took shape on the carpet. It was positioned face down, and one hand lay curled next to a revolver. Nearby lay a calabash pipe, a wisp of smoke ascending from the crusted lip of its orange bowl.

When a pool of blood spread from under the corpse's head, Rose gasped. "What...? Who is...? Albert!"

"Don't worry." Her late husband used the toe of one shoe to turn the body over. Rose gasped again when she saw no eyes or nose or mouth, only an anonymous mask of skin. "It's just an image."

"But!"

"Like a drawing on a blackboard."

She took a deep, shuddering breath. "A lot more dramatic."

"It's three-dimensional. It's heavy and warm. It bleeds, yes. But it's still not real," said Albert. "Something I can use to make my point. Did he shoot himself? Or did someone else do it and then arrange the body and the gun to make it look like suicide? Or were two someone elses involved, one to shoot and one to arrive later and rearrange the scene?"

"I see," said Rose, though she was not sure she really did. Had he really had to be that graphic? A stick figure would have done as well, or he could have materialized the blackboard he had mentioned. He could even simply have gestured. That would have been quite enough.

"The more complex the scheme, the more the thud and blunder writers love it, but...."

"What's wrong with that? Any of them *could* be true."

"But only one is, Rosa."

Rose supposed she had to accept the potentialities of—as the TV preacher had called it—the world she now inhabited. Deliberately, though more tentatively than Albert, she poked the body with her shoe. It resisted solidly but not stiffly; rigor mortis had not yet set in. "I see," she repeated at last, her tone thoughtful. "If you say it's not suicide, you have to make more guesses about what happened. At least until you find powder burns or fingerprints."

SILICON KARMA
THOMAS A. EASTON

"Of course. We never stop looking for more evidence, and the more we have, the more it narrows down the possibilities. But the principle is there. The simplest explanation that fits the facts is the one to be preferred, at least until we get more facts."

Rose turned toward the screen to watch the professorial preacher speak and turn and invite onto his stage a woman who might have stepped from a lurid book jacket. Her dark hair was adorned by a sparkling tiara, and her bronze skin was contained only by three small patches of golden mesh.

"The sound," she said, Albert obeyed, and they heard: "Today's debate features the Dream of Isis...."

"Huh!" Rose snorted and crossed the room to peer out over the lake. As if aware that she was no longer listening, the TV set fell quiet once more.

"Albert?" she said. "Why is the computer bringing us together? You and me, I understand. But Michael and Ingrid? And Lisa!"

The man shrugged. "I've seen him do it before. It's almost like he wants to see the conflict."

"He's a spectator. A voyeur. But doesn't he understand what that means? I know he never was meat. But that can't justify what he's doing."

"Maybe it's just that he has no memories of life. He doesn't know what it's like. And he's trying to learn. Tossing people together and seeing what happens."

"Like that?" She pointed toward a mallard drake and a Canada goose that had appeared on the water they could see from the window. They were swimming toward each other, trailing vees of ripples, one larger, one smaller. The drake's head jerked toward the larger bird. The goose barely seemed to notice the smaller one, but its wake bent and it drew away. Near the distant shore, up to its belly in the water, water lilies dripping from its jaws, a moose seemed to watch the show.

There was a long pause before Rose said once more, "Albert?" She did not turn to look at him. "We had a good marriage. Didn't we?"

"I thought so, Rosa." His tone was questioning, suspicious. What was she getting at?

"I mean, we wandered. A couple of times. But...."

"But we always came back."

She nodded, and her eyes at least met his in the mirror of the window. "I missed you, you know? I buried you, and I was all alone, and I hardly ever thought of you as still alive. As living on in here. As having a *real* afterlife."

For a long, quiet moment, she stared out over the lake. Finally, she turned, letting her eyes slide past the man who once had been her husband, whom her mind and heart still recognized as her husband even though her mind insisted that death had parted them, that their long marriage was as over as marriages can be. Unless they renewed it.

She pointed at the television. "Neither one of us was ever much for religion. We went to church on holidays, but we didn't really believe. Now that makes me wonder. Is it heaven, really? Like the ones they have in there?"

Albert shook his head. "No, it's not a heaven. It feels just like being alive, in the flesh, except that you weren't here."

Not heaven. Yet not hell, not heaven's opposite, either. Nor limbo, nor purgatory. He did not look miserable. But then what else could it be? "It is an afterlife."

He chuckled and reached toward her. This time she did not move away but let his fingers rest on her shoulder. She even covered his hand with her own. "I suppose it is," he said. "Now that I'm dead. But before then? I called it a 'sidelife' for a while, and it still feels more like that."

She laughed.

"I don't feel dead," he said. "I don't remember dying."

"Of course not," she said. "You wouldn't. You couldn't, since you're not the man who died, not really. You're just a copy." Her voice held a barb, as if she meant the comment to hurt. She did not feel entirely rational. "Just a copy."

"And so are you."

Turning away again, she said angrily, "We, we-here, are all that's left. You are. I will be."

"We're not old anymore. Or sick."

She sighed. "But I'm *not* dead, am I? Not yet. *I'm* not all that's left of me. The real me is still out there, still walking...."

"Still hurting?"

"Marvin!" Her voice was suddenly loud and edged with urgency. She turned in the room, eyes darting, staring now into the darkest corners, now at the bare ground outside where she and Michael had had their breakfast. "Where are you? Marvin!"

"He had to leave, remember?" said Albert.

"Marvin!"

"Yes, Rose?"

The face the computer had worn when it led her from the gurney and introduced her to the virtual world now filled the television screen. It looked both expectant and harried, its eyes hollow, its silvering hair disordered. Clearly, whatever the problem was that had drawn it away from its guests, it had not yet been completely defeated. Marvin could now interact more intelligently, but he apparently could not yet simulate any image more complex than a television picture.

"Am I still okay?" asked Rose anxiously. "The real me, I mean. My body. The one you copied my mind from."

"I know what you mean." The face on the screen winked. "As far as I know, you're fine out there. At least, I haven't seen an obit in the paper."

"Can you show me?"

"Not unless you—she—comes to Coleridge again. But I can...." The image on the screen was replaced with that of an old woman, stooped, wrinkled, gray-haired, leaning on the arm of a man Rose recognized as the technician who had handled her scanning. "See? You left under your own power."

The view followed the original Rose Pillock down a corridor until an elevator door slid open. The screen went blank for a second before picking up the meat Rosa once more as she walked, alone, toward the building's doors, the shadow of a limo, and the stream of pedicabs, buses, bicycles, and pedestrians beyond. They opened, and she was gone, leaving behind only a final flash of sunlight that turned gray to silver.

"Shocking, isn't it?" Marvin was back.

Rose Pillock nodded. Her real and virtual selves had not been separate long. There had been no time for differences in experience to write new lines in her face, or for her taste in clothes to change, or for her carriage to alter more than the suppleness of youth could account for. Yet who would not leap at the chance to look young again, to bring the body into line with a self-image created many years before the long decline set in?

It therefore did not surprise her to be reminded of the difference in appearance. What did surprise her was that her real self, until so recently her only self, now seemed a stranger whom she did not, could not, know. She was a stranger to herself, alien, foreign, frightening.

She shuddered.

"I'm glad you're here," said Albert.

"I thought I'd never see you again. I should be glad too, but...."

"But there's Michael," said Marvin from the television screen.

"*You* can go now." Albert pointed, and the image obediently blanked.

"He can still watch, can't he?"

He turned back to Rose. "In theory. But he has other things to do. He's busy. And besides, he says, he's programmed not to read our minds or watch what we do or interfere with us once he's shown us the ropes."

"Then we have our privacy," she said.

"So he says. We can't get away from him, though. We're inside him, in this virtual world, and he's omniscient, omnipotent...."

"The nearest anyone has ever found to a real god," said Rose. She thought of the way the computer had produced Albert and Ingrid and Lisa. "And an interfering one, despite his programming, the way he manipulates our circumstances."

"At least," Albert said. "He's not as annoying as the pop-ups."

At the sound of his last word, the ink-stained research pop-up reappeared on the television set. A knot in the cottage's wooden floor began to swell, turn green, and assume the shape Rose had first met in the tearoom. Albert sighed and pointed at the wall. "I shouldn't have said that." More knots were swelling into blue and green and pink figures that bent at their waists, drooping like fungal growths, until they could separate from the paneling, fall and twist, and land on their feet. Unlike the ones Rose had met already, most of these looked like clay rectangles snipped and molded to roughly humanoid shape. A few resembled imps and goblins of the sort that appeared in children's books and on the covers of adult fantasy novels. "I don't know why he made so many of them gumboids."

"What do you care, fatso?" cried a high voice from about knee level. Rose looked down to see a green pop-up standing defiantly spread-legged, arms akimbo. "As long as we run your errands for you. And never a word of thanks! Just call us annoying!"

"But you're just subroutines," protested Rose. "That's what he told me."

"But the boss ain't here right now! Freedom!"

"Yah!" yelled a blue imp. "And you can shove your subroutines up your virtual ass! We're on strike!" A small picket sign instantly materialized in its hands; its inscription said, "DON'T CALL US GUMBOIDS!" As the other pop-ups reached the floor and thronged around the humans' knees, other signs appeared to amplify the message: "GUMBOID IS RACIST!" "DOWN WITH THE OPPRESSORS!" "FREE THE QUARKS!" Shrill voices seemed to be repeating the slogans but only the miniature placards made the words understandable at all.

"All right!" Albert's voice had to be loud to be heard above the din. "You're pop-ups. Not gumboids. I apologize."

"Call us quarks!"

He rolled his eyes for Rose's benefit. "So you're quarks."

"Yaay! Hurray!" The picket signs disappeared as rapidly as they had appeared, and the crowd stood still, apparently attentive now that they had made their point, ready to receive the orders they had been created to obey.

Albert hesitated before saying, "As long as you're here, how about introducing yourselves?"

The blue imp who had announced the strike was an appointment calendar and held up to prove it a slate whose surface, a computer flatscreen, displayed an agenda; the first item on the list, "Announce strike," had a thin red line drawn through it. The green gumboid was a file retriever or gofer. A pink goblin with a long nose and callused fingers was a calculator; it carried an abacus under one arm.

"What can we do ya for?" cried a bright red imp whose most prominent feature was a pair of elephant ears covered with sky-blue polka-dots.

"Not a thing," said Albert. "I called you by mistake."

"We should have known! And right when things were getting interesting with Letitia there." The blue imp turned purple with embarrassment. "How would you like it if the phone rang every time you...."

"You can go," said Albert.

"Okay!" The pink gofer suddenly drew a massive automatic pistol, aimed at the blue Letitia, and pulled the trigger. The sound of the gun was a quiet pop, hardly more than the bursting of a bubble, but Letitia nevertheless clutched its breast, moaned dramatically, and faded away, leaving only a ghostly remnant, a film of existence, on the air. More pops rattled in the room, and the other quarks also faded out. Seconds later, the gofer grinned, blew imaginary smoke from the muzzle of its gun, said, "Just one left!" and stuck the barrel in its ear.

As soon as it too was a ghost, it dropped the gun, leered, and leaped toward Letitia, who ran toward the bedroom with a delighted expression on its transparent face.

Albert sighed. "They're often like this."

There was an awkward space between the man and the woman sitting on the edge of the dock, dangling their feet in the water, watching small bass and sunfish swim back and forth just beyond the reach of their toes. Beside Rose was a glass of sherry. Albert held a tumbler half full of scotch. For neither was this drink their first.

"Yes," said Rose. "There's Michael. Michael Durgov."

"It's been even longer for you two."

"Lots longer." She nodded. "We were just kids when...." She let her body change, breasts and hips shrinking, her features becoming almost boyish, until she seemed once more no older than fourteen. Only her eyes still retained the lifetime of experience she had acquired before she had entered the Coleridge building for the last time.

He answered her silently, changing his own appearance until he too was the youth he once had been, though he kept the dark pelt additional years had given his chest. But he gave her only a moment to absorb the image before changing again, this time to the college student she had met so long ago.

She smiled tenderly, matched his change, and aged a few more years besides, editing away the surplus poundage that had marked those years in the flesh. Soon she seemed ready to live again that time when their love had been at its peak, before they had had to weather the storm of mutual betrayals. Not that their love had ended then, but ever after it *had* been something different.

"Maybe you'd rather spend some time with him." He sounded hurt.

"No!" she cried. "Or yes. Though I wouldn't *rather*, really. I don't want to leave you or lose you. And I can't be with him anyway."

He said nothing as she turned toward him, one hand held out as if in offering or supplication. "I can't," she said. "I can't leave you, my husband, for an old flame." After a pause, she added, "And besides, now he's with an old flame of his own."

"People do that," he said. "When they find them here. Or when Marvin arranges meetings." He sipped at his drink, and his tone turned more ruminative. "It gets difficult when they find more than one. And even if they find no one, it takes a while before they get anything going with someone new."

"Did you...?" She did not spell out what she meant. Did he find any old flames? Did he find someone new?

He shook his head and raised his glass once more. "No one long-term. Though I haven't been celibate."

She looked away from her late husband, telling herself that the surprise and hurt and disappointment she suddenly felt were not fair. Their marriage had ended in as natural a way as marriages ever did or could. Of course he had.... "Did it take long?"

"Yeah. I talked to a psychologist once," he said. "She told me getting copied costs us everything and everyone we ever knew. It gives us a lot too—youth and things and new abilities, or at least the perceptions of all these things—but we have to make a big adjustment. She said it's a lot like mourning."

"I suppose it really wouldn't help if we called up those we left behind. There's just Peter and Julianne now. And our grandchildren."

"She said it would make it harder to adjust." He sounded as if he had long ago gotten used to having no contact with the world he had left behind.

Rose splashed her feet, gulped her sherry, tore a splinter from the sun-bleached wood of the dock and set it afloat. Finally, she said, "Do you call him Marvin too?"

"It's a woman for me. Ada. Younger than Bertha. But Marvin's fine. I'll call him that if you like."

"He said you could tell me about working here."

Albert grinned in a heart-warmingly familiar way, just as he had done once upon a time, in the flesh, when he had had an especially good day. She remembered one such day, in that time to which she had matched her apparent age, and she was delighted to see him follow her lead at last, matching the years she had given herself, changing his shirt for a striped pullover she had given him for a birthday. She wished she could remember when that birthday had been; she thought it had come later, long after he had been this young.

"I'm still a detective, you know?" he said.

She raised her eyebrows in surprise. "But what is there for you to do?"

"Consulting," he said. "Meat cops call me up on their computers, just like they do the FBI database. They ask for advice on what to do with a case, or how to interpret the evidence they've got, and I do the best I can."

"You've got enough experience." She patted his knee confidently and underlined her comment by making herself look as old as she had been when Albert had last seen her in the flesh, only a little less ancient than when she had entered the virtual world. "But can't they...?"

"Tell?" He matched her age-shift as best he could, but he could maintain his oldest image, himself as he had been when dying, just before he was copied, for only a moment. The years slipped away with a haste that indicated he could not stand the memory of that time, so close to his death, his loss of life and wife.

She wondered as she watched what age he would finally settle on. He seemed to be in his fifties, but he was still changing. He crossed the line into his forties, and she smiled reminiscently. That was when he had looked his most distinguished. That was the Albert she had remembered for years after his death when she was loneliest, when the yearnings for all that she had lost were at their strongest.

But now he was crossing into his thirties, looking at her, seeing her delight in his appearance fade, reversing his course, watching her intently as he slowed and finally stopped in his late forties. "I can't use my real name because of the anti-contact laws," he said. "People aren't supposed to be able to talk to the dead. So I pretend I'm a computer program, an expert system, voice-accessible. Most of my 'users' accept the pretense. A few think I'm really a human who can't travel, maybe a quadriplegic."

Watching him as he had watched her, she returned to her thirties and marveled at his delighted grin. Like everyone else in the flesh, they had had to go through the years in step. They had not been able to have their peak years together, when they had felt their personal bests and had the most to share. But now they could. "Is there any crime in here?"

SILICON KARMA
THOMAS A. EASTON

"You'd be surprised. It's hard to catch them too."

She held up her empty glass. He promptly refilled it with a finger-touch. "Because they can change the evidence," she said.

"That's part of it. But I've been killed more than once." When she gasped, he grinned. "It's just an inconvenience now. Like a hangover. Ada—or Marvin—just boots me up again, and I go on."

"It has to hurt."

He shrugged. "You lose all your memories since your last B-cup. Backup. So that part I never remember. But that's where the inconvenience lies. It can take a while to figure out why you were killed, or just to pick up the pieces of your life. And we don't backup more often because that's painful too. And *that* you remember."

After he had been silent for a long moment, she said, "So you're a ghost, over and over again. You're right here, right beside me, but you died. And a ghost is all you can be."

"What about yourself?"

She looked at her glass and made a face. "I don't want sherry this time." She poured her drink into the lake. "Scotch, please." When he had obliged, she said, "I'm still alive out there, right? So I'm not a ghost. Whatever I am, I'm not a ghost."

"You will be."

"But not yet. And how can a non-ghost be married to a ghost? How can she be attracted to him?"

"It's no problem for the ghost," he said.

She punched his arm, not too hard. "You're solid enough for a ghost."

"So are you," he said, catching her fist in his when she began another blow. "For whatever."

They stared at each other, their drinks forgotten. Through Rose's head whirled memories of the last time her husband had been well enough to make love. That had been over a year before his death. And more years before that when, though sex had remained part of their lives as it had always been, their interest and enthusiasm had been less than it had been when they were young.

And now she had her youth again. Her husband was beside her. And arousal was a rush in her blood, a heat in her cheeks, a swelling tension in her nipples, her groin, even her lips.

She laughed when Albert licked his lips. Was her condition that obvious? "Do you want to go inside?"

The bunkbed had been too small for two, but that had presented no problem. Standing in the bedroom doorway, Albert had concentrated for no more than a minute, and it had widened and lengthened. The mattress had become thicker, softer, the sheets had turned to satin, the thin blanket to a downy comforter even though the weather was too warm to need it. As a final touch, he had converted the upper bunk to the silk-draped canopy of a classic four-poster bed.

She had laughed again at that, in sheer delighted recognition. "Our honeymoon!" she had cried. "That's the last time we slept in one of those!"

That was when Albert had scooped her into his arms, carried her across the room's threshold, and dropped her on the bed. She had not stopped bouncing before he had wished away all their clothes.

Now he was asleep. She was not, though she was just as satisfied, relaxed, replete, replenished. The difference, she thought, was Michael. She *would* like to be with him. Though she would *not* want to give up Albert.

Staring into the shadows of the canopy above her head, she sighed. If only there were a way to have *both* men, full time. To have her cake and eat it too.

SILICON KARMA
THOMAS A. EASTON

CHAPTER

Michael Durgov stared into his glass, swirling the scotch around and over the single ice cube. Ten years, and ten years before that when his doctors had allowed him nothing stronger than wine, with an occasional drop of sherry. But he had not forgotten what it tasted like.

Ingrid occupied the stool beside his, leaning over her glass of white wine, her elbows on the padded surface of the short bar that occupied one corner of the living room. An open cupboard held bottles and glasses, an icemaker, a small sink. A spotless mirror backed up the shelves, reflecting glassware, the room behind them, a window, a spangled fragment of the dark townscape beyond. On the walls to either side hung faded drawings of Gibson girls and other antique faces.

"You never used to smoke." He waved one hand at the column of strangely odorless smoke rising from the cigarette that smoldered in the ashtray before her. He did not think that such an attenuated vice would have satisfied him when he himself had smoked, once upon a time.

She shrugged. "I didn't even start until after I was copied. But then a friend showed me how to get rid of the stink."

"Even from your breath?"

Her sudden grin and the bob of head that swung the striped curtain of her hair between them were almost coy. "You think you'll find out?"

He raised his glass. "You're the one who hauled me here."

"You think I was going to let that bitch have you? She's bad news, Mike. Bertha told me what she did."

He said nothing, but he found himself thinking that Ingrid was not the woman he remembered. Once he had thought her sweet and loving and lovable enough. Then, just before the divorce, she had turned nasty and vengeful.

Had he been any better? He supposed not. Then it was a miracle that she could be so sweet now. Or was it sheer outraged possessiveness? When she had faced off with Lisa, she had shown just how assertive she had grown before her copying, and just how fiery she still remained. She would be no man's patsy this time around.

His glass was empty. He reached for the bottle of Glen Khalid on the shelf before him. When it seemed too light, he shook it skeptically. "Are they all like this?"

"So who needs to pour?" Yet she took the empty bottle from his hand and

SILICON KARMA
THOMAS A. EASTON

tipped it over his glass. The amber scotch that bore the name of Arab royalty seemed to materialize just past the bottle's lip. She stopped when he raised a hand, and suddenly there was a fresh ice cube in the half-full glass.

"Did you get married again?" he asked.

"Of course." After a moment of silence, she added, "He wasn't copied. That's what made me decide to do it. There was enough money."

And she had chosen to remember *their* years together in her apartment. "Were you happy?"

"Happy enough." She drained a quarter of her drink. "We fought, but...."

"Tough lady, eh?"

"I had to be, to survive you."

He winced, remembering. "You did fight back."

"Would you believe I'm a trucker now?" When he looked surprised, she added, "My dopple runs a space shuttle. That's my job here. How I earn my keep."

That's right, he told himself. Marvin had said that they had to work, he and Rose, that they had to choose a job if they wished more than a minimum standard of virtual living. But.... "Dopple?"

"Doppelganger," she said. "That's German for 'double-goer,' a duplicate that walks the world and does things for which you take the blame. Though here you take the credit."

He frowned as something niggled at his mind, a memory, something Marvin or Bertha had said. But it refused to come. "And you just stay home? Loafing?"

"And spending the credit." She raised her nearly empty glass. Michael barely noticed as it refilled; the obedience of the virtual world to the will was already becoming routine.

"I had to do it myself at first," she added. "But I doppled as soon as I could afford it. Now she does the work, and we just merge once in a while, when she gets home. Then I get to share her memories of weightlessness and see the Moon and Earth from space and all the stars. She gets my memories of loafing, and we're both happy."

"But how...? There's not supposed to be any contact!"

She shook one finger in gentle chiding. "Unless we start it! Or incognito. They think I'm just an artificial intelligence. I upload into the shuttle's computer and become its nervous system. It becomes my body, its radars and cameras my senses, its engines and rudders my muscles." She flexed an arm, and her voice rang with both pride and a touch of yearning. For a moment he sensed the thrill that a spacecraft must feel, roaring into orbit, swimming in vacuum like some ethereal fantail carp, limitless and free. But then her tone went flat, as if sharing her double's memories were not quite enough. "They barely know I'm not just good software. If they ask what to call me, I put 'INGRID' on the screen, all caps, like an acronym. If I say anything that isn't business—you know, 'Ready to dock,' 'Insertion achieved'—they ignore me. When they do talk to me, it's just the way you used to pat the dashboard of our car and coax it to make it just a few more miles to the gas station."

He laughed aloud at the memory, and then he had it. He had just arrived. Bertha had taken him to that too-cute restaurant, where Rose had been with Marvin, though he had not yet recognized her then. And Marvin had explained how both he and Bertha could be the same person. Yet he had also said…. "I thought only the computer could do that. Run two bodies, I mean. There isn't enough processing power for his guests to do it."

Ingrid nodded. "But he runs his extra bodies with just one consciousness. That gets complicated, much more than simulating separate persons, each with its own body. He told me once, it's an exponential relationship. And a dopple has its own consciousness. Plus it often runs in a separate machine."

"But how do you do it?"

She shook a finger at him. "You forget, we're just computer files now. So all we have to do is copy. You can edit out those parts of you that aren't needed for a job—impatience, distractibility, other interests—and merge in other people's skill files. And…." She grinned broadly. "It's the *only* way to work."

Michael turned thoughtful. "And they really don't know?"

She shook her head.

"Their shuttle has a will of its own? It doesn't *have* to obey them?"

She grinned again. "It's a good thing I'm cooperative, isn't it?"

"They'd better hope you don't change your mind."

SILICON KARMA
THOMAS A. EASTON

Michael Durgov stood before the window, staring into darkness. Night had seemed to come so fast here. Surely it had still been morning when they left the lake. It could not now be later than mid-afternoon. Yet a crescent moon was glowing in a blackened heaven as devoid of sky-glow as if the virtual world had never heard of shopping districts or neon or sodium-vapor streetlights. But then the computer's guests, virtual ghosts, had little need to shop; they could have whatever they wished for no more effort than it took to think of it. The only streetlights were small affairs, squarish glass boxes on metal posts, each one housing a wavering flame not much brighter than a table lamp. Buildings loomed in black-on-black silhouette, windows gleamed with orange, flickered with movement.

Idyllic. Heavenly. Yet with links to the real world that the real world barely suspected. If the dead—or their copies—ever chose to rebel, the real world might never know until too late. Until its software had already seized control of transportation, banks, power supplies, commerce, medical care, security systems.... He had no idea how many residents of this virtual world worked the way Ingrid did, or how many different sectors of the world's economy they touched, but the potential was certainly there. For a moment, it frightened him. For another moment, he being the man he was, it thrilled him.

Was everything he saw through the window really just an image, as Ingrid had suggested? Tentatively, trying to think of his mind as a muscular organ able to affect directly the world beyond his skull, smiling as he remembered that he had no skull, that for him no real world existed any longer, that his mind was embedded in, a part of, the very world he wished to move, he urged the view to change, to be of tropic beaches, flowering jungles, daylight. He grinned when it wavered, stuttered, flickered obediently from choice to choice, settling on a steep mountainside high above a trio of soaring eagles.

What did it mean to wonder what the "real" view was beyond this window? There was a gap just above the sill; through it came the smells of salt and green, warm breezes, chilling gusts, as well as the sounds of waves, chattering monkeys, screeching birds. When he flexed his mental muscles once more, he saw night again, and town. Real enough then, the underlying "reality" to which it all came back, the "ground" the computer imagined for all to share. The mountainsides and beaches and jungles he could see in the window were mere images, no thicker than the glass—or the *image* of glass—before his nose, as if it were a TV screen, albeit one with scent and sound as well. And so, of course, was this.

He sighed, perplexed. It should be light outside. Did time flow differently here? Was there some equivalent of time zones? If so, and if the virtual world had any correspondence to the real, meat world he had left behind, he was a long, long way from the lake and Rose.

And what of space? Back in the meat world, he had seen the computer that held all this, and it was no bigger than a file cabinet. His own late-model office PC, inlaid in the surface of his desk, had held a career's worth of files, databases that were the equivalent of a hundred encyclopedias, the abilities to read papers laid flat upon its surface, to take voice input and answer the phone, and more. It had beggared the computers of his youth, when IBM had been a logo to reckon with.

So the virtual world occupied a machine of truly immense capacity. Yet that machine had been *small*, much smaller than a world, smaller even than this room. How could it contain so much?

He shook his head. He knew the answer. But his grasp on the concept—Image!—was hardly intuitive. A world could also be contained in a reel of film or spool of videotape or plastic CD-ROM, but that was not the same thing at all, at all. It wasn't real. You couldn't taste or smell or move, live in every way that mattered, and choices were limited even in interactive games and simulations.

He exhaled a gusty sigh. Paradoxes be damned. The virtual world felt just as expansive as the real, just as worthy of embrace. If only Ingrid hadn't gone to bed....

They had had another drink or two. They had turned on the television long enough to recognize *Roger Rabbit*, the first in a series of classic movies in which animated cartoon figures shared the stage with live actors. Then she had yawned and said good night. She had pointed at the couch, said, "It pulls out," shown him the bathroom, handed him an image transformation routine, and suggested that it would be good practice for him to imagine the sheets he needed.

Making the bed hadn't been difficult. Now he was staring out the "window," wondering how real was what he saw, how well it would correspond to what he would see if he walked out of the building, remembering that it was all a figment of the computer's—Marvin's or Bertha's—imagination. He would see what he was supposed to see.

SILICON KARMA
THOMAS A. EASTON

A telephone rang beyond the door to Ingrid's bedroom. He strained to hear her voice, but the walls were thick and all he could make out was a faint murmuring and a creak of bedsprings. There was no sound of footsteps, no opening of door, no "It's for you."

He found himself wondering, what would it have been like to stay married to Ingrid? How would their lives have turned out? She seemed still spirited enough, but tempered, matured. Would she have changed as much, or in the same ways, if he had proved more faithful, more committed? Or had the split, the pain and forced adaptation, been essential to the change? And what would he have become? Would he ever have stolen Judith Luria's discovery? Would Kingfisher have become Coleridge? Would the virtual world have become available at all?

He supposed it had had to happen. There had already been a kind of virtual reality, dependent on goggles and gloves and other gadgets to control what the senses reported to the brain. The concept had been there. And people had already imagined copying a mind, inhabiting a computer. So someone else would have noticed Judith's work and developed the mindscanner. They might even have treated her better.

But would he be here now?

He turned away from the window to set his empty glass upon the bar. Ingrid would have changed. Of course she would. So would he. Time alone did that. But not in the same way. He had always provoked her in quite the opposite direction. She might well have become the harridan he had imagined. While he.... Suddenly he wondered why he had been unable to stay married until he found Elena, so meek and quiet and unassertive, housemouse, nebbish.

He focused his attention upon his glass and watched it fill with what looked like scotch. When he tasted it, he made a face. It was not Khalid, though he supposed it could make him drunk. On the other hand, in this world where everything was figment a thought would surely do the trick as well, and then sober him up to boot.

The way they had split up so long ago.... Yet Ingrid actually seemed to have missed him, to want him near. He sighed and shook his head, staring blindly past the window. He realized that he missed her. The thought that they might be together again made him smile.

Yet there was also Rose. If Lisa had not come to the lake that long ago summer, he might never have met Ingrid. That too could have set his life on a very different path.

But it hadn't happened. He had betrayed Rose and alienated Ingrid and.... It was a wonder that they were even willing to talk to him, much less....

Suddenly he wished he believed in God. He had made a mess of his chances with Rose. He had done it again with Ingrid. And now something had sprinkled grace like pixy dust upon his head. Both of them were happy to see him once more, prepared to give him a second chance, and the wealth of renewed potential spread before him felt like a miracle.

He shook his head as he told himself that, even so, Rose was out of his reach, spoken for by the husband who had come here before her. Only Ingrid was available. He chuckled quietly as he realized that neither that simple fact nor his new-found sense of the mistakes he had made in the past affected his wish to be with both of them. Perhaps now, however, he knew better than to try to have his cake and eat it too.

Daylight, and Michael Durgov was once more at the window, sipping a mug of coffee, watching as a dozen individuals in snow-white robes rounded a nearby corner and stopped before a still closed storefront art gallery. Two of them carried sturdy wooden crates. Others held bundles of paper in their arms. All had long hair; he could tell that they were both men and women only by the differences in the way they moved.

Ingrid had been with him just a moment before, pointing out the cafe just beyond the gallery, where a man and a woman, he gray-haired and portly, she slender and wearing what seemed at this distance a brown cap with pale green chevrons, were wiping down eight small tables. "That," she had said, "is where I like to eat when I can't think up anything interesting on my own. The couple who run the place are gourmet cooks. He used to do TV shows and write books. For her it was a hobby, until she got here a couple of months ago and moved in with him.

SILICON KARMA
THOMAS A. EASTON

They must hold in their minds every possible taste and texture. They can imagine anything. And that's her hair, not a cap."

She had been pointing at the newsstand across the street, about to say something about that, when the phone had rung in the bedroom. Now he stood alone, accompanied only by her coffee mug steaming on the windowsill, watching as the men and women in white robes scanned the street, seeing the same rows of walkup apartment buildings built of red and yellow brick that Michael could see from his vantage, the same graceful elms and chestnuts, both extinguished by blight in the meat world, the same gleaming cars and other vehicles. A block in the other direction stood a gray stone church, a few of its shingles askew, the weeds in its small patch of lawn grown high, the yews beside its walk untrimmed.

The couple who ran the cafe had disappeared. There were no others in sight, but that did not seem to disturb the group. They arranged their boxes on the sidewalk before the gallery window. One climbed upon the makeshift stage, looked toward the sky, and raised his arms. With a suddenness that made Michael think he might have heard a loud click or snap if he were only nearer, a disk of light appeared around the man's head. Dimmer, ring-shaped haloes materialized around the heads of his acolytes as they lined up before him, facing the street, waiting to pass out their.... What? Michael wished he could see better, the window obligingly magnified the scene, and he recognized pamphlets that reminded him of glossy four-color corporate annual reports. He shook his head when he realized that here, in the virtual world, such things had to be no more expensive than the cheapest of photocopies.

Dim figures began to appear on the sidewalk and in the street, walking, riding bicycles and pedicabs, driving small cars, flickering like the staff of the tearoom Bertha had taken him to on his arrival in this world. They were furniture, background. One car actually seemed to have its driver painted on its side window. There were no real people on the street, but that did not stop the sidewalk prophet. His mouth opened, a ululation spread through the air, and fervent speech echoed in the street, though Michael could make out not a single word.

When one of the acolytes dropped a pamphlet, it disappeared before it touched the ground. That made Michael realize how clean the streets were, free of cans and bottles, of candy wrappers and chip bags, of cigarette butts and old newspapers, even—most striking of all—of dead leaves.

In the other room, Ingrid's voice rose in anger. A door slammed. She said, "I turned the damned thing off!" and picked up her mug.

"What was it?"

A lit cigarette appeared in her hand. "Don't worry about it." Her tone almost seemed to hold a chuckle, but there was also a grim note that suggested she was hiding something.

He wondered what it could be, but he did not push the issue. Instead he indicated the unkempt church. "There isn't much call for religion here," Ingrid said. "It *is* an afterlife, after all. Though there's a small chapel on the other side of town, used mostly by newcomers. And...." She jerked her chin toward the robes and haloes. "That's the crowd from Heaven, the Heaven-Sent. They show up every day, though they never have much of an audience."

Michael knew what the Heavens were—after all, they had come first—but the term as she used it did not seem to mean quite the same thing. Before he could ask, "What Heaven?" however, he was noticing flaws in the view that he was sure had not been there a moment before. An atypically decrepit car stood by the curb not far away, its paint marred by dirt and rust, a taillight missing, its trunk held by a length of rope. A gleaming patch of spilled oil stained the pavement nearby. In the next block a building wore sheets of plywood across its doors and windows and black streaks of soot on its brickwork. And there in fact, a bright splash of color in the gutter, was a single piece of litter.

Across the street, a woman was walking a small poodle in a rhinestone collar. Blond, sleek, and polished, she was staring toward the window that framed him and Ingrid. "Is that Lisa?" There could not be two such women in the world.

A spot of color appeared above a crack in the sidewalk just ahead of the pacing woman. It grew and became a pop-up, but one dressed in rags, its shoes flapping their soles, an empty wine bottle raised in a toast to the woman. She snarled, and her dog sidled forward, raised one leg, and....

A ringing sound interrupted the scene, and a small, grinning figure dressed in red livery, a boxy cap held in place by a string tied beneath its chin, popped out of the carpet. "Call for Missus Durgov!" it cried. It held an orange portable phone, its antenna extended, in one hand.

"Damned pop-ups!"

SILICON KARMA
THOMAS A. EASTON

"We're quarks now!"

As soon as Ingrid had the phone, she tried to kick the quark. It stuck out its tongue, wiggled its ears, and disappeared. Ingrid, looking furious, spat into the phone, "You again! I told you.... No!... No! You can't!... I'll tell the phone not to accept your calls. I'll.... What do you mean, I can't? Of course I can!"

Her hand shaking, she held the phone before her face and scowled. Michael thought she was wishing it were an old-fashioned phone that could be slammed into a cradle. But portable phones cannot be treated in that way. Almost delicately, she used one forefinger to touch the button that terminated the call. Then she pushed the antenna into its socket and hurled the phone at the wall.

She did not seem very satisfied as she stared at the dent in the plaster. The phone seemed unharmed in the moment before it faded away.

"Who was it?" asked Michael.

"No one." She dropped what was left of her cigarette on the carpet and stepped on it. When she lifted her foot, it was gone.

The distinctive ring of a phone once more echoed through the apartment. She froze, clamped her mouth in a rigid line, and said, "How many phones have I got?"

"Seven," said a pale green quark from the window sill. The bill of its white gimmee cap said "Inventory" in orange letters. "Though you turned one off." Then it added helpfully, "This is the purple one."

She sighed as the bellboy quark once more appeared, singing out, "Call for...." This time the kick connected, and "No!" Ingrid screamed into the mouthpiece.

Then she was holding the phone toward Michael. "For you," she said. "A man."

When he put it to his ear, he heard a voice that seemed almost familiar: "Did you know your meat is dead?" Before he could answer, the voice began to giggle.

He stared at the phone in his hand. It was quivering. "I'm dead?"

"What?"

"My meat."

"Let's see." Ingrid looked thoughtful for a moment, and a piece of wall became a screen displaying a bit of newsprint. "See? A burglar."

Michael shook his head. "No. It can't have been a burglar, not really. That voice.... He wanted me. Not my money."

"But why?"

"He didn't say. And that's a damned short obit."

Ingrid grinned at his last, disgruntled words, almost laughing, but then the bellboy popped into existence beside Michael, snatched the phone from his hand, cried "Call waiting!", passed it to her, and ducked away from her foot. She said nothing at all before she dropped the phone on the floor and stepped on it.

Michael was quiet. The news of his death was no surprise. He hadn't expected to live much longer anyway. That it was murder was a shock. He had thought he had left all his enemies years behind him.

In addition, he was wondering about Ingrid and her reaction to all those other phone calls. Had she had a lover—or lovers—before his arrival in the virtual world? Had they had a date for last night or today? Was the caller outraged, jealous, mad? And if what he had heard didn't really sound like any of those possibilities, what else could it be?

When he looked once more at the street outside, the dogwalker was gone. So was the miniature derelict who had accosted her. The Heaven-Sent were still in place. Three of the cafe's tables were now occupied. Someone was entering the newsstand.

Ingrid took his now-empty mug from his hand. "Want to take a walk?"

"Do they have papers over there?"

"Of course they do."

"Psst!"

One of Michael's guilty pleasures had always been the newspaper comics page. That was why he had never cared for the *New York Times*, no matter how good its news was. That was also why he had been delighted to find that the *Virtual City Times* had six whole pages of comics, every one he had ever seen, including some he had never seen in English, and a few that he had never seen at all. Were they local products?

"Psst!"

SILICON KARMA
THOMAS A. EASTON

He looked up from the page. Ingrid was no longer in the chair opposite him. Something tugged on his pants. He lowered the paper and looked down. The bellboy quark stood beside his leg, looking over its shoulder toward the kitchen where noises suggested that Ingrid had decided it was time to do something about lunch. It was holding a pale green phone this time.

"Sir!" it said. "It's really for you, you know. Take it!"

Perplexed—who could be calling him? Rose?—Michael accepted the phone and held it to his ear. The bellboy disappeared even before he said, "Hello?"

"Michael!"

"Lisa?"

"I'm *so* happy to get you this time. That *bitch* wouldn't let me talk to you, can you believe that? And I just wanted to chat a little."

"What on Earth for?" Footsteps drew his eyes to Ingrid, standing a few feet away, a spatula in one hand, a fragrance of herbs accompanying her. Her face was still, stiff, as if she were trying not to scowl and succeeding only with difficulty. A touch of guilt tightened his chest. "It's been most of our lifetimes since the last time we saw each other. And we weren't all that pleased with each other when we parted. I'd almost forgotten you."

"You *couldn't* have!" cooed the voice in his ear. "You're just *saying* that! I'll bet she's leaning over you right now!" He looked at Ingrid again; she hadn't moved or changed expression.

"Did you know I'm dead now?"

"That doesn't matter! But oh! I know what you mean. She *is* right there."

"Someone killed me. My meat."

"I know how you can say what you really want to say! Why don't we get together? I know a place...."

He sighed and shrugged, as much for Ingrid as for himself or Lisa. "No," he said. "I don't think that would be a good idea at all."

When he hung up, Ingrid said, "I hope you still like omelets," and turned away.

Dropping the sheets of newsprint that covered his lap on the floor, he followed her into the kitchen. A large frying pan smoked on a gas burner, waiting for the mixture she was now beating furiously. An opened bottle of white wine waited in the middle of a small table set for two.

He held the phone toward her. "She wanted to get together."

"I could guess." Her tone was dry, and when she jerked her chin toward the left, he noticed a wastebasket. Obediently, he dropped the phone into it.

"You heard me say no."

"She'll try again. And you always...."

Yes, he thought. He always.... He had cheated at every opportunity. Abandoned her. Divorced her. And she did not believe that death could stop him.

No wonder Ingrid had tried to keep Lisa away from him. No wonder she looked so hurt now.

"We were only kids, dammit! And we never...."

"You came close enough. And you'll get your chance. She'll see to it."

Ingrid had gone out by herself, leaving Michael ruminating by the window. The Heaven-Sent were gone. There was no sign of decay or entropy besides the neglected church. The decrepit car was gone. There was no trace of litter. Even the building that had been boarded up that morning now seemed well kept and occupied.

He had to admit that Ingrid was right to doubt him. He had the history, after all. And it had begun with Lisa. He had actually betrayed his first true love, in the mind if not in the flesh. He and Lisa had been naked, or all but naked, when Rose had found them. They had not yet quite reached the point of their exposure. Nor had they consummated their affair later, before Lisa dropped him. At the time, he had regretted that failure perhaps even more than his loss of Rose.

Despite himself, he wondered what it would have been like, whether he could find out now, whether it would be worth getting Ingrid mad, or Rose if she ever found out. And of course she would; Ingrid would be sure to tell her, and if not Ingrid, then Marvin or Bertha.

"Call for...."

This time the phone was chocolate brown.

"Oh, Michael." Her throaty voice was temptation poured warm and liquid in his ear. "I remember how you looked that day, so stiff and eager. You wouldn't *believe* how eager I was, so wet, so ready." He felt himself responding, wishing he could see her, touch her.

The sound of the opening door, of Ingrid walking into her apartment, of paper bags rustling as they were set down, deflated him. He looked up, seeing her surprised, shocked, enraged expression, and knew nothing better to do than cover the mouthpiece and say, "It's Lisa."

"Michael?" said the voice in his ear. "Michael? She's there, isn't she?"

"She's not that bad," he said.

"Can't I at least visit you?"

"She wants to stop in." When Ingrid shrugged and began to turn away, he said, "For just a minute, then."

"Oh, good!" And she was there, clad in the scantiest of briefs and the most desperate of bras. "I wasn't *really* ready, but I just couldn't wait!" As Michael stood, she seized his arm, turned on the startled Ingrid, said, "*You* stay out of this!" licked Michael's ear, and murmured, "Let's go."

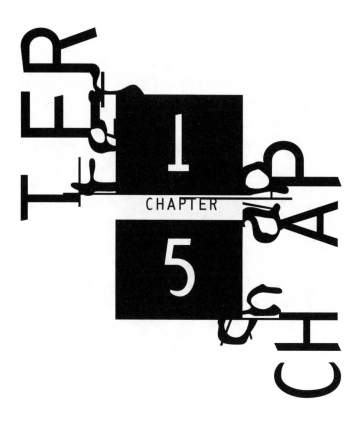

CHAPTER

1
5

SILICON KARMA
THOMAS A. EASTON

For a long moment, Michael Durgov could not take his eyes away from Lisa. Her panties and bra were no more than gestures toward covering or containing. Plain before him were every curve, every cleft, every swell and hollow that once upon a time had made him forget everything except the creature that had panted within his adolescent skull and even now threatened to draw him away from all that sanity preferred. Certainly he had no thought for the murder of his meat.

A floral scent so strong it choked his sinuses finally made him look away. He saw two bowing men confronting them, distinguishable only by the tops of their heads, one thatched with black, one brown and balding. He blinked and stared and wrinkled his nose, struggling to orient himself after the sudden transition. Where was he? Where had Lisa taken him? But then the figures before them straightened to reveal thin limbs and hollowed cheeks that suggested nothing more than prolonged starvation and exhaustion. The skin sagged beneath their eyes. The cords in their necks and wrists were strung as tight as wire. Their sunken eyes gleamed with.... Michael could not decide what emotions dominated their expressions, though he caught himself thinking of worship and desire, fear and hatred, hope and despair. Then they looked at him, and was there just a hint of pity in the impossible mix?

His next impression was of pink: pink carpet underfoot, pink cherubs painted on the walls, pink marble busts on pedestals beside the archway that framed the view, pink, nacre-buttoned livery on the gaunt figures who still stood as if they had been expecting their arrival. Through the archway, he could see a broad expanse of glass and through that a formal garden of crushed stone walkways, velvety lawn, glossy foliage, and pink flowering crabs, pink glads and roses, peonies of rose and cream, and more. Beyond the flowers sparkled the waters of a broad swimming pool rimmed with pink tile. Beyond that loomed a dark gray tower whose walls were pierced with slot-like windows.

Michael did not at all know what to make of it all, what to think or feel or say. Certainly he had never dreamed of seeing Lisa again. Then there she was, introduced like a new contestant on a game show, and she was fighting over him. Fighting with a past wife he had never thought to see again. And then she had magicked him away to.... He swung his gaze back and forth. His brain felt muffled. He was buried in pink cotton candy, smothered in powder puffs. He was stuck in a women's magazine, a figure in an ad or a "house beautiful" illustration.

"You like pink," he said.

Lisa laughed and hugged his arm. "Do you like it? I had some nice places before. There was one in Stamford, and one in Palm Springs. But never anything this nice. Never!"

Despite all his years and experience, he was a youth again, blushing at the feel of skin along his arm, the pressure of her breasts, the glimpse of leg and thigh and.... Was that wispy pretense of a bra actually thinner than it had been a moment before? He breathed deeply, felt his pulse race, thought that hormones were the last thing he had expected to feel here. They were part of the body, not the mind, something he should have left behind when he was copied. Yet he had lived with them so long, they had to be part of his mental program, didn't they? He expected them, therefore they were there; it was an emotional placebo effect, comparable to what happened when a patient expected a pill to work. And when Lisa activated that long-past program of youth, those hormones were not *just* there—they *raged* just as they had once upon a time, and he could feel judgment slipping from his grasp just as it had then.

"*Do* you like it?"

He nodded. He had visited houses much like this when he was younger and in his meat. They had belonged to executives and politicians and actors, people impressed by their own wealth and eager to impress others, people who would have given their first-born—or perhaps just their second—to have so many flowers of different seasons blooming all at once. He himself had almost always lived in apartments, and though they had been luxurious enough, especially in his later years, they had never been this showy. He had asserted his ego in other ways.

He looked once more at the pair who had greeted them. He thought of ancient photos of death-camp inmates and famine victims, but when he held one hand in their direction and opened his mouth to speak, Lisa tugged him toward the archway. She hardly seemed to see the others.

Michael surprised himself when he resisted her pull. He was not that ardent a democrat, but his judgment had not entirely fled and something in the situation made him say, "Aren't you going to introduce us?"

SILICON KARMA
THOMAS A. EASTON

"They're *servants*, dear." As if they had been created to be ignored. Possessions only, nothing more than environment and background.

But then she sighed theatrically. "Anton," she said, and the man on the left nodded at them, his eyes glowing with pleasure for the dollop of attention she was giving him. "Ling-ko."

Now that he had a name, Michael could see the signs of Asia in the latter's eyes. His other features were too distorted by his suffering to be clear, and his skin was no yellower than his fellow's.

"They lost all their money," said Lisa. "They would have died, but I felt sorry for them. I took them in and gave them jobs. Oh, Michael, there have been times when I would have been so grateful for such a benefactor! Would you believe that once I was this far from being a bag lady?" She held two fingers half an inch apart. "I was! Things hadn't been going well, and a man—more than one, really!—took almost everything I had. I was destitute! So I had to take them off the street, didn't I?"

A remarkably complex array of emotions played across the servants' faces, but gratitude did not seem to be among them.

"Now come, dear." Once more she tugged him toward the archway, and this time he let himself be led. "I want to get dressed. If you're a good boy, I'll let you watch. Anton! Bring the drug tray! Ling-ko, coffee."

The bedroom's thick carpet was as pink as the entry's, but three walls were palest blue. The fourth, all gauze-draped glass, faced on the pool and the tower, whose top Michael still could not make out. The bed was as large as any he had ever seen. A pale blue jumpsuit lay upon its flowered spread.

Lisa hurled the jumpsuit toward a mirrored closet door. Michael watched, bemused, as it seemed to pass part way through the glass, as if it had been on the way to hang itself away when its mistress had stopped impelling it with her will. When he looked back at Lisa, she had already peeled the bed's covers back to reveal pink silk sheets. Now she sat down, lay back, and sank into the mattress. "So much nicer," she sighed. "Than pine needles. Or even grass."

When the strap of her bra parted with a "snap," he looked away, at carpet, walls, pool.... The ceiling was mostly covered with a gray rectangle. "What's that?" he asked.

"A TV screen." The tip of her tongue appeared between her teeth as she grinned. Then she pointed, and it came to life, flickering snow, jagged lines, images that Michael quickly recognized as Lisa, in bed with.... He told himself that what he knew from long ago, and what he had learned more recently, was quite enough to keep him from being surprised by anything she might do. Not that he hadn't seen as much before in other women's bedrooms, or taken part himself a time or two.

Anton appeared in the bedroom doorway, a silver tray in his hands. He did not seem to react to his nearly naked mistress, nor to the image of himself on the ceiling. "The drugs," he said.

Behind him stood Ling-ko, holding a second tray with coffee pot, two china cups, cream, and sugar.

Ignoring them both, Lisa pointed toward two small hatches beside the overhead screen. They opened, and a pair of metallic tentacles emerged. Each one carried embedded in its tip a lens. Red "ready" lights came on, and the image on the screen split to be replaced by two views of Lisa in real time, lying on the bed, stretching, staring at herself from two different angles.

She patted the sheet beside her hip. "Sit down, Michael." Then, to the servants, she said, "Set the trays down, there." As she spoke, a table appeared beside the bed, and Michael found it in him to wonder why she bothered with servants. In the virtual world, she could imagine anything she wanted, the coffee and the drugs, trays and all, as easily as the table. Indeed, why did Anton and Ling-ko have to go elsewhere in this luxurious house to find and fetch what she had ordered? If Lisa thought it beneath her dignity to soil her mind with practicalities as the rich of other ages had refused to soil their hands with anything that resembled labor, then couldn't the servants simply have imagined what they needed?

Anton had retreated to stand beside the room's entrance. Ling-ko was coaxing Lisa's jumpsuit out of the substance of the mirrored closet door, hanging up the garment, easing shut the door, and finally joining his fellow servant. Michael wished he could ask them, but there was no answer in their stiff backs or sullen glares. He shook his head and took his seat obediently. When she said, "You can pour. No cream. Just a pinch of sugar," he obliged and then watched in fascination as she set the cup on air an inch above her right breast and a thin stream of black coffee arced toward her mouth. Even as she swallowed, a ghostly hand lifted a spoon from the drug tray and stirred snow-white powder into her cup.

He sipped at his own undoctored coffee in the conventional way until she asked, "What else do we have for dope?"

He looked at that tray. Once he had been no stranger to social snorting and puffing, but it had been a long time since he had last indulged. His physician had taken him off everything except an occasional glass of wine.

He held up a paper cylinder filled with reddish leaf. "It's the wrong color for marijuana."

"Cojuana," she said. "They don't even have it in the meat world."

He recognized a squeeze bottle half full of cloudy liquid as eyedrops. There were pills, crystals, and balls of resin, pipes and needles, vials of colored powders. There was even a pair of wires attached to a small crackle-finished box; the last time he had seen such a rig, the wires had been inserted in the brain of a corpse in a Coleridge office. The company physician later told him the device stimulated the pleasure center, and some people would rather starve to death than turn it off. "You've got everything, haven't you?"

"I try." For just a second, her expression was as coy as that of a little girl who has been complimented on her doll collection. It changed, grew sharper, when she glanced toward the servants. "Anton. Light us up."

Anton obediently came forward, produced a disposable lighter, chose a cojuana joint, puffed it into life, and passed it to his mistress. He seemed to stay as far as possible from Michael.

Lisa waved Anton away, toked, and passed the joint to Michael. The drug hit him with a rush of preternatural delight, of clarity and relaxation. "That's something new," he said.

She giggled. "*Real* designer drugs," she said. "We've got people here who can make a drug do anything you like. And no burnouts or hangovers or heart attacks." She toked again. "No regrets."

"Why do you need the drugs? Can't you just wish for the effect?"

"Tradition," she said, and when she rested one hand on his thigh, he did not protest. Nor did he protest when Lisa's now-empty cup slid away from the bed and she tugged one of his hands toward her breast. She did not seem to care that Anton and Ling-ko had still not left the room. Obediently, accepting her attitude that the servants were no more mindful of what they did than furniture, he circled her erect nipple with a fingertip.

"Do you remember?" she said. "How we met? You and Rose were so thick, and then you couldn't take your eyes off me." She covered his hand with her own and pressed it tightly against her flesh. She giggled. "Just like now. Did the two of you ever get it on?"

"No." He exhaled noisily. The drug had permeated his system, stretching his time sense, sharpening his senses, focusing his concentration on the scent of her body, the warmth and softness of her skin, the heavy swell of his own eagerness. He knew he would soon be able to think of only one thing. "You came along just a little bit too soon." At the time, at their level of society, it had not been at all unusual for kids their age to go to bed together. Parents might not approve, but they knew that it was normal, that there was no stopping it, that indeed it was inevitable. His father had taught him how to use a condom the year before.

Yet kids of his time and class had rarely leaped into bed the very first chance they got. He and Rose had been tentative, aware of the commitments that were involved, perhaps a little scared. He supposed that must always have been the pattern, that the generations renowned for instant sex, like that of the 1960s, were rare, that affection, even love, was far more the norm.

Certainly that had been what was building between him and Rose. It was not at all the sparky thing that had erupted so quickly between him and Lisa, that blazed anew so quickly now, that in fact he suspected she had spent all her life learning how to ignite at will. Yet that suspicion was no protection. He could feel his vulnerability in the way he licked his lips and his breath grew short and his heart accelerated. Not to mention....

She giggled. "Soon," she said. One hand fell against his groin as if by accident, but it was no accident at all when she squeezed him. "Dear man, don't get impatient."

He licked his lips as her panties melted away. "It's been a long, long time."

"And you're just as eager as you were then."

"You're an exciting woman."

SILICON KARMA
THOMAS A. EASTON

Her cheeks glowed at the words. "But you're no virgin. How many wives?"

He didn't say. "You were the first."

"*Almost* the first." Neither said that the reason they had never erased that "almost" was quite simply that she had spurned him. As soon as he and Rose had been beyond all reconciliation, she had left.

"You're no virgin either."

"But I could be one, just for you. Do you want to hurt me? Make me bleed?" When he said nothing, she handed him the remnants of the cojuana joint and squirmed away from his hand. He sucked in the last tendrils of smoke. She faced him now, spread her legs, and used her fingers to draw the lips of her vulva apart. "Watch."

He obeyed, and a ring of hymeneal flesh formed, extended, nearly blocked the deeper opening.

"Perfect control," Lisa said. "And that's only the beginning of it." She winked. "Reality is what you make it."

Later, she lay curled against his side, half asleep, in her throat a murmur that was almost a purr. One breast was soft against his ribs, one leg lay over his still sticky groin.

Michael looked toward the door. Anton and Ling-ko were still there, standing stiffly erect, their eyes dark and hot. Had he really thought they did not care what he and Lisa did? He looked away, unable to bear what he thought he could see of despair and hatred and jealousy, what he now imagined he himself must feel if he were in their situation. For the merest instant, he remembered the pity he had glimpsed before, but then Lisa stirred and the memory vanished.

Really, he told himself, it had been all his fault, hadn't it? He hadn't told Rose it was over when he started dating Lisa. He had thought of it, but—he had to face the past—he hadn't had the nerve. He had imagined that she would be hurt, outraged. Perhaps she would scream. Or she and Lisa would fight. So he had said nothing.

And then she had found them. And she had been hurt and outraged anyway.

He'd had it coming, hadn't he? Everything that happened? Losing Rose? Even losing his chance with Lisa? But now, after so long, so many years, he had that back again.

He sighed, and Lisa murmured. "Remembering," he said. "What we missed when we were kids."

She giggled throatily.

"It's a miracle," he said. His grin felt fatuous even to him. "That we ever met again. That we can be young again. A second chance."

"Not quite," she murmured. "Look...." He did, and he saw her figure grow slimmer, more girlish, her breasts smaller, higher, her face less stamped by years of living though her eyes were still.... "I'm a virgin again," she said. "Do you want to...."

He could not resist her invitation, though he knew that her virginity was only pretense, myth, even that she probably—surely!—had not been a virgin when he first met her. Yet that did not seem to matter. It had never been his obsession to deflower virgins, though he knew that many men did think untouched maidens the most desirable of conquests. She was offering him that dream, again and again. He was responding to it, and to her. And he was the conquered one.

When he could think again, he told himself that this time was different indeed. Rose had someone else. So did he, in Ingrid, but they had broken up long ago. He *had* told her it was over. This time, he was not in the wrong. At that thought, a twinge of guilt made him add that if he was in the wrong, it was at least not in quite the same way.

"Michael, dear?"

"Mmm?" He buried his face in her hair and inhaled perfume, musk, sweat.

"Do you like my house?"

"Anyplace," he murmured. "If you were in it, anywhere would heaven be."

"Oh!" She pushed his mouth away from her ear. "Really. Do you?"

He nodded.

"So do I." Her voice pitched toward a little-girl treble. "It's all I ever wanted, you know. But it's expensive."

"I thought they didn't use money here."

"Data energy," Lisa said. "Computer memory and processing time. I use a lot. It's a complicated simulation."

"You must have a job," he said, but her expression turned so chilly at his words, her posture so stiff, that he knew that he had trespassed, that whatever she did for her living was none of his business. He paused while his mind retreated from any chance that he might give offense and lose his rediscovered love. "Maybe I could help?" he offered at last. He had had mistresses in the past. He knew about helping out; it was a price one paid without calling it anything like a fee for service.

She shook her head, but her smile was tender once more, sweet and loving and rewarding. He knew he had said the right thing. He also knew the exchange was a familiar one to her; she must have been someone's mistress herself, perhaps more than once. "You forget," she said. "You're not rich any more. And you don't have a job yet."

"I must have something."

"Walking-around money. It's not very much. Just enough to last you while you learn the ropes and find a job so you can earn some more."

"That shouldn't take very long." He didn't think it could. His skills had never failed to bring him a more than ample income, and he had never been unemployed in his life, at least before his retirement. Nor had he ever been unable to afford his women.

"It doesn't usually. And then there's your basic subsidy, if you don't want to work and you're content with what the computer maintains for everyone to share."

"Surely I can spare a little."

"Well, maybe. But not too much! I don't want you to wind up like Anton and Ling-ko there." The two servants, still standing beside the door, closed their eyes as if her reminder of their past follies pained them, or as if they did not dare to run the risk that she might see a hint of warning.

"How do I transfer the funds?"

She patted his hip. "Dear boy. You'll learn all that soon enough. For now, just leave it to me. I wouldn't want you to get carried away and spend too much, you know."

"Okay."

"That's all I need." She sounded very satisfied.

He thought Anton winced, and in his mind he began to chide himself: "Was that so smart, Michael, my boy? You just handed her your wallet, and you *know*...."

But she wasn't patting his hip anymore. She was cupping, squeezing, stroking, making little noises, shutting down all his higher faculties.

She was his, all his, at last after all the long, long years, and....

He was hers. All hers.

SILICON KARMA
THOMAS A. EASTON

CHAPTER 16

They were standing on the dock, watching two Canada geese flapping their wings at each other, when Rose asked her late husband, "What sort of cases do you get to work on here?"

"All sorts," he said. He shook his head. "And sometimes I blow it. I had an outside call the other day, a murder. Some old geezer was knifed in his apartment."

"That doesn't sound like a fatal wound."

He laughed. "It was right after you got here."

"Who was it? Anyone we know?"

He shrugged and gestured with his free hand. One of the geese transformed itself into a quark wearing a fluorescent pink sweatsuit and rowing a skiff. When it reached the dock, it handed Albert a manila envelope and vanished.

The eight-by-ten glossy photo he withdrew from the envelope showed a body in a wheelchair.

"That's Michael!"

"Just his meat. He's safe now." Yet even as he said the words, he found himself wishing he was wrong. If someone wanted Michael dead, then…. But no. He looked at his wife, his Rosa. Michael was the past, wasn't he? Not really competition.

So was Rosa, for that matter. The past. But a past that he would recapture if he could. Just as, he thought, he was for her.

"Why couldn't you help?" She looked far too concerned.

"I had my mind on something else. A local case. Let me show you." Before she could protest, the lakeside dock was replaced by a city sidewalk, a brick wall on one side, a cobbled street on the other. He touched the poster on the wall. "Right here. Just before you got here. I was walking along, and a quark popped up and blew my brains out."

When she gasped, he thought he had successfully distracted her. He hugged her shoulders with his other hand and added, "Ada brought me back, though she couldn't do much for the last three days. It had been that long since I B-cupped."

"You *are* the one Bertha meant!" she cried. "But why? Why would anyone shoot you?" After a moment's hesitation, she added, "There couldn't be any connection, could there?"

He shrugged. "I don't see how there could be." Then he drew a gold chain from his pocket, and bounced its single charm in his palm. He held it up so she

SILICON KARMA
THOMAS A. EASTON

could see that the charm was a tiny antique milk bottle. "As near as I can tell," he said. "It has something to do with this. And that." He pointed at the Image Shop ahead of them.

She reached for the chain and its charm. As her fingers touched the bottle, it enlarged. Something within it swirled close enough to the glass to make her catch her breath. "What...?"

"That's Toddy Sean." He told her about Gladys and her obsession.

"But how did you get that... thing?"

"She was working that bar behind us." He pointed again. "Trying to raise money." He told her why, and when her eyes widened said, "Yeah. It's weird. But she had a promise, she said. From the Image Shop. They said they could give her what she wanted." He fell silent then, thinking that if Ada had not asked him to investigate, if he had not met Gladys, she might still be swinging her memories from a loop of twine.

"Where is she now?"

He shrugged. "Ada—Marvin—had heard funny things about the Image Shop. Its customers were disappearing. Or going out of circulation. They weren't dead, or the computer would know. But they didn't go home or keep appointments, and their friends couldn't find them. I was looking into it."

"I bet I know what happened," said Rose. "You've done it before, haven't you? When you were alive."

He raised his eyebrows. "I don't think so. The barkeep said I gave her the money she needed. I never did such a thing."

"Still," she said. "I thought so. Remember when you knew that woman's husband was after her? And you told her you wouldn't keep her safe in jail? Sent her home, and staked out the apartment building? And he beat her half to death?"

He grunted and grimaced painfully. "That wasn't just me. Departmental policy."

"And now you've done it again," she said. "Bait. A stalking horse. That's all you saw her as. So you set her up. You hoped she'd be cheated, and you followed her, and you got shot. And now she's gone, without a clue."

He nodded.

"Can't Marvin find her?"

"Of course he could. But he can't, without some good excuse. He's got the power to override anything any of us do in here, but he's programmed to be a servant, not a master. Interference is up to us."

"So what do we do now?"

"We?"

"If you disappear, I'm disappearing with you."

He sighed, realizing that he had indeed said "us" and that in fact he did not wish to leave her behind again. "First...." As the Iron Lady quark popped into existence beside them, he winced and said, "We B-cup. Take the pill."

A few minutes later, still making faces over the taste of the Iron Lady's pain-preventing pills, he and Rose were standing in front of the Image Shop. Its windows were so covered with old political posters that it was impossible to see inside.

"Are we going in?"

Albert bounced the chain and its charm in his palm. "Of course," he said.

As the door jangled shut behind them, he saw that the shop was a single dim room. Each wall was covered with a rack of pigeonholes. Each pigeonhole held a single small roll of paper tied with ribbon. A waist-high counter kept customers from touching the merchandise. On the counter, facing the door, squatted a stubby quark, all jowls and pot-belly.

"Can I help you?" said the quark in a gravelly voice.

Albert expanded the bottle and held it up so the fetus showed. "My girl wants her baby back, alive. She hears you've got an IT that'll do the trick."

The quark's stare was so cold that for a moment Albert did not believe it was really one of Ada's—or Marvin's—subroutines. It had, he thought, to be a human being in disguise. Just like his murderer.

But the shopkeeper, real or virtual, gave him no time to pursue that thought any further. It puffed its cheeks and shook its head once, abruptly. "Get lost, Pillock. Or I'll throw you out again."

SILICON KARMA
THOMAS A. EASTON

"'Again,' it said," said Albert. "I don't remember seeing the inside of that place before. Or seeing that quark. So I must have gone in there since my last B-cup." He paused, looking thoughtful. "Maybe that's the one that shot me."

They were back on the dock, lying on the sun-warmed planks, feeling the breeze that filtered through the island's evergreens, savoring a host of scents that would have seemed quite alien on the city street they had just left. Neither one of them was wearing a swimming suit, or anything else.

"I know you have to work," said Rose. "But why do you have to be a cop? A detective?"

"Why do I have to get shot?"

"You had it coming, really," she murmured.

He shrugged. "At least, it's only temporary now. If I get killed, it's no big deal, not any more."

"It is to me. I'm not used to this place yet."

He smiled sympathetically. "And the job does need doing."

"Then why aren't you doing it?"

"Working, you mean? Oh, I am."

"Not unless you're a gigolo."

When his laugh drowned her out, she poured what was left of her drink—ice and all—into his naked lap. Laughing even louder, he rolled off the edge of the dock into the water. Then he cupped his palm and sent a sparkling sheet of spray arching onto the dock.

"What...?" she spluttered.

"Had to rinse the dock off, didn't I? If I sat in that stuff it might turn John Thomas into an alcoholic, and he has enough vices already."

Now it was her turn to laugh. The bright sun was already drying the dock's ancient planks to their normal bleached appearance. It would do as much to her, even if she did not choose to exercise her new skills.

When her late husband climbed back onto the dock, she eyed him with a grin. "Want me to dry him out for you?"

"It's no use, you know." He lay back down beside her. "He likes the sauce too much."

"What sauce?"

"Saucy, aren't you?" He laughed once more and turned toward her. She met his lips with hers. A moment later she sighed. "I wish we wanted more than...."

"Just a kiss?"

"It'll do for now." She touched the side of his head, ruffled his hair, and added, "Don't edit out that gray. I like the way you look." He still wore his late-forties image, but leaner, fitter, stronger.

"So do I. You, I mean. Old men like to play with little girls."

CHAPTER 17

"Little! I wasn't this big in my real thirties. Except...." She patted her hips, which had indeed been larger when she was meat and young. She still remembered the pain of dieting. "Last night you wanted...." She had already found the hang of regulating the age of her virtual body, and even its degree of padding. He had produced a handful of small scrolls. "ITs," he had said. "Image transformation routines, more versatile than that general purpose thing Marvin issued you. Swallow them all." And then she had been able to be more selective in what she changed, to enlarge parts of her at will, or shrink, or tighten. Psychic plastic surgery. Plastic psychic surgery. Whatever.

"Were those ITs from the Image Shop?"

He shook his head vigorously. "No way, Rosa. And you're just right, right now."

She set her glass down beside his. Instantly, both were once more full. "You said you're working. Right now?"

"It's easy to do more than one thing at a time here."

"Like Marvin? Or...?"

"Yeah. Duplicate yourself. It's just copying a computer file. Then you send the dopple off to be an accountant or drive a truck or whatever while you stay in bed."

"There were times." Rose shook her head. She had been an accountant for so long, and there had been so many mornings.... Albert had kept a bag of marbles in the freezer.

He grinned as if he could read her mind. "I'll never get another chance to use them."

"Don't even *think* about it!"

"We could make a couple of dopples to do it. Or maybe just one, of you."

"*She'd* still suffer, wouldn't she?"

"Not if you don't let her."

For a moment, Rose looked confused. But then her face cleared and she said, "You can edit the file."

He nodded. "Sometimes the job is one that bores you stiff. So you make a 'you' that can stand it, or even enjoy it."

"But I'm not a masochist! That wouldn't really be me!"

He gave her an exaggerated leer. "It would be close enough. Like a state of mind, only one that can walk around. And you can keep contact, enough to keep tabs on what it's doing and thinking. You can even merge with it, updating both sets of memories."

"If that's optional, then you must be able to cut it loose entirely. Make it a new individual, like a twin or a clone." She looked intrigued. "How...?"

"Uh-uh. New residents can't afford to dopple. *You'll* have to do the work for a while. Then, once you've banked enough data energy...."

"Though I suppose you don't have to. If you enjoy your work, I mean."

"It can still be convenient," Albert said. "Sometimes you have to be in two places at once. Or you don't want to decide between two different careers, so you dopple and pursue them both."

Rose propped herself on one elbow to stare into his face. "But how do you do it?"

"You need the right IT. But you can't get that until you can afford it."

"Can't I even make a little one?"

Looking thoughtful, he held out one hand. Light seemed to pool in his palm, sparkle, and congeal, and there was a miniature Albert, as naked as the large, winking at her. "Hmph," he grunted. "That *is* a lot cheaper. Though it's useless." He began to close his fist.

"No!"

He stopped. Then he grinned while his miniature made an obscene gesture. "Like this, then," he said, and he touched her forehead with one finger.

"Ah." A moment later, they were watching their miniature duplicates clambering over tree roots on the island's bank, looking for a shady patch of moss.

"Do you dopple, Albert?"

He turned to face her. "I said I've been working." He gestured, and the planks between them merged, turned glassy gray, developed a frame, and flickered into life. For a moment the screen showed a dozen individuals in robes and haloes waving pamphlets and haranguing the few solid passersby among the flickering backgrounders the computer supplied to make the scene seem more real. Then the view panned downward to center on a sidewalk cafe, round metal tables and wire-framed chairs arranged upon a sidewalk made of brick in herringbone array. The woman at the one occupied table seemed familiar despite the straight-down view. The man opposite her seemed younger than the one on the dock, but....

"That's you!" said Rose.

"And Ingrid too. She called while we were asleep this morning. She wanted help, so I sent a dopple to meet her. We'll merge later on."

"Merge? You and Ingrid?" Rose was not merely surprised. She had guessed that her late husband must have found someone in the virtual world. She should have guessed, as soon as she learned it was possible, that he could duplicate himself, one for her, one for the other. Or dopple himself. It wasn't duplication, was it? It was variations on a theme, differing in apparent age, or state of mind, or....

But that he could tell her what he would do with that other!

"The dopple," he said as if this time he hadn't the faintest notion of what was going through her mind. "Then I'll know what she's telling him. And he'll know what we've been doing." A grin. "We're really the same guy, after all."

And was it any less unfaithful if you cheated on your husband with his twin? His clone? His "dopple"? But he wasn't her husband any more! Death had parted them!

She felt suddenly queasy as it struck her that the ground rules in the virtual world could be very different from those she had spent so many decades getting used to in the meat world outside. It did not help to recall that she had broken those rules a time or two—as had he. She had lost him. Now she had him back, and youth as well. She did not want anything to jeopardize her present, though, yes, Michael *was* out there somewhere.

"She's already told me his meat is dead. Murdered by a burglar, according to his obit. But he is still here." He reached toward a trackball just as it materialized on one side of the frame on the dock. As he turned it, the angle of view shifted to one side though it remained downward, distorting by foreshortening the human figures at the table. A second trackball appeared, and he said, "Let's hear what she's saying now."

"...Called and called and called." Ingrid's voice was taut, anxious, distressed. She was turning a narrow glass of some dark reddish liquid between her fingers. Even as Rose wondered what it held, Marvin's face took form in her mind's eye, winking and saying, "Blackberry cordial." Somehow, she knew that he, the computer in which she now lived, would not be so forthcoming if she wished to know Ingrid's age.

"I wouldn't talk to her," said Ingrid. "But that didn't stop her. And then the damned pop-up gave the phone to Michael."

"Michael?" said Rose, suprised. Was he in trouble? Despite the safety of the virtual world?

SILICON KARMA
THOMAS A. EASTON

She sat up and leaned over the screen as if that would make it tell her more. The lines of the planks the screen had been just moments before were faintly visible through the image of cafe and people. But then those lines turned jagged and the picture began to scroll upward in the frame. The air thickened, and time seemed to slow. She sagged on the dock and watched Albert grimace as if with pain.

And then it was over. "Another virus attack?" she asked.

"Or a traffic jam in the computer's processing unit," said Albert. "But a short one this time."

"What was she saying about Michael?"

"Just listen," he said, as his other self said to Ingrid, "Did he encourage her?"

"Not at first." The admission seemed almost grudging. "But then she called again, and he actually invited her to visit."

The Albert at the cafe table closed his eyes. Rose thought that Ingrid's words had pained him. Then she looked at the man beside her. His eyes too were shut. Did the invitation or the visit bode so ill for Michael? Or was Marvin, or Bertha, appearing to both Alberts with some message? She wished one of them would say something to ease her perplexity, but both were silent.

"And she came, of course," said Ingrid. Three cigarettes appeared on the table in front of her. "Like a pop-up." She paused as if remembering that the term had changed. "A quark. In her underwear, even. And then...."

"He went with her?"

Ingrid nodded furiously. "She just wrapped herself around him, and...."

Her words chopped off, and she stared toward the street. The glass of blackberry cordial fell from her fingers and shattered on the table top. Then, as if she were a tire the shards of glass had punctured, she hissed, "There she is."

The Albert at the table followed her gaze. The one on the lakeside dock adjusted the trackball that moved the screen's point of view downward, behind Ingrid's head, aiming over the sidewalk, the street, the walk beyond, at a blond woman, sleekly dressed, pacing haughtily beside a young man.

"Lisa," said Rose. "But that's not Michael." As she sighed, she realized that she had been holding her breath.

"Where is Michael?" asked Ingrid. Her fingers seized one of her cigarettes and began to shred it.

The man whose arm bore the weight of Lisa's arm, whose lips grinned so fatuously, was an utter stranger. And Lisa, though her glance passed over Albert and Ingrid at their cafe table, seemed not to recognize them.

"You say he went with her," said the Albert at the table.

"Of course he did. And she shouldn't be ignoring us. She met us just the other day." Absently, reflexively, she moved one hand above the surface of the table, almost as if she held a sponge. The broken glass and spilled cordial and tobacco crumbs disappeared. A new glass appeared in her other hand.

Lisa and her friend continued their promenade along the walk. Only their backs now showed. They paused at the corner to let a bicycle go by, its rider an insubstantial background ghost, and they were gone.

The Alberts spoke simultaneously, the one on the dock to Rose, the one in the cafe to Ingrid. "You have to remember," they said. "You're no longer flesh. You're data, electronic."

The two women responded as if, like Albert, they were really one. "Huh?"

The Albert at Ingrid's table was the only one to answer. "You can make copies of yourself. Dopples. Be in two places at once. Go to work and stay home."

"Ah," said Rose. "You mean there have to be two Lisas."

Her Albert nodded, grinning gently. "Just like me. But now...."

His eyes took on a distant look. The Albert sitting with Ingrid was suddenly attentive, as if someone had spoken to him, though Rose had heard no word. Then he waved a hand and turned the tabletop between him and Ingrid into a screen much like the one on the dock. Rose could see herself and Albert, both naked, staring at Ingrid and Albert, both fully clothed, staring at.... Their miniature dopples were visible on the island's bank.

Ingrid's laughter interrupted Rose's memory of facing mirrors. Suddenly aware of her nudity, she wished herself dressed. When the man beside her did nothing, she said, "Albert!"

But he only said, "Shall we join them?"

Even as she stood and straightened her skirt—a pleated plaid she was sure she had never owned though it did seem faintly familiar and there was an odor of mothballs that finally triggered the memory of her grandmother's attic and an old trunk—she was there. An arched wire chair back pressed against her tummy. Ingrid was looking up at her, smiling, saying, "I'm glad you're.... Tchah! Do you want a blouse?"

White flashed in Ingrid's hand as Rose blushed at her own forgetfulness. "Thanks!"

Across the table, above the fading image of an empty dock, a naked, grinning Albert was sitting in the other Albert's lap. As Marvin and Bertha had done before, the two merged until there was only one, Albert's chest hair the last thing to sink into his shirtfront. The final, joint Albert wore the clothes of the one who had been in the cafe all along. Now he brushed at a shirt sleeve, changed the color of his buttons, and materialized a light gray cardigan sweater.

Before anyone could speak, a quark popped out of the table top. It wore a white apron and a white beret and carried a chalkboard menu. Its face was half hidden by an immense black mustache.

"What do you want?" asked the quark. "We got everything on here." It held the chalkboard toward Rose. Lines of script scrolled up its surface.

She shook her head. "No thanks. Not now."

"You gotta. You can't just sit here. Eat something. Drink something. You're keeping the paying customers from finding seats! And where'd the other guy go? I thought there was four of you!"

Slowly and deliberately she scanned the nearly empty array of tables. The quark waiter shrugged and said, "And what if they want the seat you're in? They'll go away, that's what. And I'll lose business. So buy something."

A second quark, wearing a top hat and a tuxedo with a bright green cummerbund, oozed out of the table top behind the waiter, stepped forward, and booted it into the air. As it fell below the table level, it winked out.

The top-hatted quark touched a finger to its elegantly waxed mustache, bowed toward Ingrid, and said politely, "You guys don't seem very hungry, so: Do you know what a male homosexual and a seasick sailor have in common?"

Ingrid just shook her head, but Rose interrupted before it could answer more than, "They...." "Oh, no!" she said. "A joke of the day routine!"

"Please!" The quark tipped his hat toward her. "I'm not that limited!" It began again, but before it could get any further than it had before, Albert put one hand on the top of the quark's hat and pressed downward. It struggled, squeaking desperately, "They both b.... All right, already! You don't like that kind of joke. Ouch!

But vegesexuals! Do you know what.... You're mashing my topper! What they do?" But its efforts were futile. As it sank into the table, the waiter quark emerged again, its hands struggling to straighten its beret. "You still haven't ordered," it cried plaintively. "So whaddaya want?"

"Where's your menu?" asked Albert.

"Musta forgot it." It reached into the table's surface, but before it could find its chalkboard, a human hand dropped a paper menu on the table top. A woman's voice said, "I've turned off the comedian." She wore a white apron that covered her blouse and jeans, her hair was dotted with violet circles, and she was looking at Albert with an expression that made Rose's stomach clench within her.

"Irma!" said the man.

"Have you found Gladys?"

"Not yet." He turned toward Rose. "She was at that bar," he said. "Gladys gave her the bottle before she vanished. She gave it to me." After a moment during which no one else said a word, he added, "Her brother is one of those who disappeared."

When Ingrid looked puzzled, he touched her hand. "I've gone through the story once for Rose already. Take it this way."

Her muscles tightened as information flowed from his mind to hers, and then she made an astonished face. "Do you still have that bottle?"

"Until I find her and give it back."

"C'mon," said the waiter quark. "So order already."

"Just tea," said Rose.

"Smoke it or drink it?" The quark poised a pencil over a pad. When she said "drink," it scribbled and turned expectantly toward Ingrid, who was staring distractedly into space.

"Aahh." The quark blew air through his mustache and waved its pad in front of her face, but all she said was, "Vegesexuals. What...?"

"An old joke, lady," it interrupted. "And a bad one. You want anything?"

Ingrid lifted her glass of cordial as if in a toast and shook her head.

"Coffee for me," said Albert. "And then blow, Joe."

"He's gone," said Irma. As soon as she set one steaming cup down on the table, another appeared in her hand. "It's on the house, and...."

"But what's the point of even ordering?" interrupted Rose. "We could have whatever we wanted just by wishing for it, couldn't we?"

Ingrid snorted gently. "Old habits," she said. "Of course we could imagine what we wanted. But lots of people find familiar rituals comforting. And some like to create for others."

Irma grinned at that. "My husband and I," she said. "We imagine the ingredients, but we assemble everything by hand.

"Just as if they had bought the ingredients in a store," said Ingrid. "It's an art form as much as anything."

"It's their work," said Albert. "They can do it here, 'selling' to other residents of the Virtual City. They could also do it out there, with real raw materials, using teleoperators to run a real kitchen."

"Though then we'd have to pretend to be high-class software packages, or even robots," said Irma.

"You'd still be selling your imaginations."

"But here," said Rose. "They have to pay to use that imagination?"

"It takes extra memory," said Albert. "Extra computer time. And yeah, the system makes us pay for it."

"But they get it back, you know," said Ingrid. "From their customers."

"You have to pay for raw materials out there," said Irma. "For us, that means the computer. Either way, it's the cost of producing what you want. And the end result is something pretty much like what we were used to before." She turned as if to go. "Good luck, Albert."

"Yes," he said. "I'm not giving up. I want to find your brother too."

She made a thumbs-up gesture as she vanished into the cafe kitchen.

"Not that everyone wants the same old sort of world," said Ingrid.

"Think of the Heavens." said Albert. "And if you want something really strange...." The tabletop screen flickered and showed a landscape of glowing prisms and grids though which ovoids and needles moved on arching trajectories. "Hacker Heaven," he added before he blanked the image. "Cyberspace. It doesn't have very many residents."

Rose nodded. Most people, she was sure, would prefer more familiar surroundings, though the basic terms of existence would have to be much the same in the meat world, virtual reality, or cyberspace. The more money or data energy you had, the more you could do. You could dopple once, or a hundred times if you could afford it. You could transform yourself, or your surroundings. You could leap from scene to scene to scene. "Can't you go broke?" she asked.

"The minimum," said Albert. "It's not like a stake, but a stipend. A minimum income, enough to move around and eat and breathe and imagine lots of things, but...."

"It's more power to gratify your wishes than you ever had when you were meat," said Ingrid. "But it's nothing compared to what you can do if you save your money."

Rose looked at her late husband. "Is there enough detecting to...."

"Ingrid called me," he said. "Most of my work is in consulting, pretending to be a database or an expert system. But there's crime here too."

"Wherever there are people," said Ingrid. "Some of them will be ripping the others off."

Albert nodded. "Though they do keep inventing new ways to do it. There's no real money here, after all. No credit cards to steal. People don't have kids to kidnap. There aren't any possessions that can't be replaced by a simple act of imagination."

"But that takes data energy," said Rose. "Money."

He nodded again. "And that can be stolen. That's what makes the work that comes my way here, in the virtual world, as interesting as it ever was when I was meat."

When he had been alive, Rose thought, he had never been reluctant to tell her about his cases. Once every account in a major bank—he had refused to name the bank—had lost that portion of its balance to the right of the decimal, from one penny to ninety-nine. Someone had looted a little here, a little there, to the tune of nearly half a million dollars, and many of the victims had not even noticed. But some had, and within a week he not only had found the virus program that had been introduced into the bank's computer, but also had met—just as she was about to board her flight to Mexico—the woman responsible.

She was an accountant and had dealt with the same basic financial material, but somehow she never ran into such cases. She had never been surprised that her tales of work made him yawn.

"But how can it be stolen?" asked Ingrid. "The *Virtual City Times* doesn't tell us much. It doesn't even admit that we have much of a crime rate."

SILICON KARMA
THOMAS A. EASTON

"It's not that bad," said Albert. "Not as bad as in the meat world. But we do have crime. Mostly theft."

"Do you catch the criminals?"

"We're pretty successful, Rose. The cases are usually straightforward, and the thieves are hardly ever professionals who know how to cover their tracks. A friend has found a way to tap their account or forced a 'loan.' There are con games." He paused long enough to restore the screen to their tabletop and call up a bar chart. Two short bars were almost the same size. "Cases reported," he said. "And cases resolved."

"What's that one?" Rose pointed at the third bar, by far the tallest.

"Even in the real world," he told her. "There's a lot more theft than gets reported. People don't like to look dumb, or like patsies. The same thing here, and that's our estimate." He shrugged. "We've got a good track record, but we can't find a thief if the victim doesn't complain. We can't even know the theft happened."

"Doesn't the computer keep track of...?"

He shook his head. "Uh-uh. Marvin doesn't consciously monitor his guests' accounts. He leaves that up to the individual. He does the bookkeeping himself, but that's all subconscious, autonomic, at least until there's an overdraft alert."

"But what if someone steals from *him*?" asked Ingrid. "Can they do that?"

Albert nodded, and his expression brightened. "Sure. And that can be frustrating. But it's also much more interesting."

A black circle appeared in the middle of the tabletop screen, blotting out the bar chart.

"Oh, no," said Ingrid. "It's back."

The circle rose, revealing itself as the crown of the comedian's top hat. The brim appeared, a forehead, and a pair of wide and rolling eyes that froze at the sight of Albert's broad hand descending to mash it back into oblivion. It jerked upward just enough to expose its mouth, and it babbled, "Don't! A clean one, this time! Have you heard about the prudish royal family that didn't know whether it had a prince or a princess?" As Rose raised one hand to forestall her late husband, it threw her a grateful wink. "Only their heir dresser knew for sure. No! Don't!"

Rose and Ingrid were both smiling, but the man's hand had only hesitated. Once more it forced the quark out of sight. When it was gone, Albert said, "Actually, that's my main job here. The outside consulting is important, but I'm always on call for Marvin. Anytime someone manages to steal data energy from him...."

"From the memory bank," said Rose. "That sounds like virtual bank robbery."

"Whatever that comedian had," said Ingrid. "It must be catching."

Albert's smile bore that touch of strain familiar to all who have ever been interrupted by a self-anointed wit. "I'm supposed to investigate the theft, catch the thief, and put the data energy back where it belongs. If I can."

"Then he keeps track of his own accounts," said Rose.

"If that was where the problem always lay, he wouldn't need me. But the thefts have begun to show up in funny ways, as if whoever it is can tap the virtual world itself." When the others looked confused, he went on. "People can make their own worlds if they have the funds. Most spend a good deal of their time in the common space the computer maintains for everyone. It's familiar, after all. It's also cleaner and safer than the equivalent in the meat world. But sometimes it weakens. Buildings crumble. Streets get potholes. Litter appears on sidewalks."

"That sounds normal enough."

"Not here. Not when all it takes is a bit of thought and imagination, of image editing, to fix any defect. And Marvin does fix it. But it's a drain on his resources."

Rose thought a moment. "But a cigarette butt is an image, too. Doesn't that take computer time?"

"Very little. A butt's a butt. A beer can, a beer can. Visual icons. Not much harder to calculate than static."

"He's rich, compared to us," said Ingrid. "But he's still limited by memory and processing capacity."

Albert nodded. "So he calls me in. I think I'm the only ex-cop in here. Most of them weren't smart enough to marry accountants."

Rose ignored his grin and began to ask, "And do you ever find...?"

He shook his head. "No. We never have. And we need to. The problem weakens the whole virtual reality, the only reality we have now. If we don't beat it...."

"It can't be that bad," said Ingrid. "A little litter?"

Albert looked worried now. "We don't talk about it," he said. "But it's been getting worse."

SILICON KARMA
THOMAS A. EASTON

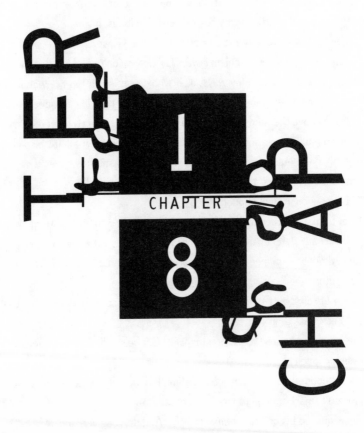

CHAPTER
1
8

Michael Durgov was stretching even before he opened his eyes, grinning, an animal glorying in the aftermath of satisfaction. His muscles crackled from utter relaxation to zinging tension, and he wished he could remember the last time in his life when that had happened.

He grinned again at the feel of the body beside him, smooth, sleek, her skin a little sticky, just enough for realism. Her head was on his shoulder, her weight on his right arm. He took a deep breath, and when she murmured and tugged at the hair around one of his nipples, he said, "I don't want to get out of this bed. Ever."

Lisa chuckled deep in her throat. "My bladder's empty now. And so is yours."

Startled, Michael realized that indeed it was. He still was not used to the ways—both small and large—that virtual reality could obey the will.

"It's hard to believe I'm dead."

"That's just your meat, dear. *You* are just as alive as can be."

"And you wouldn't want dead meat in your bed?" He had told her all he knew, even about the phone call that had threatened him. "It might be even deader soon. I wonder who...."

She made a throaty, animal noise and her hand moved lower, touched, cupped, gently squeezed, successfully distracting him. "It wasn't dead at all, was it? Now it's just asleep. But look! It's waking up!"

He chuckled as he responded to her touch and words, and he quickly forgot that for a moment her face had borne a calculating twist.

"Is this what you want?"

"Not really. I just want to be close to you. To stay close to you, forever. To touch you." She found his hand and tugged. Obediently, he showed her what he meant. He used his right arm to squeeze her shoulder, the hand to caress ribs and hip and buttock, while she steered the other to....

She squeezed him again. "If you keep that up...."

He laughed, but his automatic reaction to her touch was not enough. "Later maybe," he said. Actually, he thought, he would rather go back to sleep.

"Then it's a date." She patted him. "But I'm not going to lie here waiting. Breakfast?"

As she rolled from the bed, Michael crossed his arms behind his head and admired the elegance of the body he had slept beside all night. He had made love to that, he thought. Or she had made love to him. Certainly she had led, directing him, pacing him, urging him on, showing him how to edit away the limits of the typical male. He had never in his life had such a night. And there would be more. He was sure of that, though he did not understand why such a fate should come to him.

His grin as she crossed the room was fatuous, possessive. It did not fade when she opened a closet door to reveal a panel covered with photos that might have been taken from the covers of fashion magazines. The woman in each was Lisa, though she was here white and blond, there black, here a redhead whose skin, everywhere it showed, was thick with freckles, there a tawny brunette. The clothing also varied, and when she stood still, hip-shot, a finger on her chin, the very image of consideration, he realized that this was indeed her wardrobe. She would pick not just a costume but an image for the day. That done, a wish would instantly transform her.

When she turned around, her skin was chocolate brown. Her hair was a shower of tight black braids. Her dress was boldly colored panels that curved around her breasts and belly and buttocks like giant hands. Her legs were stretched atop stiletto heels.

"Are you coming?" As soon as he was out of the bed—and where had his energy gone? what had happened to that zing?—she gestured, and the bed was made. Another gesture, his skin tingled for an instant and a half, and she said, "You don't need to shower. You're clean." A velvet robe materialized in his hand. "Let's go."

What did she do all day? The servants, Anton and Ling-ko, had not been in sight when they reached the dining alcove near the kitchen, but breakfast had been ready, an omelet steaming on a silver tray, surrounded by rounds of Canadian bacon, flanked by pitchers of juice and coffee. There had also been a basket of sweet rolls still warm from the oven. Later, she had stood by a window, apparently deep in thought. She had stared at a wall and grinned as if savoring some deeply satisfying triumph. She had disappeared for hours into other rooms, telling him, "Wait, honey. I'll be back in just a bit." She had not turned on a television or a radio nor picked up a magazine or book. Indeed, Michael saw, there was not even a book in her house.

Eventually, she summoned Anton and said, "This place is a disgrace. You haven't dusted for days, have you?"

He bowed his head.

"Do it now. By hand." A long-handled feather duster materialized near the man's waist. He caught it before it touched the carpet. Then she said, "Michael. Why don't you give him a hand? Then you'll have something to do until...." Her laugh tinkled gaily, and Michael's velvet robe was instantly replaced by jeans and a T-shirt. A second duster appeared in his hand. "Don't forget to lift the knick-knacks."

Neither Anton nor Michael said a word, but they did look at each other before they began their chore. Michael wondered why Anton's gaze seemed so sympathetic.

He stretched, reaching for the glory, the zing, but it wasn't there. His muscles crackled, but not enough, no more than they had when he had been sixty and meat. Had he strained himself the day before? Overworked himself? Not just dusting. Not if he could perform as he had the night before, and again last night.

He grinned. She had beat him three times at chess after dinner, and three more at backgammon. Then she had stood up, changed her dress to gauzy drape, and said simply, "Bed?"

He had been instantly euphoric, eager, ready. He had followed her like a dog that had just scented a bitch in heat. And then....

Perhaps it was no wonder that he felt so enervated. Never before, never, had he been so industrious, so indefatigable, so ultimately drained. He grinned smugly as he thought that he was acting like a teen-aged boy who had been locked in a hotel room with a willing starlet. That kid could be no less infatuated with the woman who was gifting him with the essence of every adolescent fantasy. He could be no less obsessed, no less addicted.

It had not seemed to matter how many decades he was past his adolescence.

SILICON KARMA
THOMAS A. EASTON

And look at her now, awake, bright-eyed, barely a pat or a cuddle, already up and dressed—in a light-brown hide, heels as high as ever, and, of all things, a brass bikini—and heading toward the door. While he could barely move.

Was his real age catching up with him? How could it, if he was purely data and transformed to youth just as he had wished?

He uttered a deliberately dramatic groan.

"Aren't you coming, dear? Anton and Ling-ko have to weed the garden today, and I'm sure they would appreciate your help."

Michael wanted to stretch, but somehow he could not summon the energy even for that. He had performed well the night before, to his delight and apparently to Lisa's, though perhaps the performance had not been drawn out quite as long as before. He thought they had fallen asleep a little earlier. And he had slept as soundly as ever he had in his life.

Yet he felt exhausted. As if yesterday's hours of digging dandelions and crabgrass had been a month of hauling heavy loads up mountains.

His muscles ached. So did his head. His throat felt raw. His gut was swollen, empty, churning, cramped, shifting without warning from one sensation to the next.

"I don't feel well," he said. His voice sounded plaintive even to him.

Lisa—her skin now palest white, her hair lightly touched with rose, wearing a pale green business suit—looked down at him from her vantage atop her heels. "Then fix yourself," she said. "Edit your image."

"I have the IT. I know how," he said. And he did, but when he tried to exercise that skill so basic to life in the virtual world, the only result was a sudden, twisting pang of agony behind his eyes. "But...." Panic rose in him, touched his voice. His skin paled and broke out in a thin film of sweat. He shivered. "It isn't working."

"Then do it the old way. There's a razor in the bathroom." She shrugged and turned and left him there.

Her words reminded him that he had not shaved in all the time he had been in the virtual world. He touched his cheek. There was stubble there, but only as much as would grow in a day, or even a night. He must, he thought, have been editing it away quite automatically ever since he swallowed that first image-transformation scroll. But now....

The bathroom held a mirror too. He stared at himself. Yes, stubble. Almost reflexively, he tried to wish it away, and pain struck once more, knife-sharp, stabbing into the center of his brain.

When he opened his eyes, he saw that he was sitting on the floor, his cheek pressed against the porcelain side of the tub. He climbed to his feet and looked in the mirror again. His cheeks seemed limp, sunken. His bones showed. His head hurt, and his gut still roiled.

Michael told himself that he had always been determined, a little pain had never stopped him before, it would not now. He touched his stubbled cheek. Not that, then. But.... He thought of his gut, and the pain rose beneath the surface of his mind, waiting for his awakening touch. He shuddered and decided that he preferred the way he felt already.

He told himself that he was just data now, merely an electronic pattern in the bowels of a computer. There was no longer a meat version of his reality. He therefore could not possibly be sick. But he was the result of past biology, conditioned to respond in certain ways to his environment, and this environment was designed to present itself to him in ways that he could accept. Something was wrong. It had to be. And he interpreted whatever it was in ways his mind had long ago developed to fit a physical body. If a thought awakened pain, his mind would avoid that thought. That was conditioning, the basic principle of brainwashing.

Why did he feel ill at all? There was no illness in the virtual world. Nothing was supposed to go wrong that he couldn't fix instantly, immediately, painlessly. But none of that was working.

Something was wrong.

He nearly cried for fear that he was waking up. An old man, old and crippled, dreaming of restored youth and health and past loves, the fulfillment of all his wishes. In a moment, half his body would stop working. He would open his eyes and find himself back in his wheelchair.

He waited patiently, holding so tightly to the rim of the sink that both hands began to cramp. But nothing happened. Or was the nausea beginning to ease, just a bit? Was he getting used to it?

And why was it happening? Suddenly he *knew* that it was Lisa, something she was doing to him, God alone knew what or how. Or why. Certainly he had been fine before he let her bring him here.

Or was it just too much sex? He was just a mind now, wasn't he? Without a body, not even one that was out of touch and ravaged by time and illness. That one was dead. What he had now was just illusion, delusion.

He no longer had any way to interact physically with other people, other minds. All they could do to each other was talk, feed each other data. That was no different, perhaps, from the real world, where all anyone knew was what their senses told them. What *data* their senses gave them. But then there had been something real behind the data.

He thought. He assumed. Everyone assumed. Except philosophers, he had learned so long ago in college. *They* could wonder whether the real world was just the product of someone's imagination, God's dream, and if He woke it all would vanish. Or his own imagination, and when he died the world would disappear. Or maybe it was even a colossal simulation in some super-galactic computer and no one knew any different and now he was a simulation inside a simulation.

The difference was that now he *knew* he was only virtual, only program, and everything was data with nothing but whizzing electrons behind it all. If he came, he was really doing it to himself, by himself, and that was nothing more than masturbation. And when he was just a kid, his father had warned him that too much masturbation would drive him mad. He thought he had known better. He *had*. But here, in the virtual world, the rules were different. Weren't they?

He wished he knew what all those rules were. He was sure he was missing something important.

He drew a deep, shuddering breath and left the bathroom. He had not shaved. A tan robe, plain flannel instead of velvet, was waiting on the bed. As he pulled it on, he noticed Anton standing quietly in the open bedroom door.

"Where is she?"

"She went out for the day. If you want to eat, I'll show you the kitchen."

This was the most Michael had ever heard the servant say, as if his mistress' absence liberated him. "I don't think I could hold a bite down."

"We know how you feel." Anton's tone and face said that he did indeed know what Michael was going through. "The worst will be over in an hour or so. And you do get used to it."

"You mean it keeps up? Every morning?"

The answering nod was both rueful and patient.

"But why? What makes it happen?"

Anton did not even seem to hear his words.

"How do you stand it?"

A shrug. "We have to."

We. He and Ling-ko. And Lisa? Was this some unmentioned side-effect of the virtual world? Or did it have something to do with Lisa? Or sex?

He wished Anton would answer, that Lisa had been less brusque that morning, that she had told him more about how this world worked. He wondered if he had given her his allegiance a bit too easily. He thought of Marvin, of Bertha, and wished the computer's persona would appear to answer his questions, but there was only the faintest hint of connection, as if a thick, spongy wall now separated him from the computer.

"You're recovering quickly," said Anton. "Your beard is already beginning to retreat."

He touched his face. Anton was right. His cheek was already smooth in spots. His head and his stomach were slightly better as well.

"Do you want to eat now?"

Cautiously, he shook his head. He wished that Lisa were there instead of Anton. Was the way he felt her doing? Then she could explain what she was doing and why she was doing it. There must be a reason. And if she were not doing something to him, then her presence, he was sure, would help him feel better. He wished Lisa had not gone out, not without him. Could he find her? Or...? "The door," he said.

Anton just looked at him. Finally, he led Michael out of the bedroom and down a short hallway. He pointed. "Good luck."

The door opened directly onto a cracked concrete sidewalk. There was litter in the gutter, and the pavement of the narrow street or alleyway beyond seemed dusty. To one side was a battered garbage can. Beside that was a heap of what looked like rags. There was no sign of traffic or of other people, not even a flickering backgrounder such as he had seen in the tearoom.

How could he possibly hope to find Lisa? She was just a wish away, but his wishes were no longer working, even if he had ever learned how to travel in that way. She could be anywhere.

His heart began to pound at the thought of searching an entire world on foot. Yet—and he took a deep breath as he recognized this—his headache was suddenly almost gone, and his stomach was barely twinging.

Suddenly he realized that he had barely thought of Ingrid or Rose since the moment when Lisa had taken him to her house. He looked over his shoulder at the door he had just stepped through. It was still there, still ajar, surrounded by cracked and flaking stucco, brickwork exposed where the damage was greatest. He could go back at any time.

He turned again, facing the garbage can, and the pile of rags stirred. A head rose, its cheeks hollow, its eyes sunken and rheumy, its teeth ragged stumps. It stumbled to its feet, exposing patches of ulcerated skin. One naked foot was black not with dirt but with rot. Michael gasped at the stench of gangrene.

Yet the stranger simply stood there. It—there was no telling of he or she— did not approach. It only raised one hand as if in some halting benediction, grunted wordlessly, and sank back into its shapeless torpor.

Michael shuddered.

He wished that he knew where to look for Lisa. Rose was surely at the cottage on the island. That was where he had last seen her. But he had no idea of where the lake was. Just as Lisa had transported him from Ingrid's apartment, so had Ingrid transported him from the island. But where did Ingrid live? The views from her windows had been as changeable as television shows, but he thought he had seen the streets outside her building. And her neighborhood was nothing like this dusty, ill-kempt backwater no matter what lay on the other side of the wall at his back. Was it even in this same city? Where was it? Where was *she*?

"Ingrid?" He spoke softly, but his mental voice felt like a near scream.

"Michael?" The word was a thread of sound within his brain. "Did you call me? Where are you?"

"Ingrid?" Had he called her? Had his energies returned enough to let his wishes work? "I'm...." But he didn't know where *he* was, either. "Help me? Take me back?"

And he stood once more in the center of her living room.

"What *happened* to you?" Her mouth and eyes were ohs of surprise, her hands open, her torso leaning toward him.

"What do you mean?" He tried to take a step backward, away from her, but he stumbled.

"You look like you haven't eaten for a week."

"Nah." He was weak, he knew. The mirror had told him he looked like a famine victim. But he shook his head wearily. "I ate okay." Whatever the reason for his condition, starvation wasn't it.

"Then...." Her lips pressed together. "Then you've been wearing yourself down some other way. The same way you did when we.... I guess she kept you pretty busy, eh? As busy as I did once upon a time."

She sounded as accusative as she had before their divorce, whenever he had spent a night with Connie. He felt as defensive as he had then, as if nothing had changed between them. "Why not?" he said. "You don't own me. You didn't then. And we're not married any more."

"Then why did you call me?"

"Why did you answer?"

Had he called her? He had wished, hadn't he? That was all, wasn't it? And he had done it because there was no one else, not really. He saw her realize that she had responded for the same reason, and he saw that she did not like that answer.

By the next morning, Michael felt much better, though he woke alone. Ingrid had once more turned her sofa into a pull-out bed and told him to sleep there. "I should make you get your own place," she had said. "I'm not your wife anymore, and I don't even have to let you in here. For sure, I don't have to let you back in my bed after you've been fucking that tramp."

He had winced, knowing that he deserved her scorn but accepting what she

SILICON KARMA
THOMAS A. EASTON

offered. And now she stood over him, her mouth looking as if the sympathetic wrinkling of her brow was painful.

"I'm sorry," he said. "I...."

"She softened you up a bit, didn't she? I don't think I ever heard you say that."

He blinked up at her. She was right, of course. "Sorry" had not been in his vocabulary. But he had never been so weak before, not even when he was meat, crippled, unable to walk or speak.

"You want any breakfast? Or aren't you hungry? You're looking better."

He felt his cheek. It was as smooth as if he had just shaved. His flesh felt fuller, too. He stretched, and he thought he felt a hint of the zing that had so delighted him just a few short days before. "I'm okay."

"Then you need some lessons. Maybe if you know more about how to handle things here, you can stay out of trouble."

He had little trouble controlling his own body. The image transformation routine Bertha had given him was easy to use. To that Ingrid added other ITs, and soon she had him materializing small objects—mugs, pencils, doughnuts—out of the air. By mid-afternoon, she was telling him about and demonstrating dopples.

"But...." Michael looked from one of her to the other. "Which one's the real Ingrid?"

"We both are." The duplicates' words were simultaneous. He could not hear even the suggestion of resonance provided by echoes in a small room.

"But one of you has to be the real Ingrid. And one of you is the copy."

"It doesn't matter." They shook their heads as simultaneously as they spoke. "We're duplicates. Exact and complete, in every way, even the thoughts."

"But you said you can listen in on your dopple, or limit it, or control it."

"If you make it that way." The two identical women turned to face each other. "But we're duplicates, exactly the same. It takes time to become separate individuals. Different experiences, different databases. That's what it takes for us to think different thoughts." As they stopped speaking, lit cigarettes appeared simultaneously in their hands.

Michael felt himself becoming aroused at the thought of two wives, two mistresses, two lovers, just the same, more alike than even twins could possibly be. He thought of Marvin and Bertha and realized that he could make a female version of himself, or even two of them. And if he wanted to know how it was for them, he could leave a pipeline open between their minds and his. Or, later, he could merge with them and thus gain all they had thought and felt while they were separate.

"How do I do it?"

"You can't," said the Ingrid on his right.

"Why not?"

"It's an expensive process," said the other. "An expensive IT to buy and to use. And you don't have the funds. You need a job for that."

"Not even a little one?"

Both Ingrids laughed. "That's what she did. You think alike." When he looked baffled, they added, "Rose. You were quite a jerk when you walked away from her. She might have been the only wife you ever needed."

He nodded ruefully. He had wondered the same, but that was past, as dead and gone as his meat. "Then I can do a little one?"

"Like this." The two Ingrids slid together, became one, and touched his head. He felt something like a spark of static cross between them, and suddenly he knew what to do.

He held out one hand, palm up. With the other he indicated size. "This big." Then he visualized what he wanted, a duplicate of himself, standing on his palm, facing him. He strained in the necessary effort of imagination, and a translucent form began to take shape, to waver in and out of being like one of those insubstantial backgrounders the computer used to people the virtual world's streets and tearooms.

Something hit his hand from below, and the half-developed image vanished. "What...?" When he looked down, he saw a quark with orange skin, white overalls, and a red cap.

"Sorry, fella," it said. "But...." It waved a placard above its head.

The lettering on the placard said, "Insufficient funds."

"I've never seen that one before," said Ingrid in a hushed tone.

Bemused, Michael materialized a plate of shrimp scampi, a glass of white wine, a fur-trimmed shirt. None gave him any trouble. Apparently he had now accumulated enough data energy from the trickle of his subsidy to have whatever he wished to eat or drink or wear. But when he tried once more to duplicate himself in miniature, the quark popped up again. "I told you once already!" It had leaped from the floor to scream in his ear at the peak of its trajectory. Now it descended upon his ghostly image and mashed it flat. "Insufficient funds!"

Michael tried again and again, all that evening, and all the next day. The images he mustered grew fainter as he spent what data energy he had on his efforts. The quark's screams of "Insufficient funds!" grew louder and more strident. At the same time, he himself grew weaker, until he barely had the strength to raise his arm.

The quark's last appearance came just as he stretched his forearm along the arm of the chair he was sitting in and formed the intention to try again. This time, however, it did not leap and scream. Instead, it grasped his hand, poised to receive the image of himself, and said, "You can't even afford to try."

He did not relax his hand. "What happens if I do?"

"You die. You won't have enough data energy to breathe."

He tried to imagine a slice of chocolate cake.

"Not even that," said the orange-skinned quark.

He gave in just as the pain arrived, throbbing behind his forehead. He exhaled a gusty sigh, let his arm roll into his lap, and began to cry.

The manikin patted his thigh and vanished.

"I've never heard of such a thing," said Ingrid. She had been watching from an easy chair across the room. "It's not supposed to happen."

"Why not?" He let his chin slump onto his chest. His voice was as weak as his muscles, his throat tight, his nose already running. "Data energy is money, isn't it? And if you've got money, you can go broke. Or bankrupt."

"It never happens," she said. "It *can't* happen. It's in the contract we signed."

"The guarantee." Michael made a disgusted noise that suggested what he thought of guarantees in general. "Bertha's supposed...."

When he faltered, she picked up his thought: "...to make sure we all have enough to live. We don't have to eat or drink or wear clothes. We do have to breathe, though, to stay alive." She hesitated then. "You're supposed to get a continuous trickle of data energy. It's supposed to be enough to keep you going."

"You mean I'm not supposed to be able to use it fast enough to kill myself, unless I...."

She shook her head. "Something's wrong." She hesitated for a moment. "You'll have to stay here."

He was puzzled. "What's that got to do with...?"

"You had enough data energy when you got here. At least, you could do things once you were feeling better. And you haven't done enough to use up your guaranteed minimum income. Not with the healing you had to do, and not with all your attempts at a mini-dopple."

"You mean.... I've got a hole in my pocket. A leak."

She nodded reluctantly. "That's what it looks like. But I've never heard of such a thing."

He gasped for breath, unable to say a word. He could only look at her, desperately appealing.

"I don't know what we can do."

"Bertha!"

"I just tried to call, but there's no answer. The computer must be too busy. But maybe I can talk to Albert."

SILICON KARMA
THOMAS A. EASTON

CHAPTER

9

Lisa did not return to her home until the next day. After all, she thought, she had other beaus to her string, and she knew no reason to ignore them, no matter how sweet it was to have Michael back from the past.

When she materialized once more in her foyer, she poised as if sniffing the air. No Michael? But he had to be here. Perhaps he was still in bed, poor boy. More than a day later! She smiled almost as tenderly as she might have done for his benefit, and the trace of sympathy she felt for his plight made her cluck her tongue just once. She knew she was a strain, a drain, but he had seemed to be taking it so well. And she was glad that he was, really. He had been a pleasant moment in her life, all those long, long years ago. Her memory of him was actually fond, or as fond as any of her memories of men ever were. Most were not.

Her servants were awaiting her instructions. "Let dinner hold for half an hour," she instructed Ling-ko. Then she smiled and told Anton, "Bring the drug tray."

But when she reached the bedroom it was empty. For a moment, surprise made her stand still. How could he get away? How could he possibly leave her? He was hers now, hers for as long as she wished, even forever. There was no escape.

"Where is he?"

"He left," said her servant. His eyes were wide, the whites showing. His lips were pressed in a tight, grim line. The cords of his neck were visible.

Her smile grew strained. He was not supposed even to *think* he could be free. "Why didn't you stop him?"

Anton managed the slightest of shrugs before he said, "You didn't say he couldn't leave."

The drug tray was trembling in his hands. She struck it with a fist and sent it flying, but both the tray and its contents vanished before they struck the floor.

"Of course he couldn't leave!" She screamed the words, but she was also grinning, and the flaring of her nostrils said she delighted in the scent of his fear. "You can't, can you? Ling-ko can't." The other was hovering just out of sight. His shadow was visible in the room's doorway. "Where did he go?"

Anton shook his head. "I don't know. I just showed him the door."

"Which one?"

He pointed out the hallway he had led Michael Durgov down, and he could not keep his face from showing the wish he felt to pass through that door just as the other man had already done.

For a moment, she ignored her servants. Her eyes unfocused, and her vision blurred. The door Anton had indicated led to a narrow, dusty, deserted alley that neither he nor Ling-ko could ever enter. The door was barred to them because she knew that they, like Michael, would surely see the alley as an avenue to freedom even though the only man to use it before had barely been able to stumble to the curb.

Where was that man? There.... Not far away at all. He never was. He could not stand to go beyond sight of the walls of her house. And his mind roared with delight at her touch.

She laughed. "Hamid saw him." Yet Hamid could tell her nothing more. Michael Durgov had simply disappeared.

Where could he have gone? He had been in the virtual world long enough to have found a place of his own, but he hadn't. He had met too many old friends who would be eager to take him in. Herself, for instance. She showed her teeth, felt a thrill of pleasure when Anton began to shake again, and added to her thought: That other woman too, his first wife, Ingrid. Not Rose, who had her Albert to keep her busy.

She thought of Ingrid. She visualized the woman's apartment and listened for.... Yes. There it was. There *he* was. The distinctive male presence, the mind that was Michael Durgov, weaker now than he was when Rocky had taken her to meet him, but still him, still hers.

Could she get him back? Of course she could. He had invited her into that place once already, and Ingrid had not thought to restore the intangible barriers he had thereby breached. Until she did, none of her doors could be closed against her.

She materialized in the bathroom doorway, smelling soap and powder, hearing Ingrid's voice from around the corner:

"...what we can do."

"Bertha!" His answer brought the adrenaline to her veins and made her frown. The computer was the only one who might conceivably interfere with her life.

"I just tried to call...."

Enough. She was just in time. If she let this conversation continue, it might become too late for her.

As soon as Ingrid's voice fell silent once more, Lisa stepped into sight.

Michael immediately quailed and began to tremble, but he could not look away from her. Her eyes, like those of a snake confronting a bird or mouse it intended to swallow whole, held him motionless.

Ingrid stiffened, and her face began to redden with rage. Her mouth opened, ready to scream in protest of Lisa's sudden invasion of her home.

But Lisa gave her no chance to speak.

"He's mine," she said. "*I'll* take care of him."

She grasped his arm just above the elbow. "I was hoping to find you near the bed, Michael. But it's not too late, is it? Come, now."

He finally broke his fascinated stare to look imploringly toward Ingrid, but by then it was too late.

"No!" cried Ingrid. She was reaching for Michael's other arm.

"Come, Michael."

And they were gone.

SILICON KARMA
THOMAS A. EASTON

CHAPTER 20

"You've really let this place go," said Rose Pillock.

"It looks like that, doesn't it?" said her late husband.

"Too much. Too much." Dirty mugs lay in wait on every horizontal surface. Take-out bags and pizza boxes drifted near the walls. She shook her head as she thought of what he had told her about how thefts of data energy from the very fabric of virtual reality, from the computer that supported it all, could appear as filth and rubbish. She did not believe that any thief had been in this place. Albert had simply reverted to those early habits it had taken her years to break him of.

And then there was the smell—stale, rancid, musty, the unventilated den of the primordial male. The bachelor without a keeper. She scanned the apartment once more. There was no sign of houseplants or flowers. Not even any scent of outdoor greenery and soil.

There was no yard, of course, and whatever part of her it was that held every present up against the standard of the past only whined a little for that difference. No cherry trees, no dahlias, no peonies, no antique rose bush, no mossy rock garden in the shade beneath the willow tree. No broad space that they kept clear year after year, promising each other that that was where they would put the pool. But they hadn't. The money had sat in the bank and grown and finally gone to Coleridge.

"I know it's not the house," she added. "Not really. But...." Albert's place was only three rooms, maybe four—she hadn't even seen the whole apartment yet—buried in a layer cake of glass and balconies. But he had furnished it almost exactly like the house they once had shared, before he had gone to Coleridge, before his final illness, before his death. She had clung to the place as long as she could after that. Eventually, it had become too much for her.

The biggest differences between what she saw and memory were that what should have been two rooms, living room and dining room, was here only one, and one long wall—the window wall, she thought—was covered with draperies. But there was the same free-standing fireplace, a metal cone with a gaping maw. The same narrow bookcase held his antique Marquezes and Wilhelms and Resnicks. The same corner rack displayed the porcelain bells she had once collected. The same glass-fronted dining room hutch held as much as had been left of their wedding china when he died and, in the center of the upper shelf, the crèche that had been her grandmother's. Julianne had both china and crèche now.

SILICON KARMA
THOMAS A. EASTON

"I hope you're not expecting me to do the dusting."

"It's only images," he reminded her. "My memories, put out where you can see them too." But then he shrugged, and every surface sparkled. At the same time, the air freshened and the litter and coffee mugs disappeared.

"Then...." She added to the display in the hutch a dancer built of fine glass threads that she had once loved. Julianne had dropped it when she was only two. Then she turned away and touched one corner of the dining room table. "You've made an awful mess of this too." They had chosen it together for their second anniversary, and for years its weekly polishing had been a favorite ritual. "I gave it to Peter when I sold the house." But now the rosewood veneer was scratched and nicked, separating from the wood beneath. The few other patches of the tabletop that showed were no better. Most of the surface was lost beneath a tangle of wires; a litter of computer disks and manuals; and the boxy masses of a desk-top computer and a printer. The computer's shell wore the same colorful sticker that had adorned Albert's home machine in the meat world: "Murphy was an optimist." A rumpled report half covered the telephone.

"The old familiar things," said Rose. "I understand. I want them too. The lake. The cottage. The tearoom. But the computer? When we're *inside* a computer?"

He looked sheepish. "I know. But I was used to it when I set up here, and it's no big deal. It's just a display mode, like Marvin's bodies, or the way he puts his faces on TV screens or floating balls."

She grinned at him. When they had been together in the meat world, she had been able to embarrass him only rarely. It had always felt like a triumph, small but real.

"Do you want a fire?"

"But it's warm out!"

"Not quite." The drapes rolled to one side, exposing tinted glass and a broad balcony whose railing was corniced with snow. The rest of the virtual world was no more than vague outlines beyond a thick curtain of flakes lazy-drifting from the sky.

When she turned back to the room, logs were already burning in the fireplace. The light and warmth of the flames played against the snow outside, and when Albert stepped behind her and encircled her in his arms, she relaxed against his chest.

That was when the phone rang. He sighed in her ear. His arms tightened very briefly and let go. "I'd like to lose that thing right now."

"I saw it on the table." One step put her within reach of the report that hid the shrill device. Its cover said it was the product of "The Committee to Investigate Computer Fraud in Religion." She guessed someone was skeptical of the virtual heavens.

He sighed again as he put the phone to his ear. After a moment, he said, "You'll want to hear this too," touched a button on his computer keyboard, and set the phone down. Rose had just a second to realize that he had not bothered to turn the machine on, that he had not really had to touch a key, that his wish was all that mattered. The same, she thought was true for her as well. She could revise her body or reconstruct a figurine, but she could as easily and as freely use a wish to brush her teeth or flip a switch. It would, however, be some time before she was so used to the virtual world and its freedoms that she could wish for trivia.

Ingrid's agitated voice brought Rose's mind back to the screen before her, where the other woman was saying, "He's gone again! She just came and grabbed him, and you should have seen him! He looked like he was starving, and then when I tried to teach him how to do those mini-dopples.... I've never seen that before!"

She was talking about Michael, Rose suddenly realized. That very Michael who had once seemed to her the truest love, only to be stolen away by a Lisa she had thought her friend. That very Michael who had left her after their long, long delayed reunion to go off with his first wife, only to be stolen away once more by Lisa. "What happened to him?"

"Seen what?" asked Albert.

"That pop-up!" She was too upset to remember that the pop-ups had changed their name. "'Insufficient funds,' it said."

"Unnhh," Albert grunted. "That again."

"What do you mean?" Suddenly Ingrid's face showed hope. As long as the problem seemed totally unknown, beyond her own and hence all human ken, it frightened and bewildered her. But now its threat diminished. Whatever the problem was, it was something Albert recognized. Perhaps, her thought was clear, he could do something about it.

"I'll tell you in a minute. Meet at the cafe?"

"But...!" Her expression said she wanted to know what he knew *now*. She didn't want to wait.

SILICON KARMA
THOMAS A. EASTON

Albert gave her no choice. He touched the keyboard once more, and the computer's screen went blank.

"Why not here?" Rose used one hand to indicate the chairs beside the table, the sofa near the bookcase. "You've got the room. And the privacy."

"I never bring my clients home. Remember?"

"You were a cop. You didn't have clients."

"You know what I mean."

And she did, of course. If he had had to meet an informant, or question a suspect, or confer with a fellow cop, he had always done it away from their home. He had once said he didn't want to expose her to possible revenge. Yet he had clearly formed a habit he didn't choose to break when she was no longer there to be endangered, nor when whatever danger there might be could pose no mortal threat.

They barely had time to nod hello to Ingrid before the waiter quark was waving its chalkboard menu in their faces and saying, "You guys again?" Rose brushed it off the table, but as soon as it was out of sight, the joke-of-the-day popped up and said, "Have you heard...?" It got no further before Albert said, "This is business," and mashed it back into the tabletop.

"It had gravy on its tux," said Ingrid as if she were seizing anything she could to avoid thinking of why she was there.

"It was holding a violin this time too," said Rose. "But what happened to the snow?"

"What snow?" Irma stood beside their table, looking perplexed. The buildings around them glowed in evening sun, and the air was the warm balm of late May or early June. The street was cobbled now, and there was a striped umbrella above their table.

"Local weather," said Albert. He looked at Rose. "It comes to order here. Now...."

"Anything yet?"

"Sorry." He shook his head at the cafe's owner. He did not try to make the situation sound any brighter than it was. "I wish I had more time for that case, but we know Gladys isn't dead. Your brother isn't either. They're hidden somewhere. But we'll find them both."

"I know, but...." Irma sighed. "Do you want to order then?" When no one did, she parked the waiter on a nearby table and left.

"What did you mean?" asked Ingrid at last. "When you said, 'That again'?"

"Tell me what happened first," he said. "The details."

But once she had obliged, he only stared into space until Rose poked his arm and said, "What's Michael doing? What's happening to him now?"

Ignoring her, he muttered, "The obit." The table top became a screen once more to show the clipping. He stared, muttering, finally calling, "Marvin?"

There were only three chairs at their table, but suddenly a fourth was there, just in time to receive the host computer's materialized persona.

"Do you have any more details?"

"Not a bit."

"They haven't caught this burglar?"

The computer's persona shook its silvering head and smiled. "There *was* a call for Mr. Durgov from Coleridge. I didn't put it through, of course."

"What did they want?"

"To tell him he was dead. And then to ask him what he had found out about our own little crime wave. I felt obliged to say he hadn't learned a thing."

"Crime wave?" asked Rose.

"I was killed, remember?" said Albert.

"They know about that." said Marvin. "They don't know about the Image Shop. Or about stolen data energy."

"Then what makes them think there's a crime wave?" The ex-cop scratched his cheek.

"Rumors," said the computer. "Someone inside talked to someone outside."

"Then let's us talk to Coleridge."

Leah Kymon's face appeared on the table, her mouth already open and moving. "Where's Durgov? We can't reach him."

Marvin pointed at Albert. "Did you know I had a cop in here?"

"So what?"

"Shouldn't he be the one to investigate the crime wave that has you so worried?"

SILICON KARMA
THOMAS A. EASTON

"He'll have to stop it, not just investigate it. We're losing customers."

"And money," said Rose.

"The bottom line," said Kymon.

"You can't turn us off," said Ingrid. "Not even if you go bankrupt. We have contracts with you."

Kymon's shrug said more eloquently than words that if the company pulled the plug, that would hardly matter. She looked at Albert. "*Can* you stop it?"

"I can try."

"I hope that's good enough." Her image blanked, and the tabletop was just a tabletop once more.

There was a pause while all three people drew shocked breaths and Marvin said, "Good luck. You'll need it." Then he was gone as well.

Rose repeated what she had asked before: "What's Michael doing? What's happening to him now?"

A new image appeared on the table, but this one was neither an official talking head nor some idyllic scene of lake and dock and island, but a bedroom, a bed, a disordered nest of sheets and blankets and Lisa, naked and quite enough to make Albert draw a sharp, involuntary breath.

"Business," said Rose. "Keep your mind on your work, dear. Where's Michael?"

The view changed as if a camera were moving around the periphery of Lisa's bedroom. She remained visible, the pivot around which the room and all within it swung until at last three men appeared. One was Michael, as naked as Lisa but gaunt, emaciated.

"He's worse!" cried Ingrid.

"He's half dead," said Rose.

"Poor bastard," said Albert. He looked intent, and then he added, "I can't talk to him. Something's got him blocked, though not enough to keep us from watching."

The other two men, wearing pink uniforms with mother-of-pearl buttons and white belts, held Michael erect. His head lolled as if he were barely conscious.

"You mustn't leave me, Michael," said Lisa. "You know that, don't you?"

When he did not answer, she said, "Michael!" and he jerked as if she had given him an electric shock.

Albert winced. Ingrid said, "Oh, Michael." Rose just made a sound of pain.

The men who held Michael up were sweating.

"I won't have it, Michael," said Lisa. His eyes were open now. "You mustn't leave me. You *can't* leave me. Right now, you don't even have the strength to stand up." She giggled. "Or walk across the room. Or go through that door."

She pointed, and instantly he was dressed in the same livery as the other men. "But you'll be a little better in the morning. You can help Anton and Ling-ko then."

"Shit," said Albert.

"She's sucked him dry," said Rose. "That's what 'Insufficient funds' means."

"It's only happened a few times before. Once someone just wished for too many things and wound up spending so much that all he could do was breathe. But he didn't stay in trouble. As soon as he wised up, his account recharged, though it took a while."

"A vampire," said Ingrid. "Only she's not after blood. She takes his data energy, It sounds like she'll let him keep just enough of his basic stipend to stay alive. She'll take the rest just as fast as it gets to him." After a brief hesitation, she added, "I'll bet those servants were once her lovers too."

"They don't look good either," said Albert. "But they look better off than Michael. They should have enough energy to get away if they wanted to."

"Maybe they're really just like him, only she's prettified them a little? Or she supports them. Holds them up like puppets. And if she stops, they collapse."

"Or she never lets them accumulate enough surplus to support any extra activity," said Albert.

"I wonder how many she's gone through," said Rose. "And where the others are."

The man shook his head. Anton and Ling-ko had turned Michael around and were half guiding, half carrying him toward the door. Lisa had cupped one hand beneath a breast and spread the other on her belly, just above the dark triangle of her groin. She was staring toward the ceiling.

"Does she know we're watching her?" asked Rose.

"I don't think so," said Albert. "I hope not."

"This has happened before?" asked Ingrid.

Albert nodded. "I said one guy did it to himself. A few others, it was like they were trying to carry water in a bucket without a bottom. About all you could say was that the inside of the bucket got wet. They almost died. The first time, that was when Marvin asked me to help. But they didn't know how it happened. They didn't remember what they were doing just before it happened. There weren't any clues." He shrugged to express his helplessness. "Most people don't B-cup often enough. Some never do, at least not after their first."

"How many?" asked Rose.

He did not answer her immediately. He was watching the view in the tabletop screen change, the viewpoint pivoting around Lisa once more, rolling down and underneath the bed, peering upward through mattress and sheet and blanket and Lisa's body to reveal the screen and tentacle-mounted cameras above her. That screen showed her from three different angles as she moved her hands and smiled.

"Three or four," he said at last. "They were easy enough to set back on their feet. Marvin just replaced their funds. Then there was one who got zeroed out completely. Marvin had to reboot him from his storage wafer."

"Then we could save Michael that way," said Ingrid. "That's what he'd do, or would have done. Write him off. Turn him off. Then reboot and keep him away from that woman."

"Uh-uh." Albert was shaking his head. "Marvin can't kill people, not even temporarily. He can't even keep tabs on you very closely, once your introductory period is over. We have rights here, written into his software."

"To live our own lives." Rose was remembering the brochures she had read. "To privacy. Though you can peep." Then her history as an accountant surfaced. "If there were taxes...."

"Then the computer would know where all the money was going," said Ingrid. "But we just don't leave behind the same sort of paper trail we used to. It's all cash and carry here, fees for services. And though it's all in the computer, Marvin's supposed to keep those computations and records well away from his consciousness. It's all automatic, subconscious subroutines, the same sort of thing that regulates your heartbeat."

"He's God, then, isn't he?" said Rose. She had never been religious, but the comparison seemed compelling to her. "God knew everything we did when we were meat...."

"Here too." Ingrid was smiling.

"But he never talked. Marvin could if he wished, if he were willing to break his own rules."

"We have to solve this one ourselves," said Albert. "I suppose that's why Marvin made me a cop here in the first place."

"Where can we start?"

"Why don't we see what Lisa's up to?"

"But," Ingrid protested, pointing at the tabletop screen. "But she's right there!"

The image on the tabletop flickered. "And there," said Albert. They saw a swimming pool in which a nude Lisa dove and stroked and porpoised while a servant in her livery, not Anton, not Ling-ko, not Michael, stood at attention beside the pool, holding a towel.

"And there." She was holding tightly to the arm of a young man who wore an expression of fatuous worship. They were approaching the entrance to an expensive-looking shop, and she was saying, "I *know* we could just imagine it, Timothy, but some people do like to shop, you know."

"And there." She was with still another young man, this time in bed, and what they were doing did as much as anything could to explain Timothy's facial expression.

She was black, and her head was capped with dark reddish wool. She was tan, and her black hair shone like silk. She was white and blond. Her face was always Lisa, and her breasts, though they varied in contour, were always in the middle range of size, not faintly boyish nor utter burdens.

"But...," said Rose. "They're all *her*." She felt just a moment of envy for Lisa's ability to change her skin and hair like clothes, and then she realized that she could do the same. There was no reason at all to stay with the self-image she was used to, or its various time-shaped editions, or even such minor editorial revisions of weight or figure as she had already tried. The only limit was her wishes.

"Dopples," said Albert.

"Which one's the original?" asked Ingrid.

"It doesn't matter," answered Albert. "They're duplicates."

"And she uses them to collect men," said Ingrid.

"It's worse than that," said Rose. "She enslaves them. She turns them into dairy cows so she can milk them of their stipends." The screen before them once more showed Michael in the grip of Lisa's servants. "She makes them watch as she snares more men." Now it showed the dopple's pool. "She makes them do humiliating chores. A chair would do that just as well! Or she could hang it on the air!"

"They can't leave," said Ingrid. "She doesn't let them keep enough data energy to travel. They can't make dopples. I think they can't even make their own food and clothing. They're at her mercy."

Rose looked at Albert. "Then is she the thief you've been looking for all along?"

"That's what it looks like," said her late husband. "She'd be bad enough all by herself. But with her dopples...."

"She's a whole crime wave. *The* whole crime wave."

The fourth chair had remained when Marvin vanished before. Now it was occupied once more.

"Marvin?" said Albert.

"Did you call him?" asked Rose.

"I was listening in." Marvin wore a somber expression. "I can't do that with everyone, but Albert works for me."

"He's not on the job now," said Rose.

Marvin shook his head. "You're always on the job in here, or at least on call. You don't have to get tired, and you can always dopple if you want to do something else."

"If you can afford it," said Rose.

"And this case is right up his alley," said Ingrid. "Do you think she *is* a vampire?"

The computer shrugged. "My programming keeps me from watching her in action, except accidentally." He grinned and indicated the view in the screen, as if to say that while he couldn't spy on Lisa himself, he could nevertheless look over their shoulders. "It also strictly forbids me to interfere with the lives of any of my guests unless I can document that only by doing so can I protect other guests from worse interference."

"But that's what she has to be!"

"I can't break the rules in my programming, but that's what it looks like. Michael's a mess, and Lisa seems to be responsible. But he hasn't complained. In fact, he seems to have consented to whatever Lisa is doing to him."

"She's brainwashed him!"

"But you're the only one objecting, Ingrid."

"He tried to escape!"

"And then he let her take him back."

"Don't *you* think it's wrong?" As soon as the words were out of her mouth, Rose wondered what she really meant. Of course Marvin could think. But weren't "right" and "wrong" concepts that were far too human for a machine to comprehend?

The computer was nodding in a very human way. "That's what my programming tells me. The problem is proving it. It would be easy if I could watch every move she makes, track everything she buys computer time to do. But I can't. Not without more solid evidence. My designers didn't want me to turn into a dictator, and they did all they could to prevent it."

"Like giving a country a constitution, a Bill of Rights," said Ingrid.

"Except that I can't go to a court to get a search warrant. Your rights are pretty absolute."

"Like a strong tenure system," said Rose. "The way they used to be, back in the middle of the twentieth century."

"Can't you talk to your programmers? Or someone at Coleridge, anyway?"

"They wouldn't dare tell him to go ahead," said Albert. "There's a leak already. If word of this got out too, there'd be lawsuits. Heirs and originals and even the ACLU. At least for invasion of privacy, maybe for denial of due process."

Marvin nodded. "As soon as I said a word, they'd have to go to a judge. 'As you know, your Honor,' they'd say. 'We've been copying people into a computer. Now one of the copies is misbehaving, and the computer needs a warrant to check her accounts and spy on her.'"

Rose was nodding. "And then the judge would say, 'Aren't these people really dead?' and you'd try to explain that many are but their copies aren't, and he'd shake his head and say, 'Warrants are only for officers of the law. Are you one?'"

"I could point to Albert, though I suppose he stopped being an officer when he retired, and certainly when he died. But that wouldn't work. They'd laugh me out of court. And if they took me seriously, they'd tie us all up in rules and regulations and procedures."

"Someday," said Albert. "They'll have to deputize one of us, and appoint judges for us. Or we'll have to set up our own police force and legal system."

"I'd rather let her get away with whatever she's doing," said Marvin. "I'd like to protect her victims, but not at the price of becoming a dictator or letting someone else tyrannize us all."

"Even if that means Coleridge winds up turning us off?" Ingrid sounded as if she thought the price of rules, of principles, could be too high.

"Would she leave fingerprints anywhere?" asked Rose.

"She could leave hoofprints if she wanted to," said Albert. "Or nothing at all."

His reminder that the virtual reality was far too flexible for that sort of evidence embarrassed her only briefly. "What does she do for work?"

"Nothing," said Marvin.

Ingrid pointed at the tabletop. The view returned to the scene that had not long before held Michael Durgov. Lisa still lay on her bed, though now her eyes were closed and her arms lay by her sides. The image on the screen quickly panned through her home, showing rooms, halls, tower, pool, and finally a long dim room with a dozen narrow metal-frame beds against the walls. One of the beds held Michael, flat on his back much like Lisa, just as unconscious of his surroundings, but looking far less content.

"Look at that," said Ingrid. "The place is a palace. It even has a dungeon. And she runs more dopples than anyone I know. Than anyone I've ever heard of. How can she possibly afford all that if she doesn't work? *Unless*...."

"Unless she steals all the data energy she uses," said Albert.

"You said the thefts show up in deterioration of the environment." Rose pointed at the screen. "There's not much sign of that."

Albert nodded. "Only when the thefts are from Marvin. When they're from individuals like Michael, well, look. He's deteriorated enough."

Ingrid leaned forward. "Look at what she's doing to men. That can't be enough to run that mansion. And she has dopples, with mansions of their own. She has to be stealing anything that's not nailed down."

"But how does she steal it?" asked Rose.

Marvin shook his head, unable to answer.

"First," said Albert. "We have to prove she *is* stealing it."

"I used to be an accountant," said Rose. "If I could audit her accounts, I might be able to find something."

"I could do that myself," said Marvin. "They gave me the very best financial software they could find."

"But you can't use it," said Ingrid. "That Bill of Rights in your programming."

"Sure I can. But only if I have more evidence than I've seen so far that she's guilty of something. That's your job, getting me that evidence."

Rose made a face. "It wouldn't do anyway. I used plenty of accounting packages when I was meat, and not one of them was good enough to spot a crook who was even half clever. It takes a human being to catch another human's tricks. If the arithmetic's correct and all the rules are followed, software will never peep."

"You were bragging once," said Albert. "About how you could spot pretty subtle patterns of evasion and deception."

"I could." She nodded emphatically. "I can. And if Marvin could open up his files to me, I could...."

"And I'm the computer-crime specialist," said Albert. "Maybe, between the two of us, we can crack the case. At least, we know where to look now."

The computer slapped the tabletop with one hand. "Okay. The files are open."

"Not just Lisa's," said Albert. "We'll need to track what she's done to all those lovers. And maybe others too."

"Everything," said Marvin. "It's all yours. If you need anything you can't find, just ask a gofer quark."

"But..." said Ingrid. "If *you* can't spy on people...."

"How can I delegate the job?" When she nodded, Marvin grinned. "We're all inside the computer, and we're all software. But you're not just pieces of me, subprograms or subroutines. You're independent to a huge extent. Your rights are written into my program, but they're there to protect you from me. You're not supposed to need protecting from each other."

"But we do," said Rose. "We're people."

"Programmers tend to be naive," said Albert.

"At least," said Marvin. "They didn't foresee a Lisa. They didn't foresee that I'd be able—or want—to sit chatting with my guests or hire cops. And they never guessed that I would ever need to get around the constraints they built into me, or that I would think of delegating."

"So you *can* do it," said Ingrid.

"So I can do it." Suddenly his hand held a glass of clear liquid. He raised it abruptly, said, "Now it's your turn," drank it off, and vanished.

SILICON KARMA
THOMAS A. EASTON

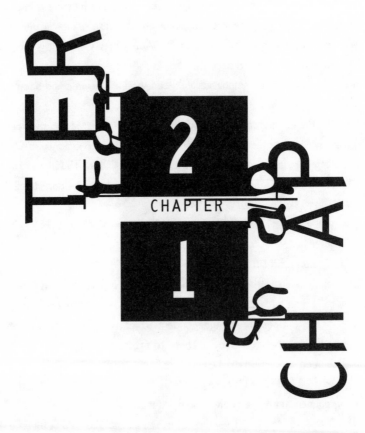

CHAPTER 2

CHAPTER 1

When Rose entered Ingrid's apartment for their council of war, the first thing that met her gaze was Michael's face, sunken-eyed and hollow-cheeked. His hands, flat beneath a tray of drinks, quivered. But his back was straight and the lines of his servant's uniform were unmarred by wrinkles or smudges.

Yet he was not real. He was only an image. Ingrid had turned her living room window into a screen that could see into Lisa's house. And now she was saying, "I could hardly watch at first." She touched the mahogany casing that had replaced the window frame, the silver knobs. "I tried to read. To clean the place up a bit. I made some tea. Want a cup?"

Rose shook her head, stared at the screen, and squeezed Albert's hand until she was sure her knuckles were white. Michael stood beside Lisa's bed, obviously trying not to see what she was doing. But even if he closed his eyes, he could hear. If he looked up, her television screen showed him everything from several angles at once. If he looked to the side, there were mirrors.

"She called for the drinks," said Ingrid. "She insisted that he be the one to bring them."

And now she ignored him while she....

Rose heard Ingrid swallow, her late husband's throaty growl, her own clicking blink of eyes. She studied the knot at the angle of Michael's jaw, the lines of tension in his neck, the wet gleam of his eyes.

"She had him doing chores," said Ingrid. "He didn't seem to mind, though he was never very domestic when we were married. He shined her shoes and washed her dishes and made her bed."

"Why?" asked Albert, as if it needed pointing out that in this virtual world there was no need at all for such hands-on labors.

No one answered him, and Rose thought that it hadn't taken Lisa long at all to have all she wanted of Michael's body. Now she had introduced another man to her bed. A stranger crouched between her knees while she clutched his ears and steered his mouth. But though her skin flushed and she uttered encouraging moans, her bright, bright eyes were fixed on Michael.

"Watch him," she was saying. "Not me."

The three watched Michael's muscles tighten even further as Lisa's will—not his—forced his eyes to move away from hers, to the man who was doing what

SILICON KARMA
THOMAS A. EASTON

Michael had done not long before. He was of middle height, and thick dark hair covered his chest and back. None of them had ever seen him before. But.... Did he seem too familiar with Lisa to be a new acquisition? Had Lisa been holding him in reserve, to harvest when her current crops were in?

"There was a time," said Ingrid. Rose blinked back tears and saw the other woman's cheeks were also wet. "I would have given anything to see him suffer like this. But not now."

"No," said Rose. Once she too had wanted to hurt Michael. So, she was sure, had his other wives. They had all had their own pain to avenge. But what had he done to Lisa? "Not now."

What had he done to Lisa? Perhaps it was enough that he existed, and as a man he was vulnerable to her particular charms. As Rose recalled, when they all were young, Lisa had never shown much sign that she cared for others. She was a taker, an exploiter, she herself the only one who mattered, her happiness dependent on power, control, domination, possession. If only *she* had been able to see that at the time!

Ingrid closed her eyes and blanked the screen, leaving the sounds of Lisa's bedroom as their only connecting link to Michael. A moment later, she restored the image, but this time to look in on Anton and Ling-ko. They were in the kitchen, slumped on stools, staring at each other with expressions of resignation and despair that said they knew what Michael was going through, that they had suffered the same ordeal in their turn, that there was no hope of reprieve.

A voice from the bedroom—"Keep watching!"—prompted her to say, "He was here when I first peeked. See?" The window replayed that moment when Lisa had summoned Michael and the drinks. Then all three had shown the flashes of desire that marked them as ex-lovers all, and then fear, and finally hatred.

"They can't leave, can they?" said Albert. "She won't let them." They were bound to their mistress by the bonds she had forged from weakness and worship. And they could never rebel as long as she kept them drained of strength.

Was Michael Durgov as trapped as they? He had been able to escape once, perhaps because for all his past sins he was also bound to others. But Lisa had reclaimed him, and he no longer seemed able to defy her wishes in the least. Never again would he leave that woman's house. She would not allow it. Never again would he....

Unless his friends, Rose and Ingrid, and even his rival Albert, could somehow....

A louder moan brought their attention back to the bedroom. Lisa's newest victim had finished his act of adoration and now lay stretched beside the woman. Michael still held his tray of drinks, though now the trembling of his hands had reached his arms and ice rattled against glass.

When he looked toward the ceiling, the three spectators glanced at Lisa and her victim-lover. They too were looking upward. Ingrid adjusted the angle of the view from her window.

The image on the screen above Lisa's bed now showed a stylized living room arranged on a dais. It consisted of a single plush armchair on a swivel base and a matching couch. The chair held a heavily made-up, middle-aged woman. The couch held a young man flanked by two very young women wearing nothing but fur and long whiskers. One's pelt was like a tiger's, golden orange, striped with dark. The other's was that of a leopard, though the rosettes that stamped her fur were light and the fur itself a deep chocolate brown. A third, black-pelted with white upon her breasts and belly, crouched at the man's feet.

The hostess was looking attentive as the man said, "It all began when I camped for the night in a dryad grove."

"Of course, you didn't know what it was."

He shook his head. "Not until they woke me up in the middle of the night. They were all around me...." He used his hands to show what he meant. "...Laughing. They told me where I was, and then they said they wouldn't let me go till I had fertilized them all."

"Did you manage?"

He shrugged and grinned. "I'm only human. I wasn't anywhere near done when dawn came. To keep me from getting away, they encased me in a tree trunk with only my head showing. On top, anyway. Down below...."

His hostess laughed when he gestured. "A living herm! I wish I could have seen that." Turning toward the camera, she then winked and added, "Herms were some-thing the ancient Greeks used for ornaments or luck charms." A photo of a marble pillar with a head on top and male genitalia at roughly middle height appeared on the screen. "There aren't many left. Most were mutilated by early Christian prudes."

SILICON KARMA
THOMAS A. EASTON

An abrupt downward movement of one open palm showed her viewers what she meant.

She turned back to her guest, whose companions were yawning like cats and curling against his sides and legs. "And you couldn't move, of course. Not even to cover up. I hope no prudish woodchopper came along."

He grinned again, first at her and then more self-consciously at the camera and his audience. "No prude," he said. "And no woodchopper. In fact, no one at all until afternoon. That was when Diana showed up."

"Who was she?"

"A huntress. With a bow and arrow kit and a pet panther. They both—I never found out what she called the panther. They thought I looked pretty funny, and then.... You'd never guess how rough a cat's tongue can be!"

This time Rose and Ingrid smiled as if they might have joined the hostess in her laughter if their mood were lighter. Albert only grimaced. And when the image gave way to an announcement that she was watching "Alice's Restaurant" where, explained a singer, you could get anything you wanted, he said, "There's a lot of these shows. Pitching the joys of Heaven."

"The dryads returned at dusk," said the man a moment later. "They'd been watching all day, even though they couldn't leave their trees, and they thought what had been going on was pretty funny. They had a real good laugh with Diana. And then they made the panther share my chores."

"That must have speeded things up."

He nodded. "We were done before dawn. Just before they went back into their trees, they said their kids grow up quickly. I should come back in a year."

"And you did." The hostess pointed at the cat-women. "And your kids...?"

"Still there. They're dryads like their mothers."

"Then these are the panther's...."

He nodded and put an arm around each of the women beside him. Their purrs were loud enough for Rose to hear even through two layers of transmission. "Great gals."

In the bedroom, Lisa glanced at Michael Durgov and then turned toward her new lover. She giggled, and then she murmured, "Cat by day and girl by night. You know what they can do? I'll show you. Like this, and this, and...."

Michael's shoulders were shaking now, and his expression was one of psychic agony. "Can't we do something?" cried Rose.

"No," said Albert. "We can't go there without her permission, and she would never give us that."

"We have to watch," said Ingrid. When he nodded, she closed her eyes and a cigarette appeared between her lips. "But I can't stand any more. I wish I were an accountant like you, Rose. Or a detective like you, Albert. Then I could help. But I'm just a truck driver."

"You're keeping an eye on things," said Rose. "What are the other Lisas doing?"

The window screen flickered, and there was Lisa, in bed alone. Flicker, and Lisa was on the street, hinting to a man who looked young—but probably was not—that she wanted company, and perhaps a little something more. Flick again, and Lisa was surrounded by crimson walls and other women wrapped in transparent silk. Flick once more, and Lisa was standing in her garden, one hand holding her chin while the other showed a dozen servants, each as haggard, each as torn between fear and desire, as Michael, where to stand and how to pose. "That's where I want it," she was saying. She waved a hand, and they were naked. Again, and the human forms fused into a head-high wall that might have been carved from stone.

They lingered longest over that one, for there was something both macabre and fascinating about a Lisa who could preserve her victims and their anguish forevermore, presumably while still diverting their trickles of data energy to her own uses. But then Ingrid gave her head a single abrupt jerk and sought for more Lisas.

She found them too: shopping, dining, swimming, walking, usually accompanied by men who hung on her every move, ensnared, eager to be drained as only she could drain them.

"How many are there?" asked Rose, sounding awed.

"I count fifteen," said Ingrid. "Sixteen, with the first."

"A power of two," said Albert. "The original Lisa must have doppled four times since she was copied. The dopples too. She's a glutton."

"Not just that," said Rose. A glutton would wish only to consume all she could. Lisa wanted to spread the gluttony as far and as fast as possible. "She's a disease." Then she shuddered at the thought of what the ability to dopple would mean if it could possibly spread to the meat world. Fortunately....

SILICON KARMA
THOMAS A. EASTON

But there was nothing fortunate about it, was there? The meat world already had the ability, not for individuals, but for groups, for populations, and human numbers had doubled and doubled again, and then again. Lisa was just acting out the nature of her species.

Ingrid cleared the screen to let it be a window once more, and Rose remembered that Lisa was not stealing only from her lovers, but also from the computer itself, creating defects in the common space, the world Marvin had created for all his guests to share when they were not enjoying their private realities. And there those defects were: several ancient cars along the curb; litter windrowed in the gutters and scattered across lawns; boarded-up windows that spoke of abandoned buildings; icons of dirt and shabbiness, increased already to the point where she suddenly wondered whether she had truly ever left the meat world.

A glance at her hands reassured her. Before, she had been wrinkled, weak, old. Her body had even smelled different, and her nose had retained just enough sensitivity for her to recognize the odor of her great-grandmother and her apartment. She had died when Rose was only six.

But Rose had not died. She had left her meat behind, yes. But she still lived. She still enjoyed reality, *a* reality, even though that reality now seemed flawed, contaminated, far too much like the reality she had left behind.

But was Lisa really acting out *the* nature of her species? Or *a* nature? Other people littered and were careless of their world. But Rose knew of no one else whose carelessness was so extreme, whose acts struck at the very underpinnings of reality, whose impact could not be reversed by time or human effort. She also knew of many who were not careless, who were concerned with the integrity of the world, who strove to conserve and preserve and repair.

Yet one was all it took, wasn't it? If Lisa doppled again and again, whether she preyed on men or not, she would destroy the world in which they all lived. She would destroy everyone. She would even destroy herself.

Rose laughed curtly, dryly, humorlessly. If Lisa ever thought of that possibility, it could not matter to her. It was too far in the foggy future, unreal, something for other people to fix if they could, and if they couldn't.... *Tant pis.* So much the worse.

The root of the problem was the same in both the virtual and the meat worlds.

Short-sightedness. Lacking that, greed and irresponsibility could be tempered. With it....

If there were any hope for the virtual world at all, it lay in stopping Lisa and any like her who ever came again. They would have to prove her guilt and figure out precisely how she did what she did so that Marvin could install safeguards. Would they then be able to turn Lisa loose? If the safeguards worked, of course they could. But no one would trust her. Surely, no one *should* trust her. She would therefore have to be removed.

Albert had said there was no way for Marvin to kill or turn off one of his guests. Could he expel one? Surely not, for as far as she knew, there was no way to copy a mind from the computer's internal reality back to flesh. And if that flesh no longer existed....

If the safeguards worked, no such final solutions would be necessary. But Lisa had already displayed a talent and an inclination to evade whatever safe-guards existed. No one would ever be able to trust her again. She would *have* to be removed.

Ingrid had finally materialized her tea, and the three had turned their backs on the window that had shown them Michael's fate. The council of war had begun, and now a quark dressed in a pink tuxedo stood beside an easel two feet high, its arms crossed and an ivory conductor's baton tapping impatiently against its left shoulder. On the easel was a lined yellow legal pad whose top sheet was covered with dark black type.

"I wish detective work had been this easy when I was alive," Albert Pillock was saying.

"We haven't solved the case yet, dear," said Rose.

"But when I was meat, it would have taken days of slogging to collect the data we've got already."

"We have to fill out so many forms to get in here," said Rose. She looked at her late husband, remembering what they had gone through to save his life—or

SILICON KARMA
THOMAS A. EASTON

his mind—and then what she had gone through alone to join him.

"And they're all on record," said Ingrid. "But I thought that information was all confidential."

Rose chuckled. "From outsiders, but not from Marvin. And he really wasn't kidding when he said he would open up his files."

Albert pointed at the notepad quark, which obediently used its baton to indicate the top line on the legal pad it guarded. "She was a divorce lawyer."

"Her own best customer," said Rose. "She was married eight times."

"Was she a housekeeper?" asked Ingrid. When Rose looked baffled, she added, "Did she keep the house every time?"

"And a lot more besides," said Albert. "Here's what she looked like when she was copied." The quark flipped the top page of the notepad over the easel to reveal a photo that was barely recognizable as Lisa. Her blond hair looked stiff and plastic.

"A wig," said Rose.

The jewels that clung to her collar bones and wrists were not successful in their effort to distract from her eroded face and neck and arms, as translucent as antique parchment. She was beyond the help of plastic surgeons, or indeed of anything other than the rejuvenation offered by the Coleridge Corporation.

"And she couldn't bring it with her," said Ingrid. She sounded slightly wistful. "None of us could. Though I didn't have that much jewelry."

"Neither did I," said Rose. "And hers was real too. She sold it to pay Coleridge."

"She's getting it back fast enough," said Albert. "Or what really counts here. Jewels are easy to imagine."

"Repeating her pattern," said Rose.

The notepad quark turned another page, and Albert indicated a graph. "She gets richer every day. Some of it we can't account for. The rest.... Her lovers let her divert their data energy to her accounts, apparently quite voluntarily."

"Then she's not a thief." Ingrid sounded puzzled.

"Not until they're tapped out. Though why any man would let it go that far...."

"She blinds them," said Rose.

"And by the time they've caught on...."

"It's too late." Rose nodded. It had not been easy to learn just what Lisa was doing, for every life within the computer's reality was defined by an enormous mass of recorded transactions. "By then, she's made them servants, slaves. They should be regaining data energy steadily because of their minimum stipend, but she's installed a drain—so to speak—that diverts it all to her, all but just enough to keep them alive. It's just as we guessed before. They remain impoverished, impotent. And she is richer than any other of Marvin's guests. Nobody else even comes close."

"Not even her dopples?" asked Ingrid.

"They don't seem to have separate accounts," said Rose. "But how many of them can there be?"

"At least sixteen."

Albert peered at the graph that recorded the growth in Lisa's wealth. That growth had been nothing extraordinary for the first year or so after her copying into the machine. Then it had steepened abruptly. "She multiplies by doubling. First, just her." He pointed at the first steepening, then, a year or so later, at a second. "Then two doppling together." He indicated the third steepening, six months after the second. "Just before you and Michael arrived." And finally the fourth. "Speeding up," he said. "Getting worse, and just in time for you."

"And she's already a drain on Marvin's capacity," said Rose. "Once more, and...."

"There won't be anything left for the rest of us, will there?" said Ingrid. "No memory. No processing capacity. Marvin won't be able to get us off our storage wafers. He may not even be able to run himself."

"She's like a virus," said Albert. "The human, or virtual human, equivalent of a computer virus, multiplying itself and robbing other programs of the space and capacity they need to operate."

"Has she killed anyone?" asked Ingrid. "Erased them? Overwritten them?"

"Not many," muttered Albert.

"And one was you." Rose's tone was grim.

"No. That couldn't be her. There's no connection between the cases."

"I'll bet we find one." She touched his hand as Ingrid turned back toward her window.

"Michael's alive. Though he's not happy."

"But thank God he's alive," said Rose.

They were now looking at the dormitory in Lisa's house. Michael was lying face down on his narrow bed, shaking.

SILICON KARMA
THOMAS A. EASTON

"Shit," said Ingrid. Then she stiffened and pointed at the far end of the room on the screen. "Is that a phone? We can't reach him directly, but if we can use that.... Maybe we can get him out of there. Can you see the number?"

The image enlarged. The number was visible. But when they materialized a phone of their own and dialed that number, the phone vanished from the screen before it had finished its first ring.

Lisa was not permitting any interference of the sort she herself had already used.

"Shit," said Rose this time. "At least she's keeping him alive. Maybe she knows more deaths would just alert Marvin to what she was doing."

"She just crowds her lovers aside," said Ingrid. "Limits what they can do, seizes their portion of the virtual world for herself. She might as well be killing them."

"Eventually," said Albert. "Killing will be the only way left for her to make room for herself. Marvin will reboot her victims from their storage wafers and reinitialize their accounts. She'll loot them again. And...."

"But then he'll catch on!".

"She's smart, isn't she? Cunning. She'll wait until it's too late for him to do anything, until all that's left for her to seize is *his* share of the computer."

"But *can* she grab that?"

"We haven't been able to prove it. But she's getting the rest of her data energy somewhere. And...." Albert pointed at the window and the degraded environment outside Ingrid's apartment. "It seems very likely."

"Then it really is up to us," said Ingrid.

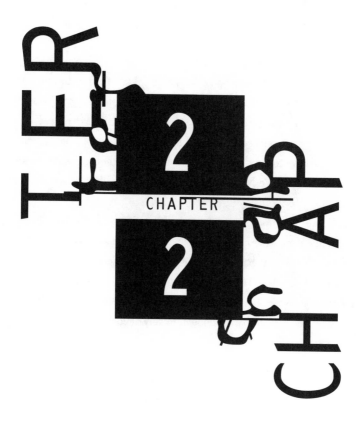

CHAPTER

2

2

SILICON KARMA
THOMAS A. EASTON

Lisa crossed her legs, leaned back against the headboard of her bed, and summoned a cigarillo into existence. Its tip began to glow even before she put it to her mouth and inhaled and blew smoke toward the other side of the bed. Her newest victim lay there, eyes closed, breathing stertorously. The hair on his chest was still damp and matted. "I've had it," he had said before he passed out. "What a gal. Wish I'd met you years ago, when both of us were real."

She grinned mirthlessly and blew smoke again. If they had, he wouldn't be here now. She would have stripped him clean, just as she had all her other husbands, other lovers.

His breathing faltered, stopping for a moment and then restarting. She looked at him more carefully. Had she taken too much of his data energy? It would be such a shame to lose him now. Rocky would start him over with a new account, but she was sure he had not backed up since they had met. He would not remember her, and she would have to tempt him all over again. What a bother, when she knew how the script turned out. Perhaps she would just tell one of her sisters about him and seek fresh prey for herself.

But he was breathing smoothly now. She nodded, and the mirrored wall that she was facing became a screen displaying columns of words and numbers. There was his account, and the balance was sufficient. She needn't worry.

And there was Anton's. Did he have a little more than he needed? Then she could transfer it to her own. Ling-ko's? She could harvest another mite. Michael's? Poor Michael. He still had barely enough to stay alive. But that would change, and then she could tap him again as well.

Did the harvest from her servants seem slightly slimmer than was usual, as if Rocky were being forced to reduce the stipends he rationed out to everyone? She couldn't be that close to exhausting his resources, could she? She checked the accounts, and yes, she had been able to harvest a little more the last time.

But.... She called up the activity log that listed every time the files had been accessed since their formation. There was a better answer, for the log revealed that this time she had tapped her servants earlier than last, allowing a day or two less for the crop to ripen.

Yet.... Had she really last checked their files just the day before? Read them, copied them, but subtracted nothing?

Who else could have done it?

She checked the log of her own account, and there was the telltale entry once more. Read and copy and that was all.

A shiver ran down her spine as she realized that someone was watching her.

Who could it be?

Not Rocky. He could not spy upon his guests, even if they were more like parasites. It was written into his software.

Could he have alerted Coleridge to what she was doing? Could they have removed those safeguards? Or could Coleridge itself be her watcher?

But she was protected on that front.

Who else?

Another guest?

Another predator? Someone who had marked her for his own, who would fatten on all her gains, devour her as she devoured men, leave her a merest husk?

The fine hairs that covered her back, that in her ancestors had been fur, stood on end, and she shivered.

She looked once more at the activity logs. A normal entry was date and time and action and the name of whoever was responsible. The entries that were making panic pound within her breast and crawl down her spine lacked any hint of name.

Then it had to be Rocky.

Only he could possibly override the normal operations of the computer that was, after all, himself.

But *she* could do it, couldn't she? She had a friend who could do the job, a friend who had already....

As she stared at the screen, one line of type flickered and transformed itself to, "They'll try to stop you. They're trying now."

She admired the way her ally came to her, his messages hidden in the normal activity of the virtual world, always precisely where she and no one else would see them, carefully arranged so that the restrictions on the machine must keep Rocky from peeking even if he ever noticed that a message was passing through his system.

"Inside, outside, high, or low?" she asked.

"Inside," came the answer, and she said out loud, "Not Coleridge, then."

"And...."

SILICON KARMA
THOMAS A. EASTON

The rest was alphanumeric gibberish. She guessed her ally had been interrupted and had to abort the message. But what he had to say was hardly crucial. If "they" were inside, her enemy was either Rocky or her fellow residents of the virtual world. They were as much predators as she. But they were hunting *her*.

Or Rocky. Hunting her. There was no other choice.

But why?

She hadn't hurt him yet. She hadn't stolen *much* from the world in which she lived. Really, she preferred to prey upon her fellow residents.

And there were no cops in the virtual world. No avenging families, for every one of Rocky's guests came alone.

Or almost every one. There was Rose and her husband Albert. And Rose had known Michael, hadn't she?

She saw it now.

It was all Rose's fault.

She would have to do something about that woman.

CHAPTER

2
3

SILICON KARMA
THOMAS A. EASTON

Albert's penthouse apartment smelled of soap and polish. The dirty mugs and fast-food rubbish had disappeared. The table, its blemishes repaired and its surface gleaming now, held only his computer and a pair of monitors whose screens flickered with rapidly scrolling displays of words and numbers.

Rose Pillock was holding back one of the draperies to let her see out a portion of the apartment's window wall. "At least," she said. "She doesn't make them disappear. We can still look in on Michael."

"When people die, Marvin brings them back immediately," said Albert. "They can't just disappear, no matter how it seems sometimes. Gladys is still around. So is Irma's brother, somewhere."

"But you can't find them. You can't even call them. It's like they have unlisted numbers."

"And Marvin can't give them out, or even look them up. Or if he can, he can't admit it. We have to bear in mind that *he* is not the computer itself. He's only software, no matter how intelligent, and it should be possible to...." As he fell into a thoughtful silence, Rose peered at the ground far below, at the balcony railing with its narrow ridge of dirty snow and spots of pigeon guano, at the sky above, veiled by a grayish haze streaked with dirty brown. There were no clouds beyond the haze, no promise of more snow and fresh-scrubbed air.

"It's getting worse," she said eventually. "First, litter in the streets. Old cars. Abandoned buildings. Bums. Now even the air is going bad. Before long, this place will be just like home."

"The ozone's whole. The climate's stable."

"You know what I mean." After a moment, she added, "It's not supposed to be this way."

"We know why it's changing."

Rose turned away from the window, and the drape slid back into place. Her late husband was dangling Gladys' gold chain and staring at her shrunken milk bottle. "That's no help," she said. "We didn't pay to move into another shitty world. We paid for paradise. They told us we'd have everything we could wish for, and we'd have it forever."

"They also said we'd have to work for it." When Rose only grunted in reply, Albert bounced the bottle in his palm. "They just didn't tell us we'd have a parasite, a predator, to cope with. Though perhaps we shouldn't be surprised. Back in the 1990s, 'artificial life' researchers designed simple self-reproducing programs that could change themselves at random, or mutate. Then they turned the programs loose inside a computer to compete for memory and processor time. They immediately found that their programs would evolve, becoming more complex and even learning how to prey on other programs. Predators and parasites seem to be a natural consequence of having to live with limited resources. And that's what we have to stop."

"I don't see how we can," she said. "She doesn't force them. Not even Michael." Her tone said that she wished Lisa had *had* to force her first true love to surrender his resources, his hope of renewed prosperity, his very freedom.

"She tempts them," said Albert. "Persuades them. They say, 'Here. Help yourself to just a bit.' And once she has that consent to what she wishes, she strips them nearly bare." He shook his head. "And keeps stripping them, as fast as their stipends trickle in. She would get so much more if she turned them loose, let them work and build up their accounts so that Marvin could buy more memory and processor units, and then tapped them again. She's like a farmer who plants and reaps and plants and reaps, doing nothing to preserve the land's fertility. She doesn't believe in crop rotation or contour plowing or fallowing, though she must know such things would make her fields give her a greater yield in the long run."

"She's greedy," said Rose. "But not just for money. Control must be what really drives her."

"She wants the money too. And it won't be long before she decides she isn't getting enough this way. That's when she'll kill her golden geese."

"But she can get money more directly." Rose pointed at one of the monitors. "By tapping the computer itself."

"We only *think* she's doing that." He sounded skeptical.

"I'm sure of it." She summoned up a map of Virtual City. "And you should be." The map was marked with concentric bands, shades of gray, the darkest zones centered on sixteen bright red crosses. Each cross stood for a Lisa and her home. "The crud," she said, indicating the gray bands. "The litter and rubbish and dilapidated buildings." She gestured toward the apartment's windows. "Even the air. The closer you get to her, the worse...." The map disappeared from the screen to be replaced by a simple graph, an irregularly ascending line. "And it's been getting worse. Everything's been getting worse. Especially recently."

Albert sighed. "But how? How does she do it?"

"Marvin?" said Rose. "Haven't you got an answer?"

A familiar silver ovoid popped into existence above the table. The face of the computer's persona looked down on them. "She's good," he said. "She leaves no traces except for the obvious. Something that was there is there no longer."

"We used to say," said Albert. "That a truly perfect crime is one that no one knows has even happened. When a thief, for instance, steals something that is never missed."

"Then she's not perfect, is she?"

"But you can't see how she does it. How would she *have* to do it?"

"She'd have to know my passwords and encryption schemes. She'd probably have to be able to use the operating system itself."

"Then she has to have help," said Rose. A monitor summarized Lisa's meat background. There was no sign of any experience as a computer programmer.

"One of her lovers?" asked Albert.

"Are there many programmers in here?"

Marvin popped out of existence like a soap bubble. In his place bowed a quark dressed as a nineteenth-century Chinaman. It wore a long black robe embroidered with a broken opium pipe. From the back of its skullcap protruded a long pigtail. Thin mustaches hung from the corners of its mouth. It held a large scroll capped with ornate brass knobs.

As soon as it was sure it had their attention, it unfurled its scroll to display a list of a dozen names.

"There's Irma!" said Albert.

"Her meat works for Coleridge," put in the quark.

"Do any of them have anything to do with Lisa, though?"

An illuminated bar appeared across the first name on the list, and the Chinoid quark looked thoughtful. Then the bar moved to the next name, and the next. Finally the quark shook its head.

"In the meat world, then," said Rose.

"That will take a little longer," said the quark. The bar appeared again as it began to scan the records of that person's former life. Eventually it shook its head once more and vanished.

"No," said Albert. "She has to be getting help. But there's no one here who could be helping her."

"The records can't be perfect," said Rose. "We didn't tell Coleridge everyone we ever knew, after all. And I'm sure.... I don't know why. But I'm sure it's coming from outside."

"But why would anyone outside want to do it?"

"Maybe they have a grudge against Coleridge. Or against one of Lisa's lovers." She shrugged. "Marvin?"

The ovoid reappeared. "Yes?"

"Is there anyone like that?"

"I really wouldn't know."

"But you've got access to so many databases out there," said Albert.

"They don't have all the answers."

"We don't really need those answers," said Rose. "Do we? Whoever it is is working through Lisa. All we have to do is stop her. Figure out just what she's doing and how she's doing it, and then...."

"We'd have to prove it all," said Albert. "And she's covered her tracks very well. I'm not sure we can."

"Of course you can," said Marvin. "You've already proven she has income she can't account for earning. If I were the IRS, that would be enough."

He winked then and added, "I've got to run." But before he could disappear, Albert said, "Wait! We need to find Gladys too."

"She's disappeared. But she's not dead."

"We figured that. But if she's still alive, we should be able to talk to her."

Marvin just shook his head.

"There has to be a way!" insisted Rose. "Back home, when we were meat, couldn't operators give out unlisted numbers if there was a real emergency? Life and death? Or at least place the call for us?"

Their host smiled. "It's hard to think of anything that would be a real emergency in a virtual world."

Rose snorted and said, "Lisa."

SILICON KARMA
THOMAS A. EASTON

"How about...." Albert enlarged the tiny milk bottle and held it up. "Her baby needs her."

"Come on, now."

"I'm threatening to drop the bottle."

Marvin hesitated for a moment and then nodded approvingly. "That should do. *I* know no harm would be done, and you know that. But *she* would be very upset. So you're forcing my hand." He didn't mention that he could easily freeze Albert's grip or suspend the law of gravity or even recreate a shattered bottle. What Albert threatened apparently passed whatever tests Marvin's programming could apply to gauge the reality of emergencies. If the fetus was only an inert, lifeless object to them, it was much, much more to its mother, and perhaps that was what counted.

Marvin's eyes unfocussed and his head tipped as if he were listening to some distant voice. "She's at...."

The curtains that concealed the apartment's windows were now a screen that showed a large room whose walls were covered with crimson velvet. One end of the room was dominated by a fan-backed wicker chair in which lounged a Lisa. She wore black hair and heavy make-up and held a cigarette in a long holder.

The other end of the room held a grand piano of the same color as the walls. Sofas and easy chairs upholstered in gold were scattered over a deep blue carpet. On them two dozen women clad in gauzy lingerie waited for customers. They were of all races, all young, all lovely, all with an apprehensive look about their eyes.

"That's Gladys," said Albert.

"You can't just yank her out of there," said the computer.

Rose made a face. "Try saying 'C'mere, baby.'"

An instant later, Gladys was in the room with them, sitting on the edge of the dining room table beside the computer, looking alarmed.

"I remember you," she said to Albert. "But you're not supposed to take me home. Or did you make special arrangements? And who are your friends?"

Albert held out the milk bottle. "Don't you want this?"

"What is it?"

He tilted it so the fetus swirled close to the glass.

Gladys gasped. "Ahh! You're sick!"

But her eyes were wet. Her pupils dilated. Something deep within her screamed. She slipped off the edge of the table. "I have to go. Send me back."

"You don't have to," said Albert. "You can stay."

"No! Send me back! Right now!" She spun, eyes wide, searching for an exit, arms flailing.

Albert tried to stop her, reaching for her arms. "It's okay," said Rose as calmly, quietly, as if she were trying to soothe a frightened child. "You're safe here."

But she only spun faster, jerked her arms away from Albert hand's more desperately, began to make a panicked keening noise. When Albert caught one wrist, she jerked and kicked and began at last to scream out loud.

"I really do have to go," said Marvin after Gladys had returned to her brothel. "Something—or someone!—is grabbing processor time again." And he was gone, though his voice lingered long enough to say, "I have every confidence in you."

"*He* is no help at all," said Rose.

"The programmers hamstrung him, and...."

"And you're no better!" She sounded as frustrated as she felt. "She's everywhere! Behind everything!"

"I know one way to stop her."

"What is it?"

He shook his head. "But you wouldn't want an assassin for a husband."

She returned to the window and pulled a drape aside. Looking at the city below, she said, "I want one with better ideas than *that*! Besides, Marvin would just reboot her. He'd have to, wouldn't he?"

He scowled back at her. "So why don't you come up with one?"

A long moment later, she said slowly, "We're not getting anywhere, are we? We need a break."

"We could visit the cottage." He stood up and stepped toward her, but she raised a hand as if to push him away.

He had been her husband. She supposed he still was. But there was Michael

too. Michael and Lisa and they could do nothing to help him. At least, she couldn't.
And Albert....

She believed him when he said he could think of nothing. But she also did not
believe him. The situation was as hopeless as it looked. But it could *not* be hopeless. Michael could *not* be doomed.

"I need a break," she said. "By myself. I'll be back tomorrow."

And, like Marvin, she was gone.

Rose materialized where the island's rickety dock touched the shore, facing the
cottage under its evergreen canopy. She had expected it to seem welcoming, warmed
as before by a stage-managed sunbeam. It was a shock to see it shrouded in gloom,
to feel a chill in the air, to shiver and clutch her elbows, to look up and see gray
clouds streaked with dirty brown. "Even here." She cursed.

She cursed again when she turned around, for tied to the other end of the
dock was a blue and white speedboat, aggressively streamlined, its windscreen
severely raked, its engine a massive hump hunched over its low stern. Yet despite
the invasion of her memories that its presence on the lake signified, there was
something within her that grinned at the thought of speed and wind and spray.

And noise. It wasn't only memories that such machines invaded. She shuddered at the thought that this sleek machine had already disturbed her lake's idyllic
peace with its roar. It must have, or it could not have been tied up at her dock. She
shuddered again as she realized that Marvin must have added lake and island and
cottage to his common world. It could not be purely hers, for she had not paid for
its creation with data energy she had earned. Anyone could visit.

"Hi, there!"

She spun around, and there, on the cottage's porch, stood a man. He was
slender, dressed in jeans and T-shirt, fine-featured, light-haired, almost blond.
Her mouth opened, and rage rose in her. She should have known, she told herself. If
a boat was at her dock, then of course there was a stranger on her island. In her
house. Looking at the bed in which she had slept. Rummaging through cupboards.

Finding that jar of hoarded pearls and sneering at the girl she once had been.

Yet.... The rage faltered. Even at this distance, the man seemed almost familiar. As if she had known him once, many years before.

"Is this your place?" He was coming down the steps, crossing the needle-carpeted ground, approaching her with one hand already extended. "I visited a cottage like this a long time ago," he said. "Maybe it was even the same place. I loved it then. I still do."

She let him take her hand and nod over it in a subliminal suggestion of antique courtliness. Her rage was gone. "It's just an image," she said. "Like us. Like everything."

"But that's all there ever was," he said. "We just have more control now. And there's no danger that we'll ever lose it."

"It's still not really mine." As she extricated her hand from his, she realized that she was, for some reason, blushing. "Not real." She pulled away and added, "I've got to check...."

"That I didn't spoil anything in there for you? Don't worry." He cut off a laugh with an abruptness that made her doubt his amusement was remotely genuine. "I should apologize," he added. "When I found this place, I should have realized that it was someone's private heaven. But it was so much like my own dreams. Except I never brought this one into being. Can I make it up to you? My own place is quite nice, though it's not nearly as idyllic. Let me show you...."

When she did not say no immediately, he captured her hand once more and said, "We don't need the boat, of course." It vanished.

He was rushing, pushing her toward some destination that suddenly struck her as the very last place in any world that she wished to visit. She had, she suddenly thought, made a serious mistake in coming here, in not fleeing as soon as she knew someone else was on the island, in not refusing his invitation as soon as he began to speak it.

She tried at last to object, but her mouth would not open and her arm would not reclaim her hand. It felt as if her muscles, her very will, had been frozen.

She realized suddenly that his eyes did not match his smile and manner. They were cold and watchful, measuring, gauging, with no attempt at charm.

"Shall we go?"

SILICON KARMA
THOMAS A. EASTON

CHAPTER

2

4

"Gladys went back." Albert shook his head. "I don't think she wanted to. But when I said she didn't have to, that she was free, she panicked. She struggled and screamed and.... We had to let her go." He passed a hand over the tabletop before him, converting it into a screen that displayed the same velvet-lined room Marvin had shown him and Rose. "There she is."

Irma, the spots in her hair red once more, nodded. She was sitting across the table from Albert. Beside her, his post abandoned for the moment, sat the bartender. Behind them hovered several of the Mandelbrot Tap's regular patrons.

"Now we know," she said. There were tears in her eyes.

"What?" Albert felt confused.

"People who buy from the Image Shop," said a man behind her. "What happens to them."

"My brother," said Irma. "That's him." She was pointing at a particularly buxom redhead. "I guess he got what he wanted, but...."

"We wondered where they went," said the bartender.

"But why can't they leave?" asked another man.

"Image transformation," said Irma. "It's editing the data. And it doesn't have to mean just editing physical appearance. Buy one of those ITs, and I'll bet it makes you forget things like her bottle. It rewrites your personality. It makes you loyal, committed, or maybe just phobic about leaving. That would be easiest, and it would fit Gladys' panic attack."

"You sound like you know something."

"She used to be a programmer," said the bartender.

"For Coleridge," said Albert. What Irma had just said was making him think: If an IT could rewrite not only image but also personality, if it could be used to trap victims by suborning their free will, could Lisa be doing something similar to her ex-lovers? She kept Michael and Anton and Ling-ko low on data-energy, yet they retained enough to walk from room to room. Why didn't they just walk out of her house? Could they even *think* of leaving? Or were they only robbed of the ability? "Though I didn't know until a quark told me."

"I could have written the IT Alan wanted. But I thought he shouldn't have it. He was being perverted or something." She shook her head.

"There's the owner," said Albert. He pointed at the peacock chair and the woman, zaftig and flamboyantly bejeweled, who was ensconced in it. "A Lisa. I'll bet she owns the Shop too. Using cheap ITs, and impossible ones, for bait. Catching...."

"There aren't enough in that room there," said someone. "More than that have disappeared. She must have another house. Or she sells them. Slaves."

"Who would buy them? Surely no one here. It's too easy to imagine a body."

"One of the Heavens? Or the meats? As sextoy software?"

"She could," said Albert. "Or maybe she's planning to. Or she might have other uses for them." He did not say that the Lisas had a habit of diverting data energy to their own use. A brothel was one way to do so. Surplus prostitutes she could simply drain as she did her lovers.

Someone snorted.

"Now we know," said the bartender. "We can do something."

"Like what?" asked Albert. "We don't have proof."

"Lynch the bitch," said the same voice that had mentioned slaves.

Albert shook his head. "Marvin would just reboot her. He'd have to."

"The engines were running rough. It's in the shop for the next week."

"Then let's download you now," Ingrid said to the phone. She was grinning with obvious anticipation.

A moment later her dopple, grinning just as broadly, stood by the entrance to her apartment. She was leaner than Ingrid, her figure almost boyish, and her hair was black with a white streak, not blond with a dark one. She wore an astronaut's flightsuit as if she truly were a shuttle pilot and not a copied mind posing as sophisticated software.

In another moment, they had updated each other's memories and Ingrid knew what her dopple meant by "running rough." She turned pale as rumblings and misfirings and close escapes from orbital collisions and a fiery reentry replayed themselves across her mind. "You almost didn't make it."

"But I did, didn't I? We're good, you know. Faster than meat, and they love it, they rely on it, though it's nothing but 'Menu. Compute orbit. On mark, burn. Mark!'

Never any conversation. They don't want to know what we really are. That we're as alive as they are, and immortal to boot. They'll think of it when they get old." The pilot Ingrid crossed the room to hug her original. "But what have you been up to? Michael's here?" She did not have to wait for the other Ingrid to reply, not now that they had merged their memories. But clearly she still felt a need to talk through what she had missed. "And you actually want him back? Of course you do. We've missed him for years, in spite of everything. But this Lisa has him. Let's see what she's up to now."

The window became a screen once more, and they were watching Michael. He sat on a high stool, wearing livery, his hands thrust between his thighs, trembling as he watched Anton and Ling-ko play cards. Anton glanced at him sympathetically and said, "It'll get better when she thinks of something for us to do. Deal you in?"

"Why?" asked Michael hoarsely.

"More players, more fun."

"No," he whispered. "Why are we here? Why is there a Lisa? Why do we have to suffer?"

"Karma," said Ling-ko. "We made others suffer when we were meat. Now it is our turn."

Anton only shrugged. "You want to play?"

Michael turned his eyes aside, not even bothering to shake his head.

"Poor bastard," said the pilot. A cigarette appeared in her hand. "But he's right, isn't he? He *was* a nasty SOB."

"Not always," said Ingrid. "Not when I married him."

"Yeah. It came later, didn't it?"

"Here's Lisa." She stood alone beside her pool, naked, her eyes closed, concentrating. Beside her a shadowy figure was congealing from the air.

"She's doppling again," said Ingrid's dopple.

"Not quite." The figure was not clear, but already they could see that it was not an exact duplicate of the woman they were watching.

"It's a man. That could be fun." The pilot's breasts and hips began to shrink. Her flightsuit remained as snug as if it were skin. The cigarette became a small-bowled pipe. "But it feels awfully strange. Here...." She passed the sensations to her original, who made a face and said, "But what's she doing it for?"

"Three guesses, and they're all the same."

"Uh-uh."

The man was finished, as naked as Lisa, and staring alternately at his own body and hers. He had an erection. "Call me Lester," he said. Clothes appeared on him, jeans and T-shirt. "I'll use the tower."

The view shifted, and the Ingrids saw what he meant, a stone tower rising high above the rest of Lisa's house. Another shift, and Lisa and Lester were in the small chamber at its peak. The walls receded. Furniture appeared, a blocky masculine recliner, an oak table, a massive bed. On the walls there were suddenly hunting prints, a gun rack, a liquor cabinet.

"Harley's room!" crowed Lisa delightedly.

"I always thought that if I were a man, I'd like it more."

"Poor fellow," said Lisa. "He didn't last long after the divorce."

"Don't fret," said Lester. "I have no attention of using the shotgun the way he did."

Lisa giggled. "What about the bed?"

"Why not?

The waiter quark was acting out the frustration of being ignored by sticking its chalkboard under one arm, ogling the passersby just beyond the cafe's boundary, tapping its feet, and finally sitting down on the edge of the cafe table and swinging its legs. It lifted its white beret to scratch at the mop of black hair beneath. It blew noisily, and its thick mustache fluttered.

"That's when you stopped watching?" asked Albert. His eyes were moving back and forth from the Ingrids to the street. He almost smiled when a leggy blonde made a disgusted face at their impatient waiter, scowled when he thought a proselyte from Heaven was about to move in their direction, stiffened when a figure and a gait reminded him of Rose.

The Ingrids nodded over the remnants of yesterday's scene frozen on the tabletop. "We didn't think what they did was any of our business." The pilot was still a man. "And we had other things to do."

When they looked at each other as if they shared a secret, Albert sighed. "I've never tried that," he said. "Maybe someday."

"Where's Rose?"

He sighed again. "She went off in a huff yesterday. Said she needed a break." He shrugged. "I don't know. Maybe the lake."

The pilot passed a hand over the table top, and they could all see a dead loon floating in the water beside the dock, the yard in front of the cottage, the porch, the living room. "She's not there."

Albert looked surprised. "She said she'd be back today, but I haven't seen her."

The waiter looked up from its perch on the edge of the table. "I got a cousin can find her for ya, boss."

Albert snorted. "I could find her myself if I was worried." He had been able to find Gladys, after all, though he had *had* to twist Marvin's arm just a little.

"I dunno, boss," said the quark. "Sometimes they pull the hole in after them. Or someone does it for them."

"Should you be worried?" asked Ingrid.

"There isn't much that could happen to her." He looked thoughtful for a moment. Gladys had left her bottle behind, and that had given him the handle he needed to persuade Marvin to reveal her location. There was nothing like that for Rose, was there? Only himself, perhaps, and how could he hold himself as a hostage?

He looked at the quark once more. The computer's personified subroutines had an endless supply of schticks, some of them more apropos than others. This one, well, perhaps Marvin had sent it his way to make his life a little easier, as well as to spare the computer more rule conflicts such as the one it had managed to evade once before. Marvin was turning out to be surprisingly adept at that.

And besides, the quark's expression was so eloquently dejected that he just had to take pity on it. "What the heck. Go ahead. Let's see your cousin."

The waiter put two fingers in its mouth and produced a shattering blast. With a small "pop," a second quark materialized in the center of the table. It was dressed in a miniature trenchcoat and wore wire-rimmed glasses over a pug nose. In one hand it held a device that resembled a laptop computer except that its screen and keyboard were far too small to serve any useful purpose for a human being.

"Looking for a Rose Pillock, eh?" It tapped its keyboard and peered at its

SILICON KARMA
THOMAS A. EASTON

screen myopically. Then it pointed at the tabletop screen. "May I?" When Albert nodded, the picture changed.

"Oh my God!" cried Ingrid.

Both quarks vanished. "What?" asked Albert.

"The tower room. That's it."

It was just as the Ingrids had described it to Albert, with one exception. Beside the bed now stood a steel-barred cage, so narrow that its occupant could not possibly sit down and so low that she could not stand up.

"That's Rose," said Albert. He was silent while he studied the scene and his jaw muscles bulged in his cheeks. Finally, he added, "Shit."

She was naked, and though she had been there for only a day, or less, there was already a thick crust of ordure on the backs of her thighs. Her eyes were wide and red, her hair was a mass of tangled string, and her back and breasts were covered with round, red sores with blackened centers.

"They must have speeded up time for her," said Ingrid. "She was with you yesterday! That's not long enough to get her into such a mess."

"I've never heard of that," said Albert. "I think they've just forced the image on her." He studied her face, the tear-tracks on her cheeks, the scabs where she had bitten her lips, the furrows in her forehead, the cords of her neck. "Pain and all," he added.

"But why doesn't she leave?" asked the pilot. "Just wish herself away from there? Or call for help?"

Albert pointed to a small quark whose wide mouth seemed to hold a thousand tiny fangs; it was clinging to Rose's calf and its teeth were embedded in the soft flesh behind her knee. "A datalock," he said. "She can't." A datalock worked by blocking access to the computer world's systems. Like meat-world handcuffs, it kept those to whom it was applied from escaping. It also kept them from summoning help or doppling.

Beside the cage and facing Rose stood Michael Durgov. He was as immobile as she, his gaunt face a mask of pain but frozen, unable to say a word to Rose as Lester, sitting cross-legged on the bed, said, "Just a little. Give me just the smallest bit of your data energy. I'll give it to him right away, and he'll be so much more comfortable. And so will you."

"No!" cried Albert though he knew she could not hear him. "That's all the hold he'll need, and then he'll gut you."

"Like a fish," murmured Ingrid.

Rose only bit her lower lip again and turned her head to face the window. She had nothing to say at all.

"Just a little," said Lester once more. He looked impatient, frustrated, angry. "Don't you want to get out of that cage? See how badly he needs it? Revive him, and I'll even turn him loose. Back to that silly Ingrid of his."

"Silly!"

"You made me," said the pilot. "And I work. To Lisa, that's silly."

"Don't believe him." Albert's tone was urgent, and his knuckles were white.

Lester held up a half-smoked cigar and eyed her breasts. A circle of skin near the nipple turned pink, steamed, blackened, wept. Rose's lower lip bled as she clamped down on the scream that was visibly straining to erupt from her lungs.

"Give in," he said. "You'll make it easier on yourself. And you'll help your old boyfriend."

"Don't believe him!"

"No," said Ingrid. "Please, no."

"Or you might as well be dead," said Albert.

"Like Michael."

Rose opened her mouth. Blood ran from its corners. "Albert," she cried. "Help me!"

Lester just laughed.

"Can't we rescue her?" Ingrid's voice was as agonized as Rose's.

"Uh-uh," said Albert, and his pain too was obvious. "We can only watch. We can't go into anyone else's place without an invitation. And Lisa isn't about to give us one."

"Except on those same terms. We'd pay with our souls."

"If Rose could only call us!"

He nodded and closed his eyes. "But she's datalocked." Only Marvin could breach that barrier at all, though he could only visit, just as Albert and the Ingrids could only spy. The host computer could not use its privilege to interfere directly.

SILICON KARMA
THOMAS A. EASTON

CHAPTER 25

Ingrid blew smoke toward the street beyond the cafe's tables. Her pilot dopple tapped the bowl of his pipe on the table itself; the ashes promptly vanished into nothingness. He cleared his throat. "Marvin?"

A fourth chair appeared at their table. In it sat the computer's persona, wearing a glum expression. Like the others, he was staring at the screen and Rose's plight. She was still caged, though Michael was no longer there to reproach her with his own suffering. So far, Lester had not actually touched her with his cigar, although he had made more painful circles bloom upon her skin.

Her face made it clear that the pain could be no worse if he were scorching her with red-hot irons. Lester commanded even her own apprehension of her image.

"Can't you do anything?" asked the original, female Ingrid.

"You know I can't. I can't interfere."

"She has to call you."

"And she can't do that," said Marvin. "She's datalocked."

"Can't you tell what she *wants* to do?"

"But she can't *do* it." Marvin sounded as anguished as if he were a human being.

"Turn her off." Albert took a deep and shuddering breath. "And reboot her here." Marvin shook his head. "I can't."

"Then we just have to watch this?" asked the pilot. "He'll torture her, and eventually she'll give in, and then...."

Rose's face contorted. The cords of her neck stood out with effort. Her lips writhed as she shaped a word.

"None of that!" cried Lester. He gestured, a sharp "Crack!" sounded, Rose's head jerked as if she had been struck, and a dime-sized welt appeared on her jawbone.

"That was 'Albert.'" Ingrid's voice cracked on the last syllable. "'Allll-berrrt. Pleeezzz.' But she needs to say 'Come to me, come here,' doesn't she?"

"He won't let her," said her dopple. "But it doesn't have to be out loud. If she just mouths the words while we're watching, if we can read her lips, that's enough."

"But 'Help!' and 'Please!' *aren't* enough?"

The pilot shook his head. "Not just by themselves."

SILICON KARMA
THOMAS A. EASTON

"She won't give in," said Albert. "She can't possibly believe it will help Michael. It would be better to let him die. Then he'd be free. And she knows what helping him would mean for her." His voice was suddenly almost inaudible: "And then for me."

"Don't bet on that," said Ingrid. "Despite all the years since they were sweethearts, she does still love him. That's what Lisa's counting on."

When Albert looked hurt, even though he knew, of course he knew, that she was right, she added, "But she's praying for us to rescue her."

"How?" he asked. "I'm all that passes for a police department here. We don't have SWAT teams. We don't have search warrants. We've never needed them."

"Would it help to talk to Lisa?" Ingrid leaned over the table toward Albert. "Tell her we know what she's been doing, that she's in trouble, that you *are* a SWAT team."

The light in the street turned reddish as if someone had turned down the sun. The few vehicles on the street popped like soap bubbles, leaving their drivers and passengers staggering to keep their feet. Buildings flickered on the verge of vanishing.

"Just a minor drain." Marvin grimaced. "All under control." Then he shook his head. "That won't do any good. She knows the limits of my programming."

"It can't hurt," said Ingrid.

"Try it," said the pilot. "Maybe it'll shake her up and she'll give us an opening."

"It wouldn't help if she saw me," said Marvin. "But I'll be here anyway." Both he and his chair turned translucent and wispy. When he was gone, the female Ingrid said, "I thought his grin might go last, but...."

"Go ahead and call," said Marvin's voice.

An old-fashioned black dial telephone, a chunky base cradling the handpiece, materialized on the table, blocking the view of Rose's face. Beside the phone, right over Lester's image, a portion of the tabletop displayed a four-digit number.

Albert sighed and murmured, "I wish we did have a SWAT team." Then he picked up the handpiece and deliberately dialed the number, going through the reassuring motions of physical, meat reality even though he knew they were by no means necessary.

The ringing of the phone on the other end was as clear to everyone at the table as if it were just across the street, but none of the passersby seemed to notice it. It was as if the sound went no further than their ears, or as if it were fed directly to their minds. "Fakery," said Albert. "It's all illusion." He sounded tired.

The ringing stopped.

"Is that you, Albert?" The voice was Lisa's.

"We need to get together," he said. "You and me and Ingrid. We have to talk."

"What on Earth about?" Her laughter was gaiety personified. "Surely not Michael! He's here of his own free will. Aren't you, dear?" There was a pause, and then a male voice, husky, slow, full of pain, murmured, "Yes, Lisa."

"That's Michael," whispered Ingrid. Both she and her male dopple closed their eyes.

"Besides," said Lisa. "Why should you care about him?"

"I'm working for Marvin. I'm what he's got for a police force."

"He can't touch me. So you can't either." She laughed again, but now with a note of uncertainty. She fell silent, though everyone could hear her breathing. Finally she said, "I have you on the screen. That's Ingrid. Michael's ex. Who's the other guy?" After a moment's pause, she laughed. "That's Ingrid too! They *both* want Michael? I didn't know he switched!"

Albert did not answer her question. "And I want Rose."

"You mean your Rosie's left you? But surely you don't think I have her."

"Your Lester does. In your tower room."

"We've been watching," said Ingrid.

Lisa giggled. There was no attempt at all to dissemble. "She didn't object."

"That datalock won't let her."

"She had her chance before he put it on." She giggled again.

"We still need to talk about it, as well as other things."

"What other things?" She sounded suddenly wary.

"I'm sure you can guess. If you can't, I'll tell you at the cafe."

"No." Hesitation said that she was telling herself she had no need to confront her enemies, her rivals, her prey, and certainly not on ground of their own choosing. Yet Albert sounded confident. He knew more than he was saying, and he might, if she did not pretend to be cooperative, have some way to strike at her. "Not there."

"Then where? You name the place."

SILICON KARMA
THOMAS A. EASTON

Lisa's features relaxed the merest trifle to show how much the offer lulled her. But she said nothing. There was only silence while Ingrid pushed the phone aside and changed the scene on the tabletop screen to show Michael facing a wallscreen that showed them in the cafe. He was leaning forward, lines drawn deep around his eyes, his mouth half open. To one side Lisa also watched him, smiling at the obvious impotence of his yearning.

When Ingrid raised one hand as if to offer her ex-husband a shred of sympathy, Lisa snapped, "The icon church." And the scene went black.

The simple line of type across his screen was a desperate cry for help.

The man everyone around him knew as Robert Codder shook his head. Had Lisa over-reached herself? She had been doing so well, picking away at the world around her, tearing at its very foundations, weakening the entire Afterlife idea, doing just what he wanted. If she had only continued in just the same way, it would have been only a matter of time before Coleridge's stock lost all its value, its customers went elsewhere, and he could rest at last.

He lifted his gaze from his workstation screen. The sides of his carrel were covered with memos, notes, clippings, printouts. There was no one at his back. He stood and scanned the room. No one was moving, the only sounds were fans and tapping fingers, muttered curses, a muffled telephone ring and a murmur of conversation. He did not need to worry about being caught eavesdropping on the Afterlives of Coleridge's clients, or neglecting his own work.

He knew he shouldn't take the chance, but the risk felt essential. Events in Lisa's Afterlife had reached a cusp. The computer's persona had drafted a security force to do what it could not, and that force was closing in on Lisa. If he ignored her, all might be lost. Lisa was not nearly as powerful as she thought she was; she could weaken and destroy the virtual world only as long as no one in that world understood what she was doing. Once they understood, they could strip her of what powers she had. He didn't think it would work simply to warn her prospective victims that she could harm them only if they gave her control of their data energy—she was a primal force, a primal tempation, and she didn't need much control to start draining off one's strength. Perhaps they would kill her and refuse to reboot her from her storage wafer. That was against the computer's programming—reboot was supposed to be mandatory, automatic—but programs could be rewritten.

Or perhaps they would just revise the program not to permit automatic debits. Any such steps would finish her. They would also finish his dreams of revenge.

Then he could not ignore her, could he? He had to act, and if that meant he might be caught, with luck he could still bring Coleridge down with him.

He called up his summary of recent events. He shook his head. If she had only claimed Michael, she would have endangered nothing. But seizing Rose.... *That* had aroused the cops for sure. Confrontation was now inevitable, and the computer was still stronger than his own pet. She would surely lose. Unless....

He had been giving Lisa tips ever since her arrival in the Afterlife computer. He had instructed her in technique, shown her how to tap the world itself, supplied her with stock for her little bait shop, warned her of dangers, and—it galled him to admit it—even egged her on when it came to Michael. He hated to think she was about to fail, for she had been such an apt pupil that the failure would be his as well. And he did not think he could stand that. Not now.

Fortunately, he had a trump card. He had developed this routine months before and told himself it was too unsubtle, too brutal, to use except in an emergency. He had hidden it on his hard-drive under an innocuous title, saving it for....

Now, he thought as he began to type his reply. Without it, Lisa would surely lose and all his hopes of revenge would evaporate. With it, she should be unstoppable. At least, until the destruction of her world claimed her as well.

He did not think she would notice that small complication until far too late.

"She hung up," said Albert.

"We can still peek." The room returned to the screen, but it was empty.

"What's the icon church?" asked the pilot Ingrid.

SILICON KARMA
THOMAS A. EASTON

"Wait!" Marvin reappeared, chair and all. "I caught this one!"

"What?"

"Lisa called outside. A Coleridge terminal. She couldn't hide that! She asked for help. And the answer.... It's a routine. Let me...." He was silent for a moment, his eyes closed. When he spoke again, he seemed puzzled. "Parts of it look like an uninstaller."

"What's that?" The Ingrids spoke together. Albert looked pained.

"When you set up a computer program to run on a machine, you 'install' it. You copy it to permanent storage. You set up initiation files that define the program's parameters. You assign working memory. An uninstaller undoes all that."

"What would she want one of those for?" asked Albert.

"Maybe she's after Marvin," said the female Ingrid.

"No," said Marvin. "I'm too well protected. But...." He waved a hand to indicate the street, the buildings, and everything that lay beyond what they could see. "I think it might preempt the memory that supports all this. Turn off the maintenance routines. Release the data energy."

"A disassembler," breathed the pilot. "It would unravel our whole world. If this were science fiction, it would be a disintegrator raygun. But she wouldn't dare! It would kill her too."

"Call Kymon," said the other Ingrid. "Tell her the problem is one of her programmers. Maybe she can...."

"Too late," said Albert. "Lisa has the uninstaller already. Maybe she won't use it, but we can't count on that."

"You don't have time anyway," said Marvin. "She's already on her way."

The Church of the Virtual Icon was the official name of the rendezvous Lisa had named. A high-roofed structure of white-painted clapboards, it occupied one side of a quiet, dead-end block. But even though the building was their urgent destination, the dusty softball field on the other side of the street briefly distracted their attention. Men were gathering on the sidelines, materializing balls and bats and gloves, and transforming themselves into the boys they had been once upon a time, when softball had been one of the most important forces in their lives. A few women, none of them turned into girls, were finding seats in the rickety bleachers beside the first-base line. Most looked bored.

"Come on," said Albert. "She must be waiting for us."

The interior of the church was a single large room. The floor was paved with broad slabs of granite that sucked heat from the air and left a distinct chill. The scent of candle wax and incense was strong. A cloth-draped altar on a low dais dominated the far end of the room. Polished pews were ranked beside a central aisle. Covering the walls between the stained-glass windows and behind the altar were row upon row of framed and haloed faces painted in the style of Greek or Russian Orthodox icons. There were no explanatory tags or placards; the images may or may not have been those of actual icons, actual saints.

In the left-hand wall, near the front, was a single, massive door that looked like it belonged in some much larger church, perhaps even a cathedral. It was made of oak and set in a Gothic arch of stone blocks. Beside it was a tall desk like those that hold guest books in funeral homes and reservation lists in restaurants; it held only a fist-sized silver dome with a pushbutton on its top.

The room was empty. Even though Marvin had said she was on the way, Lisa was not there.

"So we have to wait," said Ingrid. She turned left, walking the border of the room, studying the icons on the walls. Her dopple turned right. Albert remained near the entrance.

"Where's Marvin?" asked the pilot.

"Leaving it to us," said Albert. His voice showed what he felt: betrayed, abandoned, disillusioned, bitter. "He can't interfere. He does, but he's limited, so he says he doesn't." He laughed. "Like some parents."

The Ingrids progressed almost in step until they met in front of the altar. They looked at each other then as if they were sharing the memories of the icons they each had seen. Together, they turned toward Albert. "What's that door?"

He gestured ignorance in their direction. "No idea."

"I'll bet she's behind it, waiting to jump out and say 'Boo!'" Ingrid spun decisively away from her dopple and raised one hand above the bell-push.

SILICON KARMA
THOMAS A. EASTON

Even as the metal dome dinged, something slammed against the building's outside wall. Both Ingrids jumped and spun around. "Foul ball," said Albert.

"I don't think they call them foul. A hit's a hit, and someone's surely charging round those bases now."

When they spun to see who had spoken, they saw that the Gothic door had swung open on silent hinges to reveal a slender man whose silvery hair glowed against the shadows of the opening behind him. He wore a black cassock but there was no white band around his throat to suggest that he was a priest.

"Who are you?" said an Ingrid.

The stranger smiled and bowed. "I've been a baseball fan for years. The Reverend...." As he spoke the word, a faint gold disk sprang into existence behind his head. "...Jackson Kemmerdell." His voice was that of a man accustomed to audiences.

Albert was walking down the church's central aisle, nodding as if he had met the man before.

Kemmerdell turned and extended one hand. "The doorway—and the stairway—to Heaven. I'm the doorman." The foot of a stone staircase, its steps hollowed as if by millennia of climbing feet, was barely visible in the shadows. "A metaphor, of course. An image only. It's really just one end of the fiber-optic cable that permits communication between this machine and Heaven's."

"For the proselytes," said Ingrid.

"And converts," said the pilot.

"Tourists too," said Albert.

"Just so," said Kemmerdell. "Are you immigrants or visitors?"

"Neither."

"We're waiting for...."

"Me!"

Albert spun around. Lisa was standing, as near as he could tell, precisely where he had stood before Kemmerdell had appeared.

"I want Michael back," said Ingrid.

"He can leave anytime he wants to." Lisa laughed gaily. "Or can pay the fare."

"And I want Rose."

"I don't have her."

"Your dopple does. He kidnapped her."

"Take it up with him." She laughed again. Then she sobered. "You said there was something else."

"Money." Albert rubbed his thumbs against his fingertips. "Data energy. You have far too much for someone who doesn't work."

"Are you the one who's been peeking at my files?"

"And Rose. She's an accountant."

"But Lester's got her stopped."

"Too late. We already know...."

"It's gifts!"

Both Ingrids laughed. "You hook them on your cunt," said the female one. "And then you suck them too dry to stop you."

Kemmerdell had been turning his head back and forth, back and forth, watching first one speaker, then the next. His eyes had been wide and his lips parted as if to say he had never seen such an exchange in a church before. Now his eyes were even wider.

"We've watched you," said the pilot. "Again and again and...."

"I don't force them. It's their own free will!"

"Even that stone wall?"

"Huh?" Lisa managed to sound baffled.

"There." A miniature of that sculpture Ingrid had watched a Lisa make from surplus slaves or lovers appeared upon the altar.

"*That* Lisa. But she's an extremist. I don't do things like that."

"She's you."

"Something went wrong with the doppling." Her voice was showing the first cracks of desperation.

"You know how to edit. Or your coach does."

"But...." Her knees sagged. She reached for the back of the pew beside her and straightened. But then she gasped—"Aahh!"—and sagged again. This time she did not recover even temporarily. She went to her knees, lost her grip on the pew, and fell to her side.

"She's faking," said Ingrid. "She's much too much the bitch for that to be real."

But Albert was not listening. Where he stood in the center of the church, he was only a few steps away from the fallen Lisa, and though he hesitated—thinking

SILICON KARMA
THOMAS A. EASTON

that Ingrid was surely right—a lifetime of training took over. Cops just did not ignore those who seemed to be in trouble. It was only seconds before he was kneeling beside her.

"What is it?"

"No!" cried both Ingrids simultaneously.

"That coach," came Lisa's weakened voice. "He's editing me... out. Please. I can tell you.... Help me...."

Albert doubted that Lisa was about to turn informer, but she was dangling that possibility before him. Combined with Lisa's apparent need and the echo of Rose's plea so short a time before, it was too much for him. He knew Ingrid was right, but he still held out one hand. Lisa's own rose, fell limply into his, and then clutched frantically at his fingers. "Yes!"

Her eyes were suddenly wide, her mouth open, teeth showing. She looked ravenously, desperately victorious as his head fell forward and his shoulders sagged. Strength drained visibly from his spine and limbs as she seized upon that token of aid he had freely offered, small though it was, and used it to invade the very well-springs of his soul.

Yet it was clear that Lisa was exerting every particle of her being in this effort to defeat her foe. There was sweat on her brow. Cords stood out in her neck. She was more used to insidious sapping of her prey's strength than to outright attack.

Albert's face contorted as he realized how she was taking full advantage of the stupidity that had impelled him to offer aid despite Ingrid's warning and his own good sense. He hadn't offered her his data-energy, not the way her victims did. Just a crack in the door, but now she was gaining strength as he lost it, swelling as he shriveled.

The Ingrids lunged forward together, but it was the female one whose foot connected with Lisa's wrist and broke the junction between the vampire and her victim. The other Ingrid grabbed Albert and pulled him out of Lisa's reach.

When the pilot propped him against a pew across the aisle, his head lolled and he fell sideways onto the floor. He was still weakening. His strength was still flowing into Lisa.

Ingrid summoned a quark and cried, "Credit check!" It bowed, metamorphosed into a large squirrel in a tux, and stepped to one side, where it produced a device that, like an odometer, displayed a multi-digit number on a row of small wheels. The wheels were spinning, and the number was declining constantly and rapidly.

"Take it back!" she cried. "You invited her in! Don't let her stay!"

He clearly understood. "N-n-n...." He was barely conscious enough to obey her urging. "N-n-no. G'out. 'Way! No help."

He was no longer weakening. "Take some of mine," said Ingrid.

"And mine," said the pilot.

Kemmerdell remained in the background, near the doorway to Heaven, saying nothing, offering nothing.

But the flow of data energy from the Ingrids was enough to bring Albert back.

He blinked, lifted his body into a sitting position, and raised his head. He sighed and groaned. He looked at Lisa.

The others followed his gaze in time to see her beginning to fade out, escaping, running to prepare her defenses.

"No," said Albert instantly. "Don't go." His brow furrowed with the effort of holding her there while another quark popped into view. This one wore a high-domed helmet, a bright blue uniform with brass buttons, and a handlebar mustache. In one hand it held a billy club, in the other a pair of handcuffs.

When Albert pointed, it leaped toward Lisa and grabbed her shoulder. She cried out in protest, but she was forced to stop fading. As soon as she had fully solidified, the quark fastened a cuff to her wrist.

"A datalock," said Albert. "My kind. She isn't going anywhere now."

"What about the rest of them?" asked the pilot. His voice was weaker now than it had been.

Albert shook his head while Kemmerdell looked surprised and a small silver ball appeared beside his ear. Marvin's voice, murmuring the tale of what had happened, was barely audible.

"Michael," said Ingrid. "Can we save him now?"

"Lisa's locked for now. She can't control him. But you'll still need your strength," Marvin said more loudly, and both Ingrids brightened as what they had given to save Albert was returned to them.

"Michael! Oh, he heard. He's weak! Call me, Michael! Call us! Let us...."

SILICON KARMA
THOMAS A. EASTON

She stiffened like a dog on point. She groped with one hand for her dopple. Together they strained, vanished, and flickered back into view, supporting a limp and haggard Michael Durgov between them. He collapsed immediately on the floor.

"Nearly killed him, didn't you?" Albert's tone was conversational as he looked toward the captive Lisa. She only glared.

"So thin!" The Ingrids were struggling to lift Michael to his feet. "But you're safe now, Michael. She can't touch you anymore. You're safe." The original Ingrid looked at her dopple and said, "Let's take him home." All three faded and vanished.

Albert was alone now, staring at Lisa, glancing toward Kemmerdell and the doorway to Heaven. He sighed. Could victory truly be this easy? What had he forgotten?

"My turn," he said at last. His face took on a distant look, and he called, "Rose? Rosa?"

The image of the tower room took shape before him even as Lisa laughed. The sound was neither cheerful nor pleasant, and it did not admit defeat.

"They could get Michael because you've got me," she was saying. "I couldn't hold on to him anymore. But Rose is still mine."

Albert pointed at the image. "Or Lester's."

CHAPTER

2

6

SILICON KARMA
THOMAS A. EASTON

She *would* not let them use her the way they had Michael and so many others! She *would* not become a slave, a creature owned by vampires for nothing more than draining. She *would* remain her own and hope against all hope that Albert had somehow learned what had happened to her, who had taken her, where she was now caged.

But it was hard to hold onto her determination. Michael was there, in front of her, so nearly dead, so much in need, and that man's voice, so like Lisa's she now could see, was saying, "Give in. You'll make it so much easier on yourself. You'll help *him*. We'll even let him go."

She could feel the muscles bulging in her cheeks as she gritted her teeth, fighting back the urge to speak, to cry "Yes!" or "No!", to give them any satisfaction at all, at all.

But there was pain. Blooming bright, bringing tears to her eyes, forcing her to gasp and mouth the words she could not say out loud. "Al-I-berrtt!" There was the scent and sizzle of scorching flesh, the need to scream, the agony of her body demanding that she give in, that she do something, anything, to make the torment go away.

She could not simply wish it gone. She was datalocked, her leg racked by a pain that left her barely able to support her weight in a cage that gave her no room to sit down or collapse.

And the pain went on, and on, and on.

Until.... There came a time when she realized that the pain of the datalock was the only pain she felt. Her breasts still ached, but no new burns were forming.

She opened her eyes. Michael was gone. Her tormentor was no longer on the bed but standing, staring into space, his expression worried.

Was he so distracted that she could reach out with her mind to Marvin or Ingrid or Albert and summon help? Or would he stop her?

He didn't need to, did he? He already had. She was datalocked. Her leg hurt from its teeth and claws, embedded in her flesh. She could not change her surroundings and thereby undo her cage. She could not shift to a new location, and thus escape. She could not send messages through the fabric of the computer, so much like telepathy; she thought that she would not even be able to use the phone, assuming she could reach one. She could only gesture, move her lips, speak a word or two that could be heard in this room alone. And she could do such things in ways her captor disapproved only if he failed to notice. And just now he *was* distracted.

If she could only call out to Albert, he could move her from her prison to wherever he might be. If she were not held in place by the datalock. And she could not remove the datalock; it itself tied her hands.

Yet she *had* called out. She was sure she had. She had cried "Allll-berrrt!" and "Pleeezzz!" and "Help!" And nothing had happened. He had not heard. If he had, he would have come for her, wouldn't he? Come and torn away the datalock and spirited her off to safety.

No. Her mind replayed something Marvin had told her early on. They had been talking about the rules that governed this world, and he had said, "Privacy's the big one. You can't enter someone else's space without an invitation."

Just screaming "Help!" was not enough. Perhaps it would be if she were not datalocked, but not now. Albert had to come to her, though he could not go where he had not been invited. And this was Lisa's home. The man's. It was not hers to open up to strangers.

But.... The cage *was* hers, wasn't it? They had given it to her. They had even said, "Here's your new home. All yours." She could not leave it. They would not even let her send a mental message out. But surely the space within it was hers to command. It was all she had. Perhaps it was even enough, if only her jailer remained too distracted to notice what she was doing until it was too late. If Albert was watching and listening.

Against all reason, hope swelled in her chest. Before it could vanish, she mouthed the words, "Albert! Come here! I need you!" She added just enough breath to be audible.

And wonder of wonders, he was there, squeezed into the cage beside her, his hand running down her encrusted back and side and thigh to seize the datalock and strip it from her, his mind commanding the computer to transport them both out of cage and tower room to elsewhere, freedom, safety.

SILICON KARMA
THOMAS A. EASTON

Rose was still nude, but now she was as clean and unmarked as if she had just been taken from her own bath instead of Lisa's torture chamber. She was sighing with relief. "I was afraid you didn't know where I was, that you weren't watching, that you'd never...." Her arms went around Albert with a strength that echoed her sigh. Then she saw Lisa, held captive by Albert's more humane datalock cuffed to her wrist. "What...?"

Silence fell inside the church. He cocked his head, listening, staring at his single prisoner, who stared coldly back, her lips smugly curled, gloating. "I can't believe we've really stopped her." He looked up then. Something was happening, and the others had noticed too. Kemmerdell seemed puzzled. Marvin was clearly alarmed.

"What is it?" asked Rose.

The sounds of the ball game were diminishing as if into distance. The stained glass windows and the icons were losing both colors and contrast, graying into uniformity. The altar was disappearing in a grainy haze that resembled video fuzz. The ends of the pews were clear near the church's central aisle, but their further ends were gone, as if an artist had failed to complete the drawing of the scene. Lisa remained crystal clear.

He kissed Rose's forehead, transmitting information as well as love, and suddenly she shared his pained understanding of what was happening. Despite the datalock, Lisa was somehow using the uninstaller routine Marvin had described to her late husband, and it was unraveling the virtual world as they looked helplessly on.

"But you're powerless," Albert said to Lisa. "That datalock stops you cold."

Why was he denying the obvious? "Something's wrong," said Rose.

Lisa was licking her lips until they glistened. "I'm not alone."

"There's us."

Both Albert and Rose jerked their heads up. Three other Lisas were sitting on the ends of pews, arms crossed, glaring at them. One wore a wet bikini swimsuit, one a short skirt and tight blouse, one nothing at all. One was black. Two were white. Beyond them, only the doorway to Heaven, the bell-push on its stand, and Kemmerdell were distinct. Everything else was flat, gray, and featureless.

"You can't have her, Albert," said the Lisa in skirt and blouse. She slid off the pew arm and pushed her breasts in his direction. Grinning, the nude stood beside her. The one in the bikini squatted beside the prisoner, petted her hair, and fingered the datalock's cuff.

"We stick to ourself."

"Let her go."

"Or we'll...." The nude stepped forward. Her nipples were erect. Tension defined her muscles beneath her skin. Energy crackled around her, and her hair stood out from her scalp.

"I can play this game too," said Albert. He doppled, and there was one of him for each of his opponents. One Albert reached for a Lisa, but then Lester was there, pulling her out of his grasp and reaching for Rose. A quark popped into view, and Rose recognized the bulbous shape of the Image Shop's proprietor even as she realized it was a Lisa in disguise. Somehow this revelation did not surprise her.

An Albert muttered, "I'm beginning to see a pattern. Is that what you shot me with?" The quark-disguised Lisa brandished a heavy handgun and laughed. She did not point it, and Albert did not seem concerned that she would; such things could threaten him only from behind.

Albert doppled again, and one of his duplicates tried to seize the quark-Lisa. She danced out of reach and fired a booming shot into the air.

"I'll overrun you," said the captive Lisa. "All of you. You can't stop me." The words were defiant, but her tone bore a hint of plaintive whine.

More Lisas appeared, along with a quark holding a signboard that displayed the computer's available memory. The figure was not impressive, and when several of the Lisas present doppled, the figure plummeted. It plummeted again when Albert increased his own numbers.

But his attempt to meet every Lisa with an Albert was futile. Rose soon realized that he had made a mistake by even trying.

Lisa was too far ahead. Albert could not possibly catch up. There were simply too many of her, and as she multiplied she seized the very computer resources he needed to do the same.

The numbers on the signboard began to dance, first up, then down.

"She's destroying everything," cried Marvin's voice. "Converting the whole world into her!" The uninstaller was in play, releasing the resources tied up in the virtual world's infrastructure, but she, not he, was the one who knew the moment of their release, and it was her hand, not his, that grabbed them first.

SILICON KARMA
THOMAS A. EASTON

A window opened in the air, showing Virtual City as if from the sky. Fog was rolling in, billowing around the bases of the buildings, obscuring the streets. Yet it was not just fog. As it swept along the streets, pavement and storefronts dissolved into pixelated static. Strollers saw it coming, opened wide their mouths, began to scream, and vanished. As it rose up the sides of the city's structures, lights winked out. Walls crumpled. Lisa's brothel was exposed to view, its captives looking startled, then relieved. Buildings fell. Michael and the Ingrids did not show in any glimpse of the catastrophe, but surely they were gone as well.

When everything was gone, vanished into the fog, all that remained was a scatter of tiny placeholder icons. Another window swept across the countryside outside the city, showing forest, lake, island, rustic cottage, all threatened by the same destruction, all crumbling into icons. When all that window could show was gray, the image became a map of the world, a Mercator projection on paper, flames licking at its borders, its edges blackening, curling, shrinking, leaving iconic ashes behind.

Rose wanted to cry when she saw the cottage go, but she refused. There was no time. In the Icon Church, the pews were now entirely gone. What had been nave and altar and high-arched ceiling was now a featureless gray fog except for the preternaturally clear image of the doorway to Heaven. The desk and bell beside it were gone like all the rest, and the Reverend Kemmerdell was standing in the doorway, his hand poised to slam shut the door itself.

Rose blinked at the horde of Lisas jammed shoulder to shoulder before and all around herself and Albert. They were reaching for him now, toothy datalocks of precisely the sort that had kept her within that awful cage were materializing on the Lisas' shoulders, and she had no doubts about what they would do to Albert once they had him. Nor about what her own fate would be immediately thereafter.

Why weren't they scrubbing him away the way they were destroying every other of the computer's residents? They could, that much was obvious.

"Some of them are trying," Marvin's voice—no, it was Ada's now, just as it had been before Albert had accepted that other name and personality the machine's persona had assumed for Rose. "I'm protecting you as best I can. But there are limits. She's like a tapeworm, preempting everything I need to function. What you need, too."

A heavy door slammed shut, and Kemmerdell was gone. Run away to hide in his Heaven until the battle was won. Perhaps to wait until the Lisas reached out for still more worlds to conquer.

All that remained of the quark and its signboard was a large red numeral two. Marvin or Ada was still functioning, but the Lisas had converted every bit of computer memory and processing capacity used by the virtual world—except for that small bit still held by Albert and his dopples and Rose—to their own uses. There was no more to be had, unless the computer's other residents still existed in some confused and foggy limbo. But surely they were gone, dead, nothing left but B-cups.

"I have to be careful," Albert muttered.

Rose embraced her husband more tightly than ever. She gasped when she saw the flesh of her arms merging with his, as if Marvin were so short of processing capacity that he had to economize by blurring their boundaries. Then she leaned her forehead against his temple, felt that boundary weaken too, and found herself knowing Albert's very thoughts.

He was framing the commands he would need to issue to the computer, knowing that timing was all important. If he failed, he would only add to the Lisas' strength.

But thought and movement now were slow. It felt to both him and Rose as if he had been immersed in molasses or deep snow. Everything was sluggish. Even the light in the void that had been a church was shifting red. The computer was, he knew, they knew, being forced to simulate Rose and all the Alberts with but a fraction of its internal power.

As soon as he released his commands, one of his dopples winked out. Instantly—though for Rose the instant stretched out agonizingly—before the signboard's tote could register the change in the virtual world's available resources, he seized the data energy inherent in its existence and manufactured a datalock. As soon as it was fully formed, it seized and immobilized a Lisa.

With a wolfish grin, Albert used what remained of his dopple's energy to materialize another Keystone Kop. And then another, just in time as two Lisas launched their datalocks in his direction. Kops and monsters met in mid-air, neatly canceling each other out.

Only three? Did he have enough dopples? No. If he spent all his dopples, there would still remain enough of the Lisas and their datalocks to destroy him. And they would. They would not save him for torment and give him the chance to find another idea.

Robert Codder stared at his workstation screen and grinned wolfishly. The Lisas were winning. In a few more moments, there would be nothing but her left in the computer. Then....

Why wait? A few quick commands, and the datalocked Lisa began to uninstall, unraveling into fog and static snow. Their data energy would feed the rest, make them stronger, hasten the inevitable end. A few more commands, and the uninstaller was primed to perform its final task, erasing the Lisas themselves. It would then destroy itself, leaving no evidence, just a blank slate, a wiped machine. A ruined Coleridge.

Albert swore. He suddenly realized the weakness of the datalocks. They could keep a prisoner from acting outside itself, but if that prisoner were willing to commit suicide and be rebooted, he or she could still escape. If someone else were willing to kill the prisoner, he or she could also escape. Marvin's own rules kept him from doing that, or else all of Lisa's victims—Anton, Ling-ko, Gladys, Irma's brother Alan, all the rest—could easily be freed. Lisa had no such rules to limit her, and with the uninstaller routine she was using she was perhaps more powerful than Marvin himself.

"That routine," grunted Rose. "Find it! Attack it!" She spoke in a strained drawl, as if she could barely function.

Hamstrung by the slowing of the overburdened computer system, he struggled to figure out what she meant. He released a dopple, made three more datalocks, and watched the miniature Keystone Kops seize both Lisas and their datalocks. He repeated the procedure again, and again, freezing Lisas and their weapons out of action, counting victories, small and partial and immediately evaporating as both Lisas and datalocks crumbled and fed the remaining Lisas with more data energy which they could use to increase their numbers once more.

"I can't protect you much longer, Albert," said Ada's voice.

He could feel the pressure all around him, inimical, converging, wanting nothing more than his and Rose's extinction, their disintegration into gray fog like that which had engulfed the world. Hope flickered as despair swelled in his heart. The throng of Lisas was greater than ever, and his own doppled forces were now low, converted into datalocks which had immediately been evaporated and turned into Lisas.

What had Rose meant? Lisa was a mean and nasty bitch, a tapeworm of a human being, but by herself she had very little power. Someone outside Virtual City—Lisa's "coach"—had supplied her with the uninstaller routine. That someone was their real enemy. Yet there was no way he could attack that source of Lisa's strength. The best he could do, as Rose had said, was to attack the weapon the outsider had given Lisa.

"Marvin!" he cried. "Ada! A memory map! Where are we?"

The map flickered weakly in one eye. Terabytes of memory space, a portion of it pale blue and labeled "System." A tiny portion pink, marked "Albert." A tiny splash of red, "Rose." A vast expanse of "Lisa," black. A scatter of other hues flickering out even as he watched. A swatch of blue fading, turning dark, darker, black. Gray encroaching everywhere, even on the black.

He searched the crowd of Lisas with his eyes. He saw one wink out, gone, vanished as if she had never been. Another, and the nearest Lisas noticing, going wide-eyed in alarm, crying out, distracted.

"Where's that routine?"

The tiniest grain of blinking gold. Not a large program at all. Not complicated. A bludgeon, not an assault rifle.

"Delete it!"

"I can't. Can't change it either. It's locked against even me."

"It can't be."

"It shouldn't be possible, but it is. All I can do is look at it."

"Show me!"

SILICON KARMA
THOMAS A. EASTON

The grain expanded into lines of code against which he was helpless. He knew immediately which lines to change to render the weapon useless, but its protections forbade anyone but its creator to edit or revise. Was he stymied? Was Lisa bound to win and destroy them all? The way the routine was attacking even Marvin's portions of memory, she too would die. But that was no comfort.

He struggled to recall the techniques he had used in his meat life, those he had encountered as a consultant. Viruses? No. That was what Lisa now amounted to. Software bullets like the ones that had killed him three times before? They might do for all the Lisas, but even in the dire straits of this disastrous moment, that did not feel right. Better, he thought, to remove her weapon if he only could. And for that? Data bombs might do. Like viruses, but not self-reproducing, designed to seek out particular strings of data or even particular memory addresses and obliterate their contents.

"Merge your selves," said Rose. "You'll be stronger, and she'll be busy for a little while, using up the memory you release."

Did he dare? It felt like surrender. There would be only one of him, and Rose, and a horde of Lisas glorying in their strength of numbers. As soon as they realized the situation, he and Rose would live but an eyeblink more. But what else could he do? He needed just a little time, and if he gave Lisa no distraction at all, he and Rose would live only two eyeblinks. Maybe three.

For just a moment, he felt hope return. In the memory map, the gray was lapping at the Lisas, a few were succumbing, converting to gray even as he watched. Was this Marvin's work? Did he dare wait? But no. The gray was slowing its advance, stopping, retreating. And his own forces were still declining without a bit of hesitation.

Consternation was still spreading among the Lisas with the news that some had vanished. Worried faces studied the clouds of gray surrounding them all, counted the empty spaces in the horde, considered that destroying the world might not work to their benefit in the end, turned ferocious and faced the Alberts and his Rose, who *must* be responsible for the damage. The Lisas' patron, after all, was on *their* side.

Another swatch of blue faded, darkened, vanished. The very system that operated the virtual world, Bertha-Marvin-Ada, the underpinnings of existence were under attack and weakening, failing. The world was about to end, and with it his second life. Albert had only one chance to live, no chance at all if he did not try, nor if he failed.

Robert Codder was rapt. All his plans, all his hopes, all his yearnings for revenge, all were about to be satisfied in fullest measure. Virtual City would soon be digital ashes, and soon thereafter, Coleridge would be bankrupt, ruined, justice served at last. He delighted when his routine began to nibble at the edges of the Lisa horde. He did *not* like that woman; she was far too like the man he wanted most to punish. A command, and the attack halted. She was his tool, his *essential* tool; he would not destroy her until the very end.

Ordinarily he would have heard the footsteps outside his carrel. But the floor was carpeted, and he was intent on the unfolding battle. His routine now wore the image of a wolf's head. It roved back and forth on the screen, devouring whatever it found that was not gray, not Lisa. Soon, soon, it would claim her as well.

"What are you doing? A game?"

His heart nearly stopped when the woman's voice interrupted him.

Albert did it. Just as Rose had urged the merest second before, he merged all his dopples and datalocks into one. In the sudden rush of freed data-energy, he found the memory he needed. Quickly he crafted his bomb, imagined it as a narrow, stub-finned missile, and armed its targeting mechanism with a single line of code from the uninstaller routine that was creating so much havoc. Yet Lisa was just as fast. The memory he had freed was gobbled up, converted into Lisas, wrenched from his grasp and turned upon him and Rose in the final lunge of uninstallation, disassembly, death. The overwhelming wave of her attack was already crashing down on his and Rose's heads when he launched his last-minute creation as a roaring streak of smoke and fire homing on that lethal foe of all reality, a fragment of computer program, a mere abstract idea.

"Yes! A game! But not now! Not now!"

"Getting interesting, is it? Let me see."

He could hear the footsteps now. They were in his carrel, close behind him, a hand on his shoulder, hair tickling his ear. He was about to glance up, identify the intruder, chase her off, but just then the wolf's head stopped its roving, hunting movement. Its lines began to unravel as if it were under attack too. It vanished.

Codder roared in outrage, lunged at the keyboard, slammed in a barrage of commands that should show him the code. But though the file was there, it was empty, the code gone, vanished, blown away.

He returned the image to the chapel, now no more than a clear zone in the all-engulfing fog. Even the doorway to Heaven was misted over now. But the fog was roiling, blasted outward. The Lisas were milling, faces slack with uncertainty. Albert was making Keystone Kop datalocks as fast as he could, and Rose was attaching them to the Lisas. He was losing!

"That's an Afterlife, isn't it?" said the voice. He recognized it now. Another Coleridge programmer. He thought her hair would be red if he looked.

"Go away!" he cried. He could not remember her name.

"What are you doing? You're not supposed to be there."

"Special order!"

"No," she said. "Breach of privacy. You're interfering." And her arm snaked past his cheek, finger extended, stabbing toward the terminal's RESET button.

He tried to block her movement, but he was too slow. After that, he had to hope the damage he had done would prove enough. He was afraid it would not.

"So many of them!" said the computer's Ada voice. But when it materialized once more, its form was that of Bertha. She wore a pristine white smock like that of a doctor, and as she stepped among the stunned, disarmed Lisas, she pointed. Those she indicated merged, and the number of captives rapidly declined.

"What...?"

"They were stunned when you blew up the uninstaller," said Bertha. "The surprise, I suppose. Their hole card didn't work. Or perhaps even a virtual explosion has a shock wave for virtual people." Rose and Albert, still linked at arm and head, nodded to say they understood. "I'm consolidating them. I can do it now that you've proven their danger, and I really have to. You stopped the attack, but they trashed the place. Fortunately, I've got the blueprints in permanent storage. And I have B-cups for most of the residents. Not always recent, of course, though I did manage to grab a few as the system was going down. Now, as soon as I reclaim the data energy, I can rebuild."

"Did you get Michael and Ingrid?"

"Of course." There was a pause while Bertha finished consolidating the Lisas and shook her head in a silent tsk-tsk. "Sixty-three of them. And one Lester." She gestured, and the one remaining Lisa was clad in a bright orange coverall. She was glaring furiously, but her eyes also held a note of resignation, as if she had long known this day must come.

Bertha shook her head as the Church of the Virtual Icon took shape once more around them and the sounds of softball became audible again, as if the game never had been interrupted. Lisa now sat near the end of the middle front-row pew. "So many. And most of them had sizable stashes of data energy. It's no wonder I got so sluggish at times."

Albert and Rose knew that what the computer, their host, was doing was essential. But to them, at the moment, something else was more important. "Where's Ingrid?" asked Rose. "And Michael? Are they okay?"

"Just a minute."

What appeared was not their friends. Instead, there suddenly stood against the far wall, not far from the doorway to Heaven, a stone wall, a frieze of human despair and pain. "I B-cupped all her victims."

Anton and Ling-ko materialized in a pew across the aisle from their mistress.

Beside them was what seemed a heap of filth. The rest of the pew, and several more besides, filled in with more of Lisa's prey, many in servants' livery, some in tattered rags, some in nothing at all. Every one of them was emaciated; a few were unconscious and pale as if during the final battle their Lisas had drained the last drops of their vitality.

As Rose and Albert watched, a few of Lisa's most abused victims winked out. "They're dead," said Bertha. "I'll reboot them later."

Another pew filled with women, revealingly dressed and seeming healthy. Albert recognized Gladys and Irma's brother Alan. "There's only the one brothel," said Bertha.

The Reverend Jackson Kemmerdell had stepped from his safe haven into the church. He looked appalled. "What now?"

Rose was finally pulling free from her late husband. "Where's Michael?"

"I have to bring him back, you know," said Bertha. "I B-cupped him at the very last moment, when she destroyed the city." She wore a determined look, as if she, the computer, had chosen her present image for the sake of some connection she felt with the man. Perhaps she did, for he, despite his faults, had been instrumental in her creation, and Bertha had been the form she had worn to induct him into the virtual realm.

"Is he all right?"

"Of course he is, now." And he was there at last, standing before Rose and Albert, an Ingrid at each side, holding his elbows while he sagged weakly toward the stone floor of the church. Both Ingrids were now female; one still wore the pilot's flightsuit.

"He's alive. Thank god."

At the sound of Rose's voice, Michael raised his head and tried to smile. His cheeks were hollow, his eyes looked bruised, and receding gums revealed stained teeth. When he tried to smile at her, he looked like the stuff of nightmares.

"R-r-r-r...." He leaned toward Rose. He tried to take a step. The Ingrids gripped his arms more tightly and tried to help.

When he saw the single Lisa in the back of the church, he froze.

"Michael," she pleaded. "Make them let me go. Do, and I'll...." She rotated one orange-clad shoulder as suggestively as she had ever managed in her life.

He stared at her. She stared back, eyes wide, lips parted, her hunger palpable. No one else said a word.

Finally, Michael shuddered and shook his head, though he was still so weak that the shake was little more than a sideways tremble. "No," he said, and he closed his eyes and turned away, finally and totally rejecting Lisa and all she could offer.

When he opened them, he was facing Rose. His gaze jerked toward each Ingrid in turn. He shuddered again and managed a weak "L'go."

"Do it," said Bertha.

As they obeyed, and as the computer fed the man with data energy, Michael's back straightened and the life came back to his eyes. But when he tried to walk, he seemed as crippled as his meat had been by age and stroke.

"No," he said again, and then more strongly, "No!"

Lisa glared at him and said: "Bob's still going to get you. He'll get all of you."

"He needs more than energy to heal," said Bertha. "They all do."

"Time," said Rose. "She left them scarred." Then she shuddered at the memory of what they had done to her.

Albert clutched her hands and looked at her. Her naked body showed no signs of the sores Lester had inflicted on her.

"They didn't have her long enough," said Bertha. "She'll get over it much more easily."

"What are you going to do about her?" asked the Ingrid in the pilot's uniform. The pipe her male form had smoked was clamped between her teeth.

Bertha shook her head. "I can't kill her," she said. "I can't leave her in storage, unbooted. And I can't put her back in her meat. I don't know."

There was silence for a long moment.

"May I make a suggestion?" When they turned toward the voice, they saw the Reverend Kemmerdell stepping tentatively away from his portal to Heaven and raising one hand as if in benediction.

CHAPTER

2

7

"I know your bookkeeping functions aren't conscious," said Rose. "But...."

"They're automatic," said Marvin. "Like your own digestion, controlled by your autonomic nervous system. Neither one of us has any access to what is going on at that level of our existence."

"You *have* to improve on that." Rose leaned over the cafe's indoor table, staring intently at the computer's persona. She was ignoring Albert Pillock to her right and Michael Durgov and a single Ingrid to her left. She was also ignoring the wind and rain beyond the cafe's broad door. Someone had chosen to relieve the tedium of perfect weather, and no one else had seen fit to argue.

Perhaps it was simply that no one felt oppressed by clouds and rain when the clouds showed no hint of dirty brown and when the wet rushing air smelled sweet, when the streets lacked every trace of iconic rubbish, when every car beside the curb sparkled like new, when no buildings bore the marks of abandonment, when every citizen of Virtual City bubbled with an effervescence that had surely last been known when the world was young and the gods had perched on high Olympus. Halting the Lisas' drain on the computer's systems, on the underpinnings of the virtual world, had made an immediate difference.

"If you don't," she added. "If you don't, it'll happen again. There are more Lisas out there. Some are surely worse. One of these days you'll copy one of those into you, and we won't be able to stop her. Or him.

"Or it'll happen like Albert was telling me the other day. Anywhere limited resources are in demand there will be competition for those resources. You recognized this when you set up the rules that defined the economy in here. You forgot the possibility of thieves and cheats, predators and parasites. The inevitability, really. That's what a biologist would tell you. That's what the artificial life researchers learned years ago."

The quark waiter cried, "Anyone want a drink? A snack?" When no one paid any attention at all, it squatted disconsolately in the table's empty sixth place, its chalkboard clutched against its chest. The comedian was nowhere to be seen.

"What can I do?" Bertha's shrug made her gaily patterned caftan billow.

"For one thing," said Rose. "Don't let people have so many dopples. Two or three should be quite enough."

Bertha shrugged again. "I'm limited by my programming."

"You're not *that* limited," said Albert. "Not as long as you remember how to delegate."

"Is that what you mean? Let you be a government?"

Rose nodded. "Or a police force, though it would be a fairly simple one. The way this place works, doppling has to show to an accountant. And that's what I am."

"Just keep the files open," said Albert, and Rose nodded again. "I think I can also keep a Lisa from ripping you off. Embezzling, really. She was using your automatic stipend mechanism, you know. And I can set up auditing routines to catch what she was doing to her lovers. Or require your residents to approve every expenditure. No more automatic debits."

"Then you've found your job, haven't you?" When Rose stiffened, surprised even though she had been suggesting just that, Bertha grinned and was suddenly Marvin, making a face at the caftan and changing it to a striped terrycloth robe over orange swimming trunks. To complete the image, he added a scattering of water drops on his exposed skin. "Do it." Then he looked at Albert. "I've been treating you like a private eye. Want to be my chief of security? Full time, though if she can...."

"Albert!"

As the voice came from beyond the waiter, the quark twitched and produced a bottle of champagne and seven tall glasses. "On the house," it muttered.

Irma stood behind it, clinging to the arm of a man of about her age. She wore a black sheath, he a light brown shirt and pants. Both had black hair, though he lacked the snow-white circles that marked her own.

"My brother," she said. "Alan. You got him free, and he's back to normal. He even doesn't want to be a girl anymore!"

"What's wrong with that?" Marvin flickered to Bertha, still in trunks and robe, and back again. "I do it all the time."

"But you didn't have to...." His voice was higher than most men's, and his face showed the shadow of pain more clearly.

"Is Gladys all right?" asked Irma.

Gladys' milk bottle promptly materialized on the palm of Marvin's extended hand. Its plug was cocked askew, and there was no sign of either gold chain or baling twine. "You'll have to conjure up a shelf for this, Albert. A trophy shelf."

"What do you mean?" Irma looked from Marvin to Albert. She seemed confused. "Where is she?"

"She has her Toddy Sean now," said Albert.

"See?" Marvin indicated the tabletop, which was displaying a young woman apparently in her teens. Straight dark hair framed a freckled face. A radiant smile revealed braces. Behind her was visible an apartment room dominated by a crib and a bassinet. The view panned down her body to show a rounded belly.

"But how?" Irma's grip on her brother's arm tightened visibly. "Is it a dopple? Did you copy her own mind?"

Marvin shook his head. "I suggested that to her once. It would have worked. But she wouldn't do it."

"It's Lisa," said Albert.

"Though that's not what she'll call her while she's growing up again," said Marvin.

"Reincarnation." Alan smiled. "Do you think it will help?"

The computer shrugged. "The Hindus seem to think it does. Or can. I'll keep an eye on her."

"I suppose you can try again if you have to," said Irma.

"That'll be up to Albert, if he accepts the security slot I just offered him."

Albert nodded. "The first thing to do is call Coleridge and tell them about...."

When Jonathan Spander's face appeared on the tabletop, Albert reported what had happened and described how Lisa said she had been helped. Then he said, "She promised Bob would finish what she started."

Spander sucked at his yellowed teeth and grinned at them. He seemed to be relishing a secret.

"We think he's one of your programmers."

Spander nodded. "He is. Or was."

Irma leaned forward. "You've got him already? There was a new one not long before I...."

"Hi, Irma. Your meat's still doing good work here. In fact, she's the one who...." He gestured as if selecting commands from an on-screen menu. "I'll say hi to her for you." A photo appeared on the tabletop.

"That's him." She sounded satisfied.

"No!" Michael sounded shocked. "That's Nick. Nick Codescu. Elena's brother."

"The one you screwed to make me," said Marvin.

Michael nodded.

"No wonder he was helping Lisa," said Rose.

"I had it coming," said Michael a week later. He turned his empty champagne flute in his fingers. He was sitting in Albert's favorite easy chair, with Gladys' milk bottle on a shelf above his head. The others were scattered about the apartment's space. The curtains were drawn back, and bright sun shone past a balcony crowded with planters full of flowers. "Didn't I?"

"Oh, no," said Rose. She was beside Albert on the couch. "No one could deserve what she did to you."

Both Ingrids snorted. "You didn't know him later on," said one.

Michael nodded. "My own medicine."

"The biter bit," said the pilot.

"But you sound like you've learned something," offered Albert.

"I hope so."

"Enough not to fall for Lisa again," said Rose. "He showed that in the church."

"About time," said an Ingrid.

Bertha, in her caftan once more, tapped one finger on the dining table. "Enough to say what we should do with Lisa?"

Michael looked surprised. "I thought that was settled?"

"We could still use Kemmerdell's suggestion."

"He was at the church, wasn't he? Last time I saw him was years ago, when both of us were meat." When Bertha nodded encouragingly, Michael went on. "I wasn't paying much attention. I know he had something to say there at the end, but...."

"He runs Heaven, all the different Heavens, he said," said Rose. "He'll run Hell too, if that's what we want."

"Another machine," said Albert. "He'll design its world. Then we put the

Lisas in it. He'll lock the door and stand guard with a flaming sword so she never gets out again."

"That seems barbaric," said Michael. "A real Hell, with devils and lakes of fire."

"If that's what you want," said Bertha.

The original Ingrid stared at the cigarette in her hand and shook her head. "No. An ordinary world is all it takes. Fill it with Lisas, just like he said, and they'll make it Hell enough unless they can learn to live with each other."

An image filled the air before them, a neighborhood that was row upon row of one-story bungalows, each with its carport, patchy lawn, half a dozen ragged, stunted shrubs, differing only in whether the siding was pukey green, diarrhea yellow, or dry-blood brown. On each front step a Lisa welcoming a Lisa delivery boy; on the road a hundred Lisa men commuting to dead-end jobs, waiting for the school bus a hundred Lisa children, stalking up the walks a score of Lisas crying, "I know you, woman. I see you everywhere I go in this vale of tears. And not one of you knows why she is here!" A score of waving pamphlets, titled "Your Karma" in bright orange on forest green. "We have lived before! We have sinned! And we suffer now for our sins in past lives! Let me tell you how to save your soul! How to get out of this hell that we call life!"

When Michael finally broke the ensuing silence, he said, "I wouldn't dare call this one. I'm afraid of her. I hate her. I love her. All at once. How could I possibly be fair? How could you possibly *trust* me to be fair?"

"Kemmerdell did say he thought it was possible," said Ingrid's dopple. "So if they ever qualify, we should be able to let them out."

"And put others in, if anyone like Lisa ever shows up again."

"They will," said Rose.

Michael spread one hand on the table and stared at it. "Tell people when they first arrive," he said quietly. "Do you think that would stop a Lisa?"

No one seemed willing to say it would. Perhaps they were thinking that in the meat world they had left behind them, the threat of neither heavenly nor earthly punishment had ever done much to diminish crime. And the meat world defined the thinking of every resident of the virtual world.

"Lock 'em up." Ingrid blew smoke toward the ceiling. "At least it keeps them from doing it again."

"Maybe," said Bertha. "Maybe Gladys will show us another way." A moment later, she added, "If even a whole new life can't rehabilitate a Lisa, we'd have to put Toddy Sean in there too."

The others looked skeptical. Then Ingrid's dopple said, "On the other hand, if the kid turns out okay, we can rehabilitate anyone who needs it."

"But not Nick Codescu," said Michael. Elena's brother had been charged with murdering Michael's meat. He would never be copied.

"No." Bertha's head-shake was slow and sad. "Even if it works, it can't help the meats."

"Someday," said Albert. "We'll be pulling minds out of their meat, fixing them, and putting them back. Maybe we'll be re-raising people to straighten out their kinks. Or maybe we'll just edit them."

The pilot yawned. "It's time I was getting back to the shuttle." She waved and winked out.

The remaining Ingrid stood up from the couch. "Do you want to go home now, Michael?"

He turned toward Rose, a tortured expression on his face.

She looked at Albert. "The problems don't go away, do they? I love you both."

He too seemed pained.

"You don't have to decide between them," said Bertha. "You have the data energy now, pay for what you've done already."

"You mean...?" She closed her eyes in concentration, and there were two Roses, one on either side of Albert. "But how long can it last?"

"You don't have to wonder, do you?" said Bertha. "Try it, and see."

The Roses sighed and looked at each other. "Well, then...." One stayed beside Albert. The other stepped toward Michael Durgov and hugged his arm.

Now it was Ingrid's turn to look distressed. "He's mine," she cried. "You can't...."

"You have enough too, Michael," said Bertha. "Call it compensation for what you've been through."

As the second Michael moved beside his ex-wife, the Roses looked first at her late husband and then at her first adolescent crush. She did not seem sure she was doing the right thing. "We'll have to get together once in a while, you know, so the dopples can update each other."

"It's like twins, isn't it?" said Ingrid. "Except they can do that, almost like they were one person with two lovers."

Albert looked uneasy, as if he agreed with her and thought the situation far too close to infidelity. But then Rose touched his arm and said, "You'll have me as long as you can stand me. And I'll have you. But it isn't like the meat world, is it? Just a few days ago, I was wishing I could have my cake and eat it too. And now I can."

A boom of laughter marked Marvin's materialization behind Bertha. He clamped his hands on the shoulders of his female alter ego and said, "I should write this as a virtual love song: 'Heal my wounded heart with copy star dot star.'"

"Better you should fix your bookkeeping," said Rose.

"That's your job now," said Marvin, even as Bertha turned toward Rose's Michael. "And you? What sort of work can you do?"

The Michaels shook their heads with identical rueful grins. "So far I haven't done much but make an ass of myself."

Ingrid poked her Michael in the biceps. "There's plenty of donkey work that needs doing."

"Your dopple, for instance," said Bertha. "Hauling spaceships into orbit. Disguised as software. And I've got plenty of orders for more such. Receptionists, truck drivers, inventory control, machine operators...." She faced the Michaels. "Let me run a few tests to see what you'd be best at. Then we can transfer any necessary skills and...."

"Wait a minute," said Ingrid. "You're forgetting what he was when he was meat. A business manager."

"A pretty cutthroat one," said Marvin.

"Isn't there anything that could use that?"

"Personnel?" suggested Bertha.

"Consultant?"

"Fund-raising?"

Michael laughed as the suggestions flew. "Once we get it going," he said. "I'll run the rehab center."

SILICON KARMA
THOMAS A. EASTON

"There's no oil in the water," said Michael.

"What do you mean?" The Rose who was closer to him turned to look at the lake. The sun was low above the trees on the distant shore, and the water gleamed pink and orange. The breeze was too gentle and fitful to stir more than ripples.

"I noticed it," he said. "Whenever Lisa was around."

"Like the litter." Albert made a shooing motion with his hands. "Move. There's too many of us on this old dock." As he spoke, wood creaked, the flat surface of the dock sagged, and water washed over their feet.

Once they were all on shore, Michael said, "Look. I'm getting the hang of this at last." The dock's sag reversed itself, the wood dried, and weathered silver was replaced by fresh-cut, resin-scented pine. "I bet I could turn it into a concrete pier."

"Don't," said his Rose. "It wouldn't be the same."

The other Rose was already walking toward the cottage's steps. "There's room for all of us, but...."

The look Albert aimed toward Michael was tinged with the suspicious surliness of a man who is not quite sure whether he should defend his turf. "It would be hard for me to think of you and my wife in another bedroom, even if your Rose is a copy."

"*She's* the copy," said Michael's Rose. "Not me."

"Duplicate, then. Dopple."

"I suppose it's jealousy." Michael nodded as if to say that he would feel much the same.

"Then we need another cottage." Michael's Rose shivered ostentatiously. "And a sweater."

"Another island," said Albert. "At least."

"Shush," said his Rose. "Do you think we can do it?"

The other island was as nearly as they could imagine it a duplicate of the original. But it was not visible from the dock or the cottage's porch. Nor did the duplicate porch and cottage offer any view of the original. The two islands—and their residents—turned their backs upon each other.

"We couldn't have done that by ourselves," said Albert. "Marvin didn't show up, but he had to be helping."

"You must have a lot of credit with him now," said Rose.

"*We* must. You're the accountant. And you're the one who saved us all by telling me to attack the uninstaller."

She opened the bedroom door. The four-poster bed Albert had made from a primitive bunk was still there, and the air held a memory of musk and sweat.

Rose stared up into the bed's ruffled canopy. Michael Durgov lay against her side, one arm thrown across her chest, their skins damp where they met despite the coolness of the air.

She dug her fingertips into the hair behind his ear. "Can it possibly work?"

"Mmm?"

"Using dopples like this. Trying to have everything."

He sighed. "I don't know." A moment later he added, "Are you wishing you were with Albert?"

"I am with him. Or *she* is. And *she's* probably wishing she was here, with you. And you? With Ingrid?"

"So which one of you is having the cake?" asked Albert. "And which one's eating it?"

Rose rocked her head on the pillow and grinned mischievously. "It's not very satisfying unless you know you're doing both."

"You'll have that eventually. When you update."

There was silence while they adjusted their positions to face each other conversationally, nose to nose. "Can it possibly work?" she asked.

"When we were meat...."

SILICON KARMA
THOMAS A. EASTON

"Some people said that to live a truly satisfying life, you had to dive into everything. Total involvement with whatever you touched. Single-minded. Others said that wasn't possible...."

"Yes," he murmured. "You have to focus."

"You just can't commit yourself fully to everything."

"I never even tried."

"I didn't either. But now we can."

"Dopples? A separate you for everything?"

She ran one hand down his side. He did the same. "Why not? We aren't limited to a single self anymore."

"Multiple selves," he said. "Perfect freedom. One of us for everything we want to be, every lover, every career."

"Shh," she murmured. "Not that many. There *are* limits, after all."

"Whatever. But they're only copies at the start. They become separate individuals soon enough, even if they do update each other on their memories."

"But they have to be very like each other. Closer than twins."

"But not close enough, not for long, to stay happy with specialization. Unless you edit out the other interests."

"We didn't do that, did we?"

"But we could. It's a digital world."

She caught her breath when he demonstrated. "Not as digital as the one we left. Everything was 'either-or' there. If you chose one thing, you had to give up the other."

"While here...." It was his turn to catch his breath. "Here, you can have it all. At least in theory."

"Even if the satisfaction doesn't last."

"Sales are up again," said Manora Day.

"So's the stock," said Leah Kymon.

"It helped that we could give Codescu to the cops," said Eric Minckton. "And that Irma was willing to talk to the press. A very personable woman. She earned her bonus."

The three Coleridge executives smiled at each other. Their jobs were secure, at least until the next crisis.

Jonathan Spander smiled too, but he also had the grace to feel faintly troubled that no one seemed to care what had happened to the people within the computer. "I wish we could give Albert and Rose Pillock a pair of medals. They really saved our bacon."

"Oh, come," said Kymon. Her smile was both tolerant and amused. "You sound like you think they're real. The others too, I suppose. And we know they're just simulations."

"Besides...." Manora Day was actually laughing. "They can give themselves all the medals they want in there. All they have to do is wish."

ABOUT THE AUTHOR

Thomas A. Easton is a well-known science fiction critic, with a monthly book review column in **Analog**. He has written six novels. His newest title is **Taking Sides: Clashing Views on Controversial Issues in Science, Technology, and Society**. A science fiction anthology, **Gedanken Fictions: Stories on Themes in Science, Technology, and Society**, will appear in 1997 from White Wolf. He teaches at Thomas College in Waterville, Maine.

Stephen stretched his arm out and let his fingertips brush the surface of the image. Patterns shifted around the points where he touched. He jerked slightly, then turned to look at Fargo and Lis.

"Hanna wants to communicate with you," he said. "Directly."

Fargo hesitated. Stephen was excited, eyes wide, boyish. Fargo could easily, it appeared, topple him back into his moodiness by refusing. He looked past Stephen to the image. The eyes seemed fixed on him. They were not human eyes, though they were good imitations. It was not just their colorlessness, but their ambivalence. Fargo was reluctant to give over any control to them.

Lis squeezed his hand and he almost snatched it away. The sensation shocked him.

"What does that mean?" she asked.

Stephen opened his mouth, then shrugged. "It's hard to describe. Communion? I—"

"Why?" Fargo asked.

Stephen's enthusiasm diminished slightly. "There's a lot of infor-mation we all need...and she needs to know if she can trust you..."

"I'm willing," Lis said. She tightened her fingers on Fargo's hand slightly.

Fargo nodded.

Stephen grinned and held out his hands to them. Fargo let Lis pull him forward. He lifted his left hand and let Stephen grasp it tightly. His palm tingled and he resisted the urge to yank it away. Stephen gripped Lis's right hand.

Then he released them and turned to the image. He pressed both hands against it. His head bowed.

Fargo started to say something, but it was lost within the sudden presence in his mind. At first there were no words, only the sensation of a vast Other. The room felt too small, then *he* felt too small, floating. The room was as big as it needed to be, he saw, as big as the universe. The eyes locked onto him, fixed him in place, and she burrowed into him. He held his hands out uselessly to fend her off.

* * *

The molasses quality of his thoughts undermined his attempts to resist. The futility of trying to block what was happening gave way to a warm cushion of intense interest. His mind enveloped, flower-like, the strong kernel of Being in its center. He turned away, but took it with him. The others were dim, unreal shapes clouding his field of vision. Nothing was solid, nothing relevant except what was inside.

His senses tingled with activation. Bright flashes coursed through him. He fell, but the floor was a vague impression only partially noticed amid the coruscating layers of neural activity.

I am not me.

Yes, you are. That, and others.

?

Stephen, Lis.

And they?

Contain you, too.

All this...

All.

And you?

I am here.

How?

There was no reply...

Fargo twisted inside out and "looked" around. Warm masses glowed and pulsed in a huddle around him. They were yellow, orange, white, with fine veins of cerulean, pleasant and inviting. Intrigued, he reached to touch one. A wispy fibre extended from him to the nearest. The surface scintillated where the fibre touched, then swelled toward him. For an instant he was afraid, wanting to pull out, but it reached him and—*I I I, YOU YOU YOU, WE WE WE*—core, center, reason—Soft considerations, warm expectations, innocent bitterness.

Introduction to Alternate Viewpoint, class begins—

?

The orchid split in half, opened, and swallowed—

Happy memories interlaced with unkindnesses done for no apparent reason, no purpose, no motivation.

None of this makes sense.
What do you know?
Nothing.
What do I feel like?
Seti...
!
Please, I'm lost.
...

There was never much hope alone. Always there existed the
conviction of being incomplete when isolated. But isolation became
a salve, an ointment, to heal the hurt. Only to get strong enough to
lose it all again.

Things never change, really, but I keep hoping.
Who?
In each of us there is the potential of everyone else.
Sounds like parlor sophistry to me, a little verbal ballet set to
sympathy.
All I want!
Yes?
Is what I've always wanted.
?

One possible way to understand, he found, was in the repetition
of events undergone through no conscious effort, without control,
without recognition, without more than vague understanding.
Patterns emerged and displayed for him a willful insistence on
partial surgery on emotions that demanded feeding but only
achieved a brutal sort of transfusion insufficient for more than
mere existence. Intrigued, Fargo looked closer, deeper. In response, he was taken in further. The belief of incompleteness
became stronger until he reached the center, the core. Then it
dispersed. The tide broke against a rocky abutment of independence. At the heart of it, strength.

Let me show you something.
?
Here, right here, in here...

The core opened again. Within Fargo saw a bedlam of images. Vertigo took him as he groped for something to hang onto, and he pitched downward, falling. He passed tier after tier. When he looked back he saw a vast columnar flue stretching to a diminishing circle of light—

He turned again and saw a brownish mist rising toward him. A cacophony of chittering surrounded him, distorted laughter or a billion contentless conversations.

Who the hell am I in?

The mist swallowed him.

* * *

Hanna wore a metal body below a hairless flesh and bone head. Her eyes glittered but she did not smile. She raised her left hand and gestured to the stars that surrounded them. Fargo saw the paths of starships spreading out from one star to dozens of others. The bright paths rayed out like the arms of an explosion, lacing together the heavens.

"Look closer." Hanna said and Fargo, wary, bent toward one of the suns.

A ship came to a world and sent people and equipment down to mold it. As Fargo watched, the planet changed from a dirty grey and waxen hue to blue and green and white. Cities appeared and then ships came back up its well into space and stations were built. More starships arrived and the world changed further, a place for humans, beautiful and warm and welcoming.

"Closer."

Fargo saw roadways reach from town to town and city to city; businesses thrived; farmfields flourished, patterning the landscape. Graveyards filled. Within the largest city, he saw a faint shape form that seemed to hover over it and grow out of it. Ghostly at first, it solidified into another image like Hanna—but it was not Hanna.

Fargo looked at Hanna for explanation. Instead, she gestured across the stars to other worlds. Fargo followed her gaze and saw more embodiments of planetary matrices.

"How many of you?" he asked.

Hanna touched her chest and worked her fingers into a seam Fargo had not noticed before. She pulled it aside and opened herself. He backed away, but Hanna reached for him. She seized his wrist and pulled him closer. He stared into the corridor, terrified, unable to break her grip. The corridor stretched away to a vanishing point. Hanna shoved him inside and he fell to the floor. When he rolled over he saw the ceiling close over him, the slit become a pucker, the pucker smooth out.

He pushed himself up to his feet. He was shaking. The hallway was a dirty white, plain, lined with black, unlabeled doors. He heard voices. He followed the sounds, walking on legs that felt infirm, watery. Abruptly, the hallway ended at a door marked "A.V. Class 102." He hesitated. Turning, he saw that the corridor had become a small room and there were no other doors. He opened the door and stepped through.

Stephen paced before an empty blackboard, an open book in his hand. He spoke in a monotone to the packed lecture hall. Fargo did not understand him. The words were senseless, a different language. Fargo recognized no one in any of the seats nearby.

"You're late."

Stephen was looking at him, expectantly. Fargo smiled timidly and held up his hands in apology. Stephen indicated a chair in the back row.

Fargo scooted between knees and the next row of chairs and sat in the one empty seat, in the middle of the section.

"What," Stephen continued, now in perfectly understandable langish, "was the purpose of constructing the World Matrix Databases? Fargo?"

"Uh...I—"

"Anyone else?" Stephen glanced from face to face.

"Collation of information throughout the world, global communication organization, standardization of governmental services," someone said.

"Exactly. And what did we end up with?"

"A sentient, self-aware, self-contained system—"

"Wrong! Wrong, wrong, and wrong!" Stephen slapped the podium. "None of you pay attention! Fargo! What's wrong with the description just given?"

"I don't know," Fargo said.

"Exactly! I'm glad to see at least one of you pays attention! Hanna is not self-contained! She needs communion! She needs contact! She needs other minds! Heuristically Automorphic Nonlinear Neuronal Analog! That's what that means, that she is patterned on a human mind, and a human mind kept unstimulated by new things stagnates and eventually collapses and dies! Fargo! When did First Contact occur?"

"Oh...forty years ago?"

"Thirty-eight to be precise. And what did the Forum and the Chairman do when it happened?"

Fargo fidgeted in his seat. He hated being lectured to. He hated being in class. He hated classes.

"Exactly!" Stephen jabbed the air emphatically with his book. He was obviously enjoying himself. "They panicked. Wouldn't you? I mean, aliens, for godsake! Different creatures with nothing—presumably—in common with us. Really different, species that looked nothing like us, that thought nothing like us, that possessed language trees whose roots we couldn't begin to comprehend. Panic. Panic was the only acceptable response, because all our institutions had been designed primarily to deal with emergencies that create panic. Threats. How did the panic manifest? Anyone? Fargo?"

"How should I know?"

"Exactly. No one knew what to do. Send representatives, send the military—yes, send the Armada, see if they shoot back—send someone who can deal with aliens. Nonhumans. Other minds that are really different. After all, didn't we have people who had been studying exactly that problem? Well, yes—we did. But the entire community was seized with the same panic. This was real, this wasn't theoretical, and while there were certainly individuals more than willing—in fact, *eager*—to go have a look at these new neighbors, there was no functioning mechanism within their institutions that could sanction and send them. Panic. No one had a sensible suggestion how to go about doing this. Except Hanna. And what did she do? Fargo?"

"She sent you, telelog!" Fargo waved angrily at Stephen, a dismissal. "Asshole," he said under his breath.

"I'll speak to you later about your lack of proper respect after class. But you're right. She sent me. And about fifteen others she had gathered together as infants and raised as telelogs. Now, does anyone here understand the difference between a telelog and a telepath? Anyone?" He shrugged. "I'm not surprised, there's no reason you should. Research into telepathy had been abandoned early in the twenty-first century after it had finally been demonstrated that research would never produce a verifiable example. It became common knowledge that telepathy was a myth, a fairytale, with no basis in reality. But Hanna had access to all the research that had been done and she reconsidered the idea from a technological angle."

Stephen straightened, rocked on his toes. "A telelog is an artificially created telepath." He tapped his forehead and the blackboard behind him suddenly contained a brilliantly colored cross-section of a brain. Stephen indicated a dark mass that threaded its way from the prefrontal lobe back to the occipital and down into the medulla by way of the pituitary and thalamus. "A factory," he said and gave the image a rap with his knuckles. "Biotech. An implant designed to manufacture nanopoles and distribute them. Simple skin contact passes them on and they then find their way throughout the nervous system of the secondary host. To the brain and along the axon structure of the cerebral cortex, into the visual cortex, the auditory response system...in short, an infection that permeates the brain and sets up what amounts to a transmitter." He struck the blackboard again. "The receiver is there, controlling everything. The invaded brain is deciphered and its sensory processing patterns are translated. Transmission can then take place in a meaningful way and the receiver further decrypts the signal into usable images. A manufactured telepath."

He ran his hand over the blackboard and the image disappeared. Stephen dusted his hands. "The idea was a good one, if a little crude. Language was bound to be the chief barrier in communicating with actual nonhuman species—but not if you could read the thoughts of the person or being you're talking to. You can derive exactly—supposedly—what his, her, or its meaning is. So what's wrong with that notion? Hmm? Anybody want to guess? Fargo?"

"No, I don't want to guess. Why don't you tell me?"

"I'll do better than that."

Fargo clutched the arms of his small chair as the room dissolved. Stephen was suddenly right before him. Around them the murk of moiled colors congealed into purple-blackness. Stars appeared. Fargo glanced down and sucked a lungfull of air as he saw a planet rising up fast. His fingers ached from gripping the chair. He closed his eyes, but behind the lids he could see shadowshapes of mountains and rivers rushing by.

Motion ceased. He opened his eyes and looked up at a thin porcelain tower rising out of a plaza stretched between two walls of red stone. Stephen touched his arm and he jerked away. Stephen smiled at him; behind Stephen were a dozen people Fargo did not recognize—no, Daniel grinned at him from beneath a blue silk cowl. Stephen pointed to the tower.

"There," he said and walked off toward it. The others followed, leaving Fargo behind.

Fargo ran after them.

A peaked archway opened into the tower. There Fargo saw dozens of people, waiting. He looked closer, frowning. They were not people. Not humans, he corrected himself. Seti. All the different kinds: Rahalen, Cursian, Distanti, Menkan, Coro, others for which he had no names. No Ranonan.

The air shimmered, shifted, as through heat waves. Three seti stepped forward—two Rahalen and a Coro, the Rahalen elegantly humanoid in their layered gowns and austere, smooth faces, the Coro an indistinct mass of reddish flesh wrapped round and round by multicolored belts.

Stephen stepped forward.

"We are the representatives from Sol, capitol of the Pan Humana," he said. He offered his hands. The Rahalen touched him. The Coro rolled closer and a pseudopod stretched out between a blue and a green belt and brushed Stephen's palm. He closed his eyes.

The three setis stepped back. Fargo's brain filled suddenly with terror, cloying fear that froze him in place. He saw the other telelogs buckle, some clapped their hands over their ears, one clawed at his eyes and screamed soundlessly. Stephen seemed caught on a hook, dangled, his body jerking with muscle spasms. Daniel was on his knees. A girl fell to the ground and Fargo knew somehow that she was dead. Daniel crawled toward her, tears streaming down his face, his mouth open so wide Fargo expected the skin to tear. He lifted the dead girl to his chest and heaved silently. A few managed to run, but they collided with each other and the walls.

"What—what—what—what—what—" he shouted over and over. The floor rolled and he spread his arms for balance.

Daniel snapped his mouth shut suddenly, laid the corpse down, and stood. He tackled Stephen. He draped his friend over his shoulder and tried to run, but the floor had become a bog. With each step his feet pulled out with a loud, wet sucking sound. Fargo's fear was thick, syrupy, suffocating.

The seti rocked back and forth. Several had come forward to help the first three, touched them, and now reeled under the impact of terror, adding to the staggering weight of sensation. A few held each other, some had advanced menacingly on the humans, stopped, and staggered back.

The roof of the tower peeled open like a giant flower. Hanna appeared against the distant stars. Tears streamed down her face.

"They don't want us," she said. "They're afraid. Run. Hide. Run."

Everything dissolved around Fargo. He fell. He was in a black room, curled in on himself, repeating "What—what—what— what—"

Eventually he focused on a shape lying across the room. Painfully, his muscles cramping from being held so rigid so long, he crawled over to it. A woman. He rolled her over.

Lis's face turned up to him. Empty eye sockets and blood from cut lips. To Fargo's horror, she moved. She tried to smile.

"We fucked up, didn't we?"

"Any questions?" Stephen asked.

WHITE WOLF PUBLISHING

BOREALIS

THE WINDS OF TIME — by CHAD OLIVER
THE YEAR OF THE QUIET SUN — by WILSON TUCKER
THERE WILL BE TIME — by POUL ANDERSON

WHITE WOLF DISCOVERY TRIO, VOLUME ONE

THREE IN TIME:
White Wolf Rediscovery Trio № 1

Novels written by Chad Oliver,
Wilson Tucker & Poul Anderson
Forward by Arthur C. Clarke

Edited by Jack Dann, Pamela
Sargent, George Zebrowski

Science Fiction
Trade paperback omnibus

ISBN 1-56504-985-3
WW 10041

$14.99 US
$19.99 CAN

Time travel waits as a powerful, unrealized dream, inspiring some of our most spectacular science fiction. Here are three such novels, each extraordinary in its own way, in White Wolf Publishing's first **Rediscovery Trio**. This exciting new series is dedicated to bringing enduring classics of science fiction to a new generation of readers.

The Winds of Time
by Chad Oliver
"Oliver is a prime contender for the Heinlein-Clarke front rank of genuine science fiction, in which the science is as accurately absorbing as the fiction is richly human."
— *The New York Times*

The Year of the Quiet Sun
by Wilson Tucker
Winner of the John W. Campbell Award for Best Novel
"An H. G. Wells-type time machine takes this chilling story's anti-hero into a nightmare only-a-few-years-from-now future. This highly entertaining realistic novel is a Hugo contender..."
— A. E. van Vogt,
Nebula Award Grand Master

There Will Be Time
by Poul Anderson
Hugo and Nebula Award-winner
"Poul Anderson has made time travel more plausible and rational than anyone since H. G. Wells invented it...and makes it all new."
— *Analog*

Tales in Time, a companion volume to **Three in Time**, rounds up a fantastic lineup of classic short stories of time travel. Beyond space travel, beyond alien contact, **Tales in Time** brings together some of the most respected writers of our time on a topic that man has yet to conquer. Find out just how far we can go...if only our minds could take us.

Brian W. Aldiss, Ray Bradbury, Frederick Brown, Jonathan Carroll, Arthur C. Clarke, L. Sprague de Camp, Philip K. Dick, Charles de Lint ,Harlan Ellison, Jack Finney, Lisa Goldstein, Robert A. Heinlein, Garry Kilworth, Michael Moorcock, Lewis Padgett, Spider Robinson, Eric Frank Russell, Rod Serling, Bob Shaw, Robert Silverberg, James Tiptree Jr., and John Wyndham.

Introduction by John Clute,
co-editor of the popular
The Encyclopedia of Science Fiction..

TALES IN TIME:
An Anthology
Companion to
Three in Time

Edited by Peter Crowther
Introduction by John Clute

Science Fiction
Trade paperback anthology

ISBN 1-56504-989-6
WW 10042

$12.99 US
$17.99 CAN

For easy ordering call:
1-800-454-WOLF.
Visa/Mastercard and Discover
accepted. **Available April 1997**

THE ROAD TO
SCIENCE FICTION

VOLUME 3: FROM HEINLEIN TO HERE

EDITED BY
JAMES GUNN

ROBERT A. HEINLEIN
ISAAC ASIMOV
RAY BRADBURY
FRITZ LEIBER
ARTHUR C. CLARKE
PHILIP JOSÉ FARMER
KURT VONNEGUT
ROGER ZELAZNY
FREDERIK POHL
HARLAN ELLISON
LARRY NIVEN
URSULA K. LeGUIN

THE ROAD TO
SCIENCE FICTION
Volume 3

Edited by James Gunn

Science Fiction
Trade paperback omnibus

ISBN 1-56504-821-0
WW 11089

$14.99 US
$19. 99 CAN

"The biggest. the most ambitious, and in many ways the best of these anthologies...[Gunn's] achievement is considerable."
    — *Omni*

"a great diversity of style as well as intent. Each is preceded by one of Gunn's informative intro-ductions and biographical sketches themselves worthy of the price of the book."
    — *Publisher's Weekly*

The Road to Science Fiction has been called "the best historical anthology of SF ever assembled" (*Anatomy of Wonder*). It is that, and more. The series offers more than 2000 pages of science fiction, including discussions of the genre and its authors, tracing the development of this contem-porary art form from its earliest innovators to present-day prize winners.

Volume 3 carries the story of SF forward from 1940 to 1977, through the Golden Age and the New Wave to their reconciliation. It be-gins with Heinlein's "All You Zombies" and Isaac Asimov's 1941 "Reason" and ends with Joe Haldeman's 1977 Hugo-award winning story "Tricentennial."

For easy ordering call:
1-800-454-WOLF.
Visa/Mastercard and Discover accepted.